FORGOTTEN REALMS®

FANTASY ADVENTURE

DAUGHTER of the DROW

A Novel of the
Underdark

Elaine Cunningham

DAUGHTER OF THE DROW

Random House and its affiliate companies have worldwide distribution rights in the book trade for English language products of TSR, Inc.

Distributed to the book and hobby trade in the United Kingdom by TSR Ltd.

Distributed to the toy and hobby trade by regional distributors.

Cover art by Fred Fields.

All TSR characters, character names, and the distinctive likenesses thereof are trademarks owned by TSR, Inc.

FORGOTTEN REALMS is a registered trademark owned by TSR, Inc. The TSR logo is a trademark owned by TSR, Inc.

First Printing: August 1995
Printed in the United States of America
Library of Congress Number: 94-68147

9 8 7 6 5 4 3 2 1

ISBN: 0-7869-0165-9

TSR, Inc.
201 Sheridan Springs Road
Lake Geneva, WI 53147
U.S.A.

TSR Ltd.
120 Church End, Cherry Hinton
Cambridge CB1 3LB
United Kingdom

95-2298

Books by
Elaine Cunningham

Tangled Webs
(September 1996)

Elfshadow

Elfsong

To Judi—sister, friend, and one-woman party.

PRELUDE

here is a world where elves dance beneath the stars, where the footsteps of humanfolk trace restless paths in ever-widening circles. There is adventure to be had in this land, and magic enough to lure seekers and dreamers with a thousand secrets. Here there are wonders enough and more to fill a dragon's lifetime, and most who live in this world are content with the challenges life brings.

A few, however, remember the night-told stories that terrified and delighted them as children, and they seek out the whispered tales and grim warnings so they may disregard them. Intrepid or foolish, these hearty souls venture into forbidden places deep beneath the lands of their birth. Those who survive tell of another, even more wondrous, land, a dark and alien world woven from the fabric of dreams—and of nightmares. This is the Underdark.

In gem-studded caves and winding tunnels, turbulent waterways and vast caverns, the creatures of the Underdark make their homes. Beautiful and treacherous are these hidden realms, and perhaps chief among them is Menzoberranzan, fabled city of the drow.

1

Elaine Cunningham

Life in the dark elves' city has always been dominated by the worship of Lloth—the drow goddess of chaos—and by a constant striving for power and position. Yet in the shadows of the temples and the grand ruling houses, away from the Academy that teaches fighting and fanaticism, a complex and diverse people go about the business of life.

Here the drow, both noble and common, live, work, scheme, play, and—occasionally—love. Echoes of their common elven heritage can be seen in the artistry lavished on homes and gardens, the craftsmanship of their armor and ornaments, their affinity for magic and art, and their fierce pride in their fighting skills. Yet no surface-dwelling elf could walk among her dark cousins without feeling horror, and earning a swift and terrible death. For the drow, fey and splendid though they are, have been twisted by centuries of hatred and isolation into a macabre parody of their elven forebears. Stunning achievement and chilling atrocity: this is Menzoberranzan.

In a time some three decades before the gods walked the realms, the chaos and turmoil of the dark elves' city achieved a brief, simmering equilibrium. Wealthy drow took advantage of such intervals of relative calm to indulge their tastes for luxury and pleasure. Many of their leisure moments were spent in Narbondellyn, an elegant district of the city that boasted broad streets, fine homes, and expensive shops, all crafted of stone and magic. Faint light suffused the scene, most of it from the multicolored glow of faerie fire. All drow were able to conjure this magical light, and in Narbondellyn the use of it was particularly lavish. Faerie fire highlighted the carvings on the mansions, illuminated shop signs, baited merchandise with a tempting glow, and glimmered like embroidery on the gowns and cloaks of the wealthy passersby.

In the surface lands far above Menzoberranzan, winter was beginning to ebb, and the midday sun struggled to warm the harsh landscape. The Underdark did not know seasons and had no cycle of light and dark, but the drow still went about their business according to the ancient, forgotten rhythms of their light-dwelling ancestors. The magical warmth deep in the core of Narbondel—the natural stone pillar that served as the city's clock—was climbing toward midpoint as the unseen sun reached its zenith. The drow could read the magic timepiece even in utter darkness, for their keen eyes perceived the subtlest heat patterns with a precision and detail a hunting falcon might envy.

At this hour the streets bustled with activity. Drow were by far the most numerous folk in Narbondellyn. Richly dressed dark elves wandered down the broad lane, browsed at the shops, or paused at chic cafes and taverns to sip goblets of spiced, sparkling green wine. City guards made frequent rounds mounted on large, harnessed lizards. Drow merchants whipped their draft animals—most often lizards or giant slugs—as they carted goods to market. And occasionally, the sea of activity parted to permit passage of a drow noble, usually a female riding in state upon a slave-carried litter or a magical, floating driftdisc.

A scattering of beings from other races also made their way through Narbondellyn: slaves who tended the needs of the dark elves. Goblin servants staggered after their drow mistresses, arms piled high with purchases. In one shop, bound with chains and prompted by three well-armed drow, a dwarf smithy grudgingly repaired fine weapons and jewelry for his captors. A pair of minotaurs served as house guards at one particularly impressive mansion, flanking the entrance and facing each other so their long, curving horns framed a deadly arch. Faerie fire limned the nine-foot creatures as if they were living sculpture. A dozen or so kobolds—small, rat-tailed relatives of goblins—lurked in narrow stone alcoves, and their bulbous eyes scanned the streets anxiously and continually. Every so often one of the creatures scurried out to pick up a bit of discarded string or clean up after a passing lizard mount. It was the kobolds' task to keep the streets of Narbondellyn absolutely free of debris, and their devotion to duty was ensured by an ogre taskmaster armed with whip and daggers.

One of these kobolds, whose back was lined with the recent marks of the ogre's whip, was busily engaged in polishing a public bench near the edge of the street. So anxious was the slave to avoid future punishment that he failed to notice the silent approach of a driftdisc. On the magical conveyance rode a drow female in splendid robes and jewels, and behind her marched in eerie silence threescore drow soldiers, all clad in glittering chain mail and wearing the insignia of one of the city's ruling houses. The snake-headed whip at the female's belt proclaimed her rank as a high priestess of Lloth, and the haughty tilt of her chin demanded instant recognition and respect. Most of Narbondellyn's folk granted her both at once. They cleared a path for her entourage, and those nearest marked her passing with a polite nod or a bended knee, according to their station.

As the noble priestess glided down the street, reveling in the heady mixture of deference and envy that was her due, her gaze fell upon the preoccupied kobold. In an instant her expression changed from regal hauteur to deadly wrath. The little slave was not exactly blocking her path, but its inattention showed a lack of respect. Such was simply not tolerated.

The priestess closed in. When the driftdisc's heat shadow fell upon the laboring kobold, the little goblinoid grunted in annoyance and looked up. It saw death approaching and froze, like a mouse facing a raptor's claws.

Looming over the doomed kobold, the priestess drew a slender black wand from her belt and began to chant softly. Tiny spiders dripped from the wand and scurried toward their prey, growing rapidly as they went until each was the size of a man's hand. They swarmed over the kobold and quickly had it enmeshed in a thick, weblike net. That done, they settled down to feed. Webbing bound the kobold's mouth and muted its dying screams. The slave's agonies were brief, for the giant spiders sucked the juices from their victim in mere moments. In no more time than the telling might take, the kobold was reduced to a pile of rags, bones, and leathery hide. At a sign from the priestess, the soldiers marched on down the street, their silent elven boots further flattening the desiccated kobold.

One of the soldiers inadvertently trod on a spider that had lingered—hidden among the bits of rag—to siphon the last drop. The engorged insect burst with a sickening pop, spraying its killer with ichor and liquid kobold. Unfortunately for that soldier, the priestess happened to look over her shoulder just as the spider, a creature sacred to Lloth, simultaneously lost its dinner and its life. The drow female's face contorted with outrage.

"Sacrilege!" she declaimed in a voice resonant with power and magic. She swept a finger toward the offending soldier and demanded, "Administer the law of Lloth, *now!*"

Without missing a step, the drow on either side of the condemned soldier drew long, razor-edged daggers. They struck with practiced efficiency. One blade flashed in from the right and gutted the unfortunate drow; the strike from the left slashed open his throat. In the span of a heartbeat the grim duty was completed. The soldiers marched on, leaving their comrade's body in a spreading pool of blood.

Only a brief silence marked the drow soldier's passing. Once it was clear the show was over, the folk of Narbondellyn turned their attention back to their own affairs. Not one of the spectators offered any challenge to the executions. Most did not show any reaction at all, except for the kobold slaves who scurried forward with mops and barrels to clear away the mess. Menzoberranzan was the stronghold of Lloth worship, and here her priestesses reigned supreme.

Yet the proud female's procession kept a respectful distance from the black mansion near the end of the street. Not a house like those known to surface dwellers, this abode was carved into the heart of a stalactite, a natural rock formation that hung from the cavern's ceiling like an enormous ebony fang. No one dared touch the stone, for on it was carved an intricate pattern of symbols that shifted constantly and randomly. Any part of the design could be a magic rune, ready to unleash its power upon the careless or unwary.

This stalactite manor was the private retreat of Gromph Baenre, the archmage of Menzoberranzan and the eldest son of the city's undisputed (if uncrowned) queen. Gromph, of course, had a room in House Baenre's fabulous fortress castle, but the wizard possessed treasures—and ambitions—that he wished to keep from the eyes of his female kin. So from time to time he retired to Narbondellyn, to enjoy his collection of magical items, to pore over his vast library of spellbooks, or to indulge himself with his latest mistress.

Perhaps even more than his obvious wealth and famed magical power, Gromph's ability to select his consorts was a testament to his status. In this matriarchal city, males had a decidedly subservient role, and most answered to the whims of females. Even one such as Gromph Baenre had to choose his playmates with discretion. His current mistress was the youngest daughter of a minor house. She possessed rare beauty, but little aptitude for clerical magic. The latter gave her low status in the city and raised her considerably in Gromph's estimation. The archmage of Menzoberranzan had little love for the Spider Queen goddess or her priestesses.

Here in Narbondellyn, however, he could for a time forget such matters. The security of his mansion was ensured by the warding runes outside, and the solitude of his private study protected by a magical shield. This study was a large high-domed chamber carved from black stone and lit by the single candle on his desk. To a drow's sensitive eyes, the soft glow made the gloomy cave seem as bright as noonday on the surface. Here the wizard sat, perusing an interesting book of spells he'd acquired from the rapidly cooling body of a would-be rival.

Gromph was old, even by the measures of elvenkind. He had

survived seven centuries in treacherous Menzoberranzan, mostly because his talent for magic was matched by a subtle, calculating cunning. He had survived, but his seven hundred years had left him bitter and cold. His capacity for evil and cruelty was legendary even among the drow. None of this showed in the wizard's appearance, for thanks to his powerful magic he appeared young and vital. His ebony skin was smooth and lustrous, his long-fingered hands slender and supple. Flowing white hair gleamed in the candlelight, and his arresting eyes—large, almond-shaped eyes of an unusual amber hue—were fixed intently upon the spellbook.

Deep in his studies, the wizard felt, rather than heard, the faint crackle that warned him someone had passed through the magic shield. He raised his eyes from the book and leveled a deadly glare in the direction of the disturbance.

To his consternation, he saw no one. The magical shield was little more than an alarm, but only a powerful sorcerer could pass through with an invisibility spell intact. Gromph's white, winged brows met in a frown, and he tensed for battle, his hand inching toward one of the deadly wands on his belt.

"Look down," advised a lilting, melodic voice, a voice that rang with mischief and childish delight.

Incredulous, Gromph shifted his gaze downward. There stood a tiny, smiling female about five years of age, easily the most beautiful child he had ever seen. She was a tiny duplicate of her mother, whom Gromph had recently left sleeping in a nearby suite of rooms. The child's face was angular, and her elven features delicate and sharp. A mop of silky white curls tumbled about her shoulders, contrasting with baby skin that had the sheen and texture of black satin. But most striking were the wide amber eyes, so like his own, that regarded him with intelligence and without fear. Those eyes stole Gromph's annoyance and stirred his curiosity.

This, then, must be his daughter. For some reason that thought struck a faint chord in the heart of the solitary, evil old drow. He had no doubt fathered other children, but that was of little concern to him. In Menzoberranzan, families were traced solely through the mother. This child, however, interested him. She had passed through the magical barrier.

The archmage pushed aside the spellbook. He leaned back in his chair and returned the child's unabashed scrutiny. He was not accustomed to dealing with children. Even so, his words, when he spoke, surprised him. "So, drowling. I don't suppose you can read?"

It was a ridiculous question, for the child was little more than a babe. Yet her brow furrowed as she considered the matter. "I'm not sure," she said thoughtfully. "You see, I've never tried."

She darted toward the open spellbook and peered down at the page. Too late, Gromph slapped a hand over her golden eyes, cursing under his breath as he did so. Even simple spells could be deadly, for magic runes attacked the untrained eye with a stab of searing light. Attempting to read an unlearned spell could cause terrible pain, blindness, even insanity.

Yet the little drow appeared to be unharmed. She wriggled free of the wizard's grasp and skipped over to the far side of his desk. Stooping, she fished a scrap of discarded parchment from the wastebasket. Then she rose and pulled the quill from Gromph's prized bottle of everdark ink. Clutching the pen awkwardly in her tiny fist, she began to draw.

Gromph watched her, intrigued. The child's face was set in fierce concentration as she painstakingly scrawled some wavering, curly lines onto the parchment. After a few moments she turned, with a triumphant smile, to the wizard.

He leaned closer, and his eyes flashed incredulously from the parchment to the spellbook and back. The child had sketched one of the magic symbols! True, it was crudely drawn, but she had not only *seen* it, she had remembered it from a glance. That was a remarkable feat for any elf, at any age.

On a whim, Gromph decided to test the child. He held out his palm and conjured a small ball that glowed with blue faerie fire. The little drow laughed and clapped her hands. He tossed the toy across the desk toward her, and she deftly caught it.

"Throw it back," he said.

The child laughed again, clearly delighted to have found a playmate. Then, with a lighting-fast change of mood, she drew back her arm for the throw and gritted her teeth, preparing to give the effort her all.

Gromph silently bid the magic to dissipate. The blue light winked out.

And the next moment, the ball hurtled back toward him, almost too fast for him to catch. Only now the light was golden.

"The color of my eyes," said the little girl, with a smile that promised heartache to drow males in years to come.

The archmage noted this, and marked its value. He then turned his attention to the golden ball in his hand. So, the child could already conjure faerie fire. This was an innate talent of the fey drow, but seldom did it manifest so early. What else, he wondered, could she do?

Gromph tossed the ball again, this time lobbing it high up toward the domed ceiling. Hands outstretched, the precocious child soared up toward the glowing toy, levitating with an ease that stole the archmage's breath. She snatched the ball out of the air, and her triumphant laughter echoed through the study as she floated lightly back to his side. At that moment, Gromph made one of the few impulsive decisions of his long life.

"What is your name, child?"

"Liriel Vandree," she returned promptly.

Gromph shook his head. "No longer. You must forget House Vandree, for you are none of theirs."

He traced a deft, magical pattern in the air with the fingers of one hand. In response, a ripple passed through the solid rock of the far wall. Stone flowed into the room like a wisp of smoke. The dark cloud writhed and twisted, finally tugging free of the wall. In an instant it compressed and sculpted itself into an elf-sized golem. The living statue sank to one knee before its drow master and awaited its orders.

"The child's mother will be leaving this house. See to it, and have her family informed that she met with an unfortunate accident on her way to the Bazaar."

The stone servant rose, bowed again, and then disappeared into the wall as easily as a wraith might pass through a fog bank. A moment later, the scream of an elven female came from a nearby chamber—a scream that began in terror and ended in a liquid gurgle.

Gromph leaned forward and blew out the candle, for darkness best revealed the character of the drow. All light fled the room, and the wizard's eyes changed from amber to brilliant red as his vision slipped into the heat-reading spectrum. He fastened a stern gaze upon the child.

"You are Liriel Baenre, my daughter and a noble of the first house of Menzoberranzan," he announced.

The archmage studied the child's reaction. The crimson glow of warmth drained from her face, and her tiny, pale-knuckled hands gripped the edge of the desk for support. It was clear the little drow understood all that had just occurred. Her expression remained stoic, however, and her voice was firm when she repeated her new name.

Gromph nodded approvingly. Liriel had accepted the reality of her situation—she could hardly do otherwise and survive—yet the rage and frustration of an untamed spirit burned bright in her eyes.

This was his daughter, indeed.

Chapter 1

TIME OF TURMOIL

gnoring the muted cries of pain coming from the far side of the tower chamber, Nisstyre parted the heavy curtains and gazed down at the marketplace. The dark elf's eyes, black and unreadable in the faint light of the chamber, swept with a measured, calculating gaze over the scene below.

The Bazaar was one of the busiest places in all of Menzoberranzan, and as heavily guarded as any matron's stronghold. Today even more soldiers than usual were in evidence, keeping the peace with brutal efficiency. As captain of the merchant band Dragon's Hoard, Nisstyre usually appreciated the diligence with which the marketplace was patrolled; it protected local business and made trade such as his possible. Today, however, Nisstyre's sharp eyes also saw opportunity of another kind.

The drow merchant's lips curved as he watched a pair of guards drag away the body of a Calishite peddlar. The human's offense had been slight: he had been a little too vehement in his bartering, and his drow customer had settled the matter with a poisoned dagger. Usually Menzoberranzan's shoppers welcomed such bargaining as the sport that it was. Today, however, the volatile drow were like dry tinder awaiting the slightest spark.

To the casual observer, the bustle of the marketplace might appear normal enough. Certain goods were selling extremely well; in fact, demand for staple foods, weapons, and spell components was almost frantic. Nisstyre had seen market days like this many times before, usually up on the surface, when folk settled in for a particularly brutal winter or an expected siege. To his eyes, Menzoberranzan's drow were clearly preparing for *something*. Nisstyre doubted they knew what this something might be, but he recognized their unease and he intended to exploit it.

The Fox, his contacts on the surface world called him, and Nisstyre delighted in the name. He rather resembled that feral animal, with his sharp-featured black face, elegantly pointed ears, and unusual mane of coppery hair. He possessed his namesake's cunning in full measure. Unlike most drow, Nisstyre carried no weapons and indeed was rather unskilled in their use. His weapons were his mind—which was as agile and treacherous as the sword of a drow warrior—and his magic.

Once, many years ago, Nisstyre had lived in Ched Nasad, a city much like Menzoberranzan. Although he'd been a mage of considerable promise, the matriarchal society and the tyranny of Lloth had put limits on his ambitions—limits he did not intend to accept. He left the city and discovered a talent for trading; soon he had fought his way to the head of his own merchant band. His far-flung trade interests brought him wealth, but not the power he craved. *That* had come as a divine gift, and the divinity in question was Vhaeraun, drow god of thievery and intrigue. Nisstyre had embraced his god's directive—to establish a drow presence and power on the surface world—with all his heart. For once this kingdom was established, he, Nisstyre, planned to serve Vhaeraun as a king. But first his—and Vhaeraun's—subjects must be recruited from the ranks of the discontented drow.

In these days, discontent was rampant. Nisstyre's many informers, and his own sharp eyes, told him that. The drow of Menzoberranzan were still staggering from the disruption of magic during the Time of Troubles, and from their defeat at the hands of Mithril Hall's dwarves. They had gone to war, full of confidence in Matron Baenre and her Lloth-inspired vision of conquest and glory. And they had failed utterly, driven back into the ground by a ragtag alliance of dwarves, gnomes, and humans—lesser beings all—and by the cruel light of dawn. In the aftermath of defeat, the stunned drow felt betrayed, adrift, and deeply afraid. The powers that had ruled them so mercilessly had also kept the city secure from the dangers of the wild Underdark.

But what remained of these ruling powers? The ancient Matron Baenre, who had led the city for centuries, had erred in pursuing a surface war and had paid for this error with her life. Several of the most powerful houses were in turmoil. Under normal conditions, most of the city's drow cared little which eight houses sat on the Ruling Council. Now, however, the coming struggle for power threatened them all. Many feared the weakened and distracted city was vulnerable to attack, perhaps by the nearby illithid community, or perhaps by another drow city.

In Nisstyre's opinion, these fears were not groundless. Fully half of Menzoberranzan's twenty thousand drow had marched upon Mithril Hall, and no one knew for certain how many had returned. Few houses gave an accurate accounting of their private forces at any time, and no one wished to admit to diminished strength during this time of turmoil.

It was no secret that several of the city's strongest weapon masters—the generals of the individual house armies—were dead or missing. Nor were the losses limited to the city's professional soldiers. Hundreds of common folk had served as foot soldiers, and only a few dozen had returned to take up their labors. Magnifying this problem was the tremendous loss of life among the races who served Menzoberranzan's drow as slaves. Kobolds, minotaurs, and goblinkin had been drafted as battle fodder, and they had fallen by the thousand to the axes of Mithril Hall's dwarves and to the swords and arrows of their allies. The tasks these slaves once performed were now left undone.

Other cultures might pool labor and talents to fill the void, but such was beyond the sensibilities of the proud drow. Status was all, and no one was willing to set aside hard-won position for the common good. Menzoberranzan's drow could not unite to win the war, and they would not band together in its aftermath.

And therein, Nisstyre mused, lay *his* problem, as well. These dark elves could be motivated only by promise of personal gain. Status, power: these were the lures needed to coax the proud drow into the light. Although life was hard in the Underdark, and Menzoberranzan was facing a new and frightening level of chaos, most drow saw no other option. All the surface world offered was defeat, disgrace, and the searing horror that was the sun.

With a deep sigh, the merchant let the curtain fall and turned away to observe a spectacle of a very different nature. A drow male, a commoner of middle years and unremarkable appearance, sat bound with chains to a heavy stone chair. Around him crackled a sphere of faint greenish light, and over him loomed a black-clad drow male who stood, chanting, with eyes closed and hands outstretched. Clerical magic flowed from each of the dark elf's fingers, sizzling like dark lightning into the chained drow. The prisoner writhed in anguish as his tormentor—a priest of Vhaeraun, patron of thieves—plundered his memories and stole his secrets.

Finally the priest nodded, satisfied. The globe of light dissipated with a faint pop, and the prisoner sagged against his chains, moaning softly in a mixture of pain and relief.

Strange treatment, perhaps, for a trusted informer, but Nisstyre had little choice. The price of misplaced trust was high. In Menzoberranzan, anyone suspected of worshiping any god but Lloth was summarily put to death. Those who followed other gods, or none at all, were wise to keep their opinions to themselves.

Yet now, with their city in turmoil and their most basic assumptions suspect, there were a few drow who dared whisper the name of Vhaeraun, and who dreamed of a life free of Menzoberranzan's limitations. These drow Nisstyre was quietly seeking out. Some were like this tortured elf, whose hatred of matriarchal rule was so bitter that he would willingly endure anything to see it end. But most drow required more: something that could eradicate bitter memories and offer opportunities for power and status far beyond anything they now enjoyed.

In time, Nisstyre vowed, he would find what was needed to sway the drow of Menzoberranzan to his cause. After all, the Dragon's Hoard was famous for procuring anything, without regard for the cost.

* * * * *

Menzoberranzan was not the only land struggling with conflict and war. Far away, in a rugged land of hills and forests in the far-eastern reaches of Faerûn, the people of Rashemen knew their own time of turmoil. Magic—the force that ruled and protected their land—had recently gone treacherously awry. Ancient gods and long-dead heroes had walked the land, and a nation of dreamers had been tormented by strange nightmares and waking frenzies. Most dangerous of all, the mystic defenses crafted by the magic of the ruling Witches had faltered, and the eyes of many enemies turned once again upon Rashemen.

Of all Rashemen's warriors, perhaps none had felt this disruption so much as Fyodor. He was a young man, a pleasant fellow who had shown a steady hand at the swordsmith's forge and a steady nerve in battle. He was a hard worker, but by all reports a bit of a dreamer even by Rashemi standards. Fyodor was as quick with a song or a story as any traveling bard, and his deep, resonant bass voice often rang out over the sound of a clanging hammer as he worked. Like most of his people, he appreciated the simple joys of life and he accepted its hardships with resigned calm. His gentle nature and ready smile seemed ill-matched with his fearsome reputation; Rashemen was renowned for the might and fury of her berserker warriors, among whom Fyodor was a champion.

Rashemen's famed warriors used a little-known magic ritual to bring on their battle rages. By some quirk of fate, a stray bit of this magic broke free and lodged itself in young Fyodor. He had become a natural berserker, able to enter an incredible battle frenzy at will. At first his new skill had been hailed as a godsend, and when the Tuigan horde swept in from the eastern steppes Fyodor stood beside his berserker brothers and fought with unmatched ferocity.

All would have been well, but for another lingering memory of the time of twisted magic. Fyodor, the dreamer, continued to be haunted by the nightmares that had plagued so many Rashemi during the Time of Troubles. He told no one of this, for many of his people—simple peasants for the most part—had deeply ingrained superstitions about dreams and saw in every ale-induced night vision detailed meanings, portents of doom. Fyodor believed he knew what dreams were, and what they were not.

Tonight, however, he was not so sure. He'd emerged from a nightmare to find himself sitting bolt upright on his pallet, his heart racing and his body drenched with cold sweat. Fyodor tried without success to return to sleep, for he would face the Tuigan again tomorrow and would need all his strength. He had fought today and fought well—or so he had been told. His comrades had tipped their flasks to him and boasted of the number of barbarians who had fallen to Fyodor's black sword. Fyodor himself did not remember much of the battle. He remembered less each time he fought, and that disturbed him. Per· haps that was why this nightmare haunted him so.

In it, he had found himself in a deep forest, where he'd apparently wandered in the confused aftermath of a berserker frenzy. His arms, face, and body had been covered with stinging scratches. He had a vague memory of a playful tussle with his half-wild snowcat companion. In his dream, it slowly dawned on Fyodor that the game must have awakened his battle frenzy. He could not remember the outcome of battle, but his sword was wet to the hilt with blood still warm.

Awake, Fyodor knew the dream, although disturbing, was no prophecy of a battle to come. He had indeed tamed a snowcat once, but that had been many years ago, and they had parted in peace when the wild thing had returned to its nature. But the dream haunted him, for in it he read his deepest fear: would the time come when the battle rage gripped him entirely? Would he, in a mad frenzy, destroy not only his enemies, but those he loved?

Again and again Fyodor saw the light of life fading from the cat's golden eyes. Try as he might, he could not banish the image, or thrust away the fear that this might somehow come to pass.

And as he awaited the light of dawn, Fyodor felt the heavy weight of fate upon his young shoulders, and wondered if perhaps the dream held prophecy, after all.

* * * * *

Shakti Hunzrin slumped deeper into the prow of the small boat and glared at the two young males laboring at the oars. They were her brothers, page princes whose names she only occasionally remembered. The three drow siblings were bound for the Isle of Rothe, a mossy islet in the heart of Donigarten Lake. House Hunzrin was in charge of most of the city's farming, including the herd of rothe maintained on the island, and Shakti's family responsibilities had increased fourfold in the tumultuous aftermath of war.

Yet the dark elf's mood was grim as she eyed her brothers, unblooded youths armed with only knives and pitchforks. Traveling with such a scant escort was not only dangerous, but insulting. And Shakti Hunzrin was ever alert for any insult, however slight.

The boat thudded solidly into the stone dock, jarring Shakti's thoughts back to the matter at hand. She rose to her feet, slapping aside the hands of her unworthy escorts and climbing out of the boat unaided. Donigarten might be off the traveled path for most drow, but here Shakti was at home and in command. She stood for a moment on the narrow dock, head thrown back, to admire the miniature fortress above.

The overseer's quarters loomed some hundred feet overhead, carved out of the solid stone that rose in a sheer wall from the water. Shakti's boat had docked at the island's only good landing site: a tiny cove unmarred by the sharp and rending rocks that surrounded the rest of the island. The only way off the island was through the stone fortress, and the only way down to the dock was a narrow stairway carved into the rock wall. The water around the island was deep and cold, utterly black except for an occasional faint, luminescent glow from the creatures that lived in the still depths. From time to time, someone tried to swim these waters. So far, no one had survived the attempt.

Shakti ignored the stairs and levitated smoothly upward to the fortress door. Not only did this small flight grant her a more impressive entrance, but it also had a practical purpose. The proud drow, with their love of beauty, did not allow imperfect children to survive and had little patience for those who developed physical defects later in life. Shakti was extremely nearsighted and took great pains to conceal this fact. She did not trust her footing on the treacherous stairs, and was not certain which would be worse, the actual tumble down the steep incline, or having to explain why she had missed a step.

The overseer, a female from some lesser branch of the Hunzrin family tree, bowed deeply when Shakti walked into the vast center room. Shakti was somewhat mollified by this show of respect, and pleased to note that her brothers fell into guard position at either side of the entrance, as if she were already a respected matron.

She laid aside her own weapon—a three-tined pitchfork with a slender, rune-carved handle—and walked over to the far window. The scene beyond was not encouraging. Moss and lichen fields had been dangerously overgrazed, and the irrigation system was clogged and neglected. Rothe wandered aimlessly about, cropping here and there at the meager fodder. Their usually thick, long coats were ragged and lusterless. Shakti noted with dismay there would be little wool at shearing time. Even more distressing was the utter darkness that enshrouded the pasture.

"How many born so far this season?" Shakti snapped as she shrugged out of her *piwafwi*. One of her brothers leaped forward to take the glittering cloak.

"Eleven," the overseer said in a grim tone. "Two of those still-born."

The priestess nodded; the answer was not unexpected. The rothe were magical creatures who called to prospective mates with faint, blinking lights. At this season, the rothe's courting rituals should have set the island aglow. The neglected animals were too weak and listless to attend to such matters.

But what else could she have expected? Most of the orcs and goblins who tended the rothe herds had been taken as battle fodder, without regard for the logical consequences. These were things the ruling priestesses did not heed, expecting meat and cheese to appear at their tables as if by magic. In their vaunting pride, they did not understand some things required not only magic, but management.

This Shakti understood, and this she could provide. She seated herself behind a vast table and reached for the ledger that kept the breeding records. A sharp, pleasurable feeling of anticipation sped her fingers as she leafed through the pages. Keeping this ledger had been her responsibility before she'd been sent off to the Academy, and no one in the city knew more about breeding rothe than she did. Perhaps no one else shared her enthusiasm for the subject, but the drow certainly enjoyed the fine meat, cheeses, and wool her expertise produced!

One glance at the current page dampened both her pride and her enthusiasm. In her years of absence, the records had been written in a small, faint hand. Shakti swore, squinting her eyes into slits in an attempt to read the careless writing. Her mood did not improve as she read.

While she had been exiled to Arach-Tinilith, studying for the priestesshood and kowtowing to the Academy's mistresses, the herd had been sadly neglected. The rothe were highly specialized for life on the island, and carefully supervised breeding was essential.

Muttering curses, Shakti leafed to the back of the book, where the records of the slave stock were kept. These were considerably less detailed; in Shakti's opinion, the goblins could do whatever they liked provided their efforts produced enough new slaves. But according to the records, the birth rate among the usually fecund goblins was also dangerously low. This Shakti could not afford. House Hunzrin could acquire more slaves by purchase or capture, but such things took time and money.

17

"How many goblins remain?" Shakti asked tiredly as she massaged her aching temples.

"About forty," responded the overseer.

Shakti's head jerked up as if pulled by a string. "That's all? Herders or breeders?"

"About half and half, but all of the goblins have been herding. To help keep order, the slaves have all been moved into the main hut."

That was more bad news, for it meant the goblins lacked both the time and the privacy needed to procreate. Not that goblins required much of either, Shakti noted with distaste as she turned back to the ledger. Once again, she cursed the fate that had taken her away from the work she loved. At least the war had accomplished one thing: the rules that kept students sequestered at the Academy had been relaxed, for many of the young fighters, wizards, and priestesses were needed at home. The students had unprecedented freedom to come and go, and permission to leave was not difficult to obtain from the distracted masters and matrons.

At that moment a drow male clad in the rough clothes of a common laborer burst into the room. He slammed the heavy door behind him and bolted it in place.

"The goblins are revolting!" he cried.

The voice was familiar to Shakti; it belonged to a handsome drone who provided her with an occasional dalliance. She recognized the tone: a gratifying mixture of fear and disbelief. The faint, coppery smell of his blood drifted toward her. She was familiar with that, too. But these pleasant memories registered only on the edges of Shakti's thoughts; her concern was with the herd and her nearsighted eyes remained fixed on the page. "Yes, they certainly are," she agreed absently.

The male fell back a step, his jaw slack with astonishment. He well knew that Shakti Hunzrin was capable of a good many things, but humor was simply not among them. For a moment even the shock of the goblin uprising paled. Yet a second look at Shakti's peevish, squinting countenance convinced the drow of his error.

He brushed aside his momentary surprise and strode toward the desk. He thrust his wounded arm close to Shakti's eyes, so the myopic priestess could make out the marks of goblin fangs, the long red scores of their claws.

"The goblins are revolting," he repeated.

At last, he had her attention. "You've sent a message to the city

18

guard?" Shakti demanded.

He hesitated, a bit too long. "We have."

"And? What did they say?"

"Donigarten has it own protections," the drow quoted tonelessly.

Shakti let out a burst of bitter laughter. Translated, that meant only that the ruling matrons had more important matters on their minds than the loss of a few goblin slaves and the premature slaughter of some of the rothe. The rest of the city was safe from any unpleasantness that might occur on the island, for the only egress from Donigarten was by boat, and the only boat was secured, docked behind the office. Which meant, of course, the goblins would attack this very room.

Shakti snatched up her magic pitchfork—the weapon of choice for the Hunzrin family—and acknowledged her fate with a grim nod. It had come to this: the house nobles were forced to do battle with their own slaves.

At once there was a scrabble at the door, the sound of goblins clawing at the stone with their small, taloned fingers. The Hunzrin princes flanked their sister and raised their unblooded weapons. Shakti, however, had no intention of waiting out the little monsters. It never occurred to her she might flee. The rothe herd must be cared for, and that was what she intended to do.

So Shakti leveled her pitchfork at the door. Bracing the weapon against her hip, she covered her eyes with her free hand. The tines of her weapon spat magic. Three lines of white flame streaked toward the door, and the heavy slab of stone exploded outward with a spray of fragments and a thunderous roar.

For several moments all was a confusion of blinding light, cries of pain, and smoke heavy with the smell of charred flesh. Then the surviving goblins rallied and came on. A half dozen of the creatures roiled into the room, brandishing crude weapons fashioned of rothe bone and horn bound together with dried sinew.

Shakti's youngest brother leaped forward, pitchfork leading. He impaled the nearest goblin and flung it over his shoulder like a forkful of straw. The wounded goblin soared, flailing and shrieking, out the back window. There was a long, fading wail as it tumbled toward the luminous creatures waiting below, then a splash, then silence. Wild grins twisted the Hunzrin brothers' faces, and they fell upon the remaining goblins, pitchforks flashing as they reaped the grim harvest.

Shakti stood back and allowed the boys their fun. When the first

19

rush of goblins had been dealt with, she stepped into the blasted doorway to meet the next attack. A gangling, yellow-skinned female was the first to come. Holding high a bone dagger, the goblin flung itself at the waiting drow. Shakti coolly sidestepped the thrust and jabbed her pitchfork forward, stabbing through her attacker's uplifted arm.

At a word from the young priestess, magical lightning lit the pitchfork's tines and streaked into the goblin's body. With the first jolt, the slave's fierce scowl melted into an almost comical look of surprise. Lank strands of hair rose and writhed about its head like the snakes of a medusa, and the goblin's scrawny body shuddered convulsively. The lightning flowed on and on, and although the goblin shrieked and wailed in anguish, it could not pull free of Shakti's pitchfork. Another goblin grabbed the yellow female's imprisoned wrist—whether to rescue its companion or to steal its weapon was unclear—and it, too, was held fast by the lethal energy flow. Two more goblins, trying to edge past the shrieking couple into the room, were caught in the chain of malevolent magic.

With practiced ease, Shakti held her grip on the pitchfork and its magic. A few goblins managed to slip past the barrier of crackling energy and burning flesh. These were promptly skewered by the Hunzrin brothers and flung to the creatures waiting silently below.

Finally no more goblins came. Shakti wrenched her pitchfork from the charred flesh of her first victim. The chain of goblins fell into a smoking pile. The drow walked over their bodies and through the door, her still-glowing weapon held before her like a spear.

A few goblins—far too few!—remained, cowering and creeping slowly away. Murderous rage rose in Shakti's heart as she surveyed her disgusting foe, and only with difficulty did she refrain from striking again. The goblins were thin, exhausted, in no better shape than the cattle. The drow's practical nature acknowledged that the slaves might have seen no option other than to revolt. Yet when Shakti spoke, necessity, not compassion, governed her words.

"It is clear," Shakti began in a cool, measured tone, "there are not enough slaves to tend the herd. But what have you gained by this foolish attack? How much harder will you have to work, now that you have foolishly depleted your numbers? But know this: the rothe herd comes first, and all of you will return to your duties at once. New slaves will be purchased and all successfully bred goblin females will be granted extra food and rest privileges; in the meanwhile you will adhere to a strict schedule of labor." She hefted her pitchfork meaningfully. "Go now."

The surviving goblins turned and fled. The priestess turned to her brothers. Their eyes gleamed with excitement from their first battle. She knew just how to deepen that sparkle.

"The patrol of fighters from Tier Breche should have stopped this little rebellion before it got this far. If any of them are still alive, they've got no right to be. You, Bazherd. Take my pitchfork and lead the hunt."

The young male leaped forward to claim the powerful magic weapon. Shakti's lips firmed in a smile as she handed it over. Any blow against the drow Academy pleased her. She had no quarrel with Tier Breche in general, and usually conceded that the academies did well enough training fighters and wizards. But noble females were sent to the clerical school, and Shakti's resentment of her lot was deep and implacable. Oh, she would become a priestess, for that was the path to power in Menzoberranzan. But if another way presented itself, Shakti Hunzrin would be the first to take it.

* * * * *

At the appointed hour, every wizard in Menzoberranzan worthy of the name slipped away to a private spot to answer an unprecedented summons. One by one, each took a vial bearing the symbol of House Baenre, broke the seal, and watched as mist poured forth and shaped itself into a shimmering doorway. And one by one, the drow wizards stepped through these magic doorways. Each one emerged into the same large, lavishly appointed hall, perhaps somewhere in Menzoberranzan, perhaps in some distant plane. All the wizards knew for certain was that this was Gromph Baenre's audience chamber, and they had little choice but to attend. Even House Xorlarrin, famous for its wizardly might, was there in force. Seven Xorlarrin wizards were masters in the Sorcere, the school of magic; all seven sat uneasily on the luxurious chairs provided them.

As the wizards awaited the city's archmage, they eyed their colleagues with wary interest. Some had not seen each other since they'd trained together at Sorcere, for wizards hoarded their magical secrets to serve the power and prestige of their individual houses. Status was all, even among the city's mages. Glittering house insignias were much in evidence, and those whose heritage did not grant such a display settled for enspelled jewelry. Hundreds of gems flickered in

21

the dim light of the hall, their colors reflected in the glittering black folds of the *piwafwi* cloaks worn by all. Some of the wizards were accompanied by their familiars: giant spiders, deep bats, magically altered beasts, even imps or other creatures of the Abyss. The large room filled up quickly, yet the silence seemed only to deepen, to become more profound, as each wizard entered the magic chamber.

When the last chair had been taken, Gromph Baenre stepped out of nothingness and into the center of the room. As usual, Gromph was garbed in the glorious cloak of the archmage, a many-pocketed *piwafwi* that reputedly held more magical treasures and weapons than most drow wizards saw in a lifetime. Two magical wands were prominently displayed on his belt, and no one doubted many more were hidden about his person. Gromph's most powerful weapons, however, were his beautiful, tapered hands—so dexterous in weaving spells of death—and the brilliant mind that had brought him to the height of wizardly power . . . and doomed him to a life of discontent. In many other cultures, one such as he would be a king. And of all Menzoberranzan's wizards, only Gromph had the power to call such a meeting.

"It is not customary for the wizards of this city to gather in one place," Gromph began, speaking aloud the thoughts of all present. "Each of us serves the interests of his own House, according to the wisdom of his matron mother. This is as it should be," he said emphatically. The archmage paused and lifted a single eyebrow, perhaps to spice his assertion with a dash of irony.

"Yet, such alliances are not unknown. The city Sshamath is ruled by a coalition of drow wizards. We of Menzoberranzan could surely do as well if the need arises."

Murmurs, ranging from the excited to the appalled, filled the magical chamber. Gromph held up a hand, a simple gesture that commanded—and received—instant silence.

"*If the need arises,*" he repeated sternly. "The Ruling Council will see to the troubles of the city. Our task is to wait and watch."

Again he paused, and all present heard the silent message. The Ruling Council—the matron mothers of the eight most powerful houses—was little more than a memory. Matron Baenre, the most powerful drow in the city, was no more. Triel, her eldest surviving daughter, would assume the leadership of House Baenre, but she was young and would almost certainly face challengers. Recently, the third-ranked house had been utterly destroyed by creatures of the Abyss, but not before its renegade leader had slain the matron and the heir of the fourth house. Auro'pol Dyrr, the leader of the fifth-ranked house, had fallen during the war. Since orderly succession was a rarity, each of these houses might well be ravaged by internal strife before new matrons finally took power. These matrons would then face challenges on all sides. Seldom in the long history of Menzoberranzan had so many Council seats been open at one time, and at least a dozen houses could be counted on to go to war in an attempt to advance their status. Overall, the struggle to restore the Ruling Council could take years—years the faltering city could not spare.

"You know the problems Menzoberranzan faces as well as I do," Gromph continued softly. "If the city falls into anarchy, we wizards may well be her best chance of survival. We must stand ready to assume power."

Or to seize it.

These words were also left unspoken, but every drow in the room heard them, and marked them well.

Chapter 2

DAUGHTERS OF BAENRE

aenre is dead. Reign long, Matron Triel."
These words had been spoken many times, with varying degrees of sincerity, throughout the day as one by one the nobles, soldiers, and commoners of House Baenre filed past the fearsome black throne—a sentient wonder in whose gleaming depths writhed the spirits of Baenre victims—to pledge fealty to their new matron.

Triel Baenre herself was not an imposing sight. She was well under five feet tall, her body as slim and straight as a child's. By the standards of drow elves, she was not particularly attractive. Her white hair was long and thin, braided tightly and wrapped around her small head like a crown. She was clad simply: a long hauberk of elven chain mail draped over the simple black robe of a priestess. Yet Triel did not require the conventional trappings of royalty. She was one of the highest-ranked priestesses of Lloth in the city, and in the full favor of her goddess. The young matron exuded power and confidence, and she greeted each of her subjects with a regal nod.

In truth, Triel was not as comfortable with her new role as she appeared to be. Seated upon her mother's throne, she felt as if she were a child playacting. By the blood of Lloth, she swore silently, her feet did not even touch the floor! A minor indignity, perhaps, but to Triel's troubled mind her dangling feet seemed to be an omen, a sign she was not equal to the task before her.

Triel knew that, by any measures known to her, she should have been ecstatically happy with her elevation. She was now matron mother of Menzoberranzan's first house. Triel was no stranger to power—as matron mistress of the clerical school Arach-Tinilith, she held a position of great honor—but she had never truly aspired to her late mother's throne. The former matron had reigned for so many centuries she had seemed eternal. Even her given name had been lost to memory. To generations of drow, Triel's mother *was* Baenre, *was* Menzoberranzan. Thus each repetition of "Baenre is dead" echoed through Triel's mind like a portent of doom, until she felt she must scream aloud or go mad.

But at last the ceremony ended, and Triel was left alone to face the task of rebuilding the shattered household. It was a formidable challenge. A house's strength lay in its priestesses, and far too many had fallen in her mother's war. Many of the former matron's daughters—and their daughters in turn—had gone on to form houses of their own. In theory, these minor houses were allies of House Baenre, but their primary concern was spinning their own webs of power and intrigue.

In addition to its lack of priestesses, the first house was without a weapon master. Triel's brother Berg'inyon had gone missing during the war. As leader of the mighty lizard riders, he had led the attack on Mithril Hall's surface-dwelling allies, and he had never returned to his family home. Many drow had fallen in the terror and confusion that followed dawn, and it was not unlikely the Baenre weapon master was among them. Triel suspected otherwise. She'd often sensed that the young male's instincts for self-preservation far outstripped his loyalty to his house. Whatever the truth behind his disappearance, Berg'inyon was lost to her. He might be a mere youth—barely sixty years of age—but he was a strong fighter, and he would be difficult to replace. Lloth forbid, Triel thought with immense distaste, she might even be required to take on a patron to fill the role of weapon master!

Yet Triel's most immediate task was to choose her own successor at Arach-Tinilith. Usually the position of Academy matron went to the highest-ranking priestess of Lloth in House Baenre. After Triel, that would be Merith, a commoner taken into the Baenre ranks years ago when her considerable clerical powers began to emerge. Merith coveted the title of matron mistress, but this was simply out of the question. In any capacity, she was a potential disgrace to House Baenre. The former daughter of a streetsweeper had no understanding of the subtle nuances of protocol, no appreciation for the intricate warp and weft of intrigue. She was also sadistic in the extreme. In situations that called for a stiletto, Merith was a dwarven battle-axe. Triel expected her dear adopted sister to contract a rare, fatal illness any day now.

That left Sos'Umptu, the keeper of the Baenre chapel, as the most likely candidate. Sos'Umptu was Baenre-born, her favor with Lloth was secure, and her standing as a priestess impressively lofty. So after due consideration Triel sent for her younger sister and offered her Arach-Tinilith.

Sos'Umptu, far from being pleased at her promotion, was horrified at the suggestion she leave the Baenre chapel. Triel coaxed, wheedled, and threatened, but in the end she conceded that, at least for the time, she herself must fill both roles. Her younger sister received this decision with a relieved sigh, then glanced at the door that led toward her beloved chapel.

"No, stay with me a while," Triel said tiredly. "I must speak with you on another matter. House Baenre needs high priestesses desperately, especially nobles Baenre-born. You know I have no daughters of my own, nor am I likely to have any. I must rely on my sisters and their children to rebuild our strength. You keep the birth records; what can you tell me about our prospects? Any outstanding talents among the young females?"

The keeper of the chapel cleared her throat. "Probably the most gifted among them would be Liriel. Gromph's daughter?" she prompted, when Triel showed no sign of recognition.

Memory fell suddenly into place, and Triel's eyes widened in wonder as she considered the possibilities. Gromph's pampered, wayward daughter, a high priestess of Lloth. How preposterous, and how delightful!

From what Triel could recall, Gromph had fathered the child some four decades past and had inexplicably claimed her as his own. Liriel bore the name of her father's house, which was almost unheard of in their matriarchal society. Her mother, a useless beauty from some minor house, had disappeared, and for many years little had been heard of the child, except disapproving whispers that Gromph allowed the girl to run wild. With the onset of adolescence, Liriel had forged a place for herself in the frenetic social life of certain wealthy circles. Triel had heard tales of Liriel's exploits, which earned the girl notoriety and admiration in nearly equal parts. Although considered headstrong and capricious, Liriel reportedly had exceptional powers of mind and magic. What better use for such talents than the service of Lloth?

Triel smiled wickedly. How that would enrage Gromph! By law and custom, noble females entered the clerical college with the onset of puberty or upon their twenty-fifth birthday, whichever came first. Gromph had not required his daughter to attend—perhaps he had even forbidden it! The archmage was hardly devout in the service of Lloth, and Triel had caught glimpses of Gromph's bitter resentment toward the priestess rulers. Yet if Matron Triel commanded, Gromph would have little choice but to send his daughter to Arach-Tinilith.

And Liriel Baenre, as a high priestess of Lloth, would become not only a bright jewel in the crown of House Baenre, but also a powerful reminder to ambitious Gromph as to where the true power in Menzoberranzan lay.

Triel turned to regard her younger sister. "Why, Sos'Umptu," she said slyly, "you surprise me! I had not thought you capable of such devious subtlety."

Sos'Umptu flinched and said nothing, for she had learned through hard experience to be leery of compliments. Indeed, Triel's eyes hardened dangerously as she continued to observe her younger sister.

"It would seem," the new matron continued, "the keeper of the chapel has talents that reach beyond her chosen sphere of influence. See that your ambitions do not do likewise!"

Sos'Umptu sank into a deep reverence. "I desire only to serve Lloth, and my sister the matron mother," she said fervently.

Although it was almost beyond belief, Triel sensed the younger Baenre daughter spoke truth. The matron was not certain whether to regard Sos'Umptu's unnatural lack of ambition with relief or scorn, but she smiled at her sister and bid her to rise. "Your devotion does you credit," Triel said dryly, "and your idea has merit. Have someone find the girl and bring her here at once."

"Do you want Gromph to be present when you speak to his daughter?"

Heat flooded Triel's face until her countenance shone like an angry ruby. "I do not require my brother's blessing, in this matter or any other," she snapped.

"Of course not, Matron Triel," Sos'Umptu hastened to say, dipping into another respectful bow. "But I thought you might, perhaps, enjoy witnessing Gromph's distress?"

The dangerous glint in Triel's eyes warmed to become a comrade's gleam. "My dear sister, for the sake of House Baenre, you must venture out of your chapel more often!"

* * * * *

Meanwhile, far from House Baenre's audience hall, Gromph's daughter skipped lightly through the tunnels of the Underdark. Her eyes gleamed red as they pierced the darkness ahead, and an occasional cross-draft rippled through the thick white hair that fell in wavy locks to her waist. She was dressed for travel in boots and breeches fashioned from thin, supple leather, a shirt of quilted silk, and a vest of fine chain mail. A three-foot, barbed-tip spear rested on her shoulder, and in her free hand she carried a small bolo, which she twirled in elaborate patterns as she walked.

Behind her, well out of reach of the whirling weapon, trudged a young drow couple. The female wore the insignia of House Shobalar, a lesser clan known for the rare female wizards it produced. The other drow was an exceptionally handsome male, elaborately dressed but for the single-braided hair that marked him as a commoner. Both of these drow carried spears identical to Liriel's, and they darted wary glances here and there as they maneuvered through the field of small, sharp stalagmites that thrust upward from the rocky floor.

The tunnel was narrow, barely wide enough for three or four drow to walk abreast. Countless eons past, trickling water had carved a series of furrows into the rocky walls, leaving long, narrow stone ridges rising up on both sides of the tunnel. The passage resembled the rib cage of some giant beast, and Liriel's companions found it more than a little unnerving. They kept firm grip on their weapons and silently cursed the impulse that had led them out of the relative safety of Menzoberranzan. The Underdark was unpredictable and full of danger. Few ventured out into it without considerable strength of arms and magic. Yet when Liriel Baenre issued an invitation, how could they refuse?

Liriel was by far the most popular female in their set, a group of

28

wealthy young drow both noble and common who pursued pleasure and intrigue with typical drow passion. She was younger than most of them—still short of her fortieth birthday, which placed her in the midst of the long, tumultuous period of drow adolescence—and she possessed the fresh beauty similar to that of a human girl not yet seventeen. She also enjoyed the wealth and station of a House Baenre noble. But many of the city's young drow possessed wealth, status, and beauty. Liriel was exceptional for her ready laugh and a zest for life that was rare in grim Menzoberranzan. Admittedly eccentric in her tastes, she preferred the pursuit of adventure and magical knowledge to social intrigue. Still, few could deny her quirky charm. Many young drow vied for the chance to share her adventures. Those who survived could count on enhanced social standing, as well as a few good stories to share at that evening's round of parties.

Even with this pleasing prospect before them, Liriel's companions grew more uneasy with every step. The utter darkness of the passage did not inconvenience them in the slightest, but the silence deeply unnerved them. In Menzoberranzan, the noise of the city melted into a constant, spell-muffled murmur spiced by an occasional scream. In these tunnels their quiet footsteps thudded in their ears with a hollow, echoing sound, like stones falling into a deep well. Liriel, of course, walked like a shadow, thanks to her enchanted elven boots and two dozen years' experience with such exploration. Her gait was light and eager, her eyes fixed on the adventure ahead.

Yet Liriel was not unaware of her companions' discomfort. She knew Bythnara Shobalar well; the two of them had trained together from a young age. Gromph had apparently tired of his precocious daughter soon after adopting her, and sent her to House Shobalar to be fostered and trained by that clan's female wizards. A childhood rivalry had sprung up between Liriel and Bythnara that had followed them throughout the years. Liriel took this in stride, and in fact found it rather enjoyable. It sharpened both their efforts and added a necessary spice to their friendship. Despite their mutual interest in magic, the two had little in common. Bythnara did not share Liriel's delight in adventure or her sense of fun. The female wizard could be remote at times—and downright dull the rest of the time—but Liriel was well accustomed to the limits of friendship.

"Are we almost there?" Bythnara complained behind her.

"Soon."

"But we've been walking for hours, and by now Lloth only knows where we could be! We could *die* out here, and no one would know the difference!"

Liriel glanced back over her shoulder and winked at her friend. She did not, however, slow her pace in the slightest. "Correction, Bythnara: *you* could die out here and not know the difference."

The wizard's eyes narrowed. "Is that a threat?"

"Of course not," Liriel said mildly, turning back to the path ahead. "It's an *insult*. When I die, I'll no doubt realize *something* has changed. You, on the other hand . . ."

"Perhaps I don't run through life at your pace, but that is no matter for scorn. 'Caution is the better part of wisdom,'" Bythnara quoted in a tight voice.

"And the major part of boredom," Liriel returned lightly. "What about you, Syzwick?" she asked the male. Bythnara's latest consort was the son of a well-to-do perfume merchant. He was obscenely wealthy, highly decorative, spirited yet manageable—all qualities that made him very popular with the females in their set. "Are you having second thoughts, as well?"

"Of course not," the male said staunchly, shifting his spear to his other shoulder. "Still, we have been gone quite a long time."

"It'll be worth every moment," Liriel promised. She stopped suddenly, flinging out a hand to indicate they should do likewise. She pointed downward, and both of her companions gasped.

The trio stood on the very edge of a riverbank. Several feet below them lay a calm, dark expanse of water. The river ran deep, silent, and very cold. Its waters were said to come from lands of ice far above the Underdark. Although the air here was warmer than the water, a constant cloud of mist floated over the river like a guardian wraith.

"The boat is moored right below us," Liriel said, pointing down at a long, narrow skiff.

She leaped out over the dark water. Summoning her natural ability to levitate, she hung in the air for a moment and then floated down to land lightly at the bow of the boat. Her companions followed suit with considerably less gusto. They quickly seated themselves to calm the rocking of the craft. They knew they could not afford to tip over, and not just because of the icy waters.

For they were hunting *pyrimo*, small, fierce fish that could strip a full-grown lizard mount to the bone in minutes. These fish were extremely aggressive, known to leap from the water to attack animals that came to drink at the river's edge. So sharp were their teeth and so powerful their jaws that the first bite was often painless, unnoticed. The pain came quickly enough, though, for any blood in the water summoned dozens of the voracious fish. Hunting them was a dangerous sport, and accidents were not infrequent.

The first challenge was simply getting this far, for the tunnels that led to the river were seldom traveled and rarely patrolled. The river itself was a hazard—deceptively calm, given to sudden eddies and strong, random undertows. And the fish were dangerous even in death. Their flesh was delicate, tasty—and highly toxic. Carefully prepared, *pyrimo* were more potent than wine, and any party at which they were served instantly became an event. Fatalities among the diners did occur from time to time, but they were rare. Carefully trained chefs prepared *pyrimo* knowing their own lives depended on the result.

But the party was hours away, and before them lay the challenge of the hunt. Liriel placed a booted foot on the bank and shoved hard. Her boat, tethered to the rocky bank by a light mithril chain, glided toward the center of the river. When the craft stilled, Liriel took up her spear and stood in the prow, feet braced wide for balance. Bythnara echoed her stance in the stern, while Syzwick took a seat in the center for ballast. The boat was designed so two could hunt at a time, one on either end and well out of each other's reach. The fish attacked even when impaled, and more than one drow had been bitten by his hunting companion's speared catch. Whether by accident or design, who could say?

Liriel took two small flasks from the bag at her waist and tossed one to Bythnara. The flasks were enspelled to keep the contents—fresh rothe blood—warm. Liriel opened her flask and poured a single drop of blood into the water. To the drow's heat-sensitive eyes, the droplet appeared bright red. It would be visible for only a moment, for the icy waters would cool it quickly. Liriel readied her spear and watched intently. The glowing drop disappeared, suddenly and completely.

Liriel's spear flashed down into the water. She raised it triumphantly—a fish about the size of her hand thrashed and wriggled on the point. *Pyrimo* were impossible to see in the water, for their body temperature matched exactly that of the chill river. Clearly visible in the warmer air, the fish was a smooth oval, with silvery scales and delicate fins—a pretty thing, except for the steely, fanged jaws that spanned the width of its body.

31

"Catch, Syzwick," Liriel said casually, and with a flick of her spear she tossed the lethal fish toward the male. The drow paled and cringed away. No need: the fish slapped wetly into the box at his feet.

"If you'd missed . . ." Syzwick began.

Liriel sent him a saucy grin. "I haven't yet! Don't worry, love, the last thing I'd want to do is drop a hungry *pyrimo* in your lap," she purred. "One bite, and you'd be no good to anyone."

Bythnara's lips tightened; seeing this, Liriel suppressed a sigh. Her friend could be so possessive at times! Liriel had meant only to tease Syzwick a bit, knowing the handsome male appreciated bawdy humor. But Bythnara always mistook such remarks as statements of intent.

Syzwick did not notice the female wizard's peevish expression; he grinned lasciviously at Liriel and raised an eyebrow.

"*One* bite?" he challenged.

Liriel swept him with an appraising glance. "Perhaps two," she allowed.

Bythnara snorted and gave her flask of blood a vicious shake. Bright droplets scattered into the river.

"Don't put so much blood into the water at one time," Liriel cautioned her sternly. She could tolerate Bythnara's foul temper, but only up to a point. "You don't want to start a frenzy."

That thought sobered the jealous young wizard, and for a long time the two females hunted in silence. Perched on the very tip of the boat, Liriel worked quickly, leaning out over the water and spearing one fish after another. She herself did not care for the *pyrimo*, beyond the challenge of the hunt, but the fish had another value to her that her companions could not begin to fathom. The prospect of another hazardous adventure beckoned Liriel this day, and she was too pleased with life to allow Bythnara's snit to spoil her mood.

The boat shifted slightly, and from the corner of her eye Liriel saw that Bythnara had seated herself and put aside her spear. The female grimaced and rubbed at her neck. She reached into her travel bag and removed a small vial. She poured some pungent liniment into her hand and began to massage the sides of her neck.

A warning light flashed in Liriel's mind. She had hunted *pyrimo* many times, and well knew the strain caused by the watchful tension and lightning-fast spear thrusts. Bythnara was massaging the wrong muscles.

For a moment Liriel felt a familiar, hollow feeling in her chest, the dull empty ache that came anew with each betrayal. She quickly thrust it aside and coolly, surreptitiously studied her childhood friend. As Liriel suspected, Bythnara's massaging fingers moved in a complex, familiar pattern. The wizard was casting a spell. It was not a common spell, but Liriel had learned it just last week from her new and powerful tutor. Bythnara, of course, did not know this. Liriel's teacher had forbidden her to share with anyone the spells he taught her, and for once she blessed the greedy, paranoid nature of Menzoberranzan's wizards.

Bythnara rose, stretching, unaware her prey had sensed the hunt-within-a-hunt. The wizard's next move, Liriel knew, would be to fling out a hand and send a fireball sizzling toward the prow of the boat.

Keeping her feet spread in a hunting stance, Liriel once again summoned the natural magic of levitation. Then, in one quick, fluid movement, she rose high into the air, whirled, and threw her spear like a javelin. The barbed tip tore into Bythnara's chest, and the wizard's languid yawn turned into a rounded O of shock and pain. Arms windmilling, she toppled backward into the water.

Instantly the *pyrimo* were upon her. Liriel floated above the river's misty shroud, watching with an impassive expression as the water below her churned and roiled, turning red in the darkness as it was warmed by the blood of her treacherous friend.

When the wild rocking of the boat stilled and the waters had once again turned cool and dark, Liriel drifted back down. Syzwick still lay flat on the floor of the boat, where he had wisely thrown himself in an effort to keep the craft upright.

Liriel regarded the handsome male for a long moment as she considered what best to do with him. The scented liniment Bythnara had used had no doubt come from his father's store. It seemed likely that Syzwick had plotted with Bythnara. Perhaps the female wizard had told her consort something that might help Liriel understand the motive for this attack. If so, Liriel intended to get some answers. She kicked him, none too gently.

Syzwick scrambled onto the center seat, his eyes frantic as they met Liriel's implacable crimson gaze.

"I'll swear to anything you like," Syzwick said, the words fairly bursting from him. "I'll say Bythnara attacked you. That's believable enough, considering how much she hated you. She's always hated you—jealous, mostly—and has never bothered to hide the fact. Everyone knows it. Everyone will believe us," the male babbled on, "for she's spoken often enough of wanting to see you dead. Mind you, as far as I know she had no real plans to move against you. And I swear—I swear it by Lloth's eighth leg!—that I would never go along with such a plan, even if she'd had one and demanded my help! You know that, Liriel. All her talk about wanting you dead—it was only talk; you know how these things go."

"Yes," Liriel said in a dull, tight voice.

She knew very well, indeed. And finally, Syzwick's frantic chatter was starting to make sense. The male honestly did not know of Bythnara's attack. He had seen only that Liriel had slain his lover, and his only concern was his own survival. Murder—for such it was in Syzwick's eyes—was perfectly acceptable, even lauded, among dark elves, *provided it could not be proven.* Syzwick was a witness, and he fully expected to be eliminated. The male was pleading for his life, promising to swear that Liriel had acted in self-defense.

How ironic, she thought numbly, that in doing so he would be speaking simple truth! But she would never truly convince him of that. Nor, for her own half-understood reasons, did she want to try.

"Bythnara slipped and fell in," she said at last.

Syzwick's forehead furrowed in puzzlement, and he waited for Liriel to elaborate. When she did not, he accepted the lie with an eager nod.

"Bythnara was reaching for a fish when the boat struck one of those little eddies," he said, improvising. "We were tossed about in a circle. She lost her balance and fell. We tried to reach her, but the *pyrimo* were upon her too quickly."

He held his breath as he awaited the female's response. Slowly, a grim smile crept across Liriel's face, and Syzwick let out a sigh of soul-deep relief.

"One more thing."

"Anything!" he swore fervently.

"Planning a deed requires layers upon layers; you know this. But after the fact, do try to keep things simple, hmm?"

Syzwick was silent for a moment. "Bythnara slipped and fell in," he echoed.

"Good boy," she said dryly. "You should also bear in mind that *pyrimo* can kill in more ways than one. I would hate to see one of my dinner guests develop, shall we say, a fatal case of indigestion."

"I won't say a word," he promised. "Not ever."

Liriel nodded, and her smile hid more than she cared to

acknowledge. "In that case, let's get you and these fish back to Menzoberranzan."

★   ★   ★   ★   ★

It was turning out to be one of those days, Liriel observed, when nothing seemed to go according to plan. She'd intended to deliver Syzwick back to the city along with most of the *pyrimo* catch, then head back into the Underdark to barter off the rest of the toxic little goodies. She had several deals to make, some spells to learn, a tutorial to attend, a few scores to settle, and an assignation with a certain mercenary to keep—all before that night's festivities began. In short, it was supposed to have been a fairly typical day.

First came the hunting "accident;" then, just as she was leaving her house—a miniature castle in Narbondellyn that her father had given her on her twenty-fifth birthday—the silent alarm on her Baenre ring began to pulse.

Liriel's brow furrowed with annoyance as she dug around for the ring in the bottom of her bag. She was supposed to wear the insignia at all times, but she never wore rings. Her long, shapely hands were one of her favorite features, and she liked to ornament them with elaborate painted tatoos and glittering nail polish, but she refused to wear rings. She could hurl a knife with the best tavern cutthroat alive, and, although most drow contended jewelry did not throw off their aim, Liriel figured she took enough chances without adding that particular risk.

She found the ring and clenched it in her hand. Yes, there it was again: a silent, magical alarm, attuned to her senses alone. She'd heard it only once before, when the ring was given to her a couple dozen years ago. Every noble in Menzoberranzan carried a house insignia; House Baenre went one step further and kept each of its members on a magical leash. At the sound of the alarm, the Baenre in question was supposed to drop everything and hasten to the family fortress. Until now, Liriel had been spared such a summons. Muttering imprecations, she saddled her riding lizard and spurred it toward her ancestral home.

House Baenre was a sprawling, impressive affair. The natural rock formations were stunning enough, but over the centuries Baenre matrons had added elaborate carvings, onion-shaped domes highlighted with purple faerie fire, and a magical webbed fence supposedly woven by Lloth herself. It was, in Liriel's opinion, a bit much. Decadence was all fine and well, but this was definitely over the top.

The gate swung open at her approach and a line of Baenre soldiers bowed low. An ogre servant hurried forward to take her mount, and an escort of eight armed females—the matron mother's elite guard—led her through the winding halls toward the very heart of the castle: the Baenre chapel. This, Liriel noted grimly as she marched along in the heat shadow of her escort, was starting to look very bad indeed.

An even more impressive gathering awaited her in the chapel. There were two powerful priestesses: Sos'Umptu, keeper of the chapel, with her somber priestess robes and her pinched, pious face, and Triel, the newly elevated matron mother. Of the two, Liriel vastly preferred the boring and dowdy Sos'Umptu. The keeper rarely stepped outside her beloved chapel, but at least she was passionate about *something*. Triel, on the other hand, was a two-legged spider: cold, utterly practical, ruthlessly efficient. Gromph stood stiffly beside his sisters. Liriel took heart at the sight of her father until she noted the grim expression on his face. And looming above the Baenre siblings was a giant magical illusion, a tribute to Lloth that constantly shapeshifted from a giant black spider to a beautiful drow female. Gromph had created the spectacular illusion some fifty years ago to placate the former matron. It was rumored this tribute to Lloth had purchased the life of the impious archmage, who had angered his mother once too often. It was less well known that he'd modeled the drow female after his then-mistress. Liriel did not remember the face of her long-dead mother, but her own resemblance to the spider-drow was uncanny, and unsettling. The young drow took a deep breath and stepped into the chapel.

"Here at last," observed Triel in her tight, expressionless voice.

Liriel saluted her with deep bow. "At your command, Auntie Triel."

"*Matron* Triel," Sos'Umptu reprimanded sharply, her outrage at this lack of respect written clearly on her face. She took a deep breath and prepared to launch into the usual tirade.

But Triel waved her sister to silence. She leaned forward and fixed Liriel with a long, searching gaze. "It has come to my attention that your twenty-fifth year has come and gone. Yet you did not enter the Academy, as is law and custom for all those of noble blood. Almost fifteen years wasted in frivolity, when you should have been preparing to serve House Baenre."

Liriel raised her chin and faced the matron squarely. "I have used the time well. My father," she emphasized, glancing pointedly at the archmage, "arranged for me to have the best magical training possible."

"You have not attended the Sorcere," Triel pointed out, naming the mage school.

"Technically, no," Liriel agreed. Gromph had refused to sponsor her at the Sorcere, arguing that as the sole female there and as his daughter, she would be the target of much intrigue and would bring undue controversy upon the family. Promising her she would not feel the lack of such training, he used his power and wealth to secure for her the best tutors and gave her a generous allowance that enabled her to purchase whatever books and spell components she fancied. She cast a quick glance at Gromph, hoping he would support her. The archmage's tight, closed expression indicated she could expect no help there.

"But I *have* studied with several of the Sorcere's masters. My current tutor is Kharza-kzad Xorlarrin," she added, naming a powerful wizard who specialized in the crafting of battle wands.

Triel snorted derisively. "By all reports, you've been instructing the old he-rothe, not the other way around! Kharza-kzad's boasts have spread from the Sorcere to Melee-Magthere and even into Arach-Tinilith. Your exploits have been the talk of the Academy."

So have yours, Liriel thought with mutinous rage. It was well known that Triel had never taken a consort, and dark whispers suggested the matron mother's tastes were deviant even by drow standards. But to speak of such matters aloud would be less than wise. Nor did Liriel see any reason to either confirm or deny her tutor's boasts. She responded to Triel's baiting only with a noncommittal leer.

The Baenre matron glanced toward Gromph's scowling face, and a tiny smile lifted the corners of her mouth. "In fact," she continued softly, "I think one could say many are looking forward to the day you finally enter the Academy."

There. The old wretch had finally shown her steel. Liriel's heart sank, but she knew there was no possible way to parry the blow to come. Well, she thought grimly, she could definitely imagine worse fates. The loss of freedom would be hard to take, but she truly enjoyed the study of magic. And Kharza's boasts, although completely untrue, saved her the trouble of establishing a fun-loving reputation.

She could hit the Academy running, in a manner of speaking.

"When?" Liriel asked bluntly.

"Considering you're fifteen years late, there's no real hurry. Tomorrow will be soon enough," Triel said. Her red eyes glowed with malicious amusement.

"At your command, Auntie Triel," Liriel agreed. "I will report to the Sorcere before Narbondel reaches midpoint."

Triel's smile broadened. "I'm afraid you misunderstand, dear child," she said with false sweetness. "You will report to *Arach-Tinilith*."

"What!"

The word burst from Liriel on a shriek of rage and disbelief. She whirled to face her father. The archmage raised his hand, and the look on his face was so forbidding that his daughter's protests and entreaties died unspoken.

"It is the custom of the city, and it is Matron Triel's wish," he said stiffly.

With great difficulty, the young drow managed a nod. Furious at Triel for shunting her off to the clerical school, she was almost as angry at herself for falling into the nasty little trap the old spider had laid for her. Triel had deliberately led her to believe she would be attending the Sorcere, when all along the matron had intended to send her to the clerical school. Liriel paid little heed to Triel's words of instruction and dismissal, and was only vaguely aware of her father's hand on her shoulder, guiding her none too gently out of the chapel.

They were almost to the door when Triel called her name. Still numb with shock, Liriel turned to face the older female. All pretense of pleasantry had faded from the matron's face, and Liriel was stunned by the triumphant, icy malice in Triel's narrowed gaze.

"Listen well, my girl: once you're in the Academy you will follow the same rules as every other novice. Much is expected of you. You will excel in your studies, uphold the honor of House Baenre, and earn the favor of Lloth, *or you will not survive*. It is that simple." She gave Gromph an arch glance, and Liriel an icy smile. "But you have one last night to carouse. Do have a good time."

"*Have a good time*," Liriel mimicked bitterly as she and the archmage strode down the hall. "This, from someone whose idea of fun involves whipping people with snakes!"

Her blasphemous remark drew a shocked chuckle from Gromph.

"You must learn to guard your tongue," he admonished. "Few of the Academy's mistresses are burdened with a sense of humor."

"Don't I know it! Father, do I really have to become a priestess?" she demanded. "Can't you do anything to stop this?"

Liriel knew the words were a mistake the moment she spoke them. No one stayed healthy for long by pointing out to proud, frustrated Gromph that there were limits to his power.

The expected rage did not come. "It is *my will* you become a priestess," the archmage said coldly.

He was lying, of course, and he made no effort to hide the fact. Was her future not worth even *that* much effort?

"You have many talents," he continued, "and as a priestess you could accomplish a great deal."

"For the greater glory of House Baenre," she said bitterly.

"That too," Gromph agreed cryptically. He was silent for a long moment, as if carefully weighing his next words. "Do you know why we wizards are tolerated in Menzoberranzan?"

Liriel cast a quick, startled glance at her father. "Target practice?"

"Don't be flip with me!" snapped the archmage. "It is important you understand. Consider this: Lloth is the sole recognized deity in the city, and her priestesses rule virtually unopposed. Why does Menzoberranzan need males at all, except to breed still more priestesses? Why grant males the power to wield magic?"

"Few drow females—at least in Menzoberranzan—have the sort of innate magical talent needed for wizardry," she responded.

"So? Why tolerate wizards at all?"

The young drow thought this over. "There are limits to clerical powers," she reasoned.

"Not that any priestess would admit to it," he agreed in a sour tone. "But know this: few drow females have magical talent, and wizards have access to powers that followers of Lloth cannot manage. This power is carefully monitored by the matriarchy, of course, but Menzoberranzan needs her wizards."

The archmage reached into a hidden pocket of his cloak and drew out a small book. "This is yours. Learn it well, for you would surely go mad in Arach-Tinilith without the escape this book offers you." He paused for a grim smile. "I had this compiled for you—a task that spanned several years and cost the lives of a number of wizards— knowing this day would come."

That was quite a pitch, even for melodramatic Gromph, Liriel thought with a touch of wry humor. She took the book and opened it to the first spell. She skimmed the page, and the meaning of the symbols came to her with a rush of excitement and disbelief.

"This is a spell for summoning a gate!"

"And so is every other spell in the book," he agreed. "With this knowledge, you can travel where no priestess can follow."

Liriel leafed through the spellbook, her excitement growing by the moment. Magical travel was extremely difficult in the Underdark, and those who tried it often ended up as a permanent part of the landscape. This gift would give her greater freedom than she had ever enjoyed. Best of all, her father had foreseen this day, and prepared for it! Liriel hugged the precious book to her chest.

"I can't begin to thank you!" she cried joyfully.

Gromph Baenre smiled down at her, but his amber eyes remained cold. "Not yet, perhaps, but when the time comes I will tell you how you can properly express your gratitude. Become a priestess and seize what power you can. But never forget you are a wizard first and foremost. Your loyalty belongs to me."

The warmth fled from Liriel's heart. She held the archmage's hard gaze, and her golden eyes mirrored his. "Don't worry, Father," she said softly. "Lloth forbid I should ever forget what I am to you."

Chapter 3

FYODOR OF RASHEMEN

awn touched the snow-tipped pines, and in the faint light the mist over Lake Ashane glowed a sunrise pink. On the eastern side of the lake rose a stark, steep hill, its crest hidden in dense clouds. At the base of this hill a young man reined his sturdy little horse to a halt. His mountain pony—a shaggy, barrel-shaped beast as ill-tempered as she was strong—stomped the frozen ground and nickered irritably.

"Take ease, Sasha," crooned her rider in a remarkably deep, rich bass voice. "We have ridden through the night, you and I, but at last we have found the place."

The young man took a long, deep breath of the cold morning air. "Can you not feel it?" he murmured. "Here a mighty battle was waged and lost. Here we begin."

With that, Fyodor of Rashemen swung down from his saddle. He considered the hill before him and decided he would have to walk. Sasha might look a bit like a mountain goat—except in battle, when she resembled nothing so much as a fierce, four-legged dwarf—but the slope was too steep even for her. So he left the horse untethered

41

and began his trek up the mountain.

Winter was harsh this year, and spring late to come. The air was brittle with cold, and the snow crunched and squeaked under his boots as he climbed. But Fyodor was at home with the harsh climate. This was his land, and he had spent all of his nineteen winters within its borders. Rashemen was written in the broad, chiseled planes of his face, the straight dark hair the color of bare-limbed trees, and his winter-pale skin. Fyodor was a strong man, stocky and just a bit short of six feet. He was also a simple man; he traveled clad in layers of warm, sturdy peasant clothes and a practical cloak of dark wool. His only weapons were a blunt, roughly hammered sword of some dark metal and a three-foot cudgel fashioned from light, rock-hard driftwood. He used the driftwood club now as a staff, plunging it into the snow again and again as he hauled himself up the hill.

At last Fyodor reached the summit. He stood for a long moment, looking out over his land. Lake Ashane and the surrounding countryside lay before him, clearly visible despite the clouds that huddled over the mountaintop. To his north stretched the deep, ancient Ashenwood. Huge swaths of land lay barren, for in recent months hundreds of trees had fallen to the axes of the Tuigan barbarians. The invaders had razed large tracts of the forest to build ships for their ill-fated crossing. Fyodor shook his head in mute grief at the sight of yet another scar upon the land.

The Tuigan barbarians had swept through his beloved Rashemen, leaving pain and destruction everywhere. He had fought them, and he would be fighting still but for the command of the Witches who ruled the land. Fyodor had proven his valor in battle and had been sent away with honor. Even so, he *had* been sent away.

Fyodor accepted his fate without rancor, for none knew better than he the danger he posed to those around him. He would no doubt fight for Rashemen again, but he dared not do so until he had mastered the enemy within. Just the sight of the long-cold battlefield below him sent a familiar, dangerous heat through Fyodor's veins.

So the young man turned away from the blighted landscape and faced the task ahead. A stone tower crowned the hill; he gave it a quick glance and slogged off through the snow in search of an ancient well. Behind the tower he found a simple, circular stone wall and knew at once he had found the source of this place's unique power.

He dropped to one knee to honor the ancient, mysterious spirit who dwelt on this distant hillside. The tower had been built on this place of power several hundred years before. The Witches' magic was more potent here, and a small circle of them could protect the western boundaries of their land. From here the dreaded Witch boats were launched against any who ventured onto Lake Ashane. Unmanned and armed with powerful magic, the Witch boats attacked all who dared set sail upon the lake. With the help of the place-spirit, the Witches could even summon water wraiths: creatures of steam who had a scalding touch, and whose breath was hot enough to melt elvish steel. Fyodor had heard these stories from birth, and now he was about to see such wonders for himself.

Fyodor knelt by the well and brushed away some of the snow. He scraped together a handful of ice-encrusted soil and held it tightly in his hand. As he had hoped—and as he had feared—the memory of what had happened came to him.

He saw a circle of women, black-robed and masked, their finger-tips touching lightly as they chanted, melding their magic into one powerful spell. He watched in awe as the Witches summoned their legendary defenses against the Tuigan invaders.

Unlike the powerful women who ruled Rashemen, or the Old Ones who taught gifted men to craft wondrous magical items, Fyodor knew no magic except for that which burned in his veins and sped his sword in battle. But he did have a trace of the Sight, as did many of his people. It was an unreliable gift, as hard to command as a dream, and it often seemed to Fyodor that insights came to him just often enough to be annoying. Yet in places like this, places of power, events both wondrous and terrible left echoes for those who could hear.

Through the power of the Sight, Fyodor watched as the sorcerous Witch boats attacked the hastily built Tuigan crafts. He heard the Witches summon poisonous mists to enshroud the lakes, and call upon the giant dragon turtles that lurked beneath the waters. By the scores, by the thousands, the Tuigan died.

All this Fyodor saw, and felt a grim satisfaction at the justice the Witches meted out. Then, suddenly, the vision faded. Still attuned to the echoes of battle, Fyodor felt the remembered presence of a new power, a malevolent magic that seared and corrupted all that it touched. Yet what he saw was only the shadow of a memory; there was no image to accompany the sense of lingering evil, nothing that could tell him of the battle's end.

Fyodor cast away the handful of soil and rose to his feet. The answers he sought could be found only in the tower. Although he dreaded what he might find, he circled around to the lone door and kicked his way in.

He quickly searched the lower levels. There was no sign of the mystic circle he had glimpsed. The women's dying agonies lingered in the air of the enchanted tower, but the Witches had simply disappeared. Fyodor was not surprised; even in death, the dark sisterhood cared for its own. No doubt the women's bodies had been magically whisked away for honorable burial in the Witches' stronghold city far to the east. Yet a mystery remained: one of those women had possessed an ancient magical treasure, and that treasure had not returned to the hands of the sisterhood. It had become Fyodor's task to find it.

Fyodor continued his search until he reached the very top of the tower. The uppermost chamber of any keep was usually the most secure room, the place where treasures would be kept.

The door was open a crack, its magical defenses apparently spent. Fyodor nudged the door with his cudgel and it swung inward, creaking softly.

Immediately he was assaulted by a horrid stench: the sickly sweet, unmistakable smell of human carrion. Fyodor flung his arm across his nose to ward off the worst of the odor and pushed into the room. Sprawled about, in various stages of decomposition, were several red-robed figures. Some looked newly dead, others lay in steaming, rotting piles, and a few were little more than dust.

"Red Wizards," he muttered, and he began to understand what had happened here. Despite his youth, Fyodor had spent years fighting the powerful enemies that surrounded his land. Until the coming of the Tuigan hoard, Rashemen's deadliest foe had been Thay, an ancient land ruled by the powerful Red Wizards. Many of these wizards used magic to sustain their wretched lives far past the natural span; this would explain the many stages of decay.

But the deaths themselves? The answer to this seeming riddle was plain enough to one who had been raised in the shadow of Thay. The Red Wizards had formed a nominal alliance with the Tuigan invaders, but they were ever alert for opportunities to extend their own power. Any one of them would happily slay his fellows for personal gain. During the recent battle, these wizards had probably banded together to attack the Witches while the women were deep in their spell meld. Once they'd overcome the Witches in spell battle, the wizards had breached the tower and stripped it of its treasures. Then a single wizard had turned on the others and claimed all the treasures of the Witches' tower for himself.

A quick search of the chamber confirmed Fyodor's suspicions. There was nothing of value: no spellbooks, none of the famed Rashemi rings and wands, not a single pot of anything that resembled a spell component. The bodies of the Red Wizards had also been stripped of all magic-bearing items. The surviving wizard had taken the magical treasures of both his enemies and his allies.

No doubt this wizard had fled to a secret place, to study in private his stolen treasure until the time he had mastered enough power to return to Thay and increase his domain. Long before that day came, Fyodor would find him.

But first, he had a task to complete.

The young man dragged the dead wizards from the tower. He found a convenient, steep cliff on the south side of the hill and tossed the bodies into the ravine far below. There he left them for carrion. Fyodor did not consider giving the wizards the dignity of burial; in his land, honor must be earned. After all the bodies had been cast out of the tower, Fyodor drew water from the ancient well and sprinkled it around the defiled tower, and in each room.

When the sacred site had been cleansed, Fyodor half-ran, half-slid down the hillside. He had far to go this day, with only the promise of battle at day's end to coax weary little Sasha onward. It was well for him, Fyodor mused, that the pony loved nothing better than a fight.

*　*　*　*　*

Fyodor and Sasha spent the day searching for the renegade wizard. Although the Rashemi was a fine tracker who had hunted everything from wild rothe to the elusive snowcat, he did not really expect to find the wizard's trail. The battle was many days past, and thousands of footsteps lay buried under the fresh snow. Yet he remembered an old story, and thought he knew where a wizard alone in this forest might go.

The afternoon shadows were long when Fyodor found the first tracks. Huge, three-toed footprints, like those of a giant chicken, skittered through the forest. He followed the tracks deep into the Ashenwood. The forest was different here, quiet and watchful. The shadows were unnaturally deep, and the tall, snow-shrouded pines seemed to whisper secrets. Fyodor could sense the dark enchantment of the place, and Sasha whuffled uneasily as she slogged through the snow.

Night was falling when Fyodor found what he sought. From atop a heavily wooded hill, he glimpsed a small clearing in a valley below. In it stood a trim wooden hut. In most regards the hut was a fairly common Rashemi dwelling—tight and snug, with a thick thatched roof and brightly painted shutters. Unlike most huts, however, this one stood high off the ground on giant chicken legs. The hut strutted about the clearing as if it were a bantam rooster surveying its domain.

Fyodor slipped from Sasha's back and edged closer to the clearing. He had come this far without any real plan for defeating the wizard, but usually a solution came to him, if he pondered a matter long enough. He crouched down to watch and to wait.

He remembered the old stories, tales of a crone who had once lived in a magical hut. In the stories, the hut whirled and danced when the mistress—or now the master, Fyodor supposed—was sleeping safely within. At the moment, the hut looked as if it were patrolling the clearing. It seemed likely to Fyodor that the occupant was not home. He left Sasha on the hillside and made his way down toward the hut. It was risky, perhaps, but certainly safer than facing a red wizard's magic, or the lingering curses of the legendary crone.

At the edge of the clearing Fyodor paused and began to sing the words to a childhood verse:

> "While the mistress is asleep,
> Chicken-legs a watch will keep.
> When the mistress wanders off,
> Chicken-legs will stand aloft.
> When the mistress comes again,
> Chicken-legs will let her in.
> *Stara Baba* casts this spell,
> Listen, hut, and hearken well."

At the first note of the little song, the hut paused as if to listen. When Fyodor was finished singing, the hut ambled to the center of the clearing, folded its legs, and settled down much as a brooding hen would. The heavy front door swung open.

Fyodor silently blessed the village storyteller. Many times he had stolen away to the old man's hut to hear stories of far places and homely magic, to learn songs and to dream dreams. Some people thought the old tales and songs were meant only to entertain children, or to while away the long winter nights. Those who had learned to dream knew better.

The warrior drew his sword and walked cautiously toward the hut. Inside he found a jumble of various magics. Dusty vials cluttered the shelves, and long-dry herbs lay about on a table next to the ancient mortar and pestle once used to grind plants into potions. On the vast stone fireplace, an iron caldron bubbled and steamed despite the lack of fuel or fire, making the cottage pleasantly warm. But there was no sign of the treasure.

"Time now to think, not to dream," Fyodor admonished himself, settling down into the room's only chair. "The wizard did not carry away all the treasures of a Witches' tower in a sack."

He scanned the room, looking for something that was out of place with the simple furnishings. Finally his eyes fell upon the small, elaborately carved wooden box on the table beside him. He picked it up and raised the lid. The box was empty, but for a few bits of junk and jewelry.

Fyodor's eyes lit up. He selected a tiny golden circlet and carefully picked it up. As soon as it had cleared the edge of the box, the ring began to enlarge. It swiftly grew into a thick bracer engraved with magical symbols, large enough to fit a brawny man's forearm. The Rashemi dropped the treasure to the floor and took out a pale sliver of wood. This grew to become a wand carved from ash and painted with brightly colored symbols. On and on Fyodor went, and with each item he removed, another appeared to take its place. The pile of treasure was nearly knee-high before Fyodor found what he sought.

It was a simple trinket, a tiny golden dagger, not more than three inches long, hanging from a thin chain. The dagger's sheath was carved with runes from some long-dead language, and the metal was worn and darkened with age. Fyodor quickly hung the chain about his neck and tucked the precious thing out of sight. The Witches had made no promises, but they had suggested this ancient amulet might be the key to Fyodor's release.

Leaving the rest of the treasure heaped on the floor, the young Rashemi slipped out into the night. Immediately the hut rose and resumed its pacing.

47

Fyodor scrambled up the hill with all possible speed, for he wanted to be far from the clearing when the Red Wizard returned. He patted Sasha and swung up into the saddle. As he reined the pony away, he cast one last, triumphant glance back toward the wizard's borrowed retreat.

At that moment the shadows on the far side of the clearing seemed to stir. A single, ghostly figure emerged from the trees. And then another. Soon there were six of them, man-shaped, but so lithe of form and graceful of movement that they seemed unreal, insubstantial. Slowly, stealthily, the shadows eased away from the sheltering darkness and crept into the clearing on silent feet.

Fyodor recoiled and sucked in a silent, startled breath. Dark elves! He had heard many fearful stories about the drow, and from time to time his people encountered them in the mines deep under the rocky hills of Rashemen. He himself had never seen one. They were beautiful, with their glowing red eyes and skin so dark it seemed to swallow the moonlight. They were also hunting, and no living predator was as deadly.

Without making a sound, Fyodor slid to the ground. Although he was far from the drow band, he did not want to take any chances. To their eyes, the heat given off by a man and his horse would shine as brightly as a beacon. He led Sasha behind some snow-covered brambles and crouched to watch.

The dark elves stalked the pacing hut, their drawn weapons gleaming in the faint moonlight. One of the drow—a thin, fox-faced male with a thick mane of coppery hair—came forward. His hands traced strange symbols in the air as he chanted in a harsh, sibilant language.

"The forest is thick with wizards tonight," Fyodor murmured uneasily. He watched as the drow's feet left the ground and the figure began to float upward toward the door of the hut. As he hung suspended in the thin, cold air, the wizard cast another spell, then reached for the latch on the heavy wooden door.

"Oh, but he's going to wish he hadn't," the Rashemi observed with a wry smile. The hut had its own magical defenses, but surely the absent wizard had placed additional wards around his stolen hoard.

Disaster came quickly in the shadow of that thought. A burst of crimson light flashed from the door, sending the drow wizard hurtling backward through the air. He crashed into a pine and plummeted to the ground. Snow tumbled from the tree's branches and covered him like a thick, rounded shroud. None of the other drow came to the wizard's aid, for every eye was fixed upon the large wooden door that had suddenly appeared in the center of the clearing. Every weapon was raised for battle.

The door burst open, and from some invisible place beyond rushed tall, dog-headed warriors clad only in their own furry hides. Gnolls, for such they were, were natural enemies of elves, and they fell upon the dark-elven thieves with fierce howls and slashing swords. On and on came the gnolls, pouring through the magical portal as if they were angry bees erupting from a hive. Fyodor counted twenty before the crush and turmoil of battle made further reckoning impossible.

Fyodor's heart hammered as he watched the battle, and despite everything he had heard told of the drow he found himself hoping the elves might prevail. There were but six drow against creatures twice their size and four times their number, but how they fought! Fyodor was a warrior from a nation of renowned fighters, and never had he seen such swordcraft. He watched in awe as elven steel twirled and slashed, as the drow danced and thrust. He studied the dark elves, how they fought, how they moved. How they killed.

The gnolls fell quickly, and for a moment it seemed the drow would win the day. Then Fyodor heard a familiar, dreaded sound: the dry, thumping *whoosh* of giant wings and an eerie, wavering cry too harsh to have come from a living throat. The drow heard it, too, and they looked up into the sky. Their red eyes widened at the sight of the horror hurtling toward them.

There were simply no words to describe darkenbeasts. The monsters flew, but they were not like birds. They had been living creatures once, but transformed by a Red Wizard's magic they became twisted, deformed abominations. Fyodor had no idea what sort of animal this darkenbeast had been, but it must have been large. As the creature swept down like a swooping hawk, its outstretched wings blotted out the moon.

The darkenbeast swooped toward the tallest drow, a male who fought with two slender swords. At the moment this elf's flashing blades held off three gnolls, and as he fought he danced on a pile of gnoll bodies, whether to intimidate his enemies or to face the much taller gnolls eye-to-eye, Fyodor could not say.

Enormous talons flexed wide as the darkenbeast closed in. At the last moment, the drow dove aside with incredible agility, and the monstrous claws closed around the three gnolls. The darkenbeast lumbered into the sky with its burden. An angry cry rang out when it realized it had been cheated, and it simply dropped the gnolls. Flailing and howling, the dog-men fell to the ground. They hit hard and lay silent and broken. Huge wings beat wildly, filling the air with their thumping rhythm as the darkenbeast climbed for another attacking stoop.

Nor was the darkenbeast the drow's only problem. A vortex of tiny, sparkling crystals rose from the snow, spinning wildly and gaining mass and power by the moment. With a sharp crack, the whirling ceased and a manlike creature, eight feet tall and stocky as a dwarf, waded toward the dark elves. Fyodor muttered an oath. Skilled though the drow might be, they could do little against an ice golem.

Sure enough, the dark elves' swords glanced ineffectually off the solid ice of their newest foe. A huge white fist closed around one warrior, and the ice golem raised the drow high. The golem regarded its captive stolidly, not flinching from the blows the drow struck again and again. The dark elf's arm slowed and the blows came with less force as the unnatural cold of the golem's grip stole the drow's lifeforce. With a casual toss, the ice creature flung the dead drow aside and looked about for another victim.

Fyodor felt the hair on the back of his neck stand on end, and a prickle ran down his arms. He glanced down. The snow beneath his feet had melted to slush.

"No," Fyodor whispered. "Not again, not now."

He struggled against the rising tide of heat and fury, but it was too late and he knew it. His last conscious thought was regret for Sasha. The fierce pony would certainly rush into battle beside him. He had little hope for her life against such foes.

Then the battle rage took him.

* * * * *

Nisstyre stirred and struggled beneath his snowy blanket. Every bone and sinew ached from the fall. He had not expected this attack—his spell should have disarmed any traps on the hut's door—but then, he had never encountered the humans known as Red Wizards. He would be better prepared next time, provided he survived this attempt.

50

Finally he clawed his way out of the snowbank and drew in air with a deep, ragged breath. Then he saw the apparition storming down the hill, and he almost forgot to exhale.

A human man—or so Nisstyre assumed—rushed toward the clearing. Dark hair stood up about his head like the bristles of an enraged hedgehog, and his face was suffused with intense heat. The warrior's countenance glowed an angry red in both the light- and heat-spectrums, yet a faint, unnerving smile curved his lips. As he thundered toward the battle he thrashed the air with a long, broad-bladed sword. At first glance, the warrior appeared to be about seven feet tall, but Nisstyre was accustomed to magical illusions and he saw beyond this one. The man was in reality less than six feet tall, and although he was powerfully muscled he should not have been able to swing that enormous black sword as he did. The weapon was broad, and its edge appeared to be thick and dull, yet each wild pass cut the air with a strongly audible *swish*. By some magic that Nisstyre did not understand, this warrior was much more than he should have been.

The drow wizard struggled painfully to his feet. Although he felt and resented the strange power of this human, his first thought—and his first spell—had to address the most immediate threats. A strange, ugly dragon-thing was plummeting, with gaping jaws and out-stretched talons, toward his band of thieves.

Nisstyre flung a hand skyward. An enormous fireball hurtled toward the flying monster, and the two deadly forces collided in an explosion that shook snow from the trees and knocked the ice golem to its knees. The dragon-thing spiraled to the ground and crashed with a burst of oily flame. With a final, almost grateful cry, the creature gave up its unnatural life.

Meanwhile three drow fighters leaped upon the golem, chipping and hacking at its icy flesh. The golem flung them off as easily as a dog might shake water from its coat. It rose to its feet, and its ice-colored eyes settled on Nisstyre. The golem began its advance.

Before the wizard could summon a defensive spell, the human leaped the last few feet of his descent and sprinted through the clearing. Ignoring the drow around him, he barreled straight toward the ice golem. He ducked a swing of the golem's clublike fist and, grasping the hilt of his sword with both hands, he hauled it back for a mighty blow.

The thick black blade whistled in and struck the golem's hip with a tremendous, booming crack. For a moment it seemed as if the hit

51

had been no more effective than those of the drow. Then wavering lines rippled through the golem's body and down its leg. The massive limb crumbled into shards of ice, and the golem toppled.

The human leaped onto the fallen creature, and his black sword rose and fell again and again until the golem was reduced to a sparkling pile. That accomplished, the battle-mad human threw himself at the nearest gnoll. With one mighty swing, he struck the head from the powerful creature.

"But the sword has no edge," Nisstyre muttered, and his coppery brows knit with consternation as he scrutinized his unexpected ally.

The human had already flung himself upon a pair of sword-wielding gnolls. One of the dog-men got through the human's guard and slashed a dark red line across his thigh. The fighter did not falter, did not so much as flinch. Sweat poured from the man's red face and hung in tiny icicles from his jaw—vastly increasing his fearsome appearance—yet each swing was as powerful as the last. He did not tire; he did not concede to pain. The human would be a considerable adversary, and prudence dictated Nisstyre deal with him at once. But, since the man vented his battle lust only upon the gnolls, the drow wizard bided his time. No sense wasting the lives of his own warriors, when this human seemed so determined to die fighting.

Soon only two of the dog-men remained, easily outclassed by the five surviving drow. The fight would soon be over, the human's usefulness ended. Nisstyre began to mentally browse through his repertoire of human-killing spells.

Then, as if it sensed its defenders would soon be overcome, the hut itself entered the battle.

Running wildly about the clearing, the magical hut began to stalk the drow. The dark elves were fast and agile, and could easily have escaped into the forest. Yet Nisstyre warned them back. His outstretched hands crackled with lethal magic as he shouted at his drow band to stand and fight, on pain of death.

Like a crazed chicken, the hut chased the dark elves around the clearing, kicking and scratching. Finally it trapped one beneath a huge foot. Its claws raked at the fallen drow again and again, leaving long bloody furrows with each pass.

The human charged in. Before Nisstyre could react, the crazed warrior began to hack at the hut's birdlike leg as if he were a woodsman felling a tree. Two blows, and the hut began to stagger. Three, and the leg gave way. The hut wobbled, then toppled to the ground. It rolled several times and came to rest on its thatched roof, lying feet-upward and looking very much like a dead, one-legged bird. Then, to Nisstyre's horror, the hut simply faded away.

Hissing his rage, the drow wizard stooped and picked up a fragment of the ice golem. He spat the words of a spell and flung the shard at the human warrior. Instantly the man was encased from neck down in a thick, immobilizing crust of ice.

Nisstyre stalked over to face his unwanted ally. "Whoever you are, *whatever* you are, you cost me a fortune in spellbooks and treasure," he snarled. "Do you know how long I've been stalking that thrice-damned Red Wizard?"

Although he spoke in perfect Common, the widely used trade language of these lands, there was no spark of understanding in the trapped man's face. The human's faint smile never faltered, and his blue eyes promised death. Nisstyre realized that the magical attack had added his name to this strange warrior's list of enemies.

"How do you fight like that?" the drow demanded. "What magic do you possess?" The human did not speak, but Nisstyre did not really expect or need an answer. He would get his own.

The wizard tossed a pinch of yellow powder at the human. Immediately a faint, blue glow emanated from a point just below the man's collarbone. The other drow had crowded around to watch, and in a corner of his mind Nisstyre noted that the magic-finding spell caused all of them to glow in a dozen places as magical weapons concealed until now were revealed. He noted the measuring, wary glances they exchanged as the balance of power among them shifted swiftly and subtly. Later, he would address such matters himself.

Nisstyre pointed to the glowing dagger tucked in the belt of his strongest fighter. "Use that, and cut through the ice. I want that amulet unharmed, but break the chain if you must."

The tall drow drew his enspelled dagger and began to chip through the ice that covered the human's chest. Once the blade slipped and drew blood; the man's faint smile never faltered. Finally the drow freed the dagger pendant and broke the chain with a yank. He handed the device to Nisstyre, but the wizard shook his head.

"No. You take it and return to the Underdark. We'll study it later. I'll follow you in a day or so; at the moment I want to see if I can ascertain just where in the Nine Hells that hut went."

"And the human?"

"Leave him," Nisstyre snarled. "Let him suffer from the cold and exposure. He will die far too soon to suit me."

The wizard cast yet one more spell, and a glittering oval appeared in the clearing. He gave a few more instructions to his captain, and then disappeared alone into the forest. One by one, the drow thieves slipped through the gate on their way to distant, even more dangerous, lands.

When the last drow disappeared and there was no one left to fight, the battle rage that had gripped Fyodor faded away. He slumped in his icy prison, utterly exhausted. He never felt the pain, or the cold, or the tired muscles for as long as the battle lasted. That always came later. He had seen other berserkers die of exhaustion, or from the cumulative effect of countless, unnoticed wounds. And these were men who, unlike him, could control their battle rages and bring them on at will. Fyodor considered himself very lucky to have lived out nineteen winters.

Sasha, he noted with deep sorrow, had not been so fortunate. The fierce pony lay tangled with the body of the gnoll she had battled with teeth and hooves, but the numerous thin slashes that scored her shaggy coat did not come from a dog-man's sword. Drow steel had slain Sasha while she fought the gnoll, and for no apparent reason other than the joy dark elves took in wanton killing. A cold, lingering anger kindled in Fyodor's heart—not a remnant of the berserker rage, but the natural wrath of a man who abhorred cruelty, and who had suffered the senseless loss of a friend.

For a long moment, Fyodor was aware of nothing but his anger and his grief. Then he realized his icy prison had thinned. The terrible heat of his berserker rage had melted much of the ice and he could move a bit. The battle fury had left him, but he still had his natural strength, honed by his seven-year apprenticeship to the village swordsmith. So he bunched his muscles and pushed against the icy shell.

Moments passed, and nothing happened. Fyodor tried rocking back and forth, throwing his weight from one side to the other. Finally the ice around his feet gave way. He toppled like a felled tree, and his prison shattered when he hit the ground. He was wet to the skin and cut by the ice shards in a dozen places, but at least he was free.

Exhausted but determined, Fyodor hauled himself to his feet and collected his fallen weapons. He might not have been able to answer the drow wizard while in the grip of his battle fury, but he had understood every word. The amulet he needed was on its way to the dreaded Underdark.

Fyodor staggered toward the rapidly fading light that marked the magical doorway. Without hesitation, he stepped through the gate.

Chapter 4

THE UNDERDARK

nly one day, Liriel thought grimly as she lashed her supplies into the long, barrel-shaped craft. The life she knew would end in just one day. But until the moment this day was over, no one—not her father, not Matron Triel, not Lloth herself—would keep Liriel from living the time that remained to the fullest.

The young drow gave her boat one last inspection. It was an odd craft, fashioned of thin, lightweight metal and padded inside and out with air-filled sacks. The sides curved up, the front came to a rounded point, and ropes controlled the position of two short paddles. Next Liriel checked her cargo: the *pyrimo*, a supply of freshwater mussels harvested from the shallows of Lake Donigarten, and clams brought to the Bazaar from some distant sea. There were also a few magical items of minor value and a festive gown that had been the height of fashion two seasons past.

When all was ready, Liriel took the guide rope and dragged the boat to a small, black opening in the rocky floor. Water trickled into the hole from a crack in the wall, and the distant rush of water sounded from somewhere far below. She pointed the rounded prow at the opening and then threw herself facedown into the boat.

The craft tipped and then shot down into the tunnel, falling rapidly and gaining speed by the moment. Liriel seized the guide ropes and used the paddles to nudge and bump her way through the twisting tunnel. A spray of water shot up over the boat with each bump, and webs from the low ceiling tangled in her flying hair. The roar of water soon became deafening as the flow grew deeper and faster.

Then, suddenly, the tunnel was gone. Water flowed in from a dozen similar passages and converged into a white-water river of astonishing speed and fury.

Wild, exultant laughter burst from Liriel and was snatched away by the rush of wind and water. Few of her friends enjoyed this sport—it provided little opportunity for intrigue, and there were merely survivors, not winners—but Liriel loved every wet, bruising moment. Water-running required quick reflexes and nerves of ice. For what she had in mind, she would have need of both.

In the water ahead loomed a large black stalagmite, a thick black rock formation that thrust upward to touch the descending finger of an equally forbidding stalactite. Like mirror images, the two stone spears marked the left-hand boundary of the water-running course. Few who'd ventured beyond that marker had survived.

Liriel counted off the seconds. At the last possible moment, she pulled hard on the left-hand rope. The craft swung around hard, and the force of the onrushing water sent it into a roll. Twice, three times the barrel-shaped boat spun before it righted itself. Liriel came up soaking wet and gasping from the cold. She pulled the right oar into position and steeled herself for the jolt to come.

Her boat crashed broadside into the stalagmite and was pinned there by the force of the onrushing waters. Liriel tugged at the right oar rope with all her strength, and the boat pushed slowly away from the rock.

Now came the tricky part. Sometimes it took her two or three runs before she found her secret tunnel. But luck was with her today. Her boat was swept into the hidden undertow that rushed toward a second stone chute. The drow let out a whoop of glee and hung on for her very life.

This tunnel shot down in an almost straight drop. Liriel closed her eyes and braced herself against the sides of the boat with hands and feet, for nothing she could do now would alter her course. Then, suddenly, the tunnel was gone and Liriel's craft was free-falling through a tumbling spray of water and mist.

Her boat hit the water below in a smooth dive and plunged deep. When her descent finally slowed, Liriel scrambled out of the boat and swam upward. She broke the surface and gasped in air, then swam for the rocky shore with strong, even strokes. She rolled out onto the bank and lay there, exhausted but triumphant: she had survived one more run!

After a few moments' rest to catch her breath, Liriel sat up and surveyed her surroundings with proprietorial pride. The waterfall ended in a large, icy pond surrounded by the rocky walls of a deeply buried grotto. Caves and alcoves were scattered here and there, begging to be explored. Eerie blue and green light filled the cavern, for the rocks here emitted the strange, radioactive power that was unique to the Underdark. Such sites of power, known as *faerzress*, were highly prized by the drow and jealously guarded. This one was Liriel's alone. She earned it anew each time she made the treacherous journey.

A dry, metallic whisper came from the depth of a nearby cave, a sound like that of chain mail being dragged along rock. Then came the rapid click of taloned feet, the angry roar of some enormous creature preparing to oust the invader from its home. Liriel leaped to her feet just as the deep dragon burst from its lair.

* * * * *

Fyodor slumped against the rocky wall of the tunnel, and his eyes drifted shut. Strange, he thought numbly, how the darkness did not deepen when he closed his eyes. He opened and closed them several times and could discern no difference whatsoever. Never had he seen such blackness, not on the darkest winter night. It closed in on him, even more stifling than the narrow tunnels he'd stumbled through, or the knowledge that countless tons of earth and rock loomed over his head. This, then, was the Underdark.

He could hear the faint, fading footsteps of the drow thieves, but he could not tell from whence the sound came. Sound played tricks down here, bouncing off tunnel walls and echoing through stone. The footsteps were distorted by other noises: the constant drip of water, the rattling tumble of loose rocks and soil, the scurrying feet of small, unseen creatures. So winding were the tunnels, so full of turns and unexpected drops and climbs, that Fyodor could not even tell if the drow were above or below him. He might be a fine tracker in his own land, but he was very, very far from home.

After several moments of internal debate, Fyodor felt around in his pack and took out a stick and a strip of cloth. He wound the cloth around the end of the stick, then reached for the flask tucked into his sash. Carefully he poured a little of the liquid onto the cloth. He fumbled in his bag for flint and steel.

The sparks lit up the blackness like flashes of lightning, and the torch easily caught flame. In the sudden flair of light, Fyodor got his first good look at the Underdark.

"Mother of all gods," he whispered in a mixture of horror and awe.

He was in a cave, larger than any he had imagined possible. The ceiling arched high overhead, and long, twisted spires of rocks stabbed downward. The path he followed had a solid wall of rock along one side, and a sheer drop on the other. Just a few paces from where he stood, the pathway fell hundreds of feet into a gorge. On the far side of the divide was a lacy rock curtain resembling a giant honeycomb. Behind it Fyodor saw more paths winding up along the cliff's sheer walls and openings that could only be more tunnels. Wondrous bridges fashioned of stone and magic spanned the gorge at several levels. This place was a crossroads built throughout countless centuries by alien and unknowable cultures. Its vastness and complexity overwhelmed Fyodor as even the darkness could not.

Yet he set aside such thoughts and pressed on with his search. Dropping to one knee, the Rashemi examined the rocky floor. Finally he found a marker: a single droplet of nearly melted slush. The drow thieves had passed this way.

Fyodor followed the trail of diminishing dampness into a side tunnel, knowing as he did each step took him closer to death. He had no idea where he was and knew no way to return to the surface once he retrieved the precious amulet. He had entered the Underdark fully aware of the danger—indeed, the apparent futility—of this course of action, but what other choice did he have? Without the amulet he would die. Perhaps his time would not come for a year; perhaps it would come tomorrow.

Without warning, a giant insectlike creature darted into Fyodor's circle of torchlight. Bottle-green in hue and fully five feet in length, the monster looked like some unholy offspring of a spider and a scorpion. It had no eyes that Fyodor could see, but its excited chittering left little doubt it sensed the man's presence. Long, whiplike antennae groped here and there for its prey, and the enormous pincers on its spine-covered front legs flared and snapped repeatedly with a sound like that of steel traps closing.

Perhaps, Fyodor thought grimly, his time would come today.

* * * * *

Liriel stood absolutely still as the deep dragon stalked toward her. Both of its sharp-fanged maws dripped with hungry anticipation, and its two heads bobbed as it walked. For this dragon was a freak, a rare product of the strange radiation of the Underdark. Smaller than most of its kind—a mere fifty feet from the top of its two horned heads to the tip of its single tail—the dragon was covered with shimmering purple scales that emitted their own weird light.

The two-headed beast began to circle Liriel, like a house lizard playing with a doomed scurry rat. The head on the right wore an expression of weary resignation, the one on the left a sly, if slightly dim-witted, smile.

"Small, she is," chirped the smiling dragon head, eying the dark-elven girl. "Hardly big enough to bother sharing. I'll have this one, and you can eat the next drow that happens by, hmm?"

"Don't be such a dolt," snapped the right-sided head in a voice that was deep and gravelly, yet definitely female. "We go through this ridiculous game every time she comes. It's getting old. Eat the drow or don't, and have done with it!"

"Hello, Zz'Pzora," Liriel said, addressing both heads and holding out her hands to show she held no weapons. "I've brought you the usual goodies."

"And a gown for me?" the left head inquired eagerly. "I'll need something to wear at Suzonia's next dinner party!"

The right head rolled her eyes. "We get out so seldom," she said with dry sarcasm. "It's so important we make the right impression."

Liriel bit back a grin. The dragon was clearly confused, but she was often rather amusing. The two heads had different, distinct personalities that were almost always in conflict. The left head was vain and flighty, and liked to fantasize about visiting the Underdark cities and frolicking on the surface. The right head's persona was more typical of dragonkind. She loved solitude, treasure, and magical items. This head was the brighter of the two, and had a sharp wit and a sar-

60

castic tongue. While all dragons were dangerous and unpredictable, Zz'Pzora had a little insanity thrown in to make things interesting. Even so, Liriel had come to consider the dragon a friend. A large, dangerous, and unpredictable friend, perhaps, but no more treacherous than any of the young drow's other associates.

"I'm going to get your things now," she said, pointing toward the water. The boat had bobbed to the surface and had drifted nearly to shore. Both of the dragon's heads nodded eager agreement.

It took but a few minutes for Liriel to tow in the boat and unpack her cargo. The dragon quickly devoured the seafood, the two heads arguing all the while over the choicest tidbits. The left head squealed with delight at the sight of Liriel's cast-off gown and begged her counterpart to join her in The Change. Deep dragons were natural shapeshifters and could change at will into either snake or drow form. Zz'Pzora's drow shape had but one head, but even this form could not grant the dragon her left-headed longing for society. The drow-dragon had features that were decidedly undrowlike: round, dark eyes; a button nose; and full pouting lips. Her skin retained the bright purple hue of the dragon's scales and cast the same faint purple light as usual. In any form Zz'Pzora was, to say the least, conspicuous.

Undaunted by such limitations, the drow-shaped dragon wriggled into the gown. Hands on hips, she paced along the shore in a broad parody of a seductress's slink.

"It's very becoming, Zip," Liriel murmured, struggling to keep the mirth from her voice. "Suzonia will be consumed with jealousy."

With a happy sigh, the drow-dragon flung herself down beside Liriel, ready for some gossip. At Zz'Pzora's urging, Liriel told stories about her life in Menzoberranzan: the round of parties, the social intrigue, even the incident with Bythnara Shobalar.

A queasy expression crossed the dragon's purple, elven face. "So a wizard died to get me the *pyrimo*. I wish you'd told me that earlier!" she said in the low, gravelly voice of her right-headed persona. Before Liriel could respond to this, the drow-dragon's face twisted into a sly smile. "If you'd told me, I would have enjoyed it far more!" put in the left-headed side. "Especially if some of those fish had eaten—"

That was a bit much for Liriel. "I have to get back now," she said abruptly. "Where are my weapons?"

The drow-shaped Zz'Pzora pointed toward a small cave. Blue light spilled from the low opening, marking it as an especially powerful source of the radiant energy.

Liriel stooped and entered the small cavern. There she found the sack she'd left with the dragon two years earlier. Eagerly she opened it and drew out a small, spider-shaped metal object. The eight legs were perfectly balanced and evenly spaced, and each ended in a sharp tip. She took the weapon by one leg and hurled it at the wall of the cave. The legs bit deep into the stone.

"Perfect," she breathed. With her lethal aim, a thrown dagger could handle most creatures of flesh and bone; this new weapon could pierce the carapace of many an Underdark monster. The dark elf pried the metal spider out of the rock with her knife, not wanting to lose a single one of her new toys, and then she tied the bag of magic-enhanced throwing spiders to her belt.

Before she left the grotto, she gathered fragments of scales the dragon had broken or shed. The scales of a deep dragon were a rare and valuable spell component, and once dissolved in acid they could be used to make the prized everdark ink used by drow wizards. Since Liriel's allowance did not begin to cover her expenses, she had developed a lucrative trade of her own. These scale fragments would bring her enough gold to fund more adventures, buy more books, and learn more spells.

The elf quickly said her farewells to Zz'Pzora, and the two friends made their way to the far side of the grotto. There, in a small recessed alcove, hung a leather sling. Liriel seated herself and took a deep breath. Above her soared a long, straight shaft. The opening was too far away for her to see, but she knew from experience it would take her to a point very near the entrance to the water run. She and Zz'Pzora had rigged up a series of ropes and pulleys in this shaft. The dragon would pull Liriel up now, and return the boat to its starting point at her leisure.

Still in drow form, Zz'Pzora grabbed the ropes. The dragon's first tug sent Liriel jerking sharply upward. As the drow rose in a series of quick bursts followed by long teasing pauses, she fervently wished she hadn't exhausted her levitation spells for the day. There was no telling when the dragon's sly, chaotic persona might overwhelm the more sensible head, and it was a long way down. At the bottom of the shaft lay the crumpled remnants of old bones, a silent testament to the fate of other creatures who had fallen—or been thrown—into the shaft.

But once again, Liriel made the ascent without incident or treachery. She dropped the three pebbles that signaled the dragon of her safe arrival, then took her new spellbook from her pack and unwrapped the skins that protected it from wear and water. In the book was a spell that would enable her to establish a portal to a familiar spot of her choice. She chose Spelltower Xorlarrin.

With a mischievous smile, Liriel imagined Kharza-kzad's reaction to her latest prank. Her hands flashed through the gestures of the spell and she summoned the gate easily. Yet she lingered at the lip of the shaft, and her eyes scanned the beloved landscape of the wild Underdark. She suspected it might be a very long time before she would see it again.

* * * * *

If there was ever a time when Fyodor needed the strength of his berserker rage, it was now. Yet the familiar heat and fury did not come to the young Rashemi. He had already fought too much for one day. So he drew his sword and slowly, carefully began to back away from the enormous scorpion-spider.

But the creature seemed fascinated by the light of the torch. It made no move to attack, but as soon as Fyodor eased out of range, it skittered forward until it was back in the circle of light. The man tried this escape several times, not knowing what else to do and hoping it might tire of the game.

As it happened, the monster did just that. The result was not at all what Fyodor had hoped it might be.

One of the creature's antennae furled back, then whipped up toward Fyodor's face. Reflexively, he raised the torch to ward off the attack; antenna met flame with a searing hiss. The giant arachnid reeled back, but not before its second antenna snapped forward, low and fast. This one hit Fyodor's ankle, and the end wrapped around and around as though it were a striking whip. So quickly did the second strike come that Fyodor was yanked off his feet when the creature retreated from the torch's flame. The back of Fyodor's head hit hard on the rocky floor, and a hundred tiny, brilliant lights burst behind his eyelids.

The painful light flashed and faded in an instant, and Fyodor once again found himself in total darkness. The fall had knocked his torch from his hand. He groped around for his sword; it, too, had fallen out of reach.

Fyodor was not one to be easily discouraged, but he was beginning to dislike his chances in this fight. He drew a knife from his sash and hauled himself into a sitting position. He did not need light to know where one of the creature's antennae was.

As if sensing Fyodor's intent, the insect relaxed its whiplike hold. The flow of blood resumed in the man's numb foot, and feeling returned with a sharp, prickling rush. Perhaps, he dared to hope, the creature had lost interest in him now that there was no more light.

But then there came the quick skittering rush of many legs and a sharp, rending stab as the creature's small, beak-shaped mandibles found Fyodor's leg. The man hissed with pain and drove down hard with his knife. The weapon glanced off the creature's bony shell. He stabbed two more times, with no success. The monster clung, and its side-by-side mandibles began to grind together in an attempt to rip loose a chuck of meat. Fyodor's next thrust was into the flesh of his own leg.

Using the knife as a lever, Fyodor pried the creature's beak open. He rolled away from the grasping mandibles, several times and as fast as he could. In his wild retreat he rolled over a hard, familiar shape.

Fyodor's hand closed on his cudgel and he rose to his feet. The next time the antenna whipped forward to seize his ankle, he was ready. As long as the creature's antenna held him, he had a good idea where the rest of the body must be. Rushing forward, he began to beat wildly at the arachnid. Many, perhaps most, of his blows rang with the sound of wood on rock, but a good many of them landed on the monster's shell. Once the creature seized his ankle with a pincer; Fyodor thrashed the clawed appendage until it let go. The taut antenna also relaxed, and it seemed the scorpion-thing would release him altogether. Fyodor was not feeling so generous, himself.

The fighter planted a heavy boot on the creature's antenna, pinning it firmly to the ground. He did not dare let the monstrous insect out of the range of his driftwood club, for fear he could not see or turn aside the next attack. Fyodor redoubled his efforts and smashed with all his strength again and again into the arachnid's protective shell.

Finally he was rewarded with a cracking sound and the sudden pulpy give that suggested victory was within reach. The man continued to batter at the creature until it was reduced to a sodden mass.

Breathing hard, Fyodor reached for the flask tucked into his sash. His leg burned with cruel heat where the giant scorpion-thing had bitten him, and he knew the pain he felt now would be a pale thing compared to what must come next. He pulled the cork from his flask and tipped some of the liquid onto the open wound.

Some time later—perhaps a short time, perhaps not—Fyodor came to himself again and found he had been sleeping on a bed of cold rock. For many minutes he lay where he had fallen, piecing together bits of memory until he could recall all that had happened to bring him to this place. The terror that was the Underdark came back to him, with one thing added.

He could no longer hear the footsteps of the drow he sought.

Chapter 5

FAERIE FIRE

harza-kzad Xorlarrin's expression when Liriel breezed into his suite of rooms was all she could have desired. The wizard's thin face tightened with shock, sending ripples through the web of worry lines that creased his forehead and collected around his eyes. He also looked guilty, and his red, slightly protruding eyes scanned the tower chamber furtively as if he feared what might follow her into the room.

"I'm here for my lesson," she announced smugly.

The wizard stepped closer to examine the delicate web of spinning, glowing lights that framed the magic door. "I haven't taught you how to access a gate!" he protested in his querulous voice. "How did you do it? No one knows a gate into my rooms except—" He broke off abruptly, and in a quick nervous movement he ran both hands through what remained of his hair.

Liriel smiled and draped her arms around the wizard's neck. She would have her magic lesson, but she also had a certain, velvet revenge to exact.

"I know you haven't taught me that particular trick," she purred, "and just think of all the opportunities lost. Imagine, if I could just pop into your private study any time I pleased . . ."

The Xorlarrin wizard cleared his throat several times and backed away. "Yes. Well. Perhaps another time, I'm sure, but at the moment I am otherwise engaged."

"No, you're not," she said, and her voice was suddenly steely. "It's time for my tutorial."

Kharza sighed and raised his hands. "Very well. But first you must tell me how you learned to conjure a gate and who gave you the spell. For your own safety I must know this. Wizards are a treacherous lot, and most gates have hidden requirements, secret limitations. You can't run in and out of them on a whim, you know."

The girl produced her new spellbook and assured her tutor that "her father the archmage" felt she was ready to study and cast such magic. Liriel had discovered early in life that Gromph Baenre's name was a real conversation stopper, and she dropped it whenever it seemed likely to speed things along. As she'd anticipated, Kharza-kzad's protests evaporated at once, and they were able to get down to business with a minimum of his usual fussiness.

Together they went over Liriel's new spellbook, rehearsing arcane words and gestures, exploring the limits and the secrets of the various magical gates. Liriel threw herself into the lesson with her customary intensity, and her focus did not falter until they neared the center of the book.

"This gate goes to the surface," she murmured. The eyes she lifted to her teacher's face were wide with astonishment and wonder. "This gate goes to the surface! I had no idea such things existed!"

"Of course, my dear," the wizard said mildly. "There are many such spells. Some raiding parties use them, as do merchants. Have you never wondered how fish from the Sea of Fallen Stars, which is many hundreds of miles from here, appear fresh on your plate?"

"I have no idea how it gets from the *market* to my plate," she said absently. "But just imagine, Kharza! To see the Lands of Light with your own eyes!"

The Xorlarrin wizard frowned, troubled by his pupil's rapturous expression. "If you must talk of such things, Liriel, take care who might be listening. These spells are hoarded like rare gems, and the teaching of them is carefully regulated by the masters of the Sorcere. If it were known you were learning to access such gates, your studies with me would be quickly ended."

Elaine Cunningham

The light faded from Liriel's eyes. "They *are* ending," she mourned. "This will be my last lesson. Tomorrow morning I have to report to Arach-Tinilith."

"You, a priestess!" The wizard was clearly aghast at the thought.

"Don't get me started," she grumbled. She untied the strings that held a small leather bag to her belt. "But I did bring you a farewell gift. This bag holds the latest harvest of deep dragon scales. You can send the usual half-profit to me at my new address. Or better yet," she said slyly, "you could *bring* it to me, during one of our little assignations. I would so hate to have them end, just because I've been sent to the Academy. And think of all those who have been entertained by your boastful tales. Surely they are expecting sequels."

A look of sheer panic crossed the wizard's face, and he quickly put some space between himself and his student. Liriel might be young, but she already possessed a considerable grasp of magic and a creative flair for vengeance.

"I meant no harm," he sputtered.

"And no harm was done, dear Kharza. But I think you should know," she whispered as she swayed seductively close, "that your little stories failed to do me justice. Failed *miserably*. It's a shame, really, that you'll never learn the true limits of your imagination."

With that parting shot, the drow girl stepped into the still-glowing gate and vanished. Her light, mocking laughter lingered in the tower chamber, and it was ringing still when a thin, red-haired drow stepped into the room from an antechamber.

"That is one tigress who can draw blood with velvet paws," he observed wryly. Nisstyre, merchant captain of the Dragon's Hoard, settled down in Kharza's chair and leveled a long, speculative gaze at the older wizard. "She seems very interested in the Night Above. We should encourage that."

"Even if I wanted to, I could do nothing," Kharza said stiffly.

"Oh, but you can." Nisstyre slapped a thin, leatherbound book onto the desk. "This book contains obscure human lore—nothing of great consequence, but it may serve to whet her taste for forbidden subjects. Find a way to get it to her. If I read that girl aright, she will devour it and demand more. Then, you will introduce us. She can return here often, using that gate she conjures so nimbly, and she and I can talk."

"It is risky."

"Wizards who follow Vhaeraun take many risks," the merchant

68

returned slyly. He broke off the wizard's sputtered protests with a fierce glare. "You say you are not of my faith. Perhaps that is true. But you continue trading with me, knowing what you know about me and my work. In many circles, that could raise a few eyebrows." He chuckled briefly. "Not to mention a few scalps. Or do the matrons of Menzoberranzan still indulge in that particular pastime? I've heard a story of some minor matron who routinely scalped her patrons when she tired of them. Had the scalps tanned and sewn together, I believe, and the hair woven into a sort of wall hanging. I do hope she had the taste not to hang it in her bedchamber," he added thoughtfully. "That could prove somewhat daunting to her current favorite."

Kharza swallowed hard, although he knew by Nisstyre's sly expression that the merchant was baiting him. The Xorlarrin wizard drew his tattered dignity about him as best he could and tried to take control of the situation. "I paid you a substantial advance for the Rashemi wands you promised me," he said stiffly. "Yet you return to me without them."

Nisstyre waved the protest away. "A temporary delay. The raiding party preceded me through another gate, albeit one that brought them to a point some distance from this tower. They will arrive in the city any day."

That much was true, if somewhat misleading. Nisstyre prided himself in not telling outright lies. If Xorlarrin read in these words the promise that his paid-for goods would be delivered, well, it was not Nisstyre's fault the old drow heard what he wanted to hear.

His business over, the fox-faced merchant rose to leave. "Don't forget to give that book to the Baenre girl. In time, that little princess will convert to the path of Vhaeraun, of that I am confident." His thin lips twisted into a parody of a smile. "I never thought I would mourn the death of the old Baenre hag, but I'm rather sorry she did not live long enough to witness her granddaughter's defection!"

* * * * *

Blithely unaware her future was being decided back in Spelltower Xorlarrin, Liriel hurried to her house in Narbondellyn to prepare for her last night out. She was hosting a party that night at a mansion rented out for such affairs. A small army of servants tended to the details; she had only to show up and enjoy.

The young drow sat with unusual patience as a skilled servant

69

wove her hair into dozens of tiny braids, then looped and tied the plaited strands into an elaborately contrived whole. Liriel usually left her hair flowing free, but tonight she needed a hairstyle that could hold up to considerable abuse. Her gown for the evening was also durable and designed for movement. Pure white and daringly cut, the dress had several long slits on the skirt to allow her to indulge to the fullest her passion for dancing. Tonight's festivities would include a *nedeirra*—a wild, acrobatic dance competition—which Liriel would launch with a solo dance. Liriel loved the freedom, the sense of rhythmic flight, that she felt when dancing. In her mind, the rest of the evening's revelry, although pleasurable, would be a pale thing compared to the *nedeirra*.

When Liriel arrived at the rented mansion, her friends were already gathered. It was the custom for guests to come early, to mingle and plot and drink spiced green wine. The arrival of the host or hostess was the traditional signal for the dancing to start. Liriel walked into the room to the accompaniment of a slow, pulsing drumbeat. The *nedeirra* was beginning.

All eyes were upon her as she began to stamp a rhythmic counterpoint to the drum. Her arms started an intricate weave, and one by one other drums joined in, as well as strange percussion instruments known only to the drow. Then a deep-voiced flute began to play a strange, compelling tune, a melody that had once been sung by elves in the Lands of Light, many centuries past. Those long-dead elves would not recognize their song; its fey magic had shifted and changed to reflect the beings who now played it. Beautiful still, the music retained all of the mystery of the elven race, and none of the joy. The drow had forgotten that emotion. But they understood pleasure, and they would pursue it wildly in an attempt to fill the unrecognized void in their elven souls.

The tempo of the music quickened, and over the ragged, syncopated rhythm of the drums the flutes wailed and soared in eerie melody. Liriel twirled and leaped in time to the music, and her body dipped and swayed as she beckoned to the waiting drow. Then, with a sudden flash of magical fire, the dark dancer was outlined in faerie fire of purest white. That was the signal all had awaited, and the other drow poured onto the dance floor.

Even in dance, the dark elves competed with each other. Some used their natural ability to levitate to perform intricate soaring leaps. Others shunned acrobatics and went right to seduction, trying to draw as many greedy eyes as possible with their writhing, sensuous movements. Yet regardless of style, all the drow listened carefully as they danced; within the intricate music were hidden clues that told what was to come. The rhythm was uneven, with the strong beats coming unexpectedly, almost randomly. Those who failed to read the music aright were in danger of missing a beat. Any drow who misstepped was immediately limned in faerie fire by one of the wizards who encircled the dance floor and watched intently as the dark elves whirled and leaped and stomped. These dancers had to leave the floor to a chorus of barbed comments and mocking laughter. But their fun was not entirely ruined, for all remained on the sidelines to place bets concerning who might next follow them.

On and on went the music, with few of the skilled drow missing the complex steps. Ebony faces shone with sweat, and some of the dancers began to discard outer garments. Sometimes a *nedeirra* continued until many of the dancers dropped from exhaustion, but Liriel had other plans for the evening. From her place on the center of the dance floor, she signaled for the finale.

One of the hired wizards floated high over the dancers. His hands wove a spell, and in response the music began to quicken, speeding toward an impossible tempo. The magic touched the dancers, as well, and their feet kept pace with the pulsating music. Faster and faster they whirled, and multicolored faerie fire blinked into being on every dark elf, turning the *nedeirra* into a firestorm of dancing lights. Finally the drums joined in a roll and the flutes soared to a last keening note. Then, suddenly, the room went dark and silent.

It was a spectacular spell, and the drow applauded delightedly. Then, as was custom following a *nedeirra*, the dancers began to remove their finery. Personal servants rushed forward to collect the discarded clothing.

The party-goers were ushered, unselfconsciously naked, into another room. This was a large, low-ceilinged chamber whose walls, floor, and ceiling were honeycombed with vents. Scented steam poured into the room, cleansing the dancers and soothing weary limbs. The direction and intensity of the steam's flow changed constantly: one moment massaging with short, pulsing bursts, the next playing over the dark elves' skin like a gentle, sultry breeze. As the steam bathed the drow with a succession of pleasant sensations, they walked about, flirting perhaps, or laying multilayered traps for social rivals, or sipping from goblets of luminous green *ulaver* wine.

Elaine Cunningham

When the last jet of steam faded away, the dark elves slipped away in groups of four or five through the many small doors that lined the chamber. There, in small private rooms, they would relax on couches, exchange gossip, and score points in witty conversation as skilled servants massaged them with scented oils. Massage was a favorite treat at parties, and as near to relaxation as the ever-wary drow came.

Liriel forwent her own massage to wander from room to room, taking advantage of the small groups and the unusually mellow mood to chat with her guests. Her friends did not know she would be leaving them tomorrow, but to each one she said an unspoken farewell. In her own fashion. More often than not, sudden shrieks and gales of laughter marked Liriel's passing. Dark elves delighted in cantrips—small, harmless spells cast to play pranks upon their companions. With her wizardly training, Liriel excelled at this sport. Wherever she went, amorous hands suddenly turned icy, or scented oil changed fragrance to become the signature perfume of a hated rival. The drow, with their dark, wicked sense of humor, considered no gathering complete without a few such pranks, and tonight Liriel had spared no effect to accommodate them.

Much later, content and clad in a fresh change of festive clothing, the guests gathered in yet another hall for dinner. It was an elegant affair with several removes, each served with a different potent wine. The conversation grew raucous soon after the soup course, and here and there a few drow slipped under the tables to contemplate the evening's events or to forge new social alliances. The general anticipation accelerated as the rumor spread that *pyrimo* would be served as the final remove. Parties such as this often ended with wild merrymaking, and a *pyrimo* course almost guaranteed the celebration would reach dizzying heights of frenzy.

And so it was.

And so it continued, until the bell tolled that marked the end of the last watch. By law and custom, parties ended at the start of a new day.

Liriel stood at the door of her rented mansion and watched as her guests were helped—or poured, as the case may be—into magical litters or lizard-drawn carriages. Later, her hired servants would toss the less mobile guests out into the street, where they would be collected by their slaves and carted home. Those drow who still possessed a measure of their wits lingered in small groups about the mansion and in the street, as if loath to see the night end.

Suddenly the noisy, reeling throng of party-goers fell silent, and their various conveyances gave way to a driftdisc emblazoned with the House Baenre insignia. The magical seat floated toward the mansion in impressive silence, and Liriel's throat tightened as she watched it close in. She ran through life at a pace few could follow, yet this moment had caught her.

And how little Triel had trusted her niece's word! The matron had threatened to send someone to bring Liriel to the Academy if she were late. By Liriel's reckoning, she had hours to spare. Yet seated on the magical conveyance was no less a personage than Sos'Umptu, Triel's faithful lap-lizard and apparent lieutenant.

The driftdisc stopped at the mansion's gate and the keeper of the Baenre chapel alighted. Her face puckered with outrage as she picked her way through the crowd and the debris, and she fairly pounced upon her scandalous niece.

"I've never seen such frivolous excess, such disgraceful behavior!" she scolded.

"Really?" inquired Liriel, her eyes wide with mock innocence. "If that is so, you really ought to get out more."

Chapter 6

ARACH-TINILITH

omething must be done about that Baenre brat!" stormed Zeld Mizzrym. The priestess fairly quivered with wrath, and beneath the black and purple folds of her robe her bosom rose and fell in an indignant rhythm.

Matron Triel Baenre leaned back in her chair and surveyed the mistress in charge of the first-year students. Her raised brow warned the angry drow to tread carefully. "What has my niece been accused of this time?" she asked, pointedly emphasizing the relationship.

"More pranks," gritted out Zeld, who was apparently too angry to take the hint. "This morning Shakti Hunzrin found a field of mushrooms growing under her bed—*in* the appropriate fertilizer, I might add."

The matron mistress sighed. Liriel had spent less than three days within the spider-shaped compound, yet she was the suspected perpetrator of nearly a dozen little pranks. She was good at it, Triel had to give her that much, but the Baenre matron feared the young female would go too far. A less skilled prankster would have been caught in the act by now, and the day would certainly come when

Liriel would also misstep. Triel had plans for the talented young female, plans that did not include turning her into an ebony statue in order to instruct other students in the merit of observing proprieties.

"Can you prove that Liriel was involved?" she demanded coldly.

The mistress hesitated. "No, I suppose not. But Shakti stands adamant in her accusations, and she *does* have the right to accuse and censor a younger student."

Triel sighed again. It was not uncommon for novice priestesses to develop among themselves academic rivalries, personal vendettas, and free-floating hatreds. In fact, such was excellent training for life beyond the Academy and was seldom discouraged. But *this* was becoming a problem. Although Shakti Hunzrin was not Liriel's only victim, she was becoming a favorite target. Not that anyone cared. Shakti's family was not a major power, and even some of the wealthy commoners looked down at the Hunzrin family business, snobbishly considering the farming nobles to be little more than jumped-up clod kickers. Shakti did not help matters, with her ubiquitous pitchfork and her endless, droning monologues about the care and breeding of rothe. In addition, the Hunzrin girl was utterly humorless, vindictive to her peers, and ruthlessly vicious in her dealings with servants and younger students. The humiliating pranks played against her had evened a dozen scores and had earned Liriel a great deal of quiet applause. In short, things at Arach-Tinilith hadn't been dull.

Just last night, chapel had been disrupted when Shakti—a diligent, plodding student who was slowly nearing high priestess status—approached the altar to offer the evening sacrifice. Shakti's magical pitchfork had followed her, its tines moving in a wickedly precise imitation of her distinctive, waddling gait. Liriel had denied involvement, of course, but Triel knew what she knew. There was little the matron could do about the matter, for strangely enough, Lloth had not been displeased. It seemed even an evil goddess enjoyed a bit of dark humor now and again. In time the capricious Spider Queen would no doubt tire of Liriel's antics, but at the moment the impish female was a novelty, and she stood in the full favor of Lloth.

"We serve the goddess of chaos," Triel pointed out.

"Lloth be praised," the mistress intoned reflexively. "But someday soon that spoiled little wench will go too far!"

"And when that day comes, Lloth will instruct me," snarled Triel.

"See that you do not presume to speak where the Spider Queen does not!"

Zeld's eyes widened as she realized how badly she had overstepped. She dropped into a deep bow. "I beg your pardon, and Lloth's," she murmured, and her fingers instinctively fluttered through the rite of supplication meant to ward off the Spider Queen's disfavor.

Triel cut the prayer short. "How is Liriel progressing with her studies?"

"In some things, extremely well," the mistress admitted. Her voice was calmer now, and she chose her words with greater care. "She has an uncanny ability to learn and memorize spells. It is rumored she has been trained as a wizard."

Zeld voiced that observation with the rising inflection of a question. Triel responded only with a cold, level stare.

"You are letting her progress at her own pace, as I instructed?"

"We are, Matron Mistress. The girl has been tested carefully, and found ready to leap ahead in several areas of study. She shows an astonishing aptitude for magical travel. Today she began studying the lower planes with the twelfth-year class. At the rate she learns, she may be able to summon smaller denizens, perhaps even planewalk, before her first year is over. However," Zeld cautioned, "Liriel is disgracefully ignorant in many areas, far below acceptable standards even for a first-year novice. Her formal education has been sadly neglected. She knows almost nothing of Menzoberranzan's great history, and precious little about the worship of the Spider Queen. And while she understands social protocol well enough, she has no idea of how to conduct herself within the ranks of Lloth's clergy."

"It is your job to fill in these gaps," the matron mistress pointed out coldly. "If indeed Liriel has found time to play pranks, she is not being kept properly occupied."

Zeld stiffened, but she knew better than to argue with powerful Triel. "You have my word: House Baenre will gain another high priestess in record time."

"Excellent. I want to be kept informed of Liriel's activities."

"Oh, I'm sure you will hear of them," the mistress said dryly. "Remember, she was placed in a twelfth-year class to study planar travel. For at least part of the day, Liriel and Shakti Hunzrin will be classmates."

* * * * *

In the privacy of her dormitory room, Shakti Hunzrin hurled her treacherous pitchfork against the wall. The impact of the weapon and its clattering descent were muffled by the priestess's shrieks of rage.

The next items to take flight were Shakti's clothes. Somehow, her garments had been saturated with the scent of rothe manure, and the furious female tore them off and flung them aside. She stalked over to her washstand and sniffed at the water in the pitcher. At least *that* had not been tainted with the odor, she thought grimly. She poured some water into the basin and began to scrub herself with a sponge.

There was no doubt in Shakti's mind who was responsible for this latest indignity. She remembered the disbelief and rage in Liriel Baenre's eyes when she had commanded the new student to serve her at breakfast. Shakti had been totally within her rights to do so, yet Liriel had openly, boldly denied her the respect she had earned through twelve years of hard labor in this spider-shaped prison. And even worse, the little chit had gotten away with it!

Just another example, Shakti thought bitterly, of how badly managed the city was. The priestesses set the rules and disregarded them at will. To Shakti's eyes, Liriel could do whatever she liked, and for no better reason than the name she had inherited. A Baenre could do no wrong, it seemed, not even after the old matron had led Menzoberranzan into near ruin. But whatever else the past two days might have brought, at least they had given Shakti a focus for her rage, and her resentment, and her frustration. All that was wrong with Menzoberranzan finally had a name.

Shakti hated Liriel Baenre. The purity and strength of that emotion surpassed anything the young priestess had ever experienced. She hated Liriel for her royal birth, and for all the turmoil caused by her grandmother's long reign and disastrous war. She hated the girl for her beauty and her instant popularity at the Academy. She hated Liriel's sharp wit; whenever the wench was about, Shakti sensed there was a joke being told that she herself could not perceive. Worse, Shakti felt certain she was the butt of that joke. She hated Liriel for her quick mind, and the ease with which the girl learned things that should have taken her years of toil. But most of all, Shakti hated Liriel for the freedom she had enjoyed for fifteen years. She herself had been forced to enter the Academy at the onset of puberty. Why should a Baenre be treated any differently? For all of those injustices, vowed the Hunzrin priestess, Liriel Baenre would pay dearly.

The dark elf dressed and armed herself quickly, then slipped down the winding halls that led toward the dormitory of the first-year students. Liriel, of course, had been given her own room even though most priestesses had to coexist in twos and threes until their fifth year of study. All of the first-year students were in class, an hours-long lecture on the atrocities committed against the drow by faerie elves, followed by the usual exhortation to spread Lloth's glory by conquering first the Underdark, and then exterminating all other races of elves. It was a fine speech, Shakti thought bitterly, and as usual completely ignored by the priestesses in power. When Menzoberranzan had finally marched to battle, it was against a distant hive of dwarven drones. And what did that disastrous attempt have to do with the First and Second Directives of Lloth? Less than nothing, fumed Shakti. But if it served no other purpose, at least the indoctrination session would grant her the privacy she needed for the task ahead.

What the female intended to do was risky in the extreme, but she was in no mood to contemplate subtleties. She found Liriel's room, then cast a simple spell to raise a sphere of silence around her. After darting a quick look over each shoulder, she pointed her pitchfork at the door. Magical fire spat from the weapon's tines, and the stone portal shattered without a sound. Batting aside the dust and smoke, Shakti stepped into the room.

Her rival had spared no expense where comfort was concerned, the priestess noted bitterly. Liriel's room was hardly the spare, functional cell of a novice priestess. The narrow cot had been replaced by a floating bed heaped with silken cushions. A large, gilded chest stood against one wall, and a low study table was equipped with silver candlesticks and a supply of expensive tallow candles. Fine artwork hung on the walls, and Shakti's feet sank deep into a priceless carpet as she stalked over to the carved wardrobe. She flung open the door and began to riffle though the clothes stored inside. The black, red-trimmed robes of a novice hung crammed against one side of the wardrobe; most of the space was taken up by festive gowns, scandalous undergarments and nightclothes, and frivolous dancing shoes.

Shakti sniffed. No wonder the wench had been given her own room. If even half those clothes were put to their apparently intended use, no roommate would ever be able to sleep or study.

But most interesting to Shakti were the travel garments, the sturdy boots and the assortment of armor and weapons that were arranged in a single neat pile. It was conceivable Liriel could find time and opportunity to wear her party clothes without leaving Tier Breche, but this was gear more suited to an Underdark patrol than a coeducational debauch. Yes, it was true students had more freedom to leave the Academy these days, but it was also clear Liriel was being pushed through Arach-Tinilith with desperate, almost indecent haste. House Baenre needed high priestesses to rebuild its strength, or it would surely fall from its lofty place of power. Shakti sincerely doubted Matron Triel would approve of her precious niece leaving Arach-Tinilith for any purpose.

For the first time in nearly three days, Shakti's lips curved in a smile. At last, she had a weapon to use against her new foe. It might be some time before she caught Liriel, but now she knew what to watch for.

* * * * *

It was impossible, Liriel noted wearily, for a drow to die from sheer boredom. The fact that she sat in this chair, still alive and breathing after listening to four hours of ranting, rambling diatribe, was ample proof of that.

To her amazement, the other novice priestesses seemed to be genuinely stirred by the lecture. Murmurs of excited agreement, and even an occasional shout of "Praise Lloth!" echoed through the lecture chamber. Perhaps the other females were simply better at dissembling. Liriel doubted that, but even if it were true she had no desire to hone her thespian skills by adding her own ecstatic shouts to the general chorus. She managed to swallow every one of the sarcastic comments that popped into her mind, and that in and of itself was a sincere tribute of respect to Lloth. Such restraint was painfully unnatural for Liriel.

Yet the Academy was not *quite* as bad as she had feared. She had been allowed to bring a few simple belongings from her house, and she was granted unlimited access to Arach-Tinilith's wonderful library of tomes and spell scrolls. She longed to explore the magical treasures of the Sorcere, as well, but she had the sense to leave that challenge for another day. Apart from lecture sessions such as the one in which she currently languished, Liriel found the lessons fascinating. Clerical magic was especially intriguing, and it immediately became clear she was far beyond her classmates in ability. The spells themselves were very like those she had cast in her first few years of mage study, with one important difference: their success depended upon the favor of Lloth.

Liriel had heard Lloth's name all her life, but the Spider Queen had never been real to her. Casting her first clerical spell had changed that, instantly and dramatically. The young drow had worked wizardly magic for years, drawing upon her own innate talent and the quick mind that wrapped itself around complicated spells as if swallowing them whole. With hard work, good training, and piles of money lavished on books and spell components, she'd made herself into a credible mage. But now, when she cast her first clerical spell, she called upon Lloth, *and the goddess had answered.*

That moment was an epiphany for Liriel. The young female was not accustomed to depending upon anyone, and from her earliest years she had realized there was in truth no one there for her. She took what was offered her, but in any way that truly mattered, she walked alone and she knew it. Now, suddenly, she had the ear of a goddess!

Liriel well knew the reputation of Lloth and the fate of those who fell out of favor with the Lady of Chaos. Perhaps Lloth would someday turn against her, as well. But for now, Liriel felt gratitude, even dawning affection, for the Spider Queen. Betrayal, if indeed it came, would be nothing new to her. So Liriel said a silent prayer and did her best to tune out the strident, ranting voice of the mistress. Lloth would just have to read her heart and understand.

Finally the lecture was over. Nothing that painful could last forever, Liriel noted dryly. She darted from the hall with less than decorous haste. The next lesson was much more to her liking: studying the lower planes. Perhaps she was not free to explore the Underdark, or wander the city in the company of her pleasure-loving companions, but she was learning to look into new worlds. Now *that* had potential!

Liriel vowed she would plane-walk within the year. She had a great deal to learn before that would be possible, but the learning was a part of the journey.

So while her first-year classmates went to take their midday meal, Liriel hurried toward her room to collect her scrolls and her scrying bowl. The latter was a standard-issue affair, round and black and perfectly smooth, and it would do until she was able to have another one made to her liking. There was a fine artisan down in the Manyfolk district who could carve a bowl from a single piece of obsidian and set it in a silver holder engraved with runes and scenes honoring Lloth. For a moment Liriel wondered what might happen if such a bowl were left in Zz'Pzora's lair for a while to absorb the Underdark magic. Her eyes danced as she thought about what creatures she might summon, and what mischief they might join in making!

Then Liriel saw her shattered door, and her happy mood dissipated like spent faeric fire. Cautiously she edged closer, ready to cast a sphere of darkness around anyone she might encounter. That would slow down the intruder and give her a split second to consider her next course of action. Although the philosophy "kill them all and let Lloth sort them out" worked well enough in the world at large, the Academy had its own hierarchy and a web of intrigue she did not yet fully understand. It would not be wise, for example, to attack someone who was searching her room on Mistress Zeld's orders.

Liriel was spared the necessity of attacking, for she found her room empty. A faint, telltale odor lingered in the air, and her lips curved in a hard little smile. It might be a few days before Shakti Hunzrin realized she herself was the source of the pungent scent. Thanks to a specially tailored cantrip, the wretched she-rothe would exude the odor of manure through her pores until Liriel tired of the game and released the spell. In the meantime, this invisible manure-trail gave her an amusing way to keep track of the priestess's comings and goings.

The first thing Liriel did was check her book chest. To her relief, the lock was undisturbed. Shakti had been more interested in browsing through her wardrobe. An image of the stout priestess strutting about clad in some of the more revealing finery popped into Liriel's mind, and she laughed aloud.

She abruptly sobered and surveyed the damage. Technically, she should tell Mistress Zeld about the intrusion and have the Academy repair the door at once. That would no doubt lead to an inquiry, however, and some things were best left unexamined. Even if she *wanted* to report Shakti, doing so might focus a bit too much attention on her own recent activities. No, there was a better way.

81

Liriel hurried down to the kitchens to recruit some manual labor. As she made her way toward the dungeonlike lower levels, she reflected on her recent spate of pranks. In a corner of her mind, Liriel acknowledged that she was privileged and indulged, that she'd led a much different life from that most drow of Menzoberranzan knew. But her charmed existence had ended, and the pranks had been a last—and admittedly dangerous—attempt to deny this reality. Shakti's blatant attack signaled that she herself had pushed too far. Liriel did not intend to start a war, and she resolved to act with more discretion henceforth. She had seen the obsidian statues in the Academy's courtyard—all that remained of students who had misstepped—and she did not wish to join them.

The time for midday meal had passed, and the kitchen dungeons were quiet now. There, up to her elbows in a vast kettle of soapy water, was an ogre female. The creature was fully twice the size of the slender drow and seemed fashioned to inspire fear-tinged loathing. Muscles bulged under the ogress's leathery hide, and canine fangs jutted up from her lower jaw. Her face was set in a hate-filled scowl. Clad only in a leather apron, the ogress attacked the pots with a ferocity that suggested a mortal vendetta against dirt.

Trays of sliced raw fish lay on a nearby table, ready to be spiced and served at the evening meal. The drow selected a nice tidbit and popped it into her mouth, then turned a comrade's smile upon the ogress.

"Chirank, I have another job for you," she said.

The female's face lit up. "If Chirank do job, what you give this time?" she said in a deep growl.

Liriel held up a large gold coin. The ogre seized the coin with a soapy paw and bit down on it hard. She regarded the deep tooth marks with pleasure and grunted happily.

Seeing that the deal was made, the drow took a step forward. "You remember where my room is? . . . Good. There was a battle of sorts there, and I need someone to clear away the mess at once."

"Much blood? Drow bodies?" Chirank asked hopefully.

"Not this time," the dark elf replied in a dry tone. "All it needs is a little light housekeeping. Then there is the small matter of the missing door."

"Chirank not take," the ogress said defensively.

"Of course not. But you could, if you wanted to?"

The ogress shrugged, her animal eyes wary.

Liriel came one step closer. "Remember the room where you put the rothe manure? I want you to go there, steal the door, and hang it on my doorposts. You'll need to replace the lock, as well."

"Hard to do," Chirank bargained.

The elf held up two more coins. "You and I both know you can pick locks as fast as any halfling. No one will see you, I promise."

"You make Chirank look like drow again?" the ogress asked with a mixture of fear and fascination.

Liriel considered. It wasn't a bad idea. Although Chirank was a house slave and might well be sent into the student quarters on some errand or other, her presence might draw unwanted attention. So Liriel quickly cast the illusion that made the hulking ogre appear to be a delicate drow female dressed in the flowing robes of a high priestess. The drow pursed her lips and considered the overall effect.

"Grab that spoon over there," she suggested, pointing to a long metal ladle drying on a rack.

As the ogress did as she was bid, Liriel shaped the spell for a second illusion. The ladle in Chirank's hand changed into the snake-headed whip favored by priestesses. This one was particularly fearsome, with four angrily writhing heads and a handle fashioned from smoke-blackened bone. The ogress shrieked and dropped the whip. It fell to the stone floor with a metallic clatter.

"Hear that? It's just a ladle," Liriel soothed. "If you carry that and walk fast, no one will stay around you long enough to realize they don't recognize the face you're wearing."

The drow's reasoning made sense. Everyone in the Academy, from the lowliest slaves to the most advanced students, gave wide berth to an angry, whip-wielding high priestess. Chirank bent and gingerly picked up the writhing whip. She clanked it against her wash kettle a couple of times to reassure herself it was indeed nothing more than a harmless spoon. Finally she nodded, visibly impressed.

"You got this magic, why you need Chirank?" the ogress asked, reasonably enough. "This Shakti drow fear you, if this magic you use."

"Let's just say I prefer not to be noticed," Liriel said.

The ogress grunted in understanding. She well knew the wisdom of keeping out of sight as much as possible. Even so, she would do all the little drow asked of her, this time and any other. This drow treated her like a pack sister. They didn't trust each other, but they worked together for theft and for vengeance. That was as close to home as Chirank was ever likely to get again. And with the gold the dark elf gave her, Chirank might be able to have a dagger smuggled in. Ogres were not trusted with sharp utensils of any kind, and for good reason. Chirank was a slave and would no doubt spend the rest of her days laboring for the dark elf priestesses, but when she died it would be an ogre's death, and her body would be covered with the blood of many drow.

The ogress smiled so fiercely that her tusks pierced the magical illusion and gleamed against her drow-like face.

"Time to raid," she growled happily.

Chapter 7

OTHER WORLDS

ater that day, Liriel retired to her newly repaired and neatly swept room to attend to her studies. She had found an interesting scroll in the depths of Arach-Tinilith's library that gave a spell for conjuring a viewing portal into another plane. It was an extremely difficult spell, one that would stretch her abilities to their limits and beyond. Liriel was in deep contemplation of the scroll when a timid knock sounded on her purloined door.

Her concentration shattered, and pain erupted behind her eyelids. She swore furiously and rubbed at her eyes with her fists. If she had been attempting to cast the spell and lost her concentration, she might well have been killed by the magical backlash. Who could have been so stupid as to interrupt her at such a time? The study hour was sacrosanct, and during this time no priestess was allowed to disturb another. Yet once again came that faint knock.

Liriel pushed back her chair and stalked over to the door. She leaned close to the crack and hissed, "This had better be worth the pain I plan to inflict. Who is it?"

"It is I," came the muffled response in a familiar, querulous male voice. "Do let me in, Liriel, before someone happens by."

"Kharza?" she mumbled, startled by the unexpected visit from her tutor. She flung open the door and, seizing the wizard by the sleeve, dragged him into the room.

"I'm so glad you came! You won't believe what I'm learning to do!" she cried happily. Her anger was completely forgotten; now that Kharza-kzad was here, he could help her with her new spell. She retrieved the scroll from her desk and waved it at him. "This will let me see into other planes! Why did we never study such things?"

"Drow priestesses draw their power and their allies from the lower planes. As you know, a wizard has other sources of power," Kharza-kzad replied, absently fingering the sleeve of his robe. "We seldom call upon the power and services of abysmal creatures, and they are not really all that entertaining to observe."

Liriel grinned and sank down onto a heap of cushions. "Even so, you can help me learn the spell. Sit down, Kharza, and stop fidgeting. You're making me edgy."

The wizard shook his head so emphatically that the thin white strands of his hair leaped into disarray. "I can't stay long. I only wanted to bring you this." He drew a small, dark-bound book from his sleeve and handed it to her.

Intrigued, Liriel opened the book and held it up to catch the faint candlelight. On the pages of yellowed parchment were strange runes, angular like those of the drow language, but simpler and crudely drawn.

"What is this?"

"It is a curiosity I came across," Kharza said, speeding through the words as if they'd been well rehearsed. "A merchant of my acquaintance sold me a box of books. Some were valuable, some merely interesting. I'm afraid this is among the latter, but I thought you might enjoy it, knowing how insatiable you are."

Liriel tossed a teasing leer in his direction. "You don't know the half of it."

The wizard sighed. "An old drow's pride is his downfall," he said, ruefully quoting a familiar expression. "You will never forget my lamentable lack of discretion, will you, or tire of tormenting me?"

"Probably not," she agreed cheerfully, and then bent over her new treasure. The unfamiliar language was no barrier: a simple spell transposed the scratchlike markings into elegant drow script. Liriel skimmed a few pages, then raised incredulous eyes to her tutor.

"This book is from the surface!"

"Yes, I thought it might be," he said, shifting uneasily.

"It has stories about a people called the Rus, their heroes and their gods. There's something in it about rune magic. What is that?"

"You know of course that runes and glyphs can be enspelled and used as defenses," he began.

"Yes, yes," she interrupted impatiently. "But this is something different. This is a magic cast by shaping new runes. How is that done?"

"Of that, I know nothing, but it sounds too easy to be powerful." Kharza-kzad dismissed the notion with a sniff. "Human mages seldom—if ever—reach the level of power we know here Below. I wouldn't waste any time on the magic system of some long-dead human culture. The book, I thought, might help in some small way to satisfy your longing for far places during the time you are confined in Arach-Tinilith." He shrugged apologetically. "It seems this was hardly necessary. I had no idea you would be studying other worlds so soon."

The female's smile was brilliant and genuine. "All the same, the book is wonderful and I shall read every word. That you thought of me at all is gift enough."

Kharza-kzad cleared his throat nervously. "Then I should be returning to the Spelltower Xorlarrin. If you have no objection, I will conjure the same gate you used to enter my study."

"Why did you not come that way in the first place, instead of creeping down the halls?"

"I did not copy the spell from your book. And, despite rumors to the contrary, I did not know where your room was," he said, with an unexpected touch of dry humor. "Without a firm destination in mind, magical travel can be dangerous and unpredictable."

"Indeed. You might have ended up sharing a bubble bath with Mistress Zeld," she murmured, her face deceptively serious.

"Yes. *Ahem*. Well." The wizard hesitated, and his worry lines deepened into a look of near panic. "If you like, I can make the gate permanent so you can step into the Spelltower whenever you like. Then I can continue to help you with your magical studies, and get such supplies and goods as you require to you easily, whenever you wish." The words rushed out, and he shifted from one foot to the other as he awaited her response.

Liriel's smile froze. Although the gift of a single book had seemed genuine enough, such extravagant generosity from the wizard simply did not ring true. Kharza-kzad was cautious, fretful, and solitary by nature. He did not care for students and spent more time researching spells and creating wands than he did teaching in the Sorcere; his title of master was mostly honorary. The only reason he had agreed to tutor her at all was her father's name and influence. Neither did Kharza enjoy taking risks, yet here he was, offering to flout the rules of Tier Breche in order to continue her instruction. The old drow had a double agenda, of that Liriel had no doubt. But then, so did everyone. As long as she tread carefully, she saw no reason why she could not take what he offered.

"That is very kind, Kharza," she said. "They try to keep me very busy here, but I'm sure I can slip away sometime soon."

"Yes. Well. You do know where to find me."

The wizard's hands flashed through the gestures of the spell, and a faint oval door appeared in the room. He gave Liriel the word of power that would activate the gate, and then stepped out into the freedom of Menzoberranzan.

Left alone, Liriel sighed deeply. If Kharza had deliberately set out to avenge himself for her teasing, this would have been an inspired way to do it. Knowing escape was just one word away would be pure torture to the restless young drow. Her father had given her a book of spells so she might leave the Academy if necessary, but he had later impressed upon her the need to use such spells with extreme discretion. What he probably meant was that she was only to use them at his bidding, she thought with a rush of rebellious anger. But she had enough sense to understand the risk, and to take it only for good cause.

She lit another candle from the flame of a nearly spent stub, and then settled down at her study table to read. The book Kharza had given her was very old, and the stories were simple and rather quaint. These were the stories of a restless people who long ago took to the seas and rivers in longboats, first to pillage and terrorize, then to settle. Yet there was an energy, a love of adventure, that sang from every page. Long into the night Liriel read, lighting candle after precious candle.

She'd never given much thought to humans, but these stories fascinated her. In these yellowed pages were tales of bold heroes, strange and fierce animals, mighty primitive gods, and a magic that was part and fabric of that distant land. Liriel pored over each word, absorbing the language of that long-ago time, the thinking of the people, and their strange magic. Her excitement grew with each page.

The concept of rune magic fascinated her. Some runes were simple and could be taught; others were unique and deeply personal. A caster, she learned, had to fashion such a rune before it could be used in magic. The process was known as *shaping*. This was done in three steps—planning, carving, and activating. Over the course of a journey, or as the result of a quest or adventure, a rune would slowly take shape in the mind of its caster. Only when the rune was fully realized could it be carved. Many spells specified what surface was required. A simple rune to speed healing, for example, must be carved on the limb of an oak tree.

"What's a tree?" Liriel muttered, and then continued her study.

The final step charged the rune with power through anointing it or reciting the words of a spell. This step also seemed to be highly personal; no purchased spell scroll would yield the secret. Liriel nodded thoughtfully as she absorbed the philosophy. Kharza was right: at first consideration rune magic did seem ridiculously simple. Yet it demanded something of the caster. The magic came from a journey, whether a journey of the mind or the quest of an adventurous wanderer.

A journey. A grand quest.

A wave of longing struck her with the force of a blow. This, she realized suddenly, was what she had craved all her life. This is what all those forays into the Underdark had been about, and the endless social flitting through the city. She was a born traveler, trapped among beings who were content to live and die in a cavern that measured a mere two miles across. Wondrous though Menzoberranzan might be, it was a small place for such as she.

Liriel buried her head in her hands and struggled to keep from screaming aloud. The young female had never known despair, but it closed in on her now. The walls of her room tightened, too, until they threatened to swallow the candlelight.

Then, as suddenly as it came, the moment passed, chased from her mind by a bold plan. Liriel slowly raised her eyes to her scrying bowl.

Why not? she thought rebelliously. If she was allowed to glimpse into the Abyss and study its creatures and its fell secrets, why shouldn't she learn more about her own world? Perhaps somewhere in the Lands of Light, descendants of the Rus lived out their lives with the lusty, brawling abandon she had glimpsed in this old book. Why should she not find them and study their ways?

It occurred to her that even that might not be enough. Instantly Liriel pushed aside that thought and snatched up the precious spell scroll. She had learned to take what life offered, without reflecting overmuch on what she might not have.

So the dark elf lit yet another candle, and began to study how she might gain a window into the Lands of Light.

* * * * *

Fyodor had no idea how long he had wandered in the Underdark, for here even time seemed distorted and unreal. It was not just that he was deep below the surface, far from the comforting rhythms of the sun and the moon. The constant, raw-nerved alertness required to stay alive gave each moment an incredible clarity, so each lingered in his mind long after it should have given way to the next. In a way, the slowing of time was like that which he experienced during the berserker rage, and it was almost as exhausting.

He'd carried into the Underdark food and water enough for two days, and although he had eaten and drunk sparingly, both were almost gone. Worse, his supply of torches was nearing an end. He had seen nothing down in this land that looked as if it would burn, and that was a problem. As long as he had light, Fyodor could follow the trail of the drow thieves. He faced a hard choice: pressing on, or trying to find a way back to the surface so he could get the supplies he needed to try again.

Fyodor pressed on. The tracking was difficult, and if he faltered now he might never find the trail. Although there were five drow, they walked lightly, and any trail was difficult to follow in terrain so different from his own land.

As he pondered the difficulties of his quest, it did not occur to him to ask what he would do when he found the drow. He knew what he could do, and that knowledge spurred him on.

In his land, famed for her berserker warriors, Fyodor was a champion. He had earned respect in his land, and already there was talk of making him a *Fang*—a chieftain in charge of a band of warriors. He was respected, but he was also feared for what he was. He, in turn, feared what he might become.

One of Rashemen's most misunderstood magics involved the distillation of *jhuild*, a libation so powerful it was commonly—and accurately—called "firewine." A less potent version was distilled as a trade good, but it was definitely an acquired taste, one few foreigners cared to develop. Each berserker warrior carried a flask that held an endless supply of *jhuild* and drank it from time to time with no more effect than would be expected from any other strong distilled drink. But before battle, *jhuild* was used in a ritual that inflamed the passions and raised warriors to an impossible level of skill and ferocity. This was something Rashemi were trained to do since birth, and no one who lacked this training could successfully bring on a berserk.

Unlike his fellow warriors, Fyodor was a natural berserker. The rage came upon him without benefit of *jhuild* or ritual. He fought with greater ferocity than his brethren, but without the control. As long as the rage lasted, he could not use strategy, or change his tactics in order to aid or protect his fellow Rashemi. All Fyodor could do was attack, to slaughter his foe until no more stood against him. Someday this would mean his death, of that Fyodor had no doubt. Yet it was not death he feared. Fyodor's deepest fear was that the day would come when he could no longer tell friend from foe.

The battle in the forest clearing troubled him deeply. Before that night he had fought only to protect his people and his land. He had entered the battle frenzy for the sake of a band of drow thieves! What next: would he join Thay's wizards in storming the tower circles of Rashemen's Witches? No, it was far better he should die here, in this deep, distant land.

The path before him rose up sharply and suddenly. Fyodor scrambled to the top of the incline and lifted his torch high. Ahead the tunnel dipped and made a hard turn to the right. To his surprise, a faint light emanated from the passage.

Carefully, as silently as he could, he crept toward the light. The sound of dripping water grew louder as he went, and the air became as moist as a marshland in springtime. When at last he rounded the corner, the sight beyond stole his breath.

He was in yet another cavern. This one was smaller than the last, but stranger than any sight he had yet seen. The walls were wet here, and growing on them in strange-shaped formations were patches of moss and fungi that glowed in luminescent shades of purple and blue. The light reflected off the wet black rock and filled the whole cavern with the strange color. Fyodor held out his hand; even his skin seemed to glow weirdly in the faint bluish light.

The young warrior took a deep breath and looked around. He had come to think of the Underdark as little more than a hive of solid rock, but in this cavern grew a staggering variety of plants. Curly, dark blue ferns surrounded a small pool, and pale silvery moss hung, like a lacy veil, in draping folds from the ceiling of the cavern. Nearby, under an overhanging ledge, grew clusters of mushrooms. Fyodor crouched down for a closer look.

Never had he seen mushrooms with such colors or such odd shapes. Some looked like the mushrooms of his home forests, except they were much larger and of a deep shade of violet. Others were more ethereal, with delicate stems and thin, fluted edges that looked as if they might crumple if touched. There were puffballs, swirled with crimson and lavender, and pale mushrooms that stood like short, stout sentinels.

He might try to eat some of the odd plants, Fyodor decided, but only as an alternative to starvation. Even in his homeland mushrooms held poison; who knew what effect these strange plants might have? At least the pale, thick mushrooms were somewhat familiar. If it should come to this, he would try those first. He reached out to touch one. The mushroom twitched away and let out a shrill, whistling shriek.

Fyodor jerked back his hand. "The mushrooms scream," he muttered in disbelief. Who knew what the ferns might have to say? He didn't care to find out, but there was water beyond the fern bed and he could not afford to pass it by.

He waded through the curling blue ferns without incident, then stopped short. The bones of some long-dead wanderer lay half in, half out of the water. But such bones! They seemed to be the remains of a lizard, but the skeleton was fully the size of a paladin's war charger. Stranger still, remnants of rotted leather and bits of metal lay around the enormous bones. Fyodor leaned in for a closer look. The skeleton was intact, but for a broken bone on one leg.

The warrior shook his head as he realized what must have happened. Someone had ridden this lizard creature as a mount, and when the leg broke, the useless lizard was simply abandoned. Even the gift of death had been denied the wretched thing. Fyodor thought of Sasha, and wondered what manner of being could treat a trusted mount in such fashion.

The man bent to drink of the water, and instantly knew how death had finally come to the desperate creature. The water had a faint mineral smell. Fyodor dipped his hand in and sniffed. Once before he had smelled lime, during a season when plague took many in his village. He would never forget that terrible summer, or the scent of the lime sprinkled into the single, yawning grave. He rose and backed away from the deadly pool.

Fyodor looked around the cavern. Water ran in rivulets down the walls, and louder trickling sounds echoed through the cavern from the tunnels beyond. Surely not all of the pool's tributaries were poisonous. He had to have water soon, and this was probably his best chance of finding it. Yet the tunnels here were so twisted that the water he heard most clearly could be around the corner, or a day's walk away. His best chance, he decided, would be to continue following the drow thieves. They would also need drinking water, and perhaps they would lead him to it. So he quickly examined the tunnels leading out of the cavern and found the marks of passing elven boots.

The luminous blue glow faded as he left the cavern behind, and the pale light of his torch seemed pure and healthy in comparison. The path Fyodor followed was narrow and steep, and he soon struggled for breath in the thin, unfamiliar air. He had not gone far when he found the water. A small waterfall spilled down a rocky alcove, scattering droplets into a shallow, fast-running stream. The water followed the path for a few paces, then disappeared into a hole in the tunnel floor. Over the opening, draped from one side of the tunnel to the other, hung an enormous spiderweb. The entrapped droplets caught Fyodor's torchlight and turned the web into a thousand rainbow prisms. Fyodor noted a few tiny insects skimming the surface of the stream—a good sign that the water was potable. He tasted the water and found it sweet.

Fyodor threw himself to the ground and drank deeply. Heaving a sigh of satisfaction and relief, he reached for his water flask. His hand froze, and he cursed himself for a fool. Where there were webs, there were usually spiders, yet he had approached this gigantic web with no more sense than a fly. Eye-to-eye with the biggest spider he had ever seen, Fyodor thought he knew how a trapped fly must feel.

The spider's head was nearly as big as a man's fist, and in the faint torchlight its furred, rounded black abdomen glistened like that of a well-groomed housecat. The entire creature must have been nearly three feet across, and its eight enormous legs bent in a tense crouch.

Fyodor's startled face stared back at him, reflected a thousand times in the creature's multiple eyes. The horror he expected to feel did not come. Unlike the scorpion-thing, this creature was no mindless, ravening beast. It had an air of watchful intelligence. It was clearly as interested in him as he was in it, and just as cautious. Slowly, silently, the giant spider backed away, one leg moving at a time. When it was beyond reach it uttered a low, chittering sound and began to rise into the air.

Fyodor watched in awe as the spider slid upward on a silken thread. He had seen spiders do that many times in his world, but had never noticed the grace and beauty of the silent flight. It was uncanny that so large a creature could walk such a gossamer path. Stranger still, the giant arachnid simply disappeared in midflight, long before it reached the tunnel's ceiling.

A magic-user? he mused. If the mushrooms in this place could scream, perhaps a spider could wield magic.

Or perhaps it answered to someone who could.

That thought spurred Fyodor to action. He quickly filled his flask and hurried along the tunnel. If that spider was indeed some sort of messenger, his presence in this place would soon be noted. If he did not retrieve the amulet soon, he would surely die in this bizarre, nightmarish world. Above all, he must keep his wits about him every moment.

This much he knew: the Underdark was no place for those who dreamed.

* * * * *

The night was nearly spent before Liriel felt ready to try the spell. First she lit several candles and placed them around the edges of the scrying bowl. A conjured image had no heat, and therefore could not be seen without light. She filled the scrying bowl with water and, in lieu of the powdered substance called for by the spell, she broke an edge off one of the ancient pages of her book and crumpled it into the water.

Chanting softly, she spoke the words of the spell. The water roiled wildly, then smoothed to a glossy black. Eagerly she bent over the bowl.

In it she saw water, a vast expanse of it, rising and falling in white-crested waves. *A sea,* she thought excitedly. She had heard of such things. It was wonderful, this sea, so vast and open and full of possibilities. The water rose and fell even though there were no visible rocks and rapids to explain such movement, and cutting through the wild water was the largest, strangest boat she had ever seen.

The boat was long and narrow, fashioned of some thick, pale substance and crowned with enormous white wings that curved tightly to one side. The wings did not move, yet the boat flew through the water with exhilarating speed, sending white spray high as it cut through the waves. Most wondrous of all was the prow of the boat, which was crudely carved to resemble the head of a dragon.

So descendants of the Rus still lived, Liriel marveled, and they still traveled the seas in their far-sailing ships. Where might that dragon's wings take her, she thought longingly, if only she could travel with the restless humans! She bent low, gripping the sides of the scrying bowl with both hands as she devoured the image before her.

The boat turned sharply. Its white wings fluttered for a moment and then snapped hard to the other side. Straight ahead, visible over the rampant dragon on the prow, was an island, its edges muted by mist and the spray of water. Liriel knew about islands, for even in the city there were small islets of rock and soil in Lake Donigarten. But this place was no more like the rothe pasture than black, brooding Donigarten was like this sea. The island was huge, with a wild rock-strewn shore and sloping cliffs. And it was green, so green that beholding it hurt the eyes.

Closer and closer the island came, for the boat was flying toward it with astonishing speed. A cove came into view, a large, deeply curving bay sheltered by the tallest, strangest plants Liriel had ever seen. There were docks there, and the tiny forms of the people who waited to welcome the travelers home. Liriel felt the lure of that harbor as strongly as she had heard the call of the sea. Not blinking, hardly breathing, she gazed into the bowl.

Several more minutes passed before she acknowledged the pain smoldering behind her eyes. At first she put it down to her intense concentration; then she noticed the sky was changing color. The wondrous, vivid midnight blue was fading away to luminous silver. The sea also changed, becoming a bright, rose-touched gray that hurt the eyes. Suddenly Liriel understood what was happening.

"Dawn," she whispered in awe. "The sun approaches."

The sun. The inexorable, searing enemy that had defeated her people in battle against the dwarves, the blinding light that kept them imprisoned Below. Oddly enough, Liriel experienced none of the fear or loathing she had been taught she should feel. All she felt was a consuming lust to see such wonders with her own eyes. For such a thing, she would give anything, she vowed.

Then the reality of her life returned to her with the force of a dagger's thrust, and the enticing image in the scrying bowl winked out of view. Liriel slumped back in her chair.

No, she corrected herself; for such a thing, she would give *everything*.

She might not fear the sun, she whose eyes had been trained to candlelight from her fifth year of life. But Liriel knew what would happen to her if she walked in the Lands of Light. Her dark-elven magic would be burned away.

She'd heard the whispered stories about the disastrous surface war, and how spells went awry and spell components disintegrated with the coming of dawn. On the surface, she would be vulnerable as never before. Her magical weapons would lose their potency, as would her armor. Her innate drow powers would fade as well. Liriel supposed she could live without faerie fire, and the delicate flight of levitation, and the magical *piwafwi* that granted her invisibility. She might even be able to survive without the incredible resistance to magical attack that was a drow's birthright. She supposed she could live, but walking into such a life would be no different from a musician willingly giving up hearing, or an artist, sight.

Yes, perhaps she could have her journey into the light, but at the cost of her very identity. Dark-elven magic was more than a collection of spells and powers and weapons. It was her passion and her heritage. It flowed through her blood; it shaped her every plan and act. With it, she was drow. Without it, what would she be?

Like one asleep, Liriel rose from her table and picked up the scrying bowl. She tipped it, letting the water slowly spill out onto the carpeted floor. Then she hurled the scrying bowl aside and flung herself facedown on her bed.

For the second time in her life, Liriel wished she could weep. The first time was the day she had lost her mother. Now she mourned the loss of an open sea, and a newborn dream.

Chapter 8

THE DARK MAIDEN

iriel's sleepless night left her heavy-eyed and short of temper. Her mood did not improve as the day wore on, not even during the advanced class on the lower planes. Shakti Hunzrin was there, heavily doused with perfume to disguise the lingering scent of the pasture, but her usual scowl had been replaced by a smug little smirk, and she followed Liriel's every move with measuring, speculative eyes. The stout priestess was plotting something, of that Liriel had no doubt. Although the young Baenre was not overly concerned by this, she was in no mood to play this particular game.

Nor did she have time. Mistress Zeld seemed devoted to filling her new student's every moment with two different activities, preferably on opposite sides of the Academy. Liriel's scant leisure time had been taken away so she might attend still more classes, and even her meals were henceforth to be taken in the company of a tutor. Being lectured on the intricacies of clerical protocol was enough to destroy even Liriel's appetite. She pushed aside her food untasted, although the entree—spiced, steamed snails—was one of her favorite dishes.

Liriel literally had to run to keep up with her new schedule, and by the end of the day her arms were heaped high with spell scrolls and lore books to be learned by the following round of classes.

Not one to take abuse silently, Liriel made her way to Mistress Zeld's study, where she voiced her concerns with her usual vigor.

Mistress Zeld sat in cold silence until the Baenre princess had finished ranting. "The matron mistress bade me to make you into a high priestess in record time. I have my orders," she said in a soft, menacing tone, "*and you have yours.*"

There was little Liriel could say to counter that, so she rose to leave. She knew Zeld suspected her of the pranks, and she had thought the mistress was merely trying to keep her too busy to indulge in such mischief. If that had been the case, a little reminder of Liriel's family name and paternity would probably have been enough to bring the mistress back in line. But since this directive had been handed down from Matron Triel, there was no way Liriel could turn it aside.

Fine, Liriel concluded bitterly as she strode toward her room, heavily laden with her assignments. I'll become a high priestess before I'm forty-five, for whatever good that will do. I'll be dead of exhaustion, of course, but at least House Baenre can have the satisfaction of cremating me with one of those snake whips in my hand!

By the time she returned to the dormitory, most of the students were already asleep. The door to her room was intact and locked shut, but the faint, mingled odor of perfume and rothe droppings lingered in the hall. Liriel knew immediately her privacy had been invaded once again.

With a hiss of rage she flung aside her scrolls and books and bent to examine the lock. A quick glance told her what had gone awry. Chirank had not replaced the old lock, as Liriel had directed. All Shakti needed to enter the room was one of her old keys, for the students were not allowed to barricade their doors with spells.

Liriel cursed the ogre for her stupidity, herself for her carelessness, and the book that had kept her up all night with ancient tales and futile dreams. She jerked open the door and stalked in to access the damage.

The lock on her chest of books showed several tiny new scratches, as if someone had tried to pick it. Yet the thin, nearly invisible strand of spiderweb Liriel had stretched along one side of the chest remained unbroken. Shakti might command formidable magic, Liriel conceded, but she had a lot to learn about thievery. Inside the wardrobe all seemed to be as she left it. Not satisfied with appearances, the young wizard shielded her eyes, then cast a spell that would reveal magic.

A sphere of faint blue light blinked into view around her neat pile of travel gear. Liriel reached out to touch the glowing orb; she felt nothing, but the moment her fingertip passed through the light, the sphere popped as silently as a soap bubble. It was an alarm, set to go off when the pile of clothing was disturbed.

So that was what Shakti was up to, Liriel realized with a touch of amusement. The Hunzrin priestess intended to catch her sneaking out of the Academy. If so, she'd have to do better than that!

The dark elf waited until the blue glow of the spell faded away. Several moments passed, for there were many magical scrolls and items in her room and the telltale light made the room painfully bright. When she could see again without discomfort, she carefully, methodically searched her chamber for any other gift Shakti might have left behind.

At last she found it: hidden in the elaborate twists and folds of a wall hanging was a small, oval gem. It was an undistinguished stone, cloudy white with flecks of blue, but Liriel recognized it for what it was. Such a gem could be enspelled for any number of purposes, and was sometimes used as an aid to viewing both distant planes and nearby foes. This gem was beyond doubt some sort of scrying device.

Liriel held the stone in a tightly clenched fist as she debated what best to do. The spells needed to activate the gem were very difficult, and she adjusted her opinion of Shakti Hunzrin upward by several notches. When the priestess was not motivated by sheer rage, she could be a credible foe. Perhaps even a worthy one, Liriel mused.

There was a temptation hidden in that thought, and the young drow seized it immediately. A low, dark chuckle escaped her as the idea took hold. If Shakti wanted to try to catch her sneaking out the Academy, Liriel was more than willing to oblige.

"Very well," she said aloud, "let the hunt begin."

First Liriel conjured a sphere of darkness around the gem, effectively locking out spying eyes. That would pique Shakti's interest and get the game started. Then she quickly dressed in her travel clothes and armed herself with an assortment of small weapons and practical spells. The spellbook Gromph had given her she tucked at the top of her travel bag. By the time she was ready, Liriel had concocted a plan that gave her escape that added, piquant touch of creative revenge.

Draping her *piwafwi* around her shoulders, she slipped out into the hall. The magical cloak could grant its wearer invisibility, and in her enchanted boots Liriel walked as silently as a shadow. As quickly as she dared, she made her way toward the luxurious suites that housed Arach-Tinilith's mistresses.

One of these instructors, a newly elevated priestess from House Faen Tlabbar, was reputed to possess in full measure the wanton nature of that clan's females. Mistress Mod'Vensis Tlabbar seldom lacked for company, not with the masters and students of both the mage school and the fighting Academy so close at hand. In Liriel's opinion, the bedchamber of a Tlabbar female was an excellent place to stash Shakti's scrying gem.

That, of course, was the tricky part. To fortify her resolve, Liriel imagined what was likely to take place a few hours hence. The spell she'd cast would obscure the gem for several hours, giving Shakti ample time to take her accusations and her scrying globe to Mistress Zeld. The scene that would be revealed when the sphere of darkness faded would very likely be different than the one the Hunzrin priestess anticipated.

Liriel smiled dreamily as she visualized Shakti's expression of triumph transform into one of chagrin—and panic. She did not envy Shakti the task of explaining how and why she had intruded thus upon the privacy of Mistress Mod'Vensis. Doing so would take a much nimbler tongue than Shakti possessed!

With that pleasant thought to sustain her, Liriel crouched low and waited. The unusual silence behind the Tlabbar priestess's door suggested the evening's festivities had yet to begin.

Soon enough, a handsome young fighting student crept down the halls toward Mod'Vensis's door. Liriel wondered briefly if there was any truth in the rumor that the Tlabbar females brewed a potion that incited passionate devotion in any male who imbibed it. A good idea, Liriel supposed, if one lacked the time and talent for more conventional seduction. The behavior of the young male seemed to support the rumor, for his manner as he hurried toward the meeting with his mistress displayed more ardor than discretion.

The male moved to the door and began to tap out some elaborate code. Liriel drew her *piwafwi* more tightly around her to help muffle her heat shadow. She flexed her fingers a few times to limber them up, then crept in closer. With the stealth she had learned from her maid—an enslaved halfling pickpocket—she tucked the scrying gem into the cuff of the male's boot. The door opened, and female hands bedecked with a lethal manicure and a fortune in gems reached out and yanked the male into the room.

Smiling broadly, Liriel hurried back to her own room. Using a thin-edged knife as a tool, she quickly replaced Shakti's lock with her old one. Then she closed her door and set a simple alarm of her own: a small pyramid of drinking goblets stacked against the door. It would not be as effective as a magical ward, obviously, but if anyone tried to push open the door, the noise would at least draw some unwanted attention!

One thing remained to be determined: her destination. Liriel took Gromph's spellbook from her pouch and dropped it open on her study table. Feeling reckless and nearly giddy with the thought of freedom, she closed her eyes and stabbed her finger downward to choose the spell she would cast. She looked down and quickly clasped a hand to her mouth to hold back a shriek of pure elation.

Tonight, she was going to the surface.

Liriel spoke the word of power that brought Kharza-kzad's gate into existence. She leaped through, landing in a crouch in her tutor's suite of rooms in Spelltower Xorlarrin. Kharza was not in his study at this hour, but she followed the soft, grating sound of the wizard's snores into his bedchamber.

Not all dark elves slept, but Kharza was obviously one who did. A few drow still took their rest in the form of elven reverie, a type of wakeful meditation. With each passing century, those drow dwindled in number. The dark elves, no long able to find peace within themselves, needed the oblivion of true sleep in order to rest. That was fine with Liriel, for it was much easier to track down someone who snored than someone who merely dreamed.

She soon found the bedchamber and jumped onto her tutor's bed. Kneeling over the wizard, she seized his bedshirt with both hands and shook him awake. Kharza came out of his unelven reverie sputtering and disheveled, and he immediately groped about for some sort of weapon.

Liriel shook him again, and at last his eyes focused on his attacker. His panic melted, and exasperation flooded his wrinkled face.

"What time is it?" she demanded.

The wizard huffed. "Under the circumstances, don't you think *I* should be the one asking that question?"

She gave him another sharp shake. "No, up on the *surface*. What time is it there? At what hour of Narbondel does the sun set, and when does it return?"

Twin emotions—dread and understanding—dawned in Kharzakzad's eyes. "You are going Above? But why?"

"Call it a hunt," the drow girl said casually. She rolled off the bed and stood there, hands on hips. "Well, aren't you going to help me?"

The wizard threw back the covers. "I ought to send you right back to Arach-Tinilith," he grumbled, but he shrugged on a robe and tied it about his waist as he followed his student into his study. He assured Liriel it was early night in the Lands Above, and together they rehearsed the words and gestures of the gate spells she would need.

"I must insist upon one thing," he cautioned. "You must cast a gate that will seek out other drow on the surface. The Lands of Light are filled with hazards that you have never faced. You will be safer in the company of other drow."

"Really?" she said with cutting sarcasm. "I've never noticed that to be the case before."

Kharza did not dispute her observation. "Even so, with your House Baenre insignia and your own not inconsiderable magic, you will be welcomed by any raiding party or merchant band that knows of Menzoberranzan. You should be safe enough."

Reluctantly Liriel agreed. She did most of her exploring alone, and she did not want her first glimpse of the Lands of Light tainted by the presence of strangers. But, eager to be on her way, she cast the spell and stepped into the gate.

Instantly she was flung into a whirling, rushing tunnel, an exhilarating free-fall that went far beyond such things as speed and time and place. It was a little like water-running, but without the rocks and the noise and the jarring bumps. It was terrifying, and it was wonderful. And it was over too soon.

Liriel suddenly found herself on her knees. Her head spun, her stomach entertained second thoughts concerning her last two meals, and her hands clenched something moist and green.

"Green ferns," she muttered, recognizing the plants. "How very odd."

The sick feeling that followed the magical travel faded quickly, and the drow rose slowly to her feet. Shading her eyes with her hand, she raised her gaze slowly to the sky.

The *sky!* The glimpse her scrying bowl had given her did nothing to prepare her for this vast and endless canopy, as brilliant as the nearly black sapphires that drow loved above all gems. As she gazed up and up, something deep within her seemed to break free and take flight.

Then there were the lights! The largest and brightest must be the thing Kharza had called a moon. It was round and brilliant white, just barely peeking out from behind the distant hills. Dotting the sapphire sky were thousands of lesser lights that to her sensitive eyes showed not only white, but yellow and pink and clear light blue. If this were night, Liriel marveled, how bright could it possibly be with the coming of dawn!

And the air! It was *alive,* and it whirled about her in an exuberant rush, carrying with it a hundred green scents. Liriel stretched her arms out wide and lifted her face to the dancing wind. She resisted, just barely, the temptation to toss off her clothing and let the capricious breezes play over her skin.

The sounds that the winds brought her were just as exotic as the scents, and as enticing. She heard the low, hollow call of some unknown bird against a background chorus of repetitive, grating croaks that sounded faintly like Kharza's snoring. She crept toward the croaking sound, through a thick bed of those strange green ferns. Beyond was a pond, and the sound came from small green creatures sitting on broad leaves that floated on the water. The creatures looked a bit like fat, rounded lizards, and for many minutes Liriel was content to listen to their song. In the Underdark, lizards did not sing.

Beyond the pond was a forest, a vast jumble of plants that was a little like the groves of giant mushrooms that grew here and there in the Underdark. This one was filled not with fungi, but with tall green plants. She had seen something like these plants in her book, a rough sketch that illustrated a myth called "The Tree of Yggsdrasil." Those plants, then, must be trees.

Liriel hurriedly skirted the pond to examine one of the trees more closely. She stroked its rough skin, then plucked one of the leaves and crushed it between her fingers so she might breathe its scent.

Everywhere she looked was *green,* bright and vivid in the brilliant light of the rising moon. The vision in her scrying bowl had not fully prepared her for that. Green was the rarest color in the Underdark, and here there were so many varieties of green that the single word did not begin to cover all the shades and nuances. Liriel wandered

103

deeper into the grove, touching this tree and that, exploring the scents and textures and colors of the forest. Then, with a soft cry of delight, she bent to pick up a small, familiar object.

It was an acorn, an oft-used design in her new lore book. She stood and examined the leaves of the tree just above. Yes, the shape was right. This, then, must be an oak, the tree mentioned so often in the rune magic of the ancient Rus.

On impulse, Liriel climbed into the oak tree's arms and scrambled up as high as she could go. Finding a comfortable perch, she leaned back and gazed out over the pond below and the hills beyond. It was a wonderful thing, this tree. She could see why rune magic used the oak tree's power to aid in healing. There was a grandeur and mystery to this tree she had never seen in Underdark plants, not even the largest wild mushrooms. She thought of myconids, rare sentient mushroom-people taller than drow, and she wondered what manner of tree-creatures might dwell in this wondrous forest.

Then the scent of smoke came to her on the dancing wind, and the rich smell of roasting meat. Liriel had almost forgotten Kharza-kzad's insistence that she use a gate enspelled to seek out a drow encampment. The smoke, she supposed, must come from such a camp.

She knew she should show herself to the drow strangers immediately, before they sensed her presence and launched an attack. On the other hand, the scent of roasting meat alone did not signify she had found other People. Drow ate their food raw as often as they cooked it. She did not relish the idea of stumbling into the midst of humans or, even worse, faerie elves.

Then the music began, and Liriel knew at once the gate spell had worked as intended. The music was familiar, with an eerie, haunting melody and intricate layers of rhythm. The pure, silvery tone of the pipe was new to her, but the style was unmistakably drow.

Liriel climbed down from her oaken perch and crept through the too-green plants toward the inviting music. She paused at the edge of a small forest-cavern—a patch of open ground surrounded by trees— and gazed in wonder at the gathering before her.

There, whirling and leaping around a blazing campfire, danced a score of dark elf females. Four others hung back beyond the circle, playing silvery flutes and small drums. Without exception, the females were tall, and the muscles on their bare limbs were taut and long and powerful. Each had long, silvery hair that seemed to capture and hold the firelight. Apart from their height, these females looked just like the drow she knew in Menzoberranzan—slender, fey, achingly beautiful. They had no more concern for modesty than any of her peers, for they were clad only in scant, gossamer gowns that whirled about their legs like smoke.

The tallest of the females broke away from the group. She stood, smiling, her hands outstretched in a gesture of welcome toward Liriel's hiding place.

"Join us, little sister," she called in the drow tongue.

Just those words, and then the dark elf whirled away to resume her ecstatic dancing. Liriel, poised for a fast retreat, paused to consider the invitation. If the strange female had approached her with conversation, Liriel would have been far more wary. These drow wanted merely to dance. After a moment of fierce internal debate, Liriel decided to join the moonlit revel.

She quickly stripped off her chain mail and weapons. Dancing while armed was not only an insult in drow society, but a hazard. A single knife wielded amid a throng of leaping, whirling drow could do considerable damage, and weapons were by law and custom left beyond the circle of a dance floor. Dancing was as close to an honorable truce as dark elves could come, and therefore Liriel did not fear these drow strangers as much as she might have under different circumstances. And though she left her weapons behind, she took her magic with her. She would be safe enough.

Clad only in her leggings and tunic, Liriel leaped into the circle of song and firelight. The other drow parted to make room for her, and she fell easily into the flow and pattern of the dance.

The moon rose slowly into the sky, casting long tree-shadows into the firelit clearing. At last, the music ended and the dark elves whirled the dance to a finish. The tall female who had summoned Liriel came forward and dropped to one knee—a gesture that in Menzoberranzan signified surrender. Since Liriel was alone and this powerful-looking female was surrounded by a score of comrades, the Baenre girl took it to be an offer of peace. She accepted the gesture with her own: both hands held out, palms up, to show she held no weapons.

The strange female rose, smiling. "I am Ysolde Veladorn. These are my friends and fellow priestesses. Our campfire is yours, for as long as you would like to share it. From whence, if I may ask, have you come?"

This was strange behavior for priestesses, but Liriel was not inclined to point this out. "I am Liriel of House Baenre, first house of Menzoberranzan," she said.

That announcement was usually received with a mixture of fear and respect. A strange emotion—compassion, perhaps?—crossed Ysolde's dark face. "You have traveled far," she observed. "Would you sit with us awhile, and share our meal?"

Liriel glanced toward the campfire. One of the dark elves had taken up a harp—an instrument rare in the Underdark—and was playing softly. The other females were lounging about, laughing easily and passing around portions of the roast meat. There was a comfortable, unguarded air about these drow that Liriel found odd but strangely appealing.

"I will stay," she agreed, and then added, "Of course, I will pay for the food."

Ysolde smiled and shook her head. "That is not needed. In honor of our goddess, we share what we have with travelers."

"That custom is new to me," Liriel observed, as she followed the tall drow to the fire. "But then, I just started at the Academy."

One of the other females, a shorter, slimmer version of Ysolde, lifted her head suddenly from her meal. "Not Arach-Tinilith?"

Liriel nodded and accepted a skewer of roasted meat and mushrooms. "You know of it?"

The drow exchanged glances. "We have heard tales of Menzoberranzan," one of them said carefully. Liriel got the impression they would have liked to ask more, but Ysolde sent a calm, silencing gaze around the circle.

"Thank you for joining us in the ritual," the tall female said. "To have a stranger among us is a special offering to the goddess."

Fear knotted Liriel's throat, and she nearly choked on her first bite. Disbelief followed at once, quickly giving way to outrage. She threw aside her meal and leaped to her feet. "I might not be of your number, but you would not *dare* to offer a Baenre female to Lloth!" she snarled. "The ritual knife you raised to slay me would turn back against you!"

Every jaw dropped. Then, to Liriel's utter astonishment, the silver-haired females began to laugh.

Ysolde rose and laid a hand on the girl's shoulder. "We do not worship the Queen of Spiders. Our goddess is Eilistraee, the Dark Maiden, patron of song and swordcraft. The dance you joined was a ritual of praise to her!"

It was Liriel's turn to gape. In Menzoberranzan, rituals usually involved sacrifice of some sort. Prayers were chanted to Lloth and an occasional hymn intoned, but dancing was strictly for social events. The thought that dancing could be considered an act of worship was utterly amazing. Even more shocking was the concept that some drow worshiped another goddess. Which brought Liriel to the most basic and profoundly disturbing question of all: *there was another goddess to worship?*

Before Ysolde could continue, the sound of another musical instrument floated toward them from beyond the distant hills. It was a wind instrument, with a deep, haunting call unlike any Liriel had ever heard. The drow froze, listening.

"What *is* that?" Liriel demanded.

"The hunting horn of Eilistraee," the tall priestess replied. Her voice was hushed and her face rapt, attentive. All of the drow listened intently as the horn winded again, this time in a simple fragment of melody.

The dark elves exploded into action. They peeled off their gossamer robes and pulled on breeches and boots, tunics and deep-cowled cloaks. They strapped on weapons: swords as finely crafted and sharply honed as any Liriel had seen in Menzoberranzan, longbows many times the size of the tiny crossbows the Underdark drow used for their poison darts, and silver-tipped arrows as long as Liriel's arm. One of the drow doused the fire; another bundled up the discarded dancing gowns. An eager gleam shone in every eye as the drow prepared for battle.

Their excitement was contagious, and Liriel watched with a mixture of curiosity and envy. These strange drow were preparing for some grand adventure, here beneath the open sky.

"What is happening? Where are you going?"

"The hunting horn. It is the signal that someone nearby needs our aid," responded Ysolde. She paused in the act of strapping on a quiver of arrows and looked at the young drow. "There will be battle. If you wish to join us, we would welcome another blade."

For a moment Liriel was tempted. She was intrigued by these drow, so different from any she knew, and she felt the call of the hunt. Yet wouldn't hunting with these silver-haired females, on the bidding of this upstart Eilistraee, be an insult to Lloth? And if the Spider Queen should turn against her, Baenre or not, there would be no place for her in Menzoberranzan.

Ysolde read the girl's answer in her hesitation and sent her an understanding smile. "Perhaps that is best. You do not yet understand what we do or what enemy we prepare to fight. But remember, a rightful place awaits you in the Lands Above. You may join us any time you wish, to live beneath the sun and dance in the moonlight."

And then the drow were gone, melting into the forest with as much stealth as any Underdark patrol.

Liriel stood alone for a long moment, breathing in long draughts of the crisp night air and letting the wind play against her heated skin. Perhaps she would come here again, but only to learn and observe. Fascinating though these strange priestesses might be, Liriel was not willing to relinquish her own goddess to join them, nor could she settle down in this remote forest-cavern. If ever she should come to the surface for any length of time, it would be to travel far on some grand adventure.

That thought came to mind unbidden, and it was as appealing as it was impossible. Liriel quickly thrust it aside. She gathered together her things and prepared for her return to Menzoberranzan.

The trip back to Spelltower Xorlarrin would be more complex than the one that brought her here. That spell, although extremely powerful, only worked one way. To return she could need to take a relay of gate spells. Magical travel was unreliable in the Underdark, for areas of strong magical radiation—like the grotto where Zz'Pzora made her lair—could distort spells and throw the traveler dangerously off track.

Liriel opened her spellbook to the first of the spells. This one, Kharza said, placed a gate somewhere in the series of open caverns near Dead Dragon Gorge, some six or seven days' travel from Menzoberranzan and very near a labyrinth of caves that lay near the surface. It was an easy site to reach by magical travel, for it had much open space and no radiation magic. From there she could find the site of a second gate that would bring her to the perimeter of the city. The final spell was more difficult, and the gate had a secret to ensnare the wizard who traveled to Spelltower Xorlarrin without Kharza-kzad's blessing.

She quickly spoke the words to the spell, and darkness enveloped her like a welcoming embrace. Liriel looked around at the Underdark, at the comfortable familiarity of the tunnels and caverns. For good or ill, she was home.

An eerie, high-pitched cry sounded, reverberating off the walls of a good-sized cavern somewhere up ahead. Other voices joined in a chorus of excited, wavering hoots and shrieks. From behind her, Liriel heard an answering call. She spun around, hand on the hilt of her short sword, as two narrow slits of bright light came swooping down toward her. The distinctive violet shade—the color of glowing amethysts—could mean only one thing: a dragazhar.

Liriel threw herself flat and rolled aside. A large form swept over her, close enough for her to feel the rush of air. Her eyes, still attuned to the bright lights of the midnight sky, slipped back fully into the heat-sensing spectrum. The dragazhar, or nighthunter, flapped by on velvet black wings like those of a giant bat. The creature had the long tapered head of a scurry rat, a whiplike tail tipped with a razor-sharp triangular spike, and long curving ears reminiscent of dragon horns. With a wingspan of some seven feet, the nighthunter was one of the most dangerous of all the Underdark bats. Liriel crouched, pulled several throwing knives from their hiding places, and waited for the creature's next pass.

The expected attack did not come, but sounds of battle—repeated dull thuds and the cries of the wheeling bats—came from the cavern ahead. Ten dragazhar, she guessed from the echoing calls, a full hunting pack. Seldom did they attack anything but small animals, but whatever they'd attacked this time was giving them a good fight.

And if there was anything Liriel enjoyed, it was a good fight. Weapons in hand, the drow inched her way down the tunnel.

Faint light greeted her as she rounded a sharp turn, the pale violet light cast by certain luminescent fungi. The light increased with each step, until the tunnel was nearly as bright as the midnight sky she had left behind. The sounds of battle grew louder, too, and the mighty *thwacks* of an unseen weapon brought squeals of anger and pain from the giant bats.

This ought to be worth watching, Liriel thought happily as she scrambled down a steep, dipping curve.

Then the cavern was before her. Thick black spears of rock thrust from the floor and the ceiling of the cave, meeting here and there like bared fangs. Several dragazhar wheeled and swooped, darting between the stalactites with astonishing agility. Not one of the creatures had gone unscathed by battle. Most were scored with long, bloody lines, one had lost its tail, and yet another flopped helplessly on the cavern floor, its broken wing hanging limp. Yet the dragazhar's adversary was hidden from view.

Elaine Cunningham

She crouched low behind a rock formation and edged her away around for a better look. What she saw was more surprising than anything this night had yet shown her.

The nighthunters' bane was merely this and nothing more: a single human male.

Chapter 9

THE TREASURE HUNTER

iriel had glimpsed an occasional human in the market. A few of humankind's shadier and more desperate merchants ventured into the Underdark, but like most dark elves of her class she despised these merchants as vermin and had no dealings with them. She had never been this close to a human. Curious, she crept closer.

This one was young, about her own age as humans reckon time, or perhaps just a bit older. The man was about a head taller than she was. He was taller than most drow males and much broader. His thick muscles made him resemble a tall dwarf, but his face was beardless and finer of feature. He had none of the drow elegance of form, and in Liriel's estimation his sole claim to masculine beauty was the color of his eyes, which were as bright and clear as pale blue topaz. The man had dark, fine hair cut carelessly short and skin so pale it almost glowed in the faint light of the cavern. Liriel absently fingered a lock of her own white hair. The human was designed backward, dark where she was light, like some inverted mirror.

And the strange way he fought! He had seized one of the deepbats by the tail and was bashing at it with a long club. The man used the creature as a shield, too, by swinging it at any other bat that ventured close. The entrapped dragazhar had given up any thought of fighting and was flapping frantically in an effort to escape. The battle was not without humor, and an amused chuckle escaped Liriel.

Instantly one of the bats swerved and darted toward her hiding place. Its narrow eyes gleamed with hard, gem-colored light, and it fairly cackled with excitement as it closed in on its new, smaller prey.

Liriel leaped to her feet, a knife in each hand. She threw both knives at the same instant. With deadly precision, the knives buried themselves deep into the eyes of the attacking bat. The creature crashed into the tunnel wall and rolled to the floor in a shower of loose rocks and dirt.

Already the dark elf had her second weapon ready: a sling she'd fashioned of leather and rope. Liriel stooped and snatched up a handful of small rocks. She put one into her sling and began to twirl it. The weapon whistled as it whirled around her head, and the sudden release sent the stone flying with the speed of a fireball toward the place where the human battled the nighthunter.

The missile struck the entrapped dragazhar between the eyes. Stunned, the creature flopped forward. The man flung up his arms to shield himself from the falling beast, but the deepbat's weight was too much for him and he went down under the giant creature. His club skittered along the rocky floor.

After a moment, the human flung aside the bat's wing and crawled out. He met Liriel's amused, curious gaze, and his strange blue eyes widened with alarm. He drew a large dark sword from a shoulder strap and crouched in a defensive position. So intent was he upon the unexpected appearance of a drow that he disregarded the attack coming from the remaining nighthunters, flanking him and swooping in from either side.

Liriel pointed. "Behind you!" she shouted in the drow tongue.

The young man hesitated, perhaps not understanding her words, perhaps unwilling to turn his back on a dark elf. Liriel quickly spat the words of a spell and flung out her hand. Magical fire sped toward the human.

He dropped to the ground and rolled out of the path of Liriel's fireball. He could be quick when he wanted to; she had to give him that much. More agile than he appeared, he was back on his feet in time to see the elf's magic missile collide with the attacking bats.

One of the deepbats wheeled aside at the last moment; the fireball struck the other directly. The force of the blow flung the creature backward, and its giant wings folded together before it like prayerful hands. Liriel followed the attack with a series of thrown knives. One after another, three blades hissed through the air and sank deep into the dragazhar's eyes and heart.

The human gave her a quick, grateful nod and raised his sword to fend off an attack from the surviving deepbat. The dragazhar had circled the cavern and was closing in on the human. Fangs gleamed in the faint light as the creature dove toward its prey. The human held his sword high, ready to ward off the deepbat's bite.

That's it, Liriel thought with a stab of disappointment. The battle is over. She saw clearly what the human could not: the real attack would come from the deepbat's tail. The dragazhar's long tail was curled high and back, ready to strike with the barbed, poisoned tip. No weapon she could throw would stop it in time.

Liriel watched, helpless, as the deepbat swooped in. As she'd expected, the creature's flight curved abruptly upward, taking its body out of sword's reach. The barbed tail whipped forward.

But the man heaved the sword upward. Its heavy blade struck the nighthunter and knocked its flight askew, and the fighter lunged at the creature's striking tail. He caught it, just above the barbed tip, and hung on with both hands.

"Now what?" Liriel muttered grimly. The man had parried the attack successfully, but he had no weapon to finish off the bat.

To her amazement, he began to twirl the deepbat overhead like a giant bolo. It was an amazing defense—the force of the spin kept the bat from attacking him—but it was also woefully shortsighted. Despite his apparent strength, the human could not keep the bat circling for long, nor could he get up enough speed to successfully fling it to its death. An ogre or bugbear might have done so, had such a creature the wits to conceive the plan, but the moment this man released the bat, it would be free to fly back and attack.

Unless . . .

A quirky plan popped into Liriel's mind, and she seized it at once. Marshaling all the discipline of her magical training, she shut out the sounds of battle and traveled back in memory to her last night of freedom in Menzoberranzan. She closed her eyes and remembered the throbbing music and the faerie lights of the *nedeirra* dance. Deep in the frenzied ecstacy of the dance, she had been only faintly aware of the wizard who floated high above the floor, his hands weaving a spell that would speed the movements of the dancers into a sinuous, syncopated blur. But she had seen, and now she remembered.

Her eyes snapped open, and her hands echoed the gestures of the spell. Immediately blue faerie fire outlined the human and the bat. She heaved a sigh of relief as the magic took hold and the man's movements began to pick up speed.

Liriel took her short sword from its belt and stalked in as close as she dared. Gripping the weapon with both hands, she tensed and waited for the right moment.

Faster and faster twirled the man and the bat, caught in the grip of the dark-elven spell and limned with faerie fire. Soon the giant bat was spinning so fast it left a trailing circle of light behind it. Its shrieking wail was entirely lost in the whirl of wind. That should do it, Liriel thought. She leaped forward, her sword lashing up.

The force of the impact nearly wrenched her arms from their sockets, but the keen elven steel slashed through sinew and bone and neatly severed the deepbat's tail. Suddenly released from its spin, the creature arrowed straight toward the cavern wall and splatted there like a giant insect. The human tumbled just as violently in the opposite direction, rolling until he struck the base of a large stalactite. He lay there, either dazed or dead.

Liriel tucked her sword back into its scabbard. Her head tilted to one side as she regarded the strange male. Several minutes passed and still he did not move. She began to feel the stirrings of worry, and she crept over and stooped down for a closer look. Gingerly she reached out to touch the pale skin of his face.

His hand flashed forward and closed around her wrist. Liriel sprang backward with a startled hiss, but the man's grip was too strong to break. Her free hand sought the hilt of a knife, and her narrowed eyes fixed upon the pulsing vein in his neck. One quick slash, and she would be free.

"My thanks, lady," he said, in an unexpectedly deep, rich voice. His blue eyes, at close range, were even more startling. "If not for your magic, that monster would have gotten the better of me. It is said in my land that only a fool takes a snowcat by the tail." He glanced down at her tightly clasped wrist, and at the knife in her other hand. A wry smile twisted his lips. "If that is so, then I am twice a fool."

He spoke in Common, a language used by some merchants. It was similar to the goblin tongue, so Liriel understood it, and could speak it after a fashion. It occurred to her that she could actually communicate with this human, and in her excitement she forgot her murderous intent and her own captivity.

"How did you know how the deepbat would attack?" she demanded.

His blue eyes widened at this unexpected question. "Wyverns attack so," he said simply.

"Wyverns?"

"They are like small dragons, with pointed, poisoned tails."

Dragons, she understood, and she could picture such a creature. "And that sword," she said, gesturing with her knife toward the dull, heavy blade lying several feet away. "Why do you carry such a weapon? What good is a sword without an edge?"

Again, that faint smile. "You see the sword, how large and heavy it is. At most times, I cannot seem to hold on to it. If it were sharp, little raven, would I not cut myself when I dropped it?"

Liriel knew about ravens, too. Some wizards kept them as familiars, and the sleek black birds were both beautiful and treacherous. The comparison pleased her, even if his foolish answer did not.

She rocked back on her heels—as far back as she could go with her wrist still firmly in his grasp—and considered the strange man. A lone human, wandering in the Underdark. Either he was extremely powerful, utterly mad, or more foolish than she could have believed possible.

"What are you doing here?" she asked bluntly.

His blue eyes searched her face, and he seemed to weigh his words carefully before he spoke. "In my land, it is the custom for young men to go on *dajemma*. This is a journey to far places, so we may see and understand more of the world."

"*Dajemma*," she repeated. What a marvel, that a people would actually encourage their young to travel! She couldn't help but contrast this attitude with cloistered, xenophobic Menzoberranzan, and a fierce stab of envy and discontent pierced her.

She brushed away the sharp pain, for such was heresy, and turned her attention back to the human. The lust for exploration and adventure she understood with all her soul, but why would any surface dweller choose to travel the deadly Underdark? He had to have some motive beyond simple curiosity. Perhaps he would not willingly reveal it, but she could simply take it from his mind.

Even a novice priestess could cast a spell that allowed her to glimpse the thoughts of another. To do so, she had to touch the sacred symbol of Lloth. Yet one of her hands was firmly trapped by the human, and her other gripped the knife. She could kill him, but not before he crushed the bones of her wrist. An illithid standoff, she thought wryly, remembering the comic sight of two mind flayers facing each other, frozen by each other's mind-controlling spells. To tip the balance, Liriel reached for another weapon.

She produced her most dazzling smile and turned it full-force upon the human. "Even a snowcat—whatever that might be—must be clever enough to realize when a fight is over. Let go of me, and I shall put away the knife," she purred invitingly. "Then we can . . . talk."

The man regarded her with frank admiration, but his eyes remained wary. Then, suddenly, he shrugged and released her wrist. "I suppose there is no harm in it. Why would you help me in battle, only to turn against me now?"

Why indeed? thought Liriel wryly, noting that this man had a lot to learn about drow. On the other hand, *she* had a lot to learn about humans, and never had she had the opportunity to study one at close hand. She slowly eased away, backing up until she was beyond his reach. Only then did she tuck the knife away.

Liriel touched the symbol of Lloth that hung about her neck and silently spoke the words that would enable her to glimpse into his thoughts. Lloth was with her, and as the spell took form Liriel saw foremost in the man's mind the image of a tiny golden dagger suspended from a fine chain.

A treasure hunter, the drow thought with disgust, and she rapidly adjusted her opinion of the man downward. For the sake of a golden trinket, he had braved the Underdark alone. Not only was he human and male, but he was also apparently on the simple side.

Yet he had shown both strength and courage. Liriel admired these qualities even in lesser beings. And surely he could tell her more about the surface. It might be amusing to keep him around for a while.

With Liriel, action usually followed on the heels of impulse. She rose to her feet, her chin lifted to a regal angle. "I am returning to my city now. You will come with me," she commanded.

Her mind worked furiously even as she spoke. She would leave the human at her house in Narbondellyn, under the guard of her other servants, and then return to the Academy. No one would be the wiser. Later, she could always claim she'd bought a human slave from a merchant band. Human slaves were rare in Menzoberranzan, but not unheard of. Her tale would ring true enough.

The man studied her for a long silent moment. He clearly did not grasp her intent, for his eyes held no fear and his dark brows met in a frown of puzzlement.

"This is a fearsome land," he said slowly, "and no place for one alone. If you wish to travel together I will offer you my protection for the length of our shared path."

"Your protection?" she echoed incredulously, too stunned even to laugh. That a human, and a male at that, should offer to shield *her*—a noble female drow, a dark-elven wizard and a novice priestess of Lloth—was utterly ludicrous. "You know nothing of the Underdark, do you?"

"It would seem not," he agreed.

"Look closely," she advised him, holding her arms out wide to invite his inspection. "Black skin, white hair, pointed ears, eyes that glow red in the darkness. Stop me if any of this sounds familiar."

"You are drow," he said, still not understanding.

"Good. Very good," Liriel said approvingly. "You've heard of us, then. The drow rule this 'fearsome land'—your words, not mine—and we make the rules. If I hadn't come along just now, you'd be deepbat food. By my rules, your life is mine. It just so happens I have need of a new slave."

The man considered this, tugging thoughtfully at his ear. "But why? You say you have no need for protection."

"I want to learn more about the surface," Liriel said frankly.

"Knowledge is a good thing," he agreed, "and certainly no man could wish for a more beautiful mistress. But no man or woman of Rashemen lives as slave to another."

Liriel lifted a single white brow. "Perhaps you'll start a trend."

"Perhaps not," he said mildly, but Liriel saw the flash of anger in his blue eyes and she tensed in preparation.

The human lunged for his club. As his hand closed around the grip, Liriel snatched a knife from her sleeve and hurled it. The blade bit deep into the wood and quivered there, just inches from his hand.

Without missing a beat, Liriel conjured a small, transparent globe. Streams of light writhed inside, and the missile pulsed with barely contained power. She tossed it up and down a few times, and a meaningful smile played about her lips.

"A drow fireball," she said in a casual tone. "They explode on impact. And you may have noticed I hit what I aim at."

The human eased his hands away from the club and raised them in a gesture of surrender. "You argue well," he conceded.

The wry humor in his voice surprised Liriel. The human showed more wit than she'd anticipated. It was almost a shame to enslave such a creature.

"It would be a waste to leave you here to die," she mused, speaking as much to herself as to the human. "And die you surely would, alone and virtually unarmed. It's a marvel to me you managed to survive nearly a full day!"

"Just one day?" he echoed in disbelief.

The drow looked puzzled for a moment, but then her face cleared. "You must have come in through the Drygully Tunnel. The surface entrance is perhaps a day's travel from this cavern, but I suppose you could have wandered around for any length of time."

"Just one day's travel," the man repeated thoughtfully.

"One," Liriel confirmed. She stepped closer and prodded him with her foot. "On your feet. We're leaving, now."

He did as she bid, and instinctively the drow backed away a step. At close range, the man seemed much larger. Liriel stood perhaps two inches over five feet and had the delicate form common to elves. He was at least a head taller and powerfully built, with broad shoulders and thick-muscled arms. The drow was impressed, but not unduly concerned. With her magic and her superior weapons, she still had the upper hand.

The stranger seemed to realize this, for he gave her a respectful bow. "I am Fyodor of Rashemen, and it seems we will now travel *dajemma* together. But before I see your land, perhaps you would like to hear a story from mine?"

The drow scowled, puzzled by the strange offer. "There will be time for that later."

"Oh, but later I may not be able to recall this particular story."

That, she believed. He did seem a bit slow-witted, with his fearless eyes and slow, deliberate way of speaking. And frankly, she was starting to feel a bit curious about what he might say. There was something about his manner and the cadence of his speech that she found familiar. The stories in her new lore book had much the same flavor. So with a curt nod, she bade him proceed. The man leaned back against the rocky wall and folded his arms over his chest.

"A certain peasant was walking through the forest on his way to

118

market. He had a large sack slung over his shoulder," Fyodor began in his deep voice, sounding as calm as if he were sitting by his own fireside. "Nearby a wolf—a large, fierce predator—escaped from a trap and ran for his life, with the hunters close behind. The wolf came upon the peasant and begged him to help. So the peasant hid the wolf in his bag. When the hunters came, the peasant said he had seen no wolf. When all was safe, he opened the sack and the wolf sprang out, teeth bared."

"The man was a fool for helping such a creature," Liriel observed.

"So it would seem. The peasant begged for his life, reminding the wolf that he had saved him from the hunters. The wolf merely replied, 'Old favors are soon forgotten.'

"Now, the peasant was troubled by this dim view of life. He asked the wolf if they might ask the opinion of the next three persons they met. If all agreed that old favors are soon forgotten, the peasant would say no more and consent to being the wolf's dinner. So off they walked, and after a time they came upon an old horse—that is an animal large enough to ride—and asked whether he thought old favors were soon forgotten. The horse thought about this and agreed that it was so. 'For many years I served my master, carrying him wherever he would go, and pulling his wagon to market. Yet now that I am old, he has turned me out of the pasture to die here along the road.' The peasant and the wolf thanked the horse and went on their way. In time they came upon an old dog, lying in the shade of a tree, and they put the question to him. The dog responded at once, 'Yes, that is the way of the world. For many years I served my master, guarding his house and family. Now that I am old, and my teeth too dull to bite, he has cast me out.'

"Soon after that they came upon a fox, which is a small, clever cousin of the wolf. They told the fox what had happened between them and asked the question. But the fox replied, 'I do not believe your tale! Surely so large a wolf never fit into that sack.' And so the wolf, anxious to prove his tale, crawled into the sack. The fox grabbed the drawstring in her teeth and pulled it tightly shut. To the peasant she said, 'Quickly! Throw the sack and the wolf down yonder ravine, and then we shall discuss what payment you owe me for saving you!'

"The peasant took up the sack and swung it with all his might. As he did, he struck the fox and knocked her into the ravine along with the wolf. Then the peasant stood at the edge of the high cliff and called down to the injured fox, 'Old favors are soon forgotten!' "

Liriel laughed, delighted with the unexpected, devious twist at the end. "Do you know other stories like that one?"

"Many."

The drow nodded, silently confirming her decision to add this human to her collection of servants. She put her scowl back in place and brandished the glowing ball in her hand. "You will walk in front of me. If you try to escape or attack, I will throw this fireball at you."

"As you say," he agreed.

Together they left the dimly lit cavern and made their way back toward Liriel's gate. But the man could not walk in the darkness, and he stumbled repeatedly. Finally, near the mouth of a small tunnel, he stopped and took a stick from his pack. Striking stone against steel, he made a spark and lit the cloth-wrapped end of the stick. The sudden flair of light stung Liriel's eyes.

"Put that out," she demanded.

"Unlike you, I cannot see in the dark," he said mildly. "Nor can I walk farther without a drink. Fighting monsters and telling stories are thirsty work."

When the drow did not object, the man pulled a flask from his sash and tipped it back for a hearty swallow. He then offered the flask to Liriel. "This was brewed in my homeland. We are famed for such things. You are welcome to some if you like, but it is very strong," he cautioned her.

Liriel smirked. Many nonPeople, from orcs to deep dwarves, harbored this misconception about the seemingly delicate drow. The wines and liqueurs of the faerie elves were not unknown in Menzoberranzan, and although these might taste sweet and light, a few small glasses could send the heartiest dwarf into a snoring stupor. Drow libations—perhaps predictably—were even more potent. So she accepted the flask and took a mouthful.

The liquid had a horrid, acrid taste, and it burned her mouth as if it were molten rock. Liriel spat it out and threw the flask to the ground. The smoky brew spilled out in a spreading puddle. Immediately the man lowered his torch. The liquid caught flame with a loud burst, and a wall of fire sprang up between him and his drow captor.

Liriel reeled back, her hands clasped to her sensitive eyes. Over the roar of the fire, she heard the man's deep voice. "Good-bye, little raven. Old favors are soon forgotten!"

Anger flamed in the dark elf's heart, as bright and hot as the fire that blocked off the tunnel. How could she have been so stupid! To be tricked by a *human,* and a male at that! Her pride in her heritage of

120

drow might and magic had led her to underestimate an opponent.

As Liriel's thoughts flashed over the events of the past hour, she conceded she was probably fortunate to have lost nothing more than a potential slave. And, having wasted so much time with the human, she would be lucky to get back to Arach-Tinilith before the day's classes began. Still . . .

A slow, admiring smile spread across her face. The blue-eyed human had shown rare cunning. He'd played a good trick on her, one she would long remember.

As Liriel hurried toward the site of the second magic portal, she suspected this night's events would linger in her mind for a very long time.

Chapter 10

WANDERLUST

iriel made her way back through the Underdark without further incident, taking the relay of magical gates that moved her steadily back toward Menzoberranzan. Her last spell brought her to Spelltower Xorlarrin. When she emerged through the portal, Kharza-kzad fairly pounced on her. The wizard grabbed his pupil by both shoulders, and the expression on his face suggested he was not certain whether he should embrace her or shake her until her teeth rattled.

"Where have you been so long?" he demanded. "Narbondel's Black Death is long past—the new day approaches! I've been here the entire time you were gone, pacing, nearly out of my mind with worry!"

"Narbondel's Black Death," Liriel repeated softly, absently brushing aside the wizard's hands. On the surface world, that would be midnight. Soon dawn would come to the forest glade, and she would not be there to see it!

On the other hand, she had not realized so much time had passed, and she did not want to be away from the Academy when the spell obscuring Shakti Hunzrin's scrying stone wore off. There was always the possibility Shakti might convince Mistress Zeld she had been tricked, that someone else had sent prying eyes into Mod'Vensis Tlabbar's bedchamber. The list of suspects, Liriel knew, would be very short indeed.

"Listen, Kharza, I've got to get back to Arach-Tinilith. We'll talk later."

"That's *it*? That's all you have to say to me? After all I've been through—the terrible risk, the worry, the sleepless hours—the very least you could do would be—"

Liriel stepped through the portal, leaving the wizard fussing and sputtering behind her. Alone in the silent darkness of her own room, she reasoned Kharza would get over his ire sooner or later. *Sooner,* if he didn't have an audience. He would have larger worries if it were discovered he'd helped her slip away from the Academy on an unauthorized adventure. It was better for them both that she return at once. This way, if Zeld and her henchdrow decided to storm Liriel's room, they would find their suspected prankster at her study table, chipping away at her mountainous pile of books and scrolls with all the diligence of a mithril-mining dwarf.

With all possible speed, Liriel stripped off her travel gear and donned the black, red-trimmed robe of a novice priestess. She lit a study candle and placed a few spent candle stubs beside it, then she tossed several books and scrolls onto the floor beside her study table. The general effect suggested a long, frenzied study session had taken place. Liriel nodded in satisfaction and sat down at her study table. All that remained to be done was to actually *learn* some of this stuff.

Yet try as she might, Liriel could not concentrate on the spells that, under most circumstances, would have commanded her avid attention. The details of her adventure kept coming back to her: the wondrous lights of the night sky, the comforting strength of the mighty trees, the strange customs of the Dark Maiden's priestesses, and the peculiar encounter with the human. It was almost too much for Liriel to absorb.

In particular, the human's story kept coming back to her, playing in her mind like an insistent, remembered melody. Liriel enjoyed the unexpected, devious little twist at the story's end. It was the sort of tale that would delight most drow, were they in the habit of telling and listening to stories. The meaning of the tale, however, puzzled her greatly. When the human had offered her the story, she had been merely curious, thinking storytelling to be an odd human custom, perhaps similar to the wicked verbal thrust-and-parry beloved by the drow. But no, the human's story was too well chosen, too similar to what later occurred between them.

Like the peasant who saved the wolf from hunters, Liriel may well have saved the man's life in coming to his aid against the deepbats. By drow standards, she was more than justified in considering his life hers by purchase. Slaves were taken on much slimmer justification than that. Such as none at all.

But, "Old favors are soon forgotten," the man had told her in his story, and then proceeded to trick her and snatch back his freedom. Was the human apologizing in advance for his duplicity, or perhaps even warning her of his intentions? If that were so, Liriel mused with a touch of dark humor, the man had a dangerously overdeveloped sense of fair play!

Also troubling to Liriel was that the man's tale was in many ways similar to those she had read in her book of ancient human lore. Did all humans tell such stories? Was storytelling a natural gift of humankind, or perhaps an art form they nurtured and developed? It seemed incredible to her that this short-lived race, which she had always believed to be vastly inferior to the drow, could have such an intriguing custom.

There was another possibility, with even more potential, and it again had to do with the similarities between the man's story and the stories in her book. He had called himself Fyodor of Rashemen. Where that might be, Liriel had no idea. But perhaps the far-traveling Rus had spread their culture and their magic to the land of the blue-eyed human. Perhaps the Rashemi custom of *dajemma*, the tradition that sent young men out on a journey of exploration, was a gift from Fyodor's restless ancestors.

Perhaps. The problem was, Liriel would never know for sure. Rashemen might encourage its young people to travel and explore freely, but the drow of Menzoberranzan had other opinions on the matter.

With a sigh, Liriel pushed away the scroll she'd been pretending to read. Not bothering to remove her robe, she flung herself onto her bed for a short nap. She'd need the rest in order to face the day ahead. It would be a difficult day, for she was not well prepared for her classes. Even the pleasant prospect of learning the details of Shakti's misfired plot did not cheer her.

The new day drew near, and the sounds of early risers drifted into her room, but sleep did not come to the young drow. The reality of her situation pressed in on her, with all its disagreeable requirements. The trip to the surface had been thrilling and disturbing, but it had been an enormous risk. And for what? She was stuck in Arach-Tinilith for a good many years to come. Since the moment the webbed fence of the Academy had closed behind her, Liriel had tried to deny her fate and in doing so had taken far too many chances. If she were to survive in this grim, vicious place, she would have to give up her pranks and rein in her dark sense of humor. That would be struggle enough, but she knew in her heart she also had to resign herself to abandoning her dream of adventure in far places.

After tonight, that was.

As the dark elf nestled into her silken pillows, she knew one more wakeful night awaited her. After tonight, she would devote herself to her clerical studies. She would make peace with Mistress Zeld and apply herself to duty with a devotion that would shame even the pious, single-minded Sos'Umptu. She would become a high priestess in record time, and a credit to House Baenre. After tonight.

Please, Lloth, Liriel prayed silently as she drifted toward slumber. *Please grant me just one more night.*

*   *   *   *   *

For the first time in days, hope spurred Fyodor's steps. After a few hours' search, he found the tunnel the drow girl had mentioned. There was a small, rock-strewn cavern with a trickle of water at the bottom, and beyond, a path curved steeply upward to disappear into a hole in the rocky wall. If anything fit the name Drygully Tunnel, it was this.

He slid down into the gorge and splashed through the shallow stream. As he suspected, the hole was the opening into a tunnel. The way was steep, and the narrow tunnel curled upward in a tight spiral, but the young man fairly sprinted up the path toward the light of the sun.

He would return to the Underdark, for he had pledged to seek the amulet and he would do so for as long as he lived. Even so, the thought of a brief respite lifted his spirits immeasurably. He had not realized until now, when escape was close at hand, just how oppressive was the Underdark. It stole hope; it shut down the soul.

Yet Fyodor remembered the exuberance of the drow girl's

laughter, the avid curiosity in her golden eyes. This was someone who lived with intensity and abandon, not some soulless survivor. Yet he could not help but wonder what manner of being could thrive in such a dark and evil place. Fyodor had known hardship and danger all his life, and surviving the last few days had tested his strength and his courage. He could not begin to fathom what the Underdark would do to those who lived out all their days in its depths. The elven girl was beautiful beyond telling, as brave and capable in battle as any maid of Rashemen, but she was clearly, unmistakably drow. What that meant, Fyodor simply did not know.

Again the young fighter reminded himself he must keep alert to his surroundings, that this grim and dangerous land was no place for those who dreamed. But as he scrambled up the steep path, the dark lass was with him at every step.

*   *   *   *   *

Time in Arach-Tinilith traveled at its own pace. Liriel was certain at least two or three days dragged by during the morning indoctrination session. She silently blessed the countless vigorous, night-long parties she'd attended over the years. Without such training, she would never have developed the stamina needed to stay awake now. Even so, the girl could feel her eyes glazing over as the mistress ranted on and on. Liriel hoped the mistress would mistake her dazed expression for rapt attention.

Even the lesson on the lower planes was disappointing. The mistress conjured a viewing portal to Tarterus, which, in Liriel's opinion, was not even an interesting place to visit. It was a place of gray mists and aimless despair. The winding paths didn't seem to *go* anywhere, and the winged, dog-faced horrors who inhabited the place were fairly banal incarnations of evil. They flew, they shrieked, they tore to shreds any hapless being who ventured into their dark realms. It was all numbingly predictable.

Nor did the session provide any entertaining personal drama. Shakti was there, sullen and withdrawn, yet still clearly in the favor of the attending mistress. It would seem her failure had been a private one, Liriel concluded. Apparently Shakti had resisted the urge to run to the authorities with news of the Baenre female's supposed defection. This annoyed Liriel—she had hoped to cause Shakti embarrassment of some sort—but she was also impressed with her enemy's patience and resolve. The Hunzrin priestess was a dogged sort, obviously prepared to stalk her prey for however long it took her to uncover something sufficiently damning. Shakti was shaping up to be a credible foe. As patient as a spider, the Hunzrin priestess would be there watching, always watching, waiting for her enemy to misstep. This knowledge did nothing to brighten Liriel's mood.

The afternoon did not promise to be much of an improvement, for once again Liriel had to face the consequences of her unconventional childhood. Weapons training was required of all drow, regardless of class or gender. Liriel was deadly with anything that could be thrown, and she'd always found such expertise to be sufficient to her needs. Unfortunately bolos, slings, and throwing spiders were not in the classic repertoire of a noble female. When drow entered the Academy, they were expected to have proficiency with both the sword and the drow signature weapon: a tiny crossbow used to shoot poisoned darts. The bow was no problem—Liriel could hit whatever she aimed at—but she'd never had much interest in the art of swordcraft. As she was to learn this day, interest was optional; proficiency was mandatory.

Her swordmaster was one of the older students at Melee-Magthere. A stocky, rather unattractive male from some lesser family, he seemed alternately annoyed at having to tutor a first-year priestess and delighted to have the chance to lord it over a Baenre female.

"Your wrist is shaking," he scolded her. "Just two hours of practice, and you're tiring already!"

Liriel dropped her arm so the tip of the heavy sword rested on the floor of the practice hall. "I'm not accustomed to holding a sword," she said defensively.

"That's apparent," the male sneered. "I've seen mere children who could fight better. What have you been doing all these years?"

She pushed back a damp lock of hair and gave him a hard-edged smile. "Ask around. What did you say your name was?"

"Dargathan Srune'lett."

"House Srune'lett," Liriel mused, looking the stocky fighter up and down. "Yes, now that you mention it, I can see the family resemblance."

The male scowled, and his face heated to a livid red. The priestesses of Srune'lett were often referred to as the "fat sisters"—not in their hearing, of course—and many members of the clan, both male and female, lacked the lithe, slender form that was the drow ideal. Dargathan, it would seem, was more than a little sensitive about this

127

fact. He raised his sword in a slow, menacing arc.

"Guard position," he snarled.

Liriel faced him squarely and lifted her too-heavy weapon. Before her tired muscles could react, the male lunged in. His sword slashed open her tunic in a diagonal rip that ran from shoulder to waist. She looked down, incredulous, at the silver line of chain mail that showed through.

The girl raised murderous eyes to her opponent and held his taunting gaze for a long moment. Then she leaped at him, her sword diving in toward his heart. The male easily batted aside her thrust and danced back with a speed that belied his ungainly physique.

"*Guard position,*" Dargathan repeated, smugly this time. "Work on your stance. You're still exposing too much of your body to your enemy. Remember, left foot back, left shoulder back. Keep the target small."

Liriel gritted her teeth and did as she was told. Again and again the male drilled her on stance, walked her through the basic thrusts and parries of single-sword combat. Dargathan might lack the tightly muscled form and lightning-fast brilliance that marked the best drow fighters, but as the hours passed Liriel had to admit he was a credible teacher. The male challenged her every move, demonstrating step by step the skills a fighter would gain through years of laborious study and practice. By the standards of most races, Liriel was a competent fighter. Far more was expected of a drow. As the session went on and on, she slowly redefined her concept of swordcraft and came to realize how little she truly knew of the art. She also ached in every muscle, bone, and sinew.

"That will do for now," Dargathan said finally. "There are two main tenets of swordcraft: know the basics, and prepare for the unexpected. We've made a start on the first. With hard work and excellent instruction, there might yet be some hope for you."

With that smug pronouncement, the male sheathed his sword and strode from the practice hall. Liriel waited until he reached the door, and then called his name.

Dargathan turned back to see his pupil holding her sword like a ready javelin, high and back over her shoulder. Her eyes gleamed with dangerous light as she hurled the weapon straight at him. The sword flew hard and true, and the blade wedged deep into the crack between the doorpost and wall. It quivered there, just inches from his wide-eyed face.

"Thank you for the lesson, most excellent of instructors," Liriel said sweetly, hands on hips and stance tauntingly feminine. "But perhaps next time we should work on preparing for the unexpected?"

To further underscore her point, she snatched her bolo from a hidden pocket and began to twirl it overhead. The male turned and fled the room, his superior airs completely abandoned.

It was possible, Liriel noted as she tucked her preferred weapon back out of sight, to have a little fun now and again even in Arach-Tinilith.

*　*　*　*　*

As soon as the evening chapel was over, Liriel hurried to her room. Nothing, not even the burning stiffness brought on by her grueling practice session, could deter her from making her final journey to the surface. For her last secret jaunt out, no other destination would suffice.

Liriel quickly dressed and armed herself. She noticed as she did that her *piwafwi* had lost a bit of its luster, that her tread in the enchanted elven boots was a little less silent. It amazed her that an hour's visit to the surface could so diminish her drow magic. How, she wondered, did the priestesses of Eilistraee survive? How much of their magic, their heritage, did they abandon so they could dance in the moonlight? Were they drow still, or merely dark-skinned faerie? These were but a few of the questions she wanted to ask of the Dark Maiden's priestesses.

The young wizard quickly studied the spells she would need, then summoned the portal that would take her into Kharza-kzad's study. She hoped her tutor was already asleep so she might be spared his endless questions. But to her surprise, low, angry male voices came from the wizard's private rooms. Her natural curiosity urged her to investigate; Kharza was such a reclusive sort that the presence of another dark elf in his retreat must signal something truly momentous.

But the moonlight beckoned her with a call too powerful to be ignored, and once again she made her way through the whirling tunnel that led to the forest glade.

Again she found herself on her knees clutching the ground. Again came the startling impact of the vivid green that surrounded her on every side. And again she heard the dark elven music, the eerie, twisting melodies that were so familiar. Of course, in the Underdark, such music would not be played on a harp. The drow considered that instrument to be both insipid and disturbing. But here, in the moonlight, the delicate silvery tones of the harp sounded somehow right and fitting.

Liriel quickly made her way toward the music. The sound was easier to follow this time, for she anticipated the odd, linear path music took through the open air, and she followed it straight back toward the Dark Maiden's glade. So different, this world. Liriel was accustomed to tracing sounds that were sifted through layers of magic, that echoed and reverberated through a labyrinth of rock. Here, the source of any single sound might be simpler to discern, but the demands on her ears were so much greater.

The dark passages of the Underdark, the teeming cavern that held Menzoberranzan: though far from silent, these places were cloaked in an ominous hush. Here all was cheerful cacophony. Tiny, harmless insects chirped all around her, and plump little waterlizards sang their songs. The trees sang too, with a whispery rustle of wind-tossed leaves. The sounds of this starlit land were like its colors—too vivid, too varied. This world taxed the senses in ways even exuberant Liriel had not imagined possible. Here her every nerve felt raw and exposed. She had never felt so small, so overwhelmed.

She had never felt so *alive*.

Liriel ran through the maze of green and brown toward the firelit glade. There she found the priestesses of Eilistraee, all clad in silvery gowns and sipping from mugs of some steaming, fragrant brew. Ysolde Veladorn looked up at Liriel's approach and beckoned her closer.

"I am glad you returned tonight, little sister," she said in a joyful voice as she rose to greet Liriel. "We have another visitor, someone who is anxious to meet you."

Another drow rose to stand beside Ysolde. Liriel gasped, and the strange stories of the Time of Trouble became instantly, frighteningly real. It was whispered that Lloth had walked the streets of Menzoberranzan in the form of a tall, too-beautiful female drow. This strange female, then, could be none other than Eilistraee herself.

The drow stood fully six feet tall, and silvery radiance lingered about her like captured moonlight. Hair the color of spun silver spilled nearly to her feet, and her flowing robe flickered with its own light. Even her eyes were silver, larger than those of most drow and framed with thick, pale lashes. Her skin was as dark as Liriel's own, and it shone proudly black in the brightness that surrounded her.

Awed and fearful, Liriel sank to her knees. She had doubted any goddess but Lloth could exist, and now her unquestioning faith in the Spider Queen would mean her death. The young drow's hand crept up to the sacred symbol that hung about her neck. It marked her as a follower of Lloth, a novice priestess of the Lady of Chaos. In her homeland, those who called upon any deity but Lloth were summarily slain. She had little doubt what her fate would be at Eilistraee's hands.

Ysolde's smile faltered at the girl's strange reaction. Understanding came quickly, and consternation flooded her face. She darted forward and lifted the young drow to her feet. "Liriel, there is no need for fear. This is my mother, Qilué Veladorn. She is a priestess of the Dark Maiden, as are we all."

The tall drow smiled, and her silver eyes reassured the girl. "I hear you are a traveler, Liriel Baenre. I, too, am far from my chosen home. Join us, if you would, and perhaps we wanderers can exchange stories of distant lands."

Liriel still felt dazed, but she was drawn in by the beautiful drow's warmth and charm, and she allowed Ysolde to lead her to the fireside. For a time she was content to sit, to sip her mug of hot spiced wine, and to listen as the other females talked. The priestesses treated Qilué with great deference, and they were full of questions about her work in the Promenade Temple. Liriel's natural curiosity did not allow her to remain silent for long.

"Where is this temple? Is it in the forest as well?"

Qilué smiled. "No. The Promenade lies near Skullport, a place that has precious little in common with this peaceful glade."

"Skullport," Liriel mused. The sound of it was intriguing, tantalizing the imagination with suggestions of dangerous adventure and the promise of the open sea. "Where is this place?"

"It is an underground city, much like your Menzoberranzan, and it lies hidden far below the great coastal city of Waterdeep. Most of Waterdeep's inhabitants know little about the lands beneath their feet, and not many venture into its depths. Of those who do, few survive. It is a dangerous, lawless place." Qilué's voice was grim, and her lovely face saddened as she spoke.

"If you feel that way, why do you stay there?" Liriel asked.

"We are needed," the priestess said simply.

That was too simple for Liriel to absorb. She had been raised to examine everything for layers of meaning and motive, and it seemed to her there must be something more to the situation than Qilué was admitting. Was Skullport like the Underdark, in that the drow could not remain away for long without losing their powers?

"Can't you cast magic on the surface?" she blurted out.

Qilué looked surprised. "Yes, of course. The Dark Maiden hears and answers her Chosen wherever they might be."

Liriel nodded thoughtfully. What the priestess spoke of was clerical magic, of course, which was much different from the innate power she herself had wielded since childhood. Still, it was *something*. She wondered if Lloth could hear *her*, so far from the chapels of Menzoberranzan. Her hand crept up to the Spider Queen's symbol, and she silently spoke the words of the clerical spell that would enable her to read the thoughts of this regal drow.

Not a glimpse came to her, not a whisper. The spell did not work; the prayer went unanswered. In the Lands of Light, she was truly alone.

She looked up to see Qilué's kind eyes upon her. "Ysolde tells me you are an accomplished wizard, with many gate spells at your command. So tell me, what is your next destination?"

"This will be my last trip to the surface for many years," Liriel admitted sadly. "I am not supposed to leave Arach-Tinilith until my training is complete. So far I've been lucky, but I would be caught sooner or later. My people, to put it mildly, would not approve."

"I see. And their approval is so important to you?"

"My *survival* is important to me," she returned bluntly.

Qilué was silent for a long moment. "You have other choices."

"To dance in the moonlight," Liriel said bitterly. "That is a fine thing, but then what? What of the dawn? I would be hated and hunted by every human and faerie elf under the sun, without even the simplest magic to shield me."

She gathered up a corner of her *piwafwi* in her hand and shook the glittering cloak in Qilué's face. "Look at this: it dims by the moment. So far from the powers of the Underdark, its magic is fading. In my homeland, I can walk silent and invisible. Here I would be vulnerable, visible to all eyes. My weapons, my armor, my spell components—all would be melted by the sun."

"You would not be helpless," Ysolde put in. "You have a sword."

Liriel groaned and clasped the aching muscles of her sword arm. "Don't remind me! So what you're saying is that I would have to depend upon the least of my abilities for survival. Thank you, but no."

"You would learn new ways," Ysolde said.

"That's what I'm afraid of!" Liriel said passionately. "You don't understand at all. *I cannot abandon my heritage.* I can't forget the drow culture, or lose my innate magic, or give up all I have learned through three decades of study in dark-elven wizardry! Perhaps that might seem like nothing more than a collection of customs and powers and spells to you, but *it's what I am.*"

Qilué laid a hand on her daughter's shoulder. "Let her be, Ysolde. We all must follow the path that is given us," she said in gentle rebuke. To Liriel she said, "You have come here to learn. Since your time with us is short, why don't you ask whatever questions you might have?"

The older female's forthright, considerate manner took Liriel by surprise. Never one to refuse an opportunity, she asked about Rashemen and the customs of the land.

"Rashemen lies far to the east of here," Qilué began. "It is ruled by Witches, wise women who wield a powerful, little-understood magic. One of my sisters studied among them for a time." She paused, and a slight smile curved her lips. "Many called her Witch, but few understood why."

"The Witches of Rashemen would grant a drow such training?" Liriel asked in disbelief. "Are these humans utter fools?" In Menzoberranzan, magical secrets were carefully hoarded, grudgingly shared. This was not merely an issue of greed, but survival. Any weapon given to another drow would almost certainly be raised against the giver.

"They taught my sister," the priestess responded with careful emphasis, "knowing they had nothing to fear from her. What is your interest in this land?"

"In the Underdark I came upon a human male. He called himself Fyodor of Rashemen and told me he was on *dajemma*—a journey of exploration."

"That is their custom," Qilué agreed, "but I'm surprised one of them would venture Below. The people of Rashemen are generally fearless, but they do not throw away their lives."

"You haven't met Fyodor, then," Liriel said dryly. "He seemed pretty determined to do just that. Tell me, do you know of a people called the Rus?"

The priestess accepted the quick change of subject without comment. "There was such a people, many centuries past. Over the years they mingled their blood with the folk of many lands, so much of their language and customs have been lost. The old ways are strongest on the island of Ruathym."

"Did the Rus go so far as Rashemen?"

The priestess considered. "I am no sage, but I seem to recall that long ago, before the forests and rivers of the Anauroch turned to dust, Rashemen was overrun and settled by a race of seagoing barbarians who traveled as far inland as the rivers allowed. I had never drawn a connection between the two, but now that I consider the matter I see the ancient magics of these two lands have much in common."

She held up a hand to forestall Liriel's next question. "Of these magics, I know little. All I know is this: both cultures are strongly linked to their lands. Both draw magic from special places of power, as well as the spirits that dwell there."

Liriel nodded. She knew all too well that the Underdark had its own sites of power. It was that, perhaps more than anything, that tethered her to the lands below, for her people's dark magic drew heavily on the strange radiations of the Underdark.

"The Witches rule their land, so they must remain within its borders," Liriel reasoned. "But what of the Rus, who traveled constantly? It seems unlikely they would leave such power behind."

"Of the Rus, I do not know," Qilué admitted. "From the old tales, I would guess most of those raiders depended on the sword and the axe rather than upon magic. But the Witches can and do travel, although infrequently. My sister spoke of a unique artifact, an ancient amulet that could store the magic of such places in the event the Witches needed to leave their land."

"An amulet," Liriel repeated, thinking of the tiny golden dagger she had glimpsed in Fyodor's mind. "Do you know what it looks like?"

"Oh, yes. My sister carried it for a time, many years ago. The Windwalker, she called it. It is a tiny dagger in a rune-carved sheath."

With great difficulty Liriel cloaked her excitement. "How does it work?" she asked as casually as she could.

"I do not know all the details," the older drow said. "Syluné—my sister—told me the amulet will store magic from places of power, but only temporarily. Few Witches leave their land for very long, so that is enough for them. But legend suggests the Windwalker can make such powers permanent. How, I do not know. The knowledge has been lost."

Maybe, maybe not, Liriel noted silently. Her nimble mind leaped from one possibility to another, weaving the disparate threads into a new and hitherto unsuspected whole. If the far-traveling Rus had settled Rashemen, the Windwalker could well have been of their making. If this were so, then rune magic was the key to the amulet's power. If the amulet Fyodor sought was indeed the Windwalker, then this ancient device was somewhere in the Underdark. If she could find it, perhaps she could adapt it to store her own magic. And why not? The drow's inherent magical powers, and the magic of most of their crafted items, were magnified by the radiations peculiar to the Underdark. Was that not a form of place magic?

If, and if again. There were far too many 'ifs', but in her excitement Liriel was not discouraged. For the first time, her dream of travel and exploration in the Lands of Light seemed within her grasp. Some drow—such as these priestesses—might abandon their heritage and forsake the Lady of Chaos, but that was not an option for Liriel. She loved the wild beauty of the Underdark, and although she longed for adventure in the world beyond, she wanted to be able to return home. If she could find this amulet and test its powers, there might be a way for her to come to the surface whole, on her own terms: silent, unpredictable, mysterious, powerful, magical, deadly. Drow.

On impulse, Liriel reached forward and embraced the regal female. "I have to leave now, but I can't tell you what this visit has meant to me!"

Qilué regarded the girl's excited face and shining golden eyes for a long moment. "The Promenade Temple," she repeated softly. "Remember that name, if ever you should need it."

Chapter 11

FALSE TRAILS

leet and silent, Liriel ran through the forest back toward her magical gate. Her flight surprised a strange creature, a large dun-colored beast with enormous brown eyes and a pair of many-pronged horns. The animal bounded off and was soon lost among the trees. For just a moment Liriel paused to watch the graceful creature. Any other time, she would have followed it, perhaps to hunt, perhaps just to learn more about the strange and fascinating beast. Tonight a more important prize awaited her.

She had an idea where the Windwalker amulet might be, and her time to find it was short. Quickly she stepped into the gate that returned her to the Underdark. The magical flight was swift and brief, and it brought her near the place where she and the human had joined in fighting the deepbats.

Liriel retraced her steps to the glowing cave where she had met Fyodor of Rashemen. There was a mystery here, one that she must solve. She crouched down to examine the body of a deepbat the human had slain.

Even in death, the creature was imposing. The crumpled wings spanned a good seven feet, and the dagger-sharp fangs jutting from the deepbat's slack mouth were fully the length of her fingers. It was a marvel the human had managed to kill such a creature, but even stranger that the giant bats had attacked at all. Although they were dangerous in the extreme, dragazhar were highly intelligent creatures who rarely attacked anything larger and more threatening than a scurry rat. Something must have happened to embolden or threaten them, to force them beyond their normal behaviors.

Seizing the dragazhar's wing with both hands, she hauled the creature over onto its back so she might examine its underbelly. There she found the answer she sought. Scoring the creature's abdomen and legs were several long, thin cuts: the interweaving marks of twin blades. Such wounds were too fine, too precise, to have been inflicted by the human's dull blade. Drow steel had marked the dragazhar.

She examined the bodies of three other dead bats and found similar markings, including the telltale poison darts from a drow crossbow. These bats had most likely come across Fyodor as they fled from another, larger battle. After tangling with a band of drow fighters, a lone human must have seemed very easy prey.

This discovery supported one of her suspicions: in pursuit of the amulet, Fyodor had followed a band of drow into the Underdark. What the man planned to do once he caught up with the drow, Liriel could not begin to fathom. He fought well enough, but he was one lone human against the deadliest fighters of these deep realms!

It did not occur to Liriel to ask what she herself might do, alone against a band of drow fighters. After all, she was a Baenre princess and a wizard, and deadly determined to find the Windwalker amulet.

She searched the rocky floor until she found a series of blood drops leading out of the cavern. Some of the bats had survived Fyodor's sword and cudgel, and one of them had been wounded badly enough to leave a trail. Since wounded deepbats invariably returned to their lair, she suspected its flight would retrace the path that had brought it to this cavern. Liriel conjured a globe of faerie fire so she might follow the trail. Excitement sped her steps as she traced the way toward the site of the first battle.

The blood-drop trail ended in a vast, dark cavern. There was no light here, none of the phosphoric rock or glowing plants that lit what she had come to think of as Fyodor's cavern. But Liriel saw well enough. Patterns of heat in the air, in the rock, gave the grim landscape a precision and nuance the light-sighted could not begin to imagine. In the Underdark, even the coldest stone held some heat.

And the corpses of two drow males, as cold as their stone tomb, gave off the dull, bluish glow peculiar to lifeless flesh.

Liriel hurried toward the dead elves. She dropped to her knees and began to search the bodies. Her efforts turned up a number of fine knives and trinkets, but not the amulet she sought.

Swallowing her disappointment, the female sat back on her heels and considered the situation more closely. The males had been commoners, and neither wore an insignia that claimed alliance to one of Menzoberranzan's noble houses. They were well armed, but even so it was odd there were only two. Liriel dared the Underdark alone because of the magic she commanded, but only drow wizards went out in such scant company. These males had no spellbooks, no bags of strange components, no wands or other magic weapons. They were definitely trained fighters, probably thieves, and nothing more.

Both of the dead males had suffered strikes from the dragazhar's fangs and wing claws, but none of these wounds were deep enough to prove fatal. These drow had likely been killed by strikes from the deepbats' poisonous tails.

Liriel rose to her feet and conjured another globe of faerie fire. Holding it high, she surveyed the cavern. The bodies of a dozen dragazhar littered the cavern, attesting to a long and bitter fight. Was it possible these two drow had fought alone?

But no, there were weapons scattered on the cavern floor, more than these two dead drow could possibly have wielded. Two fine matching swords, slender and carved with runes, caught Liriel's eye. She stooped and ran her fingers along one of the shining blades; magic throbbed through the sword like a pulse. These were priceless weapons, the pride of the drow who had wielded them. She abandoned the idea that the surviving drow had fled, leaving the bodies of their two comrades behind. No dark-elven fighter would leave such weapons unless he was long past need of them.

A few paces beyond the discarded weapons, Liriel saw a spattering of cold, dried blood. She searched for several moments before she found the next splotch, some ten feet away. Suddenly she understood what had happened here.

Deepbats usually took their prey back to the lair for leisurely snacking, especially if they felt threatened. A battle with drow would certainly qualify as that—Liriel marveled the dragazhar had persisted so long against such odds. They must have needed food very badly. It was odd, though, that they'd left two bodies behind.

After a moment's hesitation, Liriel once again began to follow a bloody trail. The deepbat lair must be very close. As large as the dragazhar were, they could not carry the bodies of full-grown drow very far.

As she suspected, the cave was not far away. Its mouth was placed high on the rocky wall of the tunnel, a near-horizontal slit that seemed too narrow to admit the giant bats. Liriel leaped up, grabbed the ledge, and hauled herself up for a peek.

Only a few adult dragazhar were in the cave, asleep and hanging by their tails from the cavern's ceiling. There were also many young, perhaps forty or more. These baby dragazhar were rather cute, with their well-groomed, jet black fur and plump, small bodies. They hung sleeping in a neat row, by all appearances sated and content.

Liriel nodded as several pieces of the puzzle fell into place. The necessity of feeding so many young had driven the dragazhar to attack a drow party. The bats had left the two poisoned dark elves behind, probably because the baby dragazhar could not feed upon poisoned flesh. Judging from the number of young, Liriel estimated the cave was home to several hunting packs of bats—at least three or four score of adults. That was certainly enough to destroy a small party of drow fighters.

She carefully scanned the low-ceilinged cave. Few drow ventured into such areas, but those who did claimed they were veritable treasure troves. Liriel had a very specific treasure in mind.

The drow cast a cautious glance over each shoulder. The tunnel was dark and silent for as far as she could see. The bats were out hunting again, except for the few nursemaids left behind to tend the young. Liriel realized her chances were not good; on the other hand, they'd never be better.

Liriel pulled herself up onto the ledge. Clutching her *piwafwi* close, she edged into the lair. The acrid smell of bat guano assaulted her, and she blessed the enchanted boots that allowed her to walk without the sickening crunch that should have heralded her intrusion. She had not gone far when her foot nudged something soft. She crouched for a closer look.

It was the body of a tall drow male—or what remained of him. Fine chain mail had turned aside the fangs of the deepbats and left the torso mostly intact, but the limbs were little more than bone. Two other bodies lay nearby, in no better condition than the first.

If Liriel had needed a reminder of the importance of stealth and silence, she could not have asked for a better one. Carefully she patted down the partially eaten bodies. She found a good supply of poisoned darts and several very nice knives. Usually she would have taken such items, but these bodies would be searched later, and she did not want anyone to suspect she had already been in the cave.

Several moments passed before Liriel found what she sought. One of the dead drow wore a leather pouch, suspended from his neck by a long thong and hidden beneath the chain mail vest. In the bag was a three-inch dagger, tucked into a rune-carved sheath that hung from a broken chain. Clutching the amulet triumphantly in her hand, Liriel backed out of the lair.

She hurried back to the relative safety of the glowing cavern and examined her trophy more closely. Yes, it was the very trinket she had glimpsed in Fyodor's mind. She understood now how such a thing could lure a man into the Underdark. This, if it was indeed the Windwalker, was a unique magical treasure, an artifact from a long-gone era of strange and powerful sorcery. Finding such a thing was a worthy life quest. Possessing it was worth all the risks Fyodor had taken.

Would take. With that thought, Liriel's triumph evaporated and her face creased in a scowl. Of course the human would return, and if *she* had found the dead merchants, he might also. The man had certainly shown himself to be strong and resourceful. But without the benefit of elven boots and the shielding invisibility of a *piwafwi*, he would no doubt join the drow fighters as food for the deepbat young.

Liriel did not stop to ponder why she should care about the matter one way or another. There was no time to waste, and she quickly formulated a plan that would accomplish what needed to be done. She took out her spellbook and summoned the magic gate that led to Kharza's tower. What she had in mind would require the wizard's help.

But Kharza was not alone when she stepped into his study. Her tutor sat behind his desk, his pale-knuckled hands clasped tightly before him. Lounging in a chair nearby was a drow male, probably the most strikingly exotic dark elf Liriel had ever seen. His long, copper-colored hair was bound back in a single thick tail, and in the faint candlelight his eyes gleamed as black as his ebony-hued skin. His angular face was defined by fine, high cheekbones, a sharply pointed chin, and a thin blade of a nose. He was slender and richly dressed, and his manner suggested both pride and power. Liriel took in all this with a glance, and just as quickly dismissed him. Another time, she might be interested, but now more important matters absorbed her attention.

"Kharza, we must talk," she said quickly, glancing pointedly at the stranger.

Before the wizard could respond, the red-haired drow rose to his feet and swept Liriel a polite bow. "I would greet you, lady, but I do not know your name and house," the male said. "Kharza-kzad, would you be so kind?"

The wizard's worry lines deepened into veritable canyons, but he launched into the formulaic introduction. "Liriel of House Baenre, daughter of archmage Gromph Baenre, may I present to you my associate Nisstyre, captain of the merchant band Dragon's Hoard."

Nisstyre's black eyes lit up and he bowed again. "I was not expecting such an honor. Our mutual friend assures me you were pleased with his recent gift?"

"The book of human lore," Kharza said reluctantly, noting Liriel's blank expression. "Nisstyre was the source of it."

"And I would be happy to supply you with others, if you should so desire. The Dragon's Hoard is famous for procuring anything, regardless of cost. I'm sure the wizard would be happy to attest to our discretion. We have been supplying his house for many years."

Such arrangements, Liriel knew, were not uncommon. Many of the noble houses sponsored merchant bands, for such was their only tie with the world outside Menzoberranzan. In turn, the threat of retaliation from some powerful matron granted the merchants a degree of security they might not otherwise have enjoyed. Liriel recognized at once the value of such an ally, and she turned the full force of her smile upon the exotically handsome male.

"I do not require any books tonight, but perhaps you can help me with another matter. I need to hire some discreet muscle."

The merchant lifted one copper-colored brow. "There are mercenary bands in this city, I believe."

"Yes, and most answer to some matron or other," she said, dismissing that possibility. "This is personal, and private."

"I see. What, exactly, did you have in mind?"

"I found a drow patrol in the tunnels, killed in battle with dragazhar. I want some of the bodies moved to the mouth of the Drygully Tunnel, along with a few of the dead bats. There you will set the scene to make it appear the battle occurred in that place."

Nisstyre studied the girl for a long moment. "Such a thing could be done, but I fail to see its purpose."

Liriel's chin rose to a regal angle. "Accept the task or decline it, but do not presume to question me."

"A thousand pardons, lady," the merchant murmured without a trace of sincerity. "And if I accept, I trust you can fund such an expedition?"

He casually named a price; it was steep, but not nearly as high as Liriel would have expected.

"You shall have that and more," she promised. "I can give you your fee now, in gold or gems as you wish. I will also show you the location of the dragazhar lair. You're welcome to all the treasure you care to dig out of the bat guano. I don't lay claim to any of it. In addition, I counted some forty dragazhar young. Deepbats are popular companions to wizards; harvest a few of the young for training as familiars, and you'll earn your fee again, some twenty times over. All this you may have, provided you do as I say—without question. Do you accept these terms?"

Nisstyre smiled. "With pleasure."

"Excellent. Kharza, I need you to come, too."

The wizard balked. "I, enter a dragazhar lair?"

"Well, why not? What good is magic unused?"

"But—"

"If we disturb the deepbats' food supply, they will attack. Count on it. And from what little I could see, I'd say the cave holds a large community, at least six hunting packs. We'll need an extra wizard."

"I believe I can assist you there, my lady," broke in the merchant. "Like yourself, I am well versed in the Art."

Liriel looked the copper-haired male up and down, and she believed his claim. Merchant captains often possessed great wealth and influence. No one could attain a position of such power without considerable might of arms or magic, and this one did not have the look of a fighter. He was too thin, too finely drawn, almost effete in his elegance.

"Will he do, Kharza?"

"His skills are adequate," the old drow said grudgingly.

Liriel nodded. "Good. Let's get started, then."

"What, now?" the merchant inquired.

"Of course now!" she snapped. She snatched up an hourglass from Kharza's desk, turned it over, and set it down with a thunk. "I must collect some things from my room. Get three of your best male fighters—three, no more—and meet me here before the sands run out." With that, she conjured the portal to Arach-Tinilith and fairly leaped into it.

"How interesting," Nisstyre said, turning mocking black eyes upon his host. "You did not tell me Liriel Baenre has been to the surface."

"How did you—" Kharza-kzad broke off suddenly and bit his lip in consternation.

"How did I know?" the merchant mocked. "It is obvious, my dear colleague. Not the particulars, of course, but the general idea is plain. As you may know, the Drygully Tunnel leads to the surface. The little princess wishes to discourage someone from following her back into the Underdark. What better way than to stage a fearsome battle? Scatter the bodies of a few drow fighters, several monstrous bats, and the most intrepid of surface dwellers who stumbles upon the scene might think twice about pursuit. Quite ingenious, really. What I would like to know," he said thoughtfully, "is what foe she considers worthy of such effort."

"I'm sure I have no idea," the Xorlarrin wizard said, folding his arms across his meager chest. "And I'm even more certain I don't care to find out!"

The merchant rose from his chair. Placing both hands on the desk, he leaned down to look directly into the old wizard's face.

"Risks," he said in a confidential whisper. "Every follower of Vhaeraun must be prepared to take them."

With that final taunt, he left Kharza-kzad alone to sputter out his usual denials. It was an odd game, but one Nisstyre enjoyed playing. In time, perhaps Kharza would become so accustomed to the insinuations that he would come to think of himself in those very terms. This was unlikely, to be sure, but a Xorlarrin wizard, a master of the famed Sorcere, would be a prized addition to Vhaeraun's band.

The merchant hurried from the Spelltower Xorlarrin to his rented house near the Bazaar. Now that he had met Liriel Baenre face-to-face, he was more interested in her than ever. She thought for herself, followed her own rules. No slave to the fanaticism that paralyzed so many of Menzoberranzan's drow, she was a prime candidate for conversion to the ways of Vhaeraun. Granted, she had in full measure the haughty arrogance of noble females, but that could change in time. In fact, the task of humbling the little princess greatly appealed to Nisstyre.

First, of course, he would have to win her over. That she would hire him for this task was a stroke of purest luck. It was also ironically amusing, for of course the dead drow Liriel had described were his own lost thieves. She had saved him the trouble and expense of hunting them down.

Nisstyre did not mention that fact to her, and he saw no reason to enlighten her now. He hurried to his hired barracks and selected three of his strongest fighters. When they had been briefed and armed, he led them swiftly back to Spelltower Xorlarrin.

Liriel was there already, fairly bursting with impatience. She looked the males over and pronounced them adequate. With Kharza-kzad's help, she sent the drow fighters into the gate toward their dead comrades. Nisstyre she left to his own resources. If he was not wizard enough to handle such a task, it was better she knew it now. When her forces had gathered, she led them to the site of the dragazhar battle and quickly laid out her plan.

"Five drow came into this cavern. Two of them you see dead before you; the other three are bat food. Now, we can do this one of two ways. We can retrieve what's left of the three drow in the cave and risk rousing the deepbats, or the three of you can help stage a false battle, then leave a fresh trail to the surface and beyond."

The fighters exchanged glances. Two of them were plainly relieved at this turn of events—not even the most battle-thirsty drow relished the idea of fighting the deadly bats—but the third, a tall drow with short-cropped hair and a tattooed cheek, sneered in open contempt.

"This was not your original offer," Nisstyre pointed out. "What of the dragazhar lair? The treasure, the baby deepbats?"

"My original offer specified you would do as I say, without questions," Liriel said impatiently. "After this task is accomplished, I will show you the cave. You can harvest the bats and treasure later, on your own time."

The merchant accepted her terms with a bow. "As you say. But I am curious why I am here, if there is to be no battle with the dragazhar."

"Who says there won't be?" she retorted. "You wouldn't ask if you knew how close the dragazhar cave is. The longer you stand there talking, the greater the risk."

"I see." Nisstyre considered for a moment. "I know of another opening to the surface, not far from the Drygully Tunnel. It is nearer, and it is a shorter path to the Night Above. Shall I have my fighters use it?"

Liriel agreed readily. She did not want Fyodor of Rashemen to meet the three drow on his way back. That the human would be back, she did not doubt, and he would be no match for these three trained and well-armed drow. Perhaps he could track Nisstyre's band to the surface; perhaps he could even catch up with them. But she doubted it. More likely he would follow them as long as the trail lasted, and then once the trail was lost he would go on his way, seeing no reason to return to the alien dangers of the Underdark. That suited her perfectly.

So Liriel supervised the fighters as they hoisted the two dead males and carried them to the mouth of the Drygully Tunnel. Nisstyre came in handy after all, casting spells of levitation that floated several of the giant bat carcasses to the cavern. The wizard also arranged the faux battle scene with gory flair and an artistic eye. In all, Liriel was pleased.

One more thing remained to be done. Liriel selected the largest of Nisstyre's fighters, the bold male with the dragon tattoo festooning one cheek. In her estimation, this one could best survive what she had in mind. Also, the fighter had made little effort to hide his disdain for this errand. Liriel was not accustomed to such insubordination from a servant and she did not want to see his attitude go unrewarded.

So she ordered the fighter to remove one of the leather bracers that protected his forearms. He did so, and as he held out his arm to her a curious, slightly mocking smile played about his lips. Liriel grabbed his wrist and squeezed it, hard.

"What is your name, and what do you find so amusing?" she demanded.

"I am called Gorlist. I destroy my enemies; I do not waste time laying false trails for them to follow," the drow said with no little pride. For good measure, he tightened his fist, so the muscles in his arm swelled and rippled impressively. The display of strength broke Liriel's grip with contemptuous ease.

"No false trails," she echoed with a touch of dark humor as she renewed her grip on the fighter. "Funny you should say that, Gorlist."

In a single lightning-fast movement, Liriel drew a knife and slashed a long, deep line across the male's arm. Gorlist's eyes widened incredulously as blood gushed from the cut. He snatched his arm from her grasp.

"Do not bind it; do not try to stanch the bleeding in any way," she instructed him. "Leave a trail to the surface even a heat-blind idiot could follow. Note that I do not insult you by asking you to leave a *false* trail. Real blood, I'm sure, is much more to your liking."

"But the loss of blood! I may not survive to reach the Night Above!" he protested.

"Oh, stop whining. You don't have to bleed all the way to the surface. Just mark the trail to the right tunnel, that's all I ask," she said impatiently.

Gorlist's outraged scowl did not lessen. Apparently, this male did not know his place; Liriel was more than happy to remind him. She took hold of his wrist again. With the forefinger of her free hand, she traced the edge of the cut with one finger.

"If I had wanted to kill you, I would not have cut you there," Liriel said. Using his blood as ink, she slowly, teasingly traced another line on his arm, this one a fraction to the side. "I would have cut you *here*."

A knife appeared suddenly in her bloodstained hand, and she pressed hard against the line she had drawn. She met the male's angry glare with a cold smile and a challenging gaze.

Nisstyre intervened. "And we are grateful for your expertise," he said as he gently disengaged his fighter's wrist from Liriel's grasp. "You, Gorlist, will do as you are bid. The three of you, go with all haste to the surface. And after that?" he asked, turning the question to Liriel. "Where shall they go?"

She paused, not sure how to answer. Her only thought had been to lay a trail out of the Underdark, and she did not know of any surface destination to give them. Wait: yes, she did.

"Waterdeep," she said decisively.

The merchant captain's thin lips curved in a smile. "Well chosen. It is a long trip, but one they would soon make regardless. The Dragon's Hoard has a base near that city."

"In Skullport?" Liriel asked, thinking it more likely the drow merchants would thrive underground than in a human stronghold.

Nisstyre's smile broadened. "For a noble female of Menzoberranzan, you know much of the wider world. I would not be surprised if we should meet again soon, my dear Liriel."

"Not unless you plan to enroll in Arach-Tinilith," Liriel responded, using a tone of voice designed to quench the too-familiar spark in the wizard's black eyes. "I shall be there for a number of years."

"Such a waste," the merchant said fervently.

"Such blasphemy," Liriel returned lightly. "But since you are not of Menzoberranzan, perhaps Lloth will overlook your words. Now, perhaps you'd like to see the way to the dragazhar lair?"

Nisstyre followed the girl to the narrow tunnel that led to the deepbat cave. He noted the confident way she moved through the wild terrain, her utter lack of fear despite the fact that they were merely two against the dangers of the wild Underdark. The young female was clearly a seasoned adventurer with a lust for the unknown. Yes, he could lure this one up into the Night Above, Nisstyre assured himself complacently. A push, a nudge, and she would be his.

And, by extension, Vhaeraun's. In some matters, even the God of Thieves had to take second place.

Chapter 12

Trollbridge

yodor followed the steep tunnel path for many hours, with little sense of how much time actually passed. When he could no longer run, he walked, and he rested what little he dared. After a time—how long or short he could not say—the path leveled off and ended in a small cave.

The darkness here was less intense, and when Fyodor put out the last of his torches, he found he could see well enough. After a quick exploration he found the exit, a small opening just slightly higher than his head and not much larger than a badger hole. Fyodor used his sword to chip away at the rock and soil. When he thought the opening might suffice, he grabbed the edge and hauled himself up. Slowly, laboriously, he eased his shoulders through the opening. Finally he rolled out, exhausted but exultant. For a long moment he merely lay there, breathing hard and taking stock of his surroundings.

The ground beneath him was hard and rocky, and the walls of a ravine rose steeply on either side of him. By the smooth, round stones around him he knew this to be a dry riverbed. Something or someone must have diverted the river, for at this time of year the water should have been rushing along, swollen by the melting ice and snow. The air was crisp, but much warmer than when he had last seen daylight. Either he had been wandering in the darkness much longer than he would have thought possible, or he had emerged many miles from the Ashenwood and the magical gate that had taken him into the Underdark.

Fyodor lifted his eyes upward. A deep tangle of trees met overhead, and through the thick green curtain he glimpsed the faint pink and silver glow of sunrise. Dawn was breaking. It was the most beautiful sight he had ever seen, and one he had not expected to see again. Thanks to the drow girl, he had found his way back to the sun. He therefore owed her his life, not once, but twice over.

He rose and scrambled up the steep bank, searching for anything that might tell him where he was. The forest around him was thick and dark, but ahead to the west the foliage around the dry riverbank dwindled to a low growth of brambles and newly leafed bushes. It was springtime here, and the season was much further along than in his native Rashemen.

Fyodor made his way quickly along the riverbank toward the forest's edge. A hill sloped down before him into a low, fertile valley. There were meadows, already thick and lush, and a vast tangle of berry bushes dusted with white flowers. Even more encouraging were the fields of rye growing beyond, for the carefully tended crops spoke of a nearby settlement.

The young warrior nodded in satisfaction. Despite his joy in finding a way to the surface, he was determined to return to the Underdark as soon as possible so he might pick up the trail of the drow thieves. Even if the settlement were no more than a few farmhouses, he could purchase what supplies he needed for his journey. The silver coins he had earned during his apprenticeship still hung heavy in his purse. With long, eager strides, he took off in search of the village.

He had not gone far before he heard the busy sounds of hammers and saws. Beyond the fields huddled a cluster of buildings within a sturdy wooden palisade. Fyodor hurried to the gate and knocked loudly.

A small portal opened, and a stern, gray-whiskered face glared out at him. "Who are you, and what do you want?" the man demanded coldly.

"I am a traveler seeking to purchase supplies," Fyodor replied.

"Hmmph! Too early for that," the guard grumbled, but he eyed the young man with a slightly less glacial expression.

Fyodor glanced back toward the east. The sun had broken over the forested hills and was shining over the grainfields in long, slanted rays. "The morning is young," he agreed, "but I can hear that your village is already hard at work."

"Getting ready for the spring fair, we are," the guard offered. "The river's gone down a mite, and merchants will be coming through any day now. Where did you say you hailed from?"

"My homeland is Rashemen."

"I heard tell of it," the guard said, and his eyes narrowed in speculation. "You be one of them crazy berserker fighters?"

For a moment Fyodor was uncertain how best to answer. Many people feared the warriors of Rashemen, and they might well deny him admittance to their village. He desperately needed supplies and could not afford to lose this opportunity. On the other hand, it was his custom to speak the truth.

"I am, sir, but I fight only when I must."

"Hmm. Well then, it might be that the townsfolk can sell you what you need."

The wooden gate swung open, and Fyodor gazed in puzzlement at the strange village beyond. Cattle and goats were penned in small enclosures, munching dried winter fodder despite the lush grazing in the meadows beyond the village walls. Buildings lined the street: strong, sturdy wood-and-stone structures that lacked any of the homey comfort of Rashemi cottages. There were no painted shutters, no carefully tended beds of herbs and flowers to brighten these dwellings. No storks nested on the roofs, which were fashioned not of neatly woven thatch but of hard, dark slate. There was not a touch of color, not a bit of beauty. All stark wood and stone, the town reminded Fyodor of a forest in midwinter.

Its inhabitants were no less grim. No small clusters of villagers stood about in courtyards, sharing mugs of steaming *kvas* along with the morning's gossip. Men and women rushed about, tending to business and speaking to each other only in terse, sharp words, when they bothered to speak at all. Dozens of villagers were busily shoring up the walls of the palisade, nailing crossbars into place and caulking every narrow crack with thick, reddish clay. Others were building rows of wooden booths on both sides of the main street, and the din of their pounding hammers filled the morning air. Still others were laying out goods of their own for sale: woolen blankets and skeins of undyed yarn, simple pottery, dried fish and game, wheels of cheese, pots of honey and barrels of mead. These activities were clearly those of a village preparing for a spring market, but there was none of the joyful anticipation that would have marked such preparations in Rashemen. The atmosphere here would have been more appropriate to a people besieged.

"Where is this place, and what is it called?" Fyodor asked curiously. "You must forgive me, but I have wandered far and have lost my bearings."

The guard gave him a sharp glance. "Village is called Trollbridge, and it's a half day's travel from nowhere on every side. Trade routes and rivers everywhere, and us smack dab in the center of it all, like the itch you can't quite reach on the middle of your back," he grumbled.

"Trade routes?" Fyodor prodded.

"To the north of us is Evermoor Way, the travel road what goes from Tribor up to Silverymoon. Just beyond is River Dessarin. Dead Horse Ford crosses over the Ironford Path, what cuts up to the Calling Horns hunting lodge. Where'd you come in from?"

"The forest."

It was the best answer Fyodor could give, and apparently it was a good one. The one man's eyebrows flew upward, and he nodded, visibly impressed.

"Ain't many men can travel alone through the High Forest. I thought them stories about berserkers got kinda tall, but getting out o' that place alive takes more than what most men have got. And it's no wonder you're feeling turned around. A man can wander a lifetime in that forest and never find his way out."

Although the names of the roads and rivers meant nothing to him, Fyodor *had* heard of the High Forest. It was a deep, magical woodland, incredibly ancient and vast, and it lay many hundreds of miles from his homeland. This knowledge was staggering, but he accepted it as he did most things: with fatalistic calm and an eye toward what needed doing.

"I would be grateful if you can tell me where I might buy supplies," he said.

The guard puckered his lips thoughtfully as he eyed Fyodor's heavy sword. "It'll be three, mebbe fours days before the caravan comes in," he said casually. "Might be you can stay on until then? We got work to be done, if you'd care to sign on for a few days' pledged hire."

It was on the tip of Fyodor's tongue to ask why the man thought he might be needed. The townsfolk worked at a frantic pace; at this rate, the booths would be finished by highsun. And why, for that matter, would he be required to sign a pledge to remain for the agreed-upon time? Was not a man's word good enough for these grim-faced villagers?

"A meal, then," Fyodor asked, sidestepping the guard's question. "Does Trollbridge have an inn?"

The guard's eyes took on a hard glint. "So you'll be staying. Good, that's very good." He hailed a passerby, a tall, rangy man who wore a stained linen coat and a dour expression. "You, Tosker! Take this man over to the Steaming Kettle and tell Saida to treat him well."

The man pulled up and looked Fyodor over. His eyes took note of the young man's weapons, measured the width of his shoulders. "You a sellsword?"

Sir, I am not."

That was all Fyodor cared to say on the matter, and more than he could say in a civil tone. In Rashemen, warriors fought only when they must. It was no small thing, the taking of life, and the young warrior had nothing but contempt for those who killed for profit.

"Oh. Well, come along anyway," the man said grudgingly.

Fyodor followed his reluctant guide down a narrow side street to the inn. Not at all like the cozy, homelike taverns of his land, this was a big barn of a place, with thick stone walls and long, narrow windows paned with leaded glass. A wooden bar ran the length of one wall, and along it stood a row of stools. About half the seats were taken by village folk who'd stopped for a quick meal of dark ale and steamed grain porridge.

The Rashemi took a stool beside his guide. Saida, the innkeeper, bustled over to them with a steaming bowl in each hand. She was a plump, brisk matron with nut-brown hair, and she wore a no-nonsense expression and a thick shawl of practical gray wool. But the vest she wore over her chemise was tightly laced and bright red. It was the first glint of color Fyodor had seen in this dismal place, and he took that as an encouraging sign. He greeted the woman pleasantly. "Good-day, Saida. Can you tell me where I can buy some travel supplies?"

"I've got plenty of supplies on hand," she replied. "What do you need?"

Fyodor listed dried trail food, a length of rope, and as many pitch torches as he could reasonably carry. Tosker choked on a mouthful of ale and turned narrowed eyes on the young man.

"Sounds like you're planning to go Below. Only a fool would do that."

"Yes, you are probably right," Fyodor said mildly, and took a long pull at his mug. The brew was bitter, but it filled his too-empty stomach with a pleasant heat.

"If it be drow you seek, you needn't leave this accursed valley to find them," came a quavering voice from the corner of the room.

Fyodor turned. A wizened man hauled himself out of his chair and staggered toward the bar. His face was crisscrossed with old scars, and the lid of one eye sank deep over an empty socket. Though the morning was young, he had clearly been drinking for some time and was already long past the point of discretion.

"Be quiet, you old fool," Saida snapped.

But the man stumbled closer to the bar, too deep in his ale and his memories to be deterred by her words. "Every year they come," he muttered, his scarred face haggard with remembered horrors. "Every year. Can't never tell when, but usually they strike during moondark."

Fyodor did some quick calculations. The moon had been waning the night he followed the drow thieves into the magic gate. If he had wandered in the Underdark for three or four days, then this would indeed be the time of the new moon. That would explain the repairs to the walls, the penned animals, the general sense of foreboding. But what of the frantic preparations for the spring market?

"If your village is in danger, is it not strange to hold a fair?" he asked. "Or are the merchants in these lands not afraid of such a threat?"

"They would be plenty afraid, if they knew about it," Saida said grimly. "The caravans have usually come and gone by now. But the river's high this year, and the caravans late in coming. They don't like to stop here, us being so far off the path and all. If the drow attack while the merchants are here, it will likely be the last spring caravan to come through Trollbridge. And then, I ask you, what are we to do?"

A man several seats from Fyodor slammed down his mug. "All

the more reason why we should hunt down the drow fiends before they can strike," he growled. "Stake their bloody corpses out in the fields to scare away the crows."

A muttered chorus of agreement rose from the bar, and the sheer hatred in the villagers' voices sent a prickle of revulsion down Fyodor's spine. He pushed aside his half-eaten bowl of porridge, his hunger forgotten. He was about to ask Saida the cost of the meal when the dark-bearded man to his left elbowed him.

"You're a likely-looking young fellow. If'n you know how to use that sword you carry, you might do well to stay around Trollbridge a few days. One man's nightmare is another man's opportunity, I always say."

The bearded man drew a leather thong from beneath his jerkin. Suspended from it was a dark, triangular bit of leather. Although it had been dried and tanned, it was unmistakably an elven ear. The man brandished the trophy in Fyodor's face.

"The wizard rulers of Nesme are ready to pay good silver for every black ear we can bring 'em. You with me, son?"

Fyodor dared not answer. If he spoke his mind, the black-bearded man would surely attack him, and the young warrior knew he would meet drawn steel with the cold fury of a berserker rage. Fortunately, the bounty hunter did not press the point.

"Good silver!" the man repeated to the room at large. "Yet here we sit with our hands in our breeches! Why huddle within walls every moondark? It's time to hunt!"

"They say drow are hard to kill," put in another man, a lank fellow with a quiver of arrows slung over his shoulder. He patted the quiver strap. "But I'm thinking they'll die when you shoot 'em, same as any other wild beast."

Tosker shifted uneasily on his stool. It was clear all this talk of battle did not sit well with him. "Better yet, we could find out where they come out, and seal them in."

"And what would *you* know about that?" snapped the bounty hunter. He leaned forward over the bar to level a glare at Tosker. "You know the farmlands, but when was the last time you stepped foot beyond the fields? There are more caves in these hills and woodlands than a dog has ticks. A man could search a lifetime, and not find a place where the drow come out!"

Fyodor knew of such a place, but he could not bring himself to speak. In less than two days' march, provided they had the courage to enter the Underdark, these folk could find the cavern were he had encountered the drow girl. He could guess what would befall the lass should these hard, bitter people find her, and he wanted no part of that.

There was no doubt in Fyodor's mind that the people of Troll-bridge had suffered at the hands of dark-elven raiders. He suspected the drow committed almost as many atrocities as the stories credited them with. But he had been to war, and he knew what horrors mankind was capable of committing. He had not given up on his own deeply flawed race, and he was not about to condemn every member of another.

Young as he was, Fyodor trusted himself to make such decisions on one person at a time. His limited Sight gave him an occasional glimpse into what was or what might be. He did not depend solely upon it, but he had learned he was as good at reading character as many a wiser man. Even so, the dark elven girl was a mystery to him. Her laughter had been purely elven, a magical sound that reminded Fyodor of faerie bells and delighted babies. Treacherous she certainly was, and as deadly in battle as the stories of drow had led him to expect. Yet she was not animated obsidian, or some walking, breathing caricature of evil. Fyodor had been startled by the look on her face when he spoke of *dajemma*. For a moment he saw a kindred spirit behind those strange, golden eyes. Even more troubling was the fleeting but certain conviction that this girl could become as powerful—and as important—as the Witches he had been raised to revere. Most disturbing of all was the sense that his destiny was somehow linked with hers. Yet she was drow! Fyodor did not know what dark secrets might be veiled in such beauty; he only knew he could do nothing that might give the dark-elven girl to these vengeful townsfolk.

So Fyodor kept his peace and finished his breakfast amid the morose company of the villagers. When he had eaten his fill, he bought from Saida the things he would need. The innkeeper charged him more than the goods should have cost, but he did not take the time to bargain. As precious as his moments in the sun had been, they were time stolen from his quest.

As soon as he could reasonably slip away, Fyodor left the village of Trollbridge behind and retraced his steps into the forest. He found the cave opening and wriggled his way inside. The sudden darkness closed around him, and he lit the first of his pine-pitch torches. On impulse, he searched around for a rock big enough to seal the opening, and he hoisted it into place. Then, holding his torch high, he began the steep descent back into the Underdark.

Chapter 13

BOTTLED DARKNESS

lowly, carefully, Liriel tried to pull the tiny dagger from its rune-carved sheath. Three days of almost constant study had passed, days that had impressed upon the young wizard the hazards and challenges inherent in her quest.

There was no doubt in her mind that the amulet was an artifact of great power. She had cast several formidable spells upon the amulet, spells that should have shown her the meaning of the tiny runes carved on the sheath. All were in vain. A magic more potent than hers protected the ancient secrets. And the amulet's chain, which had been broken when she'd taken it from the body of the drow thief, had simply healed itself. New links had grown to fill the gap, but so perfectly matched were they to the weathered gold that Liriel could no longer tell where the break had been. She had never heard of a magical item that could repair itself unaided. As she tugged at the tiny dagger, her concern was less for the delicate amulet—which could clearly take care of itself—than for the magic such an action might unleash.

Yet try though she might, she could not pull the dagger free.

Dagger and sheath might as well have been carved from a single piece of metal, so tightly were they bonded together.

With a sigh, Liriel slumped against her chair. She had come too far and risked too much to fail now.

Getting the amulet had been the easy part. Finding time to study it had been a far greater challenge. She'd not dared approach Triel for a leave of absence, knowing the matron mistress would almost certainly deny the request out of hand. The best hope Liriel had was to keep the matter from Triel's eyes altogether. There were rumors of several challenges to House Baenre's position, so the harried matron had more important matters to attend than following her niece's every move. And if Liriel's instructors, and Matron Zeld in particular, believed the matron mistress had sanctioned the girl's absence, they would not challenge Triel's decision.

On the other hand, the Academy matrons might very well be curious and seek answers in a less direct fashion. They might be loyal to Triel, but they also kept an eye to the advancement of both their houses and their careers. Liriel fully expected to have the eyes of a dozen noble houses prying into her business, trying to discern what House Baenre might consider important enough to warrant granting one of their females time away from Arach-Tinilith's training.

And so it had been. Liriel and Kharza-kzad had placed layers of wards about her Narbondellyn home, and the air about her fairly crackled with frustrated magical probes. In the three days since she'd left Arach-Tinilith, two of her servants had disappeared. Liriel did not expect to see them again, and indeed they would be of little value to her after their abductors had finished extracting what information they could. But for the intervention of two powerful wizards—the reluctantly supportive Kharza-kzad and the archmage himself—Liriel would not have been left in peace this long.

For yes, she had decided to risk involving her father in this plan. Doing so created an extremely ticklish situation. Gromph Baenre had the influence necessary to get her out of Arach-Tinilith, yet the Academy's matrons would assume he would not dare to do so unless it was at Triel's bidding. Liriel knew that proud Gromph would not appreciate this reminder of his limitations, and that he would not act on her behalf unless there was potential gain.

So she'd told him enough about her trip to the surface, including the information on the priestesses of Eilistraee, to whet his interest.

She stressed there were drow on the surface who could cast magic, who had powers that those who dwelt below did not know. She promised to learn what she could from them and bring this knowledge back to him. Gromph had questioned her closely, and only when she'd agreed to act as his emissary to the drow community above did he agree to help her.

At least he'd agreed. How he would explain his actions to Triel if the matter came to light was *his* concern; Liriel was more than content to let the two Baenre siblings fight it out. Still, the expression on her father's face when she'd spoken of a rival deity made her wonder if it had been wise to involve him. What use would ambitious Gromph make of this information?

Nor did she trust Kharza-kzad. Like Gromph, he had his own agenda. This had been made abundantly clear by the wizard's gift of a gate that would enable her to slip out of the Academy at will. Before that, Liriel had assumed the old wizard's interest in her had been strictly personal, that he enjoyed their association for the bragging rights it gave him. Even if he had not told one lying tale, it was apparent he found the company and attention of a beautiful young female gratifying. But there was more. Liriel was convinced her tutor had plans of his own, and that he wished to make her a part of his unseen design.

Still, she needed Kharza-kzad. As a master of the Sorcere, he had access to scrolls and books denied most wizards, and Spelltower Xorlarrin was as well equipped a magical laboratory as Menzoberranzan could produce. This, it seemed, was due in no little part to the wizard's constant and secret trade with the merchants of the Dragon's Hoard.

Which was yet another risk that Liriel had taken. She'd sent for Nisstyre and asked him to sell her every book of human lore he could buy or steal on extremely short notice. Possession of these books was illegal, of course, and even though such an exorbitant purchase would bring her to near-ruin Liriel saw no alternative. She dared not ask specifically for books of rune lore for fear that doing so would show too much of her hand. The black-eyed merchant was also a wizard, and he knew more about the Lands of Light than any of Menzoberranzan's magic-wielders. He would be more likely than Kharza, even more likely than Gromph, to put together what she planned to do.

Nisstyre, however, had been nothing but helpful. He brought

159

several boxes of books to her and bid her take whatever she liked and return the rest at no cost. He offered to answer any questions she might have about the Lands of Light, and even hinted he would be pleased to act as her guide. He hinted at a great many things, actually, with a boldness that few males of Menzoberranzan would have dared. Although Liriel had little interest in a personal liaison with the copper-haired merchant, she might have taken him up on one or two of his other offers if she'd had the time.

Time. With a sigh, Liriel cast a quick glance at the glowing sands in her hourglass. What little time she'd purchased was almost out, for sooner or later the too-busy Triel would hear of her niece's absence and force her back into Arach-Tinilith. In truth, three days of freedom was more than Liriel had expected.

She had used her stolen time well. She had committed to memory maps of the lands above her, learned more about the people and their ways. What she did not learn, however, was how the amulet in her hand could be turned to her purpose.

Aimlessly, Liriel twisted at the dagger. To her amazement, the tiny hilt turned in her hands and the weapon came free of its sheath.

The dark elf examined the golden object and received her second surprise. It was not a dagger at all, but a small chisel. The tool remained bright and sharp-edged, with not a hint of corrosion despite the water that filled the bottom of the sheath.

"A chisel," she murmured. "Of course!"

The dark elf seized her book of rune lore and paged through it with growing excitement. Near the end she found a crudely drawn picture of an ancient, sprawling oak. The tree was called Yggsdrasil's Child, and its thick, gnarled trunk was marked with the runes of a thousand spells. According to the text, only the most powerful runes could be carved on this tree, and only with tools forged by powerful runecasters and blessed by the gods of the ancient Rus.

Liriel raised the tiny chisel and regarded it with awe. Was it possible she held such a thing in her hand? She studied the picture closely. Yes, some of the markings on the ancient oak were identical to those on the amulet.

But could she, a drow of the Underdark, use this tool to carve a spell onto the sacred oak? The casting of a rune was not like the wizardly spells she wielded with ease and authority. A rune such as she would need was not learned from a scroll, but carved into the mind and heart. And the tool for such a task was a long and perilous journey, such as the ancient Rus had undertaken to expand both their domains and their magical power. Only through change and growth, through hard-won insight, did such a rune come to the caster.

Shaking with excitement, Liriel picked up a large parchment scroll and smoothed it flat. It was a map of the northlands, and according to Nisstyre it depicted the lands that lay above the Underdark she knew. Her finger found the distant city of Waterdeep and then traced a path across the sea to Ruathym. On that island lived the ancestors of the Rus. And on that island stood Yggsdrasil's Child, the ancient sacred oak tree.

This, then, was her destination. If her journey yielded her the rune she needed, she would cast the spells that would give her permanent possession of her drow magic.

First, though, she would have to carry this magic across the miles to Ruathym. The droplets of water trapped in the sheath had suggested an answer to that problem, for her book of rune lore contained many stories of sacred wells and springs. Water was plentiful in the Underdark and had little potency beyond its common, life-sustaining nature. But Liriel's dark homeland had its own places of power.

* * * * *

"Liriel Baenre, you have finally gone utterly and completely mad!"

This pronouncement, coming as it did from an insane, two-headed purple dragon, lacked some of the impact it might otherwise have had.

"I'm telling you, Zz'Pzora, this will work," the young drow insisted as she chipped away at the wall of the grotto with a small mithril pick. "Just try to hold steady for another minute or two."

"Hold steady, she says," grumbled the dragon's right head, literally talking to herself as she addressed her other head. "What does the drow think we are, a hummingbird?"

The left head's answer was lost in the noise of yet another ringing blow and the thumping *whoosh* of the dragon's wings as the creature struggled to maintain its position. A warm, strong updraft helped hold the dragon aloft, but hovering in one place was extremely difficult for any dragon under the best of circumstances.

Zz'Pzora's task was complicated by the added weight of the drow who straddled the base of the dragon's dual necks. Liriel was not all that heavy—most deep dragons considered a ninety-pound drow a snack, not a burden—but Zz'Pzora was small for her kind. Nor did the drow balance herself well. She leaned far to the side, and each time she pounded the rock her hold on her dragon mount became just a bit more tenuous. At any moment, the reckless dark elf would take them both crashing to the floor of the grotto.

"Look around you," the dragon's right head begged. The creature dipped dangerously close to the cavern floor, and she beat her purple wings frantically until she had regained her position. "The entire cavern glows with energy! Take something that's easier to get at."

Liriel shook her head and pounded again. A thin crack appeared in the rock, outlined by an eerie blue glow that shone even through layers of magic-dead stone.

"This is the best place, Zip, and you know it," the drow said in a distracted voice. More careful now that the rock had given way, she tapped gently at the wall, slowly enlarging the network of spreading cracks. "The Banshee's Needle holds more magic than any ton of rock in this place."

The Banshee's Needle, a slender bit of glowing rock that seemed to hold and condense the radiations of this hidden cavern, was so named for the banshee—an undead drow female—that had once haunted Zz'Pzora's lair. The banshee was gone long before Zz'Pzora's time; the dragon's mother had vanquished the undead elf in a horrendous magical battle that may well have contributed to her future offspring's unusual appearance. Whatever the case, the mutant dragon did not like to think about the matter too deeply or too often.

At that moment Liriel dropped her pick to the rocks below and began to painstakingly peel away the layers of rock with her hands and a knife. Zz'Pzora flinched at the metallic crash of mithril meeting stone.

"That could very well have been us, you know," the right head pointed out.

"I'm hurrying," Liriel assured the dragon. The drow was well aware of the precarious nature of her situation. She wished she could have brought Kharza along to aid her work with spells of levitation, but the fretful old wizard would likely have died of fright during the trip. Water-running was not a sport for the timid.

Liriel could have floated up to the Banshee's Needle under her own power, but doing so would have exhausted her ability to levitate for the rest of the day. The drow still had to make the long trip up the shaft, and she had to rely on Zz'Pzora to hoist her up. It was not unlikely that the dragon, in a fit of pique, might "accidentally" lose her grip on the rope. So Liriel clung to the dragon's purple neck with one hand as she tapped away at the wall of glowing rock.

Suddenly brilliant blue light bathed the grotto—the Banshee's Needle was free of its rocky sheath. The drow worked even more quickly now, for neither her light-sensitive eyes nor her dragon helper could take much more of this. She carefully inserted the tip of her knife under the exposed sliver of stone and pried it loose. The amulet hung ready about her neck; she dropped the glowing bit of stone into the sheath and quickly twisted the dagger-hilted chisel back into place.

"Got it!" she exulted. "Let's go down."

"Tiamat be praised!" grumbled the dragon, both heads joining in unison in an oath invoking the god of dragons. The creature swept down toward the cavern floor and skidded to a grateful stop.

Liriel slid off the dragon's shoulders and began to gather up her magical items. If the renewed glitter of her *piwafwi* was any indication, her things had more than regained the magic they'd lost in her two moonlit visits Above. And so soon! Usually a new item needed to bask in such sites of power for years in order to become imbued with magic; an item whose magic had been lost completely needed at least a year to regain potency. For the first time, Liriel felt truly confident her plan would work.

"Now what?" the right head inquired. "After all the trouble we've gone through to get that thing, you could at least tell me what you plan to do with it."

"I'm going on a long journey, Zz'Pzora," Liriel said happily.

"Good!" huffed the dragon heads in unison. The purple creature settled back on her haunches and folded her arms across her chest in an oddly elven gesture. "You're much more trouble than you're worth," her right head added caustically.

The drow raised a single eyebrow. "And I'll miss you, too," she returned with equal warmth. "But I won't be making the trip for some time, not until I've finished my training at Arach-Tinilith. As a high priestess, I'll have the power and status I'll need to come and go as I please."

"In that case, you'll be coming again soon?"

Liriel shook her head. "I'm sorry, Zip, but I don't dare leave the

Academy again. I'll come to see you as soon as my training is finished."

"Hmmph."

Zz'Pzora pouted. There was no other word for it. The sulky expression looked a bit out of place on the scaly, fearsome faces of the purple dragon, but Liriel found it rather endearing.

"The years will pass quickly, you'll see; my training and my journey will soon come to an end. When I return, would you like me to bring you something from the Lands of Light?" she wheedled, thinking that perhaps naming her destination would lift Zz'Pzora from her dark mood.

The dragon's reptilian eyes—all four of them—widened in surprise. A crafty smile spread across the left head's face. Until now, the practical right head had dominated the dragon's words and actions, but finally something had ignited the interest of the dragon's flightier half.

"Yes," the head said, and the decisive tone sounded odd in its chirpy, little-girl voice. "Find me a way to get to the surface."

Liriel blinked. "Actually, I was thinking more along the lines of a spellbook, a treasure of some sort."

"Nevertheless, you have offered, and I have answered."

Again that decisive, passionate tone, so unexpected of Zz'Pzora's left-headed persona. Even the dragon's right head looked at her counterpart with amazement.

After a moment's shared silence, the drow shrugged. "All right, Zip, I'll do what I can."

Promises of both drow and deep dragon were easily made and seldom kept, but Zz'Pzora seemed satisfied with this response. Liriel gathered up the rest of her magical items and took her place in the shaft. For once the dragon hoisted the drow up without any of the sudden jerks or teasing pauses that usually defined the trip. When the drow reached the top, she heard the faint, distant sound of the dragon's two voices raised in a haunting song of farewell.

For the first time, a touch of sadness tainted Liriel's excitement, and she began to ponder all she would leave behind. She was not entirely sorry the trip lay several years in the future. There was still so much to do, so much to learn and experience, in her native Menzoberranzan. And the more powers she gained, the more she could take with her into the Lands of Light. Yet, whenever her time came, Liriel knew she would be traveling alone in a strange land.

Perhaps, the drow mused as she stepped through the gate that would bring her back to Spelltower Xorlarrin, she might try to keep her promise to the dragon after all.

Chapter 14

SHAKTI

hree days!" raged Shakti Hunzrin, hurling her water pitcher at the door of her room. The fine earthenware shattered with a satisfying crash and a cascade of dust and splinters. This did little to improve the drow's mood; there was scant pleasure to be had in the destruction of inanimate objects. She continued to pace the room restlessly, feeling as thoroughly out of sorts as a dwarf in water.

The priestess had wasted much time and several good spells watching the comings and goings of her Baenre rival. All that effort was for naught. The matron mistress had, against all logic, simply given her precious niece a leave of absence. And for what? By all reports, Liriel had barricaded herself in her home. No doubt the little princess needed time to recover from the rigors of a full five days at Arach-Tinilith, Shakti concluded sourly.

But *three days?* She herself had been granted only a few hours' leave here and there, and that only to attend the pressing concerns of her family business.

Suddenly Shakti stopped her restless pacing. Perhaps, she

mused, a few hours might be enough.

She straightened the folds of her robes and impatiently smoothed her hair back into place—she had a habit of tugging at it during her rages. Her slippers crunched the shards of broken pottery as she stalked from the room in search of Matron Zeld.

*   *   *   *   *

"Why do you need the time away, and why do you come to *me*?"

They were reasonable questions both, and Shakti was prepared for them. "It is breeding season for the rothe," the Hunzrin priestess explained. "No one knows more about the matter than I. Not even the rothe themselves," she added proudly.

Mistress Zeld's brow furrowed at that strange pronouncement, but she quickly decided not to pursue the matter. "But you are a twelfth-year student, nearing high priestess status. I have no authority over you."

Shakti leaned forward. "But you *can* give me permission to leave. It is to both our advantages that I go. I can bring back information."

"I must admit, I have little interest in the social life of cattle," the mistress said in an acid tone.

The young priestess fell silent, struggling against her rising anger. She had not expected the mistress to be so difficult. By all appearances, Mistress Zeld held little affection for Liriel and would not be displeased to see her young student brought down. If doing so could bring trouble to House Baenre, so much the better.

"May I speak frankly?"

Zeld's lips curved in ironic amusement. "That would be refreshing."

It could also be deadly, and knowing this, Shakti chose her next words with care. "Arach-Tinilith is the strength of our city, the glory of Lloth. For centuries untold, the students were not allowed to leave the Academy until their training was completed. Now, in these troubled times, individual houses need all the talents at their command, including those of their youngest members. Even so, permission to leave the Academy is not granted lightly, and not without some greater gain in sight."

Mistress Zeld listened carefully, hearing the words that Shakti left unspoken. "And you are saying your need is great enough to justify your release."

Elaine Cunningham

The Hunzrin priestess dipped her head in a respectful bow. "Not as great, perhaps, as the plans and designs of some of the greater houses."

"I see." Zeld leaned back in her chair and considered the younger female. Finally, the young priestess had stated her intent, and done so with impressive subtlety. Of course, Mistress Zeld had understood Shakti's motivation from the start, and she stalled merely to force the Hunzrin female to lay some inducements on the bargaining table. Shakti was not alone in wondering what plot House Baenre had in mind that would require the involvement of Gromph's wizard daughter. Many had tried to discover this—without drawing fire from the powerful first house—and so far all had failed. Perhaps the singleminded, hate-filled young priestess could do better. If Shakti failed, it would be no great loss. But if she succeeded, Zeld's own clan would be pleased to receive this information, and she herself would surely be rewarded for Shakti's efforts.

"You have my permission to leave, provided you return in time for chapel. There are other conditions, of course."

"Naturally."

"You will give me a full report upon your return. Leave out nothing."

Shakti nodded respectfully and rose to leave. "The Hunzrins have purchased new breeding stock to revitalize the herd. We plan to introduce both wild rothe and the larger, surface rothe into the line. We expect good results from this mix. I will be happy to bring you a copy of the breeding records. This might be useful, if ever you should be questioned about your decision to grant me a leave of absence."

"Your attention to detail is commendable," Zeld said dryly. "There is one more condition. If you fail, we did not have this conversation."

A grim smile firmed Shakti's lips. They understood each other perfectly, without a direct word being spoken. "I understand your reticence," she said softly. "Rothe breeding is hardly a popular topic of conversation. I have noticed no one has quite the same enthusiasm for this subject as I do."

"Not even the rothe, most likely."

But Shakti, in her hurry to leave, did not hear the mistress's arch comment. It would have been lost on the serious young priestess, anyway.

168

And this, Zeld concluded, was just as well. Shakti was talented, devious, hardworking, and utterly vicious. Young though she was, the Hunzrin priestess didn't miss much, and she was proving herself to be a formidable enemy. Had she been blessed with a bit more perspective, which often manifested itself in dark humor, she would have been far more dangerous. Even without it, she was definitely a female to watch.

Every drow, even the powerful mistresses of Arach-Tinilith, kept an eye open for potential rivals.

*   *   *   *   *

Trust Liriel Baenre to have a house right across from Narbondellyn's most infamous festhall, Shakti thought with bitter scorn. Seated in a plushly cushioned alcove and shielded from view by the curtains that draped it on all sides, she shifted the heavy velvet and peered out across the street at her enemy's miniature castle.

In her hand she gripped the moonstone she'd had enspelled to seek out her rival, the same stone that had inexplicably ended up in Mistress Mod'Vensis Tlabbar's bedchamber. Retrieving it had been no little matter, and at the moment Shakti regretted the effort. The stone's magic could not penetrate the veil of spells hiding Liriel from view. Shakti had tried clerical spells, as well, but Lloth did not respond to her entreaties. Whatever plot House Baenre had in mind, it had apparently found favor with the Lady of Chaos.

That made matters all the more difficult, for Shakti's only hope of gaining access to Liriel's castle was by physical means. Her spies had reported seeing the girl leave the place early that day, but who knew how long she might stay away? If Shakti was to find a way in, she must do it soon. The nearsighted priestess squinted frantically, but she could see nothing from this distance that would help her.

With a hiss of frustration, Shakti left the festhall and hurried across the street. Like many of Menzoberranzan's drow, she traveled swathed in her *piwafwi*, her face hidden by the deep cowl of her hood. She was all too aware, however, that her stout figure and distinctive, ungainly walk made her conspicuous, and she did not want to be seen examining the house too closely. One pass, two at the most, was all she dared risk.

At first Shakti saw nothing that might help her. The houses in this city, even those of the commoners, were virtual fortresses

169

protected by magic and ingenious hidden devices. As far as she could see, there was no way in. Then suddenly, she detected a movement in the seemingly solid stone of the front door. A tiny swinging door poked up and outward, and the mottled red and black head of a lizard poked through the opening. Its tongue flicked out to taste the breeze, and it darted off into the shadows.

The priestess smirked. Finally, the chink in her rival's defenses! She'd heard rumors the spoiled princess kept a menagerie of exotic pets brought from distant places in the Underdark, even from the Lands of Light. This door was no doubt designed to allow Liriel's collection of pet lap-lizards to come and go as they pleased.

It was possible this door also had magic wards. Shakti would never know for certain unless she tested it.

So with all possible speed, the priestess made her way to the home of a certain wizard, a commoner of considerable skill whose talents were for hire. Granted, there were priestesses in her family who wielded more powerful clerical magic than her own, and two or three who might be able to cast the needed spell. But that would mean invoking Lloth—a dangerous enterprise at any time and utter insanity when the purpose was a direct attack against a Baenre female. Besides, this was a personal matter and Shakti did not wish to involve her family. Among the drow, it was far less expensive to buy a service than to accept a favor. The price for the latter was never quite what one expected it to be.

Within the hour, Shakti and her hired wizard slipped through a back door in the Hunzrin compound. She led the mage to the barracks that housed the clan's soldiers. She selected a soldier—a dispensable male, of course—and explained the task before him.

"You will enter the home of Liriel Baenre through the door used by her collection of pet lizards. This wizard here will shrink you to a fraction of your normal size."

"How small?" the soldier ventured.

Shakti held out her hands, one above the other, measuring a distance of about six inches between them.

The male blanched, his face paling nearly to blue in the heat spectrum. "But the lizards—" he began.

"You are armed," she snapped. "The soldiers of House Hunzrin have been trained to handle foes greater than lap-lizards!"

The soldier considered the wrath on the priestess's face and decided that the safer course would be to hold his tongue and do as she said. Never mind the fact that to a six-inch drow, a large gecko was nearly as fearsome a foe as a dragon!

So he inclined his head in a gesture of respect and acceptance. "As you command, Matron—" the male paused, letting his intentional error linger in the air like incense. "*Lady* Hunzrin," he corrected.

It was an obvious ploy, a ridiculous currying of favor that would have earned him a sharp cuff—or worse—from most drow females. But even a lowly soldier could recognize the ambition, the pride, on this one's face, and the singleminded fervor exceptional even among the fanatic drow. Shakti would hear only the implied compliment in the male's words, and not the mockery.

As he'd anticipated, the young priestess received his flattery with a complacent smile. She nodded to the wizard, who handed the soldier a small vial.

"When you are safely inside, drink this potion. It will reverse the spell and return you to your normal size," the wizard instructed.

"Be certain you are not seen," Shakti added. "Kill the servants only if you must. Once you are sure we will not be detected, you may let me in through the back. The doors will almost certainly not be warded from the inside."

At a nod from the priestess, the wizard began to cast the spell. Eyes closed, he half sang the arcane words in a long, drawn-out chant, all the while sweeping the air with elaborate gestures. Shakti sat calmly through the spell, patient for once despite her eagerness. Considering the price of this spell and the reputation of the wizard, she'd expected a bit of a show.

Through it all, the soldier stood at attention: tense, stoic. The chant rose to a high, wailing note, and the wizard ended the spell with a flurry of hands and a brief flash of purple light.

Smoke, the same eerie purple hue as the vanished light, wafted from the wizard's outflung hands. It streamed unerringly to the soldier and surrounded him, head to foot, like a drow-shaped cloud. Immediately the cloud began to move inward, compacting itself against the soldier's body and pressing him on all sides.

The male's eyes bulged as the magic haze tightened around him. Slowly, inexorably, the drow's body began to give under the pressure. Agony twisted his face, and his mouth opened in a shriek of anguish. On and on it went, the shrinking and the screaming.

Shakti leaned forward, her eyes gleaming with twisted pleasure as she watched. Finally the male was small enough to suit her purposes, and she stopped the wizard with a nod. The purple smoke dissipated at once, and the soldier, now small enough to sit on Shakti's hand, slumped to the floor.

"By the way, this may hurt," the mage said casually.

The priestess took in the wizard's sated expression, the perverse delight in his eyes, and saw opportunity written there. Even in vengeance, Shakti was a frugal manager, as canny as any merchant in the city.

"Your fee," she said, handing the wizard coins totaling slightly less than the agreed-upon amount. She nodded pointedly to the tiny drow on the floor, and her single raised eyebrow suggested the wizard had already been amply paid by the pleasure his spell brought him.

The wizard did not argue with her silent logic. He took the offered coins and, with a final satisfied glance at his handiwork, slipped out into the darkness that was Menzoberranzan.

Shakti stooped and picked up the soldier, marveling at how fragile the fighter was at this size. She could crush him merely by tightening her fingers. Only with great effort did the priestess restrain from following the tempting impulse.

Instead she promised herself a treat when this was over: a dozen tiny soldiers, acting out a battle to the death for her amusement. How marvelous, how godlike, that would feel! How thrilling, the sense of power! It would be as if she were touching the very shadow of Lloth. Such a thing was more than an amusement, the young priestess rationalized; it would be an act of devotion, and well worth the high price of the wizard's spells.

Shakti tucked the male into the front of her robe. He should be secure enough, clinging to the chain of her house insignia and wedged in her ample cleavage. It pleased her, this blatant reminder of the power females wielded over lowly males.

Shakti Hunzrin was not one for subtleties.

* * * * *

The Hunzrin priestess stooped, under the pretense of picking up a dropped package, and surreptitiously placed the miniature fighter near Liriel's front door. As instructed, he sprinted toward the lizard door and pressed it inward.

Shakti took a deep breath and began to walk away. She would circle around and approach the house from the back. If all went well, her tiny spy would admit her to the Baenre girl's castle, and she would search the place quickly, before its owner returned.

A sound came from behind her, a high piping cry that sounded like the squeaks of a wounded scurry rat. Shakti froze, and swore. The tiny door had been trapped, after all.

She spun around and glared furiously at the small figure staggering toward her. She snatched up the drow male and held him close to her eyes. Protruding from his body was a dart, such as those the drow used in their tiny crossbows. Considering his current size, the male might as well have been impaled upon a three-foot spear. And he'd been gut-shot, one of the more painful and lingering deaths.

Shakti swore again, and her eyes darted to the street. A patrol of lizard-mounted drow approached, making their silent rounds of the city.

"You were worried about lizards," she hissed at the tiny male. "Yet if you were to live long enough, you would be grateful you met this one."

With those words, she tossed the drow soldier in the path of a passing lizard mount. The creature's long, slender tongue whipped out and curled around the unexpected morsel. Back it snapped, so quickly that the lizard's rider did not notice what his mount had eaten.

Once again Shakti retraced her steps to the Hunzrin complex. Now that she knew the nature of the traps guarding the door, she would send in another servant, one far more valuable than a male soldier.

* * * * *

Less than an hour later, Shakti stepped triumphantly through Liriel's back door. She regarded the creature who had let her in with a mixture of pride and revulsion. Its face was a hideous parody of a drow visage. Dark blue in color, with long pointed ears that looked almost like horns, the head could well have belonged to some creature of the Abyss. But its body was that of a thick snake, nearly ten feet in length and covered with dark blue scales. The creature's swaying tail ended in a barbed, poisonous tip. This was a dark naga, one of the rarest creatures of the Underdark and a valued ally of House Hunzrin.

"Pay Ssasser now," hissed the naga in an airy, whistling voice. He bared his fangs in a grin of anticipation, and his long pronged tongue flicked out. "Ssasser's servitude to Hunzrin family over."

"That was not the terms of our agreement. When I have Liriel Baenre under my power, you will be free," Shakti reminded him.

The creature scowled, and then it brought forth a tremendous belch. Its thin lips pursed and it spat a small dart at Shakti's feet. "This did Ssasser swallow, when through the door Ssasser came. A good trap, it was. If Ssasser knew not about the magic trip-wire, dead might Ssasser be."

Shakti kicked the dart aside. Among the dark naga's many talents was the ability to swallow virtually anything without harm. Weapons, poisons, spellbooks—all were safely stowed in the internal organ that allowed the naga to carry whatever it needed. Granted, catching a crossbow-fired dart was a bit out of the ordinary, but the naga had clearly been up to the challenge.

"Cost Ssasser, it did, the spell of invisibility," the dark naga hinted.

"And you will have another, at no additional charge," the priestess promised. Above all its other weapons, the naga was prized for its magical ability. The high cost of developing its natural magic often forced the nagas into servitude. This creature was in debt too deeply to buy its way free of the Hunzrin family anytime soon, so Shakti felt she could be generous.

She bade the snake-thing return to House Hunzrin, and then began the search of the castle. Liriel's home was, as Shakti expected, a virtual den of dissolution. Since the Hunzrin priestess had little interest in luxuries, she gave most of the house scant attention. The one room she wanted was the study.

And in it, she found what she sought. Books were rare and expensive, but Liriel had more than her fair share of them. Most, beautifully bound in rare leathers and embossed with elegant drow runes, were neatly organized on shelves. Shakti gave these no more than a glance. She was more interested in the crude, battered books that seemed to be scattered everywhere.

Books were stacked on the study table, piled against the wall, tossed about on the floor. And such books! Many of them were about humans and human magic—subjects strictly forbidden in Menzoberranzan.

Elated with this discovery, Shakti hugged one of the damning volumes to her chest. Drow had died for lesser offenses, and the possession of these books was enough to bring serious trouble even to a member of House Baenre. But that was not quite enough for Shakti; she wanted to know *why* Liriel sought this information about the surface world.

No one took such risks motivated only by intellectual curiosity. Was House Baenre planning another strike against the surface? Or perhaps seeking an alliance with a group of humans? If either of these things proved true, the city would almost certainly rise up in rebellion.

Shakti tossed the book aside and reached for another. Instantly she froze as loose pages fluttered from the discarded book.

The priestess stooped and picked up a page. It was fine vellum parchment, covered with small, elegantly formed drow script. Even without light, the nearsighted priestess could read the page, for it was written in everdark ink, the rare, glowing ink used only by the most powerful and prosperous of drow wizards.

As she read, her excitement grew. These were Liriel Baenre's notes, written in her own hand! Shakti scanned page after page, and the emerging picture surpassed her darkest dreams of vengeance.

Liriel Baenre had found a way to take her innate drow powers to the surface. She'd found an amulet, a human artifact of some sort, that granted her this power.

The pages fluttered unheeded from Shakti's hands as the importance of this discovery struck home. She read in these handwritten pages Liriel Baenre's death warrant. Most of the city's drow would cheerfully kill to possess such magic. And then what might happen? For good or ill, such a thing could change Menzoberranzan forever.

But how, wondered Shakti, had Liriel done such a thing? Eagerly the priestess took up one book after another. Finally, tucked between the pages of a particularly battered volume, she found what she sought: a handwritten bill signed only with a faint, familiar design. Shakti recognized the mark of the Dragon's Hoard.

A wild grin twisted Shakti's face. She knew the merchant band well. In fact, she had recently acquired a new rothe stud from the Dragon's Hoard, a white ram whose compact size and unusually fine fleece marked him as the property of House Zinard, a family of the drow city Ched Nasad. The rothe was stolen, of course, for the Zinards would never part with such a valuable animal.

It was whispered around Menzoberranzan that contraband

goods of almost any kind could be had from the Dragon's Hoard. The merchant band protected the many secrets of its clients, but surely Shakti could find a way to make one of the merchants talk. She was as talented at torture as any drow in Menzoberranzan. Oaths of secrecy, even fear of death at Captain Nisstyre's hands, would mean little to the unfortunate male who fell into her hands.

* * * * *

Before the bell rang to summon Lloth's faithful to chapel, Shakti had extracted some fascinating information from her chosen captive. The merchant had known nothing about Liriel Baenre, but he'd spoken eloquently on the subject of his employer.

Nisstyre, it seemed, was not just any merchant captain. He was a wizard trained in the schools of Ched Nasad, who had fled the city many decades past rather than submit to the mind-searching test of loyalty to Lloth. Shakti thought she might know why.

In his last, agonized moments, the tortured drow had confessed that he himself was a follower of Vhaeraun, the drow god of intrigue and thievery. It seemed unlikely the servant would dare to follow such a god without the knowledge and consent of his master. This gave Shakti a powerful weapon to use against Nisstyre, but oddly enough the female was not inclined to wield it.

The concept of a rival deity fascinated her. She had never entertained such thoughts, knowing it was her lot to become a priestess of Lloth. She had always resented this, but had never seen another way.

Now, for the first time in her life, Shakti began to move past discontent toward ambition. The city teetered on the brink of anarchy. What better time than this to break the power of Lloth's priestesses? And what better tool than a rival deity? If this Vhaeraun had a powerful, hidden following in the city, perhaps she could find something that would persuade them into open warfare against the faltering matriarchy. Even more delightful, a proven connection between Vhaeraun's followers and House Baenre could very well topple the threatened first house. Liriel would not survive such a conflict, of course, but even that delightful prospect paled before the larger picture emerging in Shakti's mind.

Anarchy was all well and good, and necessary to bring about sweeping change in Menzoberranzan society, but *someone* would have to bring the city back to order. Shakti was supremely confident of her management skills, but she also realized that no one person, no one faction, was strong enough to regain control. Her family controlled much of the city's food supply, and that was a powerful tool. She would also need strong allies and ties to the world outside the city. Who better to provide both than a powerful merchant captain who was also a wizard?

And for that matter, who better to snatch Menzoberranzan from the hand of Lloth but Vhaeraun, the drow god of thievery!

The female nodded slowly. Sometime very soon she would pay a visit to this Nisstyre.

Chapter 15

COUNCILS AND CONSPIRACIES

ach day at Arach-Tinilith ended in the Academy chapel, in a session of prayer and praise to the goddess of the drow. Although the services took many forms, they were always eerie, impressive affairs. The chapel itself inspired awe, carved as it was from a single mass of black stone. Circles of seats surrounded a central platform, each row higher than the last so all could see the dark altar. Eight curving beams buttressed the circular room and met at the top of the domed chamber, becoming part of an enormous sculpture of a spider with the head of a beautiful drow female: a favored form of the Spider Queen. Faerie fire outlined the gigantic spider and cast shadows across the sea of dark faces below.

All of Arach-Tinilith gathered there, from the matron mistress to the lowliest novice priestess, and the rhythmic chanting of hundreds of dark-elven voices echoed throughout the high-domed chamber. And of all the voices raised, perhaps the most fervent belonged to Shakti Hunzrin, who had tucked within the folds of her robes papers that could not fail to destroy her hated rival.

The chanting gathered speed and power as the time for the dark ritual grew near. One of the older students slowly approached the altar, carrying before her a silver tray. On it lay a drow heart, still throbbing with life newly taken. It was the heart of a male, which was usually considered a lesser sacrifice, but this night the ritual had a special power. This night the sacrifice fulfilled one of Lloth's most brutal requirements.

Devotion to the Spider Queen was all-important, superseding any personal loyalty. Lloth was especially offended by the possibility that one of her priestesses might become too fond of a lowly male. So from time to time, a priestess was commanded to slay her lover, a matron to sacrifice her house patron, a mother to offer up the sire of her children. Knowing this, the drow had learned to be wary of giving and receiving affection; the penalty was too cruel for all involved. But as the young priestess approached the altar, the hard set of her face and the blood on her delicate hands proved she had been equal to the task.

The priestess lifted the tray high, and the thunderous chant rose to a single, keening note. In voices as haunting and high-pitched as elven flutes, the drow females began to sing a ritual song of summoning. Matron Triel Baenre stepped forward, robed in the somber black of a high priestess. Her voice, magically enhanced to match the power of the assembled singers, chanted a low-pitched prayer in weird counterpoint to the song.

Tonight the song and the chant were largely a formality, for Lloth rarely spoke now except to the most powerful of her priestesses. It was whispered in Menzoberranzan that the loss of so many priestesses in the war and in the struggle for position that continued to this day had diminished the very power of the goddess. In times past—before the Time of Trouble, before the disastrous war—ceremonies such as this were often rewarded with some manifestation of Lloth's approval: a new spell, the creation of a magical item, the summoning of a scurrying rush of spiders, even an appearance of one of the goddess's minions. On rare occasions, the avatar of Lloth herself appeared to her faithful. But it seemed as if those times had passed.

Suddenly the faerie fire died, plunging the chamber into utter blackness. The song and the chant fell silent, and every eye was fixed in fearful fascination upon the faint glow dawning in the very heart of the chapel.

In the midst of the room, where the altar had been but a moment before, stood a huge, hideous creature. Its formless body resembled a mound of half-melted wax, and large bulbous eyes shone with baleful red light as it glared out at the assembly.

A mixture of elation and dread gripped Lloth's faithful. This was a yochlol, a creature from the lower planes and a handmaiden of the Spider Queen. For good or ill, the yochlol's appearance meant Lloth's eyes were upon them.

"Anarchy."

The yochlol's voice was faint and airy, a mere wisp of sound, yet every ear in the room heard the single word of warning.

The creature's body shifted and flowed, and an armlike appendage shot toward the student priestess and knocked the silver tray from her still-uplifted arms. The sacrificed heart flew across the room to land in the lap of an aged priestess. In the utter silence the sound of the tray hitting the stone floor was a ringing portent of doom.

The yochlol oozed forward and snatched up the heart from the old priestess's bloodstained lap. It held the sacrifice aloft.

"Another life taken," the creature hissed. "Do you think this carnage pleases Lloth?"

Triel Baenre stepped forward and sank into a respectful bow. "For centuries untold, this has been the custom of the drow, by the command of Lloth. Teach us where we have erred."

"Too much blood stains the streets of Menzoberranzan," announced the yochlol in its otherworldly whisper. "Too few drow remain, yet you slay each other without thought for the consequences. In your selfish ambitions, you have endangered all. By the decree of Lloth, this striving between houses must cease. Likewise, the struggle for personal power within each house must end. Until Lloth instructs otherwise, there is to be peace among her followers. Tonight, at the hour of Narbondel's Black Death, the twenty most powerful houses that remain will gather together in Qu'ellarz'orl."

The yochlol named them in turn, from House Baenre down to House Vandree. "So you are ranked by the word of Lloth, and so you will remain until it pleases the goddess to release you from this enforced peace. Any house that has not settled its affairs and chosen a matron by the appointed hour will be summarily destroyed," the creature admonished. "Go now, each to her own house, and carry with you tne word of Lloth."

Another tremor passed through the yochlol's form, and the handmaiden melted into a bubbling puddle. Steam rose from the seething mass, forming into a multitude of wraithlike spiders and floating up toward the carved image of Lloth that surrounded the chapel with its stone embrace. Then, as suddenly as it had come, the manifestation of the yochlol was gone.

The drow priestesses sat stunned and silent. Lloth, the Spider Queen, the Lady of Chaos, was calling for peace! No one was sure what to make of such a thing!

Again Matron Triel broke the silence. "You have heard. At the appointed hour, we will meet at House Baenre."

Scowls met this announcement. The yochlol had decreed the gathering take place in Qu'ellarz'orl. This, the most prestigious district of Menzoberranzan, took its name from the tiny cave that served as a meeting chamber for the Ruling Council. Every female in the room aspired to sit in that chamber, and most of them understood this meeting might realistically be their only chance to do so. Nonetheless, no one dared to protest the directive of the matron mistress. By the word of Lloth, Triel Baenre was still matron of the first house. There were practical considerations, also, for in all of Qu'ellarz'orl, only the vast Baenre chapel was large enough to house such a gathering.

So the drow slipped away into the darkness. As each female hurried to her family fortress, she pondered how best to turn these new developments to her own advantage. The strange, unnatural peace would end in due time, and much could be done in preparation for that delightful day.

* * * * *

A lone figure stood at the base of Narbondel, the natural stone pillar that supported the vast cavern and marked the passing of time. Gromph Baenre, the archmage of Menzoberranzan, waited and watched as the magical heat in the core of the pillar sank toward its lowest point. Soon it would be midnight—Narbondel's Black Death—and he would cast the powerful spell that started the process anew.

Although there were none about to see and envy him, Gromph's proud stance suggested he was keenly aware of the impressive picture he made. The magnificent cloak of the archmage, a glittering *piwafwi* whose many pockets held more magic than all of the Sorcere, was draped proudly about his shoulders. Jeweled broaches adorned his shoulders and held the cape in place. The archmage touched one of them, a fist-sized sapphire that held the magic needed to enspell the city's timeclock.

Gromph knew he was striking even without the trappings of power. Tall and handsome, as fit and youthful in appearance as any student of the fighting school, he could draw eyes to him in admiration as well as in fear and respect. And he was greatly feared, for in all of Menzoberranzan no wizard was as mighty as he. This dark hour was uniquely his, and the casting of this spell was a daily, private celebration of his own power.

The wizard began to meditate, to gather his thoughts in preparation for the casting. Then, from the corner of his eye, he noted a driftdisc floating down the broad street toward him. Behind it marched not the usual armed escort, but a group of robed priestesses.

Gromph frowned as he recognized the matron of Barrison Del'Armgo, the second-most powerful house of Menzoberranzan. What might she be doing at this hour, riding forth in state?

His puzzlement grew as he noted another driftdisc approaching from elegant Narbondellyn. Close behind it were several slave-carried litters. More priestesses came, some mounted on lizards, others on foot. They streamed past him on all sides, nearly all the priestesses of the city, moving with quiet determination toward the Baenre fortress.

Rage, hot and fierce, burned in Gromph's heart. It was obvious an important meeting had been called, and he had not been included, or even informed. Something momentous was happening, and he must know what it was.

He grasped the house insignia that hung about his neck, and spoke the words that would transport him with the speed of thought to the Baenre stronghold. To his utter astonishment, nothing happened. The powerful archmage of Menzoberranzan stood alone in the center of the dark courtyard, barred from his family home.

Because he could do nothing else, Gromph turned to the cold stone pillar and began to recite the words of the spell.

* * * * *

Triel Baenre sat at the heart of the Baenre chapel, looking out over the dark faces before her. Although this was her stronghold, her kingdom, she felt ill at ease with the task ahead and was not sure how to begin such a meeting.

For good or ill, the decision was taken from her. A small, rather wizened drow female made her way boldly toward the Baenre throne. The other priestesses fell back to make room for her, and even Triel rose to her feet and offered the seat of honor to the newcomer.

For the old drow was Hesken-P'aj, the matron of House Symryvvin and the most powerful priestess in all of Menzoberranzan. Although her house had been ranked a mere eighteenth for centuries untold, the matron had a power that all recognized and respected. Hesken-P'aj was often called "the eyes of Lloth," and on the rare occasions she ventured from her house she was granted great respect.

But Hesken-P'aj waved away Triel's offer of the throne. "I have been sent to speak, not to rule," she said impatiently. The old female turned to the assembled priestesses, clearly eager to have her say and be off.

"To each new matron, Lloth sends congratulations. Rule long and well, and restore the faith of Lloth to its former power. You have already heard there is to be no more war in Menzoberranzan. The city must be restored. No priestess shall slay another, and all healthy drow children must be reared, even the males. Until Lloth directs otherwise, the Ruling Council will enforce these new laws."

The old drow then named the eight matrons who would lead the city. "See that you rule well," she admonished, "for Lloth's peace is temporary and easily broken. Know that those who break peace for their own advancement will be destroyed. Those who extend Lloth's reign will be rewarded. That is all I have to say." With those words, the matron became as insubstantial as mist and faded from sight.

Triel cleared her throat. "All have heard. Now that the Ruling Council has been established, all future meetings will be restricted to the Eight. If any of you have words to speak that concern this general council, you may do so now."

Shakti Hunzrin leaped to her feet. Such a moment might never come again, and she meant to seize it with both hands. Lloth might have averted anarchy for the moment, but Shakti would do what damage she could.

"Something has come to my attention that concerns each drow present," Shakti began. "A novice priestess has dabbled in strange magic, human magic. To what purpose, I cannot know. This priestess possesses an amulet, a human artifact of great antiquity that allows her to carry drow magic up into the Lands Above."

Shakti took several sheets of parchment from the folds of her robe and held them high. "I have here the proof, written in this priestess's own hand. This magic is wielded by Liriel, of House Baenre. To this council I give my discovery, and the task of deciding what must be done with it."

There was a moment—just a moment—of blank and utter shock. Then the meeting exploded into chaos. The priestesses received this news with wildly varying opinions. Some argued excitedly about the possibilities, others loudly called for the death of the Baenre traitor, still others—grim-faced—muttered prayers to Lloth.

Finally Matron Triel rose to her feet. Despite her lack of physical stature, all eyes turned upon her as she stood before them, her small face blazing with wrath.

"Silence!" Triel thundered.

Silence fell, complete and immediate. The single word carried the force of a spell, and not one person in the chapel could have spoken even if she had dared to try.

"This is disturbing news," the Baenre matron admitted. She spoke in a cold, perfectly even voice, but the look she gave Shakti was one of pure malice. "Of course you all realize this discovery puts me, personally, in a most difficult position. Liriel Baenre's actions took place under my rule, and it hardly matters whether she acted with my approval or without my knowledge. I am grateful indeed for Lloth's peace," Triel added honestly and pointedly. "But in the spirit of this new unity, we will discuss what might best be done, and we leave the decision in the hands of Lloth. You," she said, pointing toward a stunningly beautiful female seated with the delegation from House Faen Tlabbar. "Speak your mind, Matron Ghilanna."

The newly elevated matron rose in a whisper of silk and the gentle tinkle of silver jewelry. House Faen Tlabbar had suffered more inner turmoil than most, for both its former matron and her heir had been slain. All the city knew Ghilanna had won her position through a vicious, bloody battle with her seven sisters, yet the female's delicate appearance was completely at odds with her deadly reputation. Ghilanna Tlabbar was tall and slender, as vain of her appearance and reputedly as wanton in her habits as any Tlabbar female. Unlike most of the priestesses in attendance, she dressed not in somber robes but in an exquisite black gown. Black seed pearls and fine embroidery graced the tightly molded, daringly cut bodice, and the entire length of her legs was clearly visible through the gossamer layers of her skirts. Yet her lovely, painted face was set in grim lines.

"This new magic could mean the end of matron rule," Ghilanna said bluntly. "The people of Menzoberranzan submit to our rule—at least in part—because they lack options. Few can survive in the wild Underdark for long, and indeed such a life would hardly be worthy of the name. Nor is there a place for us in the Lands of Light. Recent events have proved that dramatically. But consider this: if wizards could cast their spells on the surface with all the power they wield Below, what would keep them under our command? Their eyes are trained to the light, and with their magic they could survive, perhaps even thrive, in the world above.

"Even the commoners," Ghilanna continued earnestly, "the artisans and the soldiers, might be tempted to try to carve out a place for themselves Above. And why not? The lowliest drow has at her command powers that a human wizard might envy. We possess a natural resistance to magic that is the envy and horror of other magic-wielding races. Their spells slide off us like so many drops of water. Invisibility, silence, darkness, invulnerability to magic—these things are the heritage of every drow. Never forget that few can match the deadly skill of a drow fighter—and who among us is not trained in arms? Consider all these things, and ask yourselves how many drow would remain in Menzoberranzan, under our rule, if they knew they had the power to thrive elsewhere."

Mez'Barris Armgo, the matron of House Barrison Del'Armgo, was the next to receive Matron Triel's permission to speak. As ruler of the second house, Mez'Barris was clearly furious such permission was necessary. To add to this insult, the young matron of a lower house had spoken first! Yet Triel had firm control of the assemblage, and the best Mez'Barris could do was vent her ire on the upstart Tlabbar matron. The look she cast over the lovely female was one of utter disdain.

"That was a fine speech," sneered Mez'Barris. "Trust Ghilanna to bring style and flair even to blasphemy. And blasphemy it was—only thus can we describe her words," Mez'Barris shouted in ringing, impassioned tones. "Do we or do we not rule by the grace and power of Lloth? The Spider Queen is not threatened by a girl-child's magical trinket, and neither are we, her priestesses!"

She sat down amid a murmur of agreement.

"I agree with Matron Mez'Barris that this discovery poses little threat to the matriarchy. Quite the contrary. This could benefit us all," put in Matron Miz'ri. Her clan, House Mizzrym, was notable for its trade contacts, its willingness to deal with nondrow, and its delight in treacherous double-dealings. The matron's red eyes held a hard gleam now as she considered the delightful possibilities.

"With this trinket, as you call it," Miz'ri went on, "we could go into the Lands of Light armed as never before. Who could stand before our merchant bands, our raiding parties? Consider the wealth! This new magical device is a tool, like any other. We have it, and we should use it."

Kyrnill Kenafin rose to speak. Her house was currently ranked tenth, but her arrogant manner and cruel, crimson eyes marked her as the tyrant she was. In House Kenafin, priestesses reigned supreme, and they took immense delight in subjugating and terrorizing the house males.

"This talk of commoners, males, and wizards wielding such a thing is utter nonsense. Do they dare to handle a snake-headed whip of a high priestess? Of course not! Likewise, if the priestesses of Lloth claim this new magical item as our own—as well as all copies made at our command—who will gainsay us?" Kyrnill punctuated her question with a hard, cocky smile.

"I would like to know," began Ker Horlbar, one of the two ruling matrons of House Horlbar, "why this claim was brought against House Baenre in defiance of Lloth's peace?"

Several of the drow priestesses exchanged arch glances. The Horlbar clan depended upon agriculture for their wealth and position, and their chief rival in this pursuit was House Hunzrin. Lloth might declare peace, but her followers would still find a way to strive against each other.

"It is not my purpose to accuse the first house," protested Shakti, again rising to her feet. "This discovery goes beyond the ambitions of any single drow. It *may* be even more important than increasing the wealth and position of House Horlbar."

This barbed response brought a chorus of mocking laughter and some scattered applause from the assembled drow. Even some of the priestesses who had frowned when Shakti first rose to speak sent approving nods and long, measuring glances her way. The young female was not yet a high priestess, nor her mother's heir to House Hunzrin. In Menzoberranzan, power was not given, but seized. Any female willing and able to do so was worthy of serious consideration.

The discussion went on for some time. Triel listened as each priestess spoke, but no answer came to her. Even if her own house had not been involved, this discovery had more depth of possibility, more layers of danger and implication, than even a drow could fathom so quickly.

At last she turned to Zeerith Q'Xorlarrin. The regal female was renowned for her diplomatic skills and was often called upon to mediate in disputes between houses. Even now Zeerith sat serene amid the controversy. This situation would surely test even her fabled judgment.

"What do you say on this matter, Matron Zeerith?" Triel demanded. She was confident the matron's judgment, although seemingly impartial, would honor the long-term alliance between houses Xorlarrin and Baenre. "Speak, and we will accept your counsel as if it came from the mouth of Lloth."

The matron rose. "Clearly, we need to know more about this human artifact. Since it is an instrument of magic, I suggest it be entrusted to the collective masters of the Sorcere. Only the mage school has the resources needed to study and reproduce such an item. They will do so, of course, under the close supervision of the Ruling Council. Until a decision is made, we must keep this knowledge from the common folk. I say any priestess who speaks of this amulet outside of this room, except to the master wizards of the Sorcere, will be punished by the Ruling Council and suffer loss of rank and honor, with the threat of worse to follow when Lloth's peace is revoked."

Most of the drow nodded, silently accepting Matron Zeerith's decree.

"Now, as to the young novice who started all of this," continued Zeerith unexpectedly. "By the decree of Lloth, no priestess can slay another. It seems to me that Liriel Baenre has not yet reached that status, and she is therefore not protected by the Spider Queen's decree. Furthermore, Liriel Baenre has shown herself to be a wizard of considerable power, yet she has not submitted to the mind-search tests required to determine her loyalty to Lloth. For both these offenses, I call for her death. That is my decision, and, by the word of Matron Triel, it is the will of Lloth."

This decree, so unexpectedly harsh from the subtle, conciliatory Xorlarrin matron, sent a ripple of dark murmurs through the room.

"No."

The single word shocked them all into silence. Sos'Umptu Baenre, the usually reticent keeper of the Baenre chapel, walked to the center of the room. She stood before the altar and faced them all, her slender form rigid with certitude. "No," she repeated. "This is *not* the will of Lloth."

Triel rose from her throne, shaking with wrath. She was not happy with Zeerith's sentence, but she had pledged before all the powers of Menzoberranzan to follow the Xorlarrin matron's advice. Her authority had already been sadly undermined by this whole affair, and the unexpected defiance of loyal Sos'Umptu was more than the beleaguered young matron could bear.

"You defy me?" she raged, bearing down upon her younger sister. "How is it that the Queen of Spiders speaks to you, against the wisdom of your own matron mother?"

"Lloth speaks to us all," Sos'Umptu said stoutly. The priestess turned and pointed to the magical image of Lloth, the shapeshifting spider that hovered over the altar. The priestess waited until the illusion shifted to the form of a drow female. "Look at her face."

For the first time Triel noticed the illusion's striking resemblance to her errant niece. There was no way she could miss it now, for the eyes of the drow female were no longer the glowing crimson typical of dark elves. They were a strange, very distinctive shade of amber. And the lips of the magical image were curved in a smile of dark amusement.

All those who had seen Liriel Baenre recognized the significance of the transformation, and whispers spread the meaning of this manifestation to all present.

"We serve the Lady of Chaos," Sos'Umptu said softly, pointing to the golden-eyed image before them. "For good or ill, Liriel Baenre has found the favor of Lloth. Remember the words of Matron Hesken-P'aj: those who find other ways to extend Lloth's reign will be rewarded. Perhaps Liriel has found such a way. What this new magic will bring us, we cannot yet know. But see before you the will of Lloth, and go your way in peace."

* * * * *

The meeting ended soon after Sos'Umptu's pronouncement, and the priestesses of Menzoberranzan slipped away into the darkness.

Zeerith Q'Xorlarrin, the matron mother of House Xorlarrin, was one of the first to leave the Baenre compound. She pulled the curtains of her slave-carried litter shut and settled back against the cushions. Only then did she give vent to her emotions, hissing curses against

House Baenre and its three generations of female fools.

She had gone to war at old Matron Baenre's side, and she was still seething over what had occurred in the tunnels beneath Mithril Hall. Auro'pol, the matron of the powerful House Agrach Dyrr, had been killed by a creature of the Abyss at the command of the former Baenre matron. The war itself had been disastrous, but it was the death of Auro'pol—which was most assuredly not sanctioned by Lloth—that convinced Zeerith Q'Xorlarrin the first house no longer deserved its position. Triel Baenre was due for trouble when Lloth tired of peace, of that Zeerith was certain.

In the meantime, there were certain things Zeerith could do. She had risked much with her harsh pronouncement: her informal and unspoken alliance with House Baenre, her reputation as a fair and impartial diplomat. She had been publicly rebuked in a most dramatic fashion, and that did not sit well with the proud matron. Yet she had not lost entirely. The new magic would be entrusted to the Sorcere, where seven Xorlarrin wizards served as masters. No house in Menzoberranzan possessed more wizardly might than Xorlarrin, and whatever secrets the wizards uncovered would be whispered in the ears of Matron Zeerith before they were revealed to the Ruling Council.

The opportunity for revenge against House Baenre was not entirely lost either. Perhaps no priestess of Lloth could move directly against young Liriel, but more drow died from poisoned daggers and wizardly spells than from the high priestesses' snake-headed whips.

Comforted by these pleasant thoughts, Matron Zeerith smiled and relaxed against the litter's silken cushions. She had a task in mind for her dear brother Kharza-kzad. By all reports, the old fool was unduly fond of his beautiful young student.

And why, thought Zeerith, should females alone bear the burden of sacrificing those nearest their hearts?

* * * * *

From the window of his dark study, Gromph Baenre watched the city stir to life. While most of Menzoberranzan slept, he often passed the hours this way, alone in his Narbondellyn mansion. He did not sleep—he had never been able to sleep—and now he relied upon the magic that kept him youthful to sustain his life without benefit of rest. During his first few centuries of life, Gromph had found ease and restoration in the deep, wakeful reverie that was his elven heritage. For many decades now, despite the formidable discipline of his magical training, the ability to enter this waking trance had eluded him. The archmage of Menzoberranzan had forgotten how to dream.

So he sat alone, filled with sullen wrath and seething with the endless frustration that defined his existence. His mood did not improve when the magical alarm on his Baenre house insignia began to pulse with a silent, insistent summons. It seemed his dear sister Triel finally required the pleasure of his company.

For a long moment, Gromph toyed with the idea of defying the summons. Yet he dared not. Triel reigned in House Baenre, and his life would be worth nothing if he incurred her wrath.

Not that his life was worth so very much now, Gromph concluded bitterly. For once not bothering to don the robes and cape that proclaimed his powerful office, the archmage spoke the words that would take him to House Baenre.

He found Triel pacing about the family chapel. She leaped at him, her eyes wild, and seized him by the forearms.

"Where is she?" the matron demanded. "Where have you hidden her?"

Gromph understood at once, for over his sister's head loomed the magical image of Lloth, crafted by his might and magic. The beautiful illusion smiled down at him with sardonic amusement in its golden eyes. *His* eyes, and those of his unexpectedly resourceful daughter.

The wizard pointedly disengaged the matron's grasping hands. "You might be more specific," he requested coolly. "There is no shortage of females in Menzoberranzan."

"You know who I mean," spat out Triel. "Liriel is not at Arach-Tinilith. You gave her permission to depart, and left me to look the fool. Tell me why she left, tell me where she is, tell me everything she has done!"

Gromph shrugged. "Liriel said only that she had personal matters to attend. It is not my custom to question the actions of a Baenre female."

"Enough!" shrieked the priestess. "There is no time for such games. Where is Liriel, and where is the artifact?"

There was a moment of stunned silence. "Liriel said nothing of an artifact," Gromph said slowly.

Triel believed him. The familiar, covetous expression on the wizard's face convinced her beyond doubt. Artifacts were rare, even in magic-rich Menzoberranzan, and it was unlikely Gromph would permit his daughter to possess such an item if he knew of its existence, and its dangerous power.

"Then you don't know Liriel has found a way to take drow magic to the Lands of Light," she stated.

Gromph shook his head slowly, more in wonder than in denial. "I did not know what she had, what she planned to do. Of course I would have taken it from her."

"And so you must," insisted Triel. "If you do not, the artifact will end up in the Sorcere, its secrets open to all. Find it and bring it here. You and I alone will share its power, to our personal benefit and to the glory of House Baenre."

"And what of Liriel?"

Triel shrugged. "Half of Menzoberranzan is seeking her. With or without your involvement, the girl is not likely to live out the day. No one will know whose hand dealt the blow, and it is better her efforts strengthen House Baenre."

"But what of that?" Gromph asked, gesturing toward the golden-eyed image of Lloth that loomed over the altar. "Seldom does Lloth speak so clearly. Surely it would be folly to ignore such a sign."

"Look again," Triel said dryly.

Even as she spoke, the image shifted and the eyes took on their usual crimson gleam. An instant later, they were amber once again.

Gromph understood at once. The Lady of Chaos delighted in pitting her followers against each other, not only for her own pleasure but in the belief that the strongest drow emerged from the struggle. Liriel might have found Lloth's favor, but that was no guarantee of a long, happy life.

The archmage did not hesitate. "It will be done," he agreed.

"What, no regrets?" Triel mocked him.

"Only that I did not act sooner, and alone," he said bluntly.

The matron smiled, recognizing the truth of his words. "That time is past, dear brother," she purred. "We have an alliance now, you and I."

She tucked her arm companionably into his and drew him out of the chapel. "We have much to discuss, for it has been an eventful night. Lloth has decreed the city be at peace so we might rebuild our strength. For now, House Baenre retains its rightful place, but we must shore up our defenses against the day this peace will end."

Gromph allowed his sister to lead him away. He knew Triel was manipulating him, appealing to his desire for power and influence. Yet as he strolled from the chapel, arm in arm with the deadly female, he knew the alliance would be a true one for as long as it benefited them both.

* * * * *

News of the meeting and its events spread fast, traveling from the great houses even into the humble homes and businesses of the Manyfolk district. Before the great timeclock Narbondel marked the beginning of the new day, nearly everyone in Menzoberranzan knew Lloth had declared a time of truce. No one knew exactly what to make of this, and throughout the city speculations and rumors were served up along with the morning meal.

In his tower chambers overlooking the Bazaar, Nisstyre pondered these new developments. On the one hand, the break in the constant, striving warfare promised better trade, and that was certainly good news for the Dragon's Hoard. But the merchant's real purpose, his life quest, would not be served if Lloth regained her full strength in Menzoberranzan.

He was not pleased when his lieutenant came to the door with news that a Hunzrin priestess demanded audience. Nisstyre had no desire to see any member of the Spider Queen's clergy. But before he could give the order to have the female sent away, she pushed past the lieutenant and strode into the room.

The priestess stood stiffly before his desk, her arms full of books. Nisstyre leaned back in his chair and took in the unpromising details: the purple-trimmed black vestments of a student priestess, the symbol of a minor house, and the fanatic expression on her pinched face.

"Yes?" he inquired. The single word managed to convey a staggering lack of interest or encouragement.

"I am Shakti of House Hunzrin. And you," hissed the priestess, "*you* do not worship Lloth!"

Nisstyre's coppery brows rose. "I take it the art of conversation is not among the subjects taught at Arach-Tinilith."

"You are also a wizard," Shakti continued, inexorable in her purpose. "A powerful wizard, yet you have not taken the test of loyalty to Lloth required by all who practice magic in this city. You stir up discontent among Lloth's faithful, and turn them to Vhaeraun, that so-called god of thievery. For any one of those offenses, you could be dipped in melted cheese and staked out for the scurry rats to devour!"

"Hmm," Nisstyre murmured appreciatively. He considered this scenario for a moment, no doubt tucking it away for future use, before he turned his attention fully upon his visitor.

"I will say this for you, priestess, you have a creative touch where torture is concerned. And yet," he added, leaning forward and fixing her with his unnerving black gaze, "some might call you unwise. Suspecting me of such power, you come here, to my place, to threaten me?"

"I'm here to do business," she corrected him. "I want you to hunt down a certain female. I will pay you well."

He waved away this offer. "Surely there is someone more suitable to the task than the captain of the Dragon's Hoard. The city does not lack for assassins and bounty hunters."

"You will notice I did not ask you to *kill* the female," Shakti said with careful emphasis. "I ask only that you find her and bring her possessions to me. What you do with her is entirely up to you, so long as she is not seen in Menzoberranzan again. Surely you can handle so simple a task."

"So could a mercenary band, at a much lower price. The city has many such bands. Go hire one of them."

"I cannot," she said reluctantly. "I cannot risk word getting back to any of the city's matrons. Lloth has forbidden one priestess to slay another."

"I begin to understand your dilemma," Nisstyre said with a touch of amusement. His reputation for handling questionable deals with great discretion had brought him many similar offers over the years. "How unpleasant for you, being forced to do business with a suspected heretic. But why me, especially?"

Shakti threw the books on his desk. "You sold these books. They tell of the surface world and are forbidden in the city!"

"So we're back to threats now," the merchant observed. "I must say, this is getting rather tiresome. Unless you have something interesting to offer me—"

"I offer you Liriel Baenre!"

Nisstyre received this announcement with a moment's silence.

"You needn't shout," he admonished the young priestess. He kept his face carefully impassive except for the faint, sardonic smile that curved his lips. "I admit the offer has a certain appeal, but of what practical value is a Baenre princess to a merchant band?"

Shakti put both hands on the desk and leaned in. "Liriel Baenre carries a magical device that could be very helpful in your work. It is a matter of much conflict among the priestesses of Lloth. I can say no more about it at this time, but bring it to me, and I will share its secrets with you."

"But you are a priestess of Lloth."

"That, and perhaps more." Shakti met his gaze squarely. "From time to time, a cleric of Lloth is sent into a rival church as a novice, to act as the eyes of Lloth. The Spider Queen permits this spying, and sometimes encourages it. It may be possible for a priestess of Lloth to work with those who follow Vhaeraun. Information can be spoken both ways, to the benefit of all. It is an enormous risk. I am willing to take it."

Nisstyre gazed at Shakti Hunzrin for a long time, weighing her sincerity and considering the immense value of her offer. He measured the hatred in her voice when she spoke Liriel's name, the fanatic gleam in her eye, and decided to accept the alliance. But, unlike the priestess, he was not willing to speak so openly, or commit himself to so dangerous a course.

"The Dragon's Hoard is famous for acquiring nearly anything, regardless of the cost," he said, choosing his words carefully. "I will get you your princess, but I warn you, the reward had better be worth the trouble."

"Trust me," she agreed grimly.

The concept was so ludicrous that both merchant and priestess burst out laughing.

Chapter 16

HUNTERS

lone in his study, Nisstyre pondered the strange alliance he had made. He had accepted Shakti Hunzrin's offer, not only to place a spy in Lloth's stronghold of power, but also to learn more about the magical device the priestess had mentioned. He thought he knew what this device might be.

The wizard thought back to the battle in the forest of Rashemen and the amulet he had taken as his sole prize. When his patrol did not return to Menzoberranzan with the amulet, Nisstyre had written off the entire excursion as a loss. Then came his meeting with Liriel and the recovery of his lost patrol. Nisstyre did not find the amulet on the bodies of the drow soldiers, nor on the two slain in the cavern, nor among the skeletal remains he had later recovered from the deepbat lair. He'd assumed the amulet was lost somewhere in the cave, perhaps even ingested by a dragazhar. Liriel's attention seemed to be focused entirely on her unknown foe, and on the need to ensure that this enemy did not follow her into the Underdark. It did not occur to Nisstyre that Liriel might have taken the amulet. Apparently, it should have.

The last person to possess the amulet had been an impossibly strong human warrior, a man Nisstyre had left to die in the forests of Rashemen. The drow wizard had assumed the amulet's magic caused the human's fierce battle rage. If that were so, what use could Liriel make of it, and why should the priestesses of Menzoberranzan should want it so desperately?

Nisstyre pushed back his chair and strode from his study. In all of the city, there was one drow who might have the answer to these questions.

* * * * *

Kharza-kzad Xorlarrin paced his room, frantic with worry and indecision. Zeerith Q'Xorlarrin, his younger sister and liege matron, had left him just moments before after a most disturbing interview.

Liriel, it seemed, had gotten herself into very serious trouble. The old wizard had been afraid something like this might happen to the impetuous young girl. To some extent, Kharza-kzad blamed himself. If he had understood more about his student's plans, perhaps he could have done something to avert this disaster. He knew Liriel had been to the surface, of course, and that she had acquired some new magic there. He had not imagined Liriel might have found a human artifact, and he would never have thought anything human-made could possess much power or cause such controversy.

To take drow magic to the surface! Kharza-kzad was staggered by the implications of such a thing. But that prospect, fearful though it might be, was not the thing that put the old wizard into a frenzy of grief and worry.

He excelled in the creation of magical wands, particularly those used for battle. His wands were the prized possessions of many a battle wizard, and hundreds of Menzoberranzan's enemies had fallen before his magic. Yet he himself, Kharza-kzad Xorlarrin, had never killed.

The old wizard was not sure how many drow could make such a claim, and he was quite certain few would boast of it. He had never really considered the matter before, never envisioned those who would fall before his wands of destruction. Now he rued his isolation, his dedication to his solitary craft. Had he witnessed a few battles, wielded just one of his own weapons, perhaps he would be better prepared to take the life of his student. For Matron Zeerith had ordered him to hunt Liriel down, take the amulet, and leave no trace of its former owner.

It did not occur to Kharza-kzad that he might refuse Zeerith's command. He was a drow of Menzoberranzan, a lowly male despite his power and his honorary position at the Sorcere, and he was bound by law to honor the will of a ruling matron.

The wizard's fingers, wizened and dry, clasped the grip of the wand tucked into his belt and he steeled himself for what must be done. Yet the familiar object felt foreign in his hand, as foreign as the dreadful task before him.

*　*　*　*　*

In a locked room in the Hunzrin fortress, shielded by magical wards to keep out the prying eyes of her kin, Shakti chanted the words of a clerical spell. It was risky to invoke Lloth in her cause, but if the goddess was not truly with her, Shakti preferred to know this now.

The young priestess had been one of the last to leave the Baenre chapel after that eventful meeting. House Hunzrin's humble rank had ensured that she had a seat near the back of the room, and she had lingered there to observe the other priestesses, to watch who exchanged conspiratorial glances and who stalked out scowling with rage. And in the shadows of the chapel she, Shakti Hunzrin, had seen what few of Menzoberranzan's priestesses divined: the true will of Lloth.

The enormous magical illusion, the shapeshifting spider-drow, looked out over the Spider Queen's faithful with golden eyes and the face of Shakti's hated rival. Yet when the chapel was nearly empty, the illusion shifted again, and the drow eyes flickered back and forth from amber to crimson. To Shakti, the message seemed clear.

The Lady of Chaos had rejected the death sentence that Zeerith Q'Xorlarrin had laid upon Liriel. In its place, a contest had been declared. Lloth's favor was a capricious thing, a prize awarded to the most resourceful and devious. At the moment, Liriel Baenre seemed to wear that crown. Shakti intended to take it from her.

So she chanted a prayer to the dark goddess of the drow, asking for a spell of invisibility to enshroud her servant. Ssasser, the dark naga, waited eagerly at her side. The snakelike creature was coiled before an ornate mirror, and the faint light from candle sconces set into the mirror's frame glittered on the naga's blue-scaled body. Eyes closed, Shakti chanted the final words of the spell. A hiss of unmistakable delight and triumph signaled that Lloth had answered her prayer.

197

Elaine Cunningham

Shakti opened her eyes: the naga was gone.

The priestess raised her pitchfork and waved it before the mirror. Instantly the image of the naga appeared in the glass. The creature's hideous face furrowed in a scowl, and its long thin tongue flicked out toward its reflection.

"Don't fret, Ssasser. But for this reflection, you're invisible," Shakti informed the naga. She knew better than to let the magic-wielding creature out of her sight entirely. The naga was a virtual slave to House Hunzrin, but it was as evil and treacherous as the drow it served. Ssasser would welcome a chance to slay a Hunzrin priestess; indeed, the sly creature began to slink away from the telltale reflection.

"Stay by the mirror, where I can see you," snapped the priestess. "Listen well: you will return to Liriel Baenre's home. Search the place for anything that will help you track her. Return to the Hunzrin compound with the information you gain. Then I will give you a pair of quaggoth to aid you in the hunt. When you kill Liriel and bring me her amulet, you will earn your freedom."

The dark naga's mirrored face brightened at this news. Quaggoth were huge, white-furred, bipedal creatures that looked like the impossible offspring of ogres and bears. They were not particularly intelligent, but they were fierce hunters, strong and cunning in battle. Some drow enslaved them as soldiers or guards. Ssasser loved to command, and with such troops he would surely accomplish the delightful task of slaying a female drow.

"Ssasser hear all that Shakti mistress say. Ssasser hunt now?" the creature implored.

At a nod from the drow, the naga darted toward the small tunnel that led out of the room and wound downward through the walls of the compound.

Shakti smiled, pleased by the dark naga's eagerness. She had a high opinion of the Dragon Hoard merchants, and her decision to work with Nisstyre was not made lightly. Still, there were other hunters at her disposal, and she was determined to put every one of them on Liriel's trail.

* * * * *

In the hills north of the village of Trollbridge, Fyodor of Rashemen crouched low behind a scattered pile of rocks and peered into a small cave. The sun was rising behind him, but the morning was chill and the rocky soil white with a late frost. The young warrior blew on his hands to warm them and settled down to watch and wait. He had hunted for days; now for the first time, his quarry was within sight.

A spark flared in the depths of the cave, and then another. In moments a tiny campfire let off meager light. There was no smell of cooking meat, but that did not surprise Fyodor. The drow, it would seem, ate their food raw. He had followed these three through the forest, and more than once he'd come across game they'd recently slain. Although he had never lost their trail, not once did Fyodor see the remnants of a campfire. He was rather surprised the dark elves risked one now. Of course, daylight was coming, and a small fire, lit for warmth in this cave on a remote hillside, was unlikely to be spotted.

Before the arrival of each new day, the drow found shelter from the sun. The rough countryside was studded with caves, but this was the first time Fyodor had actually found their hiding place. He'd hunted the drow for days now, starting in the Underdark cavern strewn with the bodies of giant bats and dark elf warriors. Something about the battlefield disturbed him; what exactly, he could not say. He had searched the bodies of the two slain drow and had not found the amulet on either. This did not surprise him, for surely the survivors would take such a treasure with them. So he had followed the bloody footsteps of the three surviving drow to a steep tunnel that led him up into rugged, rocky hills. The drow headed west, traveling throughout the night with speed that Fyodor, following their trail by day, could barely match.

But now his time had come. When the drow emerged from the cave with the coming of night, Fyodor would claim his amulet, or he would die.

*   *   *   *   *

The dark naga cowered in a corner, wary despite the spell of invisibility hiding him from view. Ssasser had slipped into Liriel's castle as he'd done before, easily overcoming the trapped door by swallowing the crossbow-fired dart. He did not fear the servants that tended the drow female's abode, for his servitude to the Hunzrin family had purchased him a considerable amount of magic. But the powerful being in the Liriel's study was far beyond the naga's strength.

Gromph Baenre, the most famed wizard in the city, was seated at his daughter's table. Books were scattered about his feet, and his face was fixed in a fearsome scowl.

His long black fingers moved through the gestures of a spell, and he muttered arcane words with the precision earned by great power and much practice. Ssasser paid little heed to the gestures—since the naga lacked hands, such knowledge would do him little good—but he listened carefully to the spell and repeated it to himself silently, several times, until he was certain he had it right.

So intent was the creature on his stolen lesson that he did not at first notice the result of the spell. Smoke flowed into the study, seemingly from the carved stone walls. The cloud tugged free of the wall and formed into a drow statue of living stone.

"I can find nothing of value here," the wizard said, waving his hand impatiently over the piles of discarded books. "Find the girl's servants and see what you can learn from them about her whereabouts."

The golem bowed and strode from the room, its feet clicking with every step. Ssasser shrunk back beyond the reach of those stone boots, then slithered forward eagerly to see what the archmage might do next. Seldom did the naga have the chance to observe such a powerful wizard, and the creature hoped Gromph might demonstrate another spell.

But the drow wizard did not oblige. He ran his hands through his long white hair in a gesture of supreme frustration; then he sat in silence, deep in his own thoughts. At length he took a small book from a pocket of his glittering cloak and, after flipping through a few pages, he tossed it onto the table.

"I cannot do this alone," he murmured to himself, "not even with a copy of the spellbook I gave her. Using these gates, Liriel could be nearly anywhere. I cannot leave the city myself. And yet, can I trust such spells to another wizard?"

Gromph rose and began to pace the room. "No," he concluded at length. "If I cannot find the girl before she learns of her danger and flees the Underdark, she is lost to me, and her magic with her."

A clatter arose from the floor below. The scream of a halfling slave came to them clearly, a wail of pain that quickly faded into an earnest babble of words. The wizard smiled and strode from the room to see what information his stone servant had extracted from Liriel's maidservant.

The invisible naga slithered with frantic haste toward the table.

His fanged maw opened wide and he lunged for the precious book. He swallowed it, gulping several times to speed its way down his gullet toward the safety of an internal organ that housed, at the moment, two spell scrolls, several vials of poisons and potions, a small mithril axe, a rather nice dagger, and the crossbow dart he'd recently swallowed. Ssasser could regurgitate any one of these items at will. For good measure, the naga swallowed a large map of the surface world. With this, he would convince his Hunzrin slavemistress he had the knowledge needed to track down the renegade female.

The spellbook he would keep as his reward, and his secret.

* * * * *

Far from the tumultuous drow city, Liriel skipped lightly through the dark passages of the Underdark. She was tired but supremely happy. Now that the Windwalker amulet was in her hands, enspelled to hold the unique magic of the Underdark, she would return to Arach-Tinilith to hone her powers in preparation for her journey into the Lands of Light. The years of training ahead did not seem so long now, or the burden of her clerical studies quite so heavy. She wished, fleetingly, that there was someone with whom she could share her success. But that was not the way of the drow, and Liriel's spirits were too high for her to entertain regrets over something that could never be. The young drow conjured the gate that would take her back to Spelltower Xorlarrin and, with a sigh of satisfaction, she stepped into the portal.

Kharza-kzad was there to greet her, but he did not seem his normal fussy self. The wizard stood tense and still. His sparse hair, which usually stood in wild disarray, had been neatly combed, and even the wrinkles in his face seemed less pronounced. He seemed strangely determined, oddly composed.

"Do you have any idea what you have done?" he said in a tight, mournful voice.

Liriel froze, momentarily stunned by the realization that Kharza had somehow found her out. But of course she could get around the wizard; she had charmed him into her way of thinking many times before. "Of course I know what I've done! It's quite marvelous, actually. I've found a way—"

"You've signed your death warrant, that's what you've done!" he interrupted. "Are you so naive you think the rulers of Menzoberranzan would allow you to wield such power? What drow would not kill to possess this ability for herself?"

The girl blinked in puzzlement. Few of Menzoberranzan's drow ventured into the Underdark, other than the patrols ordered to keep the surrounding tunnels clear of enemies. Few dark elves shared her curious nature, her love of adventure and exploration for its own sake. And certainly no one wanted to travel the Lands of Light on a quest for knowledge, in search of a rune of power. For that matter, what drow of Menzoberranzan knew of rune magic? It was by purest happenstance that she herself had pieced together the story of the Windwalker. No one could know what the amulet meant to her, or what it could do.

Understanding came to her quickly. Of course they could not know! The drow no doubt believed the amulet was like most magical items in the city, that the mere possession of it by a wizard or priestess of sufficient power would be enough to unleash its spells! No wonder Kharza said many would kill for it!

"But the amulet would do them little good! Its magic is not like anything we know," she said earnestly. "Let me explain—"

"Don't," Kharza said bluntly, abruptly raising both hands in a silencing gesture. "The less I know about this amulet, the better my own chances of survival."

Liriel's eyes dropped to the battle wand in her tutor's right hand, then lifted slowly to his resolute face. The truth struck her: Kharza meant to kill her.

The wizard took a step closer, his empty hand stretched out toward her and his wand held back and low, like a ready sword. "The amulet must go to the Sorcere for study. Give it to me now."

Her hand closed around the tiny golden sheath that hung over her heart. She tried to speak and found she could not, so dry was her throat and so tight the pain in her chest. Liriel had suffered many betrayals in her young life, but none had come upon her more unexpectedly than this. She knew that Kharza, in his own way, cared about her, perhaps more than anyone ever had before. She had come to rely on this, and something approaching trust had developed between them. But among drow, trust invariably brought betrayal. Liriel recognized the depth of her folly and accepted her punishment.

With the courage and defiance expected of a dark-elven noble, the girl lifted her chin to meet death. Her fingers tightened around the amulet, and with her free hand she formed her final words in the silent language of the drow.

Strike now. The amulet will survive. You can pick it out of the ash.

Kharza-kzad lifted the wand and pointed it at her. They stood facing each other in tense, aching silence for many long moments.

Then, unexpectedly, the wizard swore a ripe oath and flung the magical weapon aside. "I cannot," he mourned.

Liriel watched in disbelief as her tutor's hands flashed through the gestures of a spell. A gate, a glittering diamond-shaped portal, appeared in the center of the room.

"You must leave Menzoberranzan," the wizard insisted, pushing her toward the shining door. "It isn't safe for you to remain here. Take your new magic to the surface and live there as best you can."

"But—"

"There's no time to argue. Go now."

Stunned into obedience, Liriel stepped toward the gate.

"Wait!" shrieked Kharza, lunging forward to drag her back. He mumbled to himself for a moment, busily ticking off the numbers to nine on his fingers.

"Just as I thought," he muttered. He seized a bellpull hanging on the wall and tugged at it urgently.

A male servant came in prompt answer to the summons. Kharza seized the drow and thrust him into the glittering gate. There was a flash of light, and the acrid smell of burned flesh filled the room as the unfortunate servant disappeared.

"Every ninth person through that gate is incinerated," Kharza-kzad explained absently. "As I have told you before, no magical portal is without protection and without danger."

The familiar, pedantic tone of her teacher's voice broke through Liriel's trancelike state of shock. She threw herself into the wizard's arms, and they stood together in a brief, desperate embrace. Neither was moved to speak, for there were no words in the drow language for such moments.

Kharza-kzad put her gently away. "Go now," he said again.

The young drow nodded and stepped toward the gate. She lifted a hand in farewell and disappeared into the shining magic.

The wizard's thin shoulders rose and fell in a heavy sigh. He turned away, his movements slowed by the unfamiliar weight of sadness and loss, leaving the gate to fade in its own time. As he did a stray bit of metal caught his eye. Ever tidy, the old drow bent to pick it up. It was a brass wristband, embossed with the symbol of House Xorlarrin, and it was all that remained of the drow servant.

The wizard slid the bracelet onto his own wrist. It was too large for him, but he regarded the trophy with pride.

"How delightful," he murmured, turning his arm this way and that so the polished brass sparkled in the candlelight. "I managed to kill someone, after all."

Chapter 17

WEAPONS

’m so delighted to have found you still here. I rather thought you’d have run to the safety of the Sorcere by now.”

Startled, Kharza-kzad whirled to face his unwelcome visitor. As his eyes settled upon the copper-haired drow—who was sprawled with insolent ease in Kharza’s own chair—the wizard bitterly cursed the day he’d started trading with the merchant. Once again Nisstyre had slipped into Spelltower Xorlarrin, using the gate they had established many years ago for that purpose, without invitation or permission. It had become a frequent, disturbing practice.

“What do you want?” Kharza-kzad demanded.

The merchant smiled and propped his feet up on the study table, paying no heed to the pile of scrolls dented by his boots. “No more than any other drow in the city. I want Liriel Baenre’s amulet.”

The wizard willed himself not to let his eyes slide to the faint, nearly faded outline of the gate that had taken Liriel to safety.

“I’ve no idea how rabble like you heard such news, but it will do you little good,” he said with a good deal more bravado than he felt.

Even flushed with the excitement of his first kill, Kharza-kzad had no real wish to raise his battle wands against another wizard. He knew success in battle involved more than might of arms and magic; it required instincts he himself had never tested, much less developed. His best chance of avoiding such a conflict, he believed, would be to utterly discourage the merchant wizard.

"By the word of the Ruling Council, the amulet was taken to the Sorcere for study," Kharza said, deliberately invoking all the powers of Menzoberranzan. "Unless you plan to apply as a student there, it's well beyond your reach."

"I think not," Nisstyre said calmly, ignoring the older drow's insults. "Somehow I doubt the amulet has made its way to the Sorcere. You are here, after all. And, if I am not mistaken, awaiting a visit from your student."

"Such a visit would be welcomed, but it is unlikely. Liriel is at Arach-Tinilith," lied Kharza-kzad.

"Not so, I'm afraid. My sources at Arach-Tinilith assure me Liriel is hiding somewhere in the city, or in the Underdark nearby. Or perhaps," the merchant said slowly, "she has already escaped into the Night Above."

Nisstyre rose to his feet and bore down upon the wizard. "Tell me what you know," he hissed.

In response, the Xorlarrin wizard snatched a wand from his belt. If ever he'd had any compunction over killing, it did not show now in his hard, narrowed gaze. Blue fire sizzled down the length of the weapon and hurtled in a ball of light and power toward the copper-haired merchant.

To Kharza's astonishment, the fireball passed right through Nisstyre's body and struck the far wall of the chamber. It exploded silently, showering the carpet with bright sparks. The fire caught, and flames licked upward at the walls. A priceless tapestry hanging there began to smolder and smoke.

Kharza realized the Nisstyre standing before him was no more than a magical projection. The younger wizard's true body was elsewhere, perhaps far from Menzoberranzan, more likely in this very room. Kharza whirled, looking frantically for his enemy, but there was no other sign of the red-haired drow.

"Do you have the courage to join me in the open?" mocked Nisstyre's image. "Or shall the two of us raze Spelltower Xorlarrin to its foundation?"

So it had come to this: he had no choice but to fight. Strangely enough, Kharza-kzad felt none of the fear he'd expected. A surging elation swept through his ancient frame, and he glared steadfastly at the projected image of his nemesis.

"I am ready," he said simply. "You have only to choose the site."

"It is chosen, and I await you." The magical projection extended one slender, apparently solid hand. "Give me a personal item, a ring or some such, so I might attune the portal to you."

Kharza-kzad did not consider this demand unreasonable, for he knew magic gates had an endless variety of requirements. Some demanded an offering of gold or gems, others granted transport only at certain times, still others required spells or rituals. He had not heard of a need for attunement, but it was not inconceivable. So he stripped a gold and onyx ring from his finger and dropped it into the outstretched hand.

At once the Xorlarrin wizard felt the magical swirl of a teleportation spell surround him, carrying him off with a rush of power and movement such as he had never experienced. Kharza had seen little need for magical portals in his long life. He could summon a mere five or six, and on only one occasion had he used one himself: the brief trip from Liriel's room at Arach-Tinilith to Spelltower Xorlarrin. Of course, he knew enough about general magical principles to help Liriel practice the gate spells in her new book, but he had not bothered to copy any of the spells or learn them himself. He regretted that now, for this new experience was exhilarating beyond words.

Suddenly he felt solid stone beneath his feet, and he found himself in a vast, uninhabited cavern. As he looked around in awe, the wizard realized this was his first time out of Menzoberranzan. Under less dire circumstances, he would have been fascinated by the wild stone landscape, untouched by magic or artifice, and by the seething pool of melted rock that bubbled and spat far below him.

Kharza-kzad shot a glance upward. His eyes were not accustomed to such distances, nor was his mind equipped to register them. But he perceived high overhead a distant light, a brilliant snatch of blue that could only be the sky of the Lands Above. Nisstyre, it seemed, had chosen the heart of a live volcano for their confrontation. So be it, thought Kharza, and he steeled himself for the fight to come.

"Show yourself," he shouted. "Let it begin!"

In response, a bolt of liquid stone rose from the pool and shot toward him. Kharza crossed his forearms before his face and spoke a single word of power. A rounded shield, glimmering black but as transparent as glass, sprang up between him and the onrushing lava. The glowing stone hit the magical shield with a tremendous hiss, cooling instantly to become a solid wall of protection.

With insolent ease, Kharza cast a spell that shattered the wall into pebbles and dust. He stood there, his arms crossed and a faintly bored expression on his wrinkled face.

Mocking applause echoed through the cavern, and Nisstyre stepped into view. The copper-haired wizard stood on the far side of the lava pool, on a ridge of rock roughly on eye level with his foe.

"I believe the first round is a draw," he conceded with a slight bow.

"And the second will be mine," Kharza assured him. The wizard took a sticky pellet from a hidden pocket of his robes and hurled it high into the air. The pellet exploded, and what had been merely a wad of spiderweb expanded into gray lines of magical force. Sticky tendrils shot off in all directions, seeking solid stone and quickly finding purchase. In less than a second the entire cavern was enmeshed in a giant, shadowy web. The web trembled far over the heads of the wizards, like a giant canopy. A large sticky drop slowly broke free to fall with a hiss into the lava pool below.

Nisstyre's face, which glowed red in the darkness of the cavern, paled nearly to gray as the web of shadows magically stole his body's warmth. His features registered the pain of the bone-deep chill, and his hands moved with agonizing slowness as he formed the gestures of an answering spell.

The Xorlarrin wizard did not wait for the attack; he chanted the words of a summoning. Giant spiders appeared at his command and scurried across the sticky gray web toward their assigned prey. They slipped through the strands and began to descend on silvery threads toward Nisstyre.

"A fit death for a heretic!" exulted Kharza-kzad as the venomous spiders, so beloved of the Lady of Chaos, closed in.

"Do you really fight for the honor of Lloth?" sneered Nisstyre.

The younger wizard's hand swept slowly forward in a menacing arc, not at the spiders, but at the web itself. Kharza had expected this to come sooner or later, for only a magical attack could dispel the web. To his astonishment, the copper-haired wizard unleashed not a pulse of fey energy, but a bolt of simple fire.

Simple, but effective. Flames raced along every strand, setting the entire web ablaze. The web of fire was a glorious, dazzling sight, and Kharza marveled as he beheld it. It was also, he conceded, a brilliant strategy. The heat and the punishing light of the fire forced him to deal with the burning web. This would give his enemy time to marshal his own magical strength, to recover somewhat from the magical chill. Fortunately, Kharza was well prepared for the task.

Shielding his eyes with one hand against the brilliant light, the wizard drew a fist-sized obsidian sculpture from a pocket of his robes. As was befitting of a master of the Sorcere, he possessed an Amulet of Plelthong, an ancient and powerful drow device that commanded many attacks and defenses. Kharza spoke the words that would unleash the needed force. He raised the amulet—the graven face of a smiling drow wizard—and pointed it toward the flaming web.

The obsidian lips pursed, and the drow-shaped amulet spat a stream of cold blue light upward. The magic expanded, becoming a cone of power that engulfed the fire and extinguished it. The web remained, but it was blackened and brittle. The charred bodies of the spiders dangled and swayed for a moment, then fell toward the waiting lava.

Kharza allowed himself a smile of triumph and just a moment's celebration. Too long: a black dart sped toward him and pierced his uplifted hand. His priceless amulet was knocked from his grasp to roll amid the common stones.

The wizard let out a shout of pain and outrage, but he had learned the danger of hesitation. Without bothering to pull the needlelike dart from his hand, he snatched a wand from his belt and pointed it upward.

As he had anticipated, two more of the death darts had taken flight, and yet another was in Nisstyre's hands. The merchant wizard did not hurl the final dart. He mockingly lifted it to his lips and tossed it into the air as if throwing a kiss. He did not bother to aim, and he did not need to. Magically enspelled to seek out their target, the long black weapons circled the cavern and swooped toward the Xorlarrin wizard like birds of prey.

Kharza squeezed the grip of his wand once, twice, and then a third time. He held the wand steady in case its fourth and final attack was needed. But his aim was true, and three globes of light flew to meet the incoming darts. The wizard summoned his natural power of levitation and rose at a sharp angle, putting as much distance between himself and the coming impact as he could.

Elaine Cunningham

The globes struck the death darts and exploded, one after another, in spectacular bursts of greenish light. Acid spat from the globes, corroding the black metal and sending droplets of green acid and liquid metal to the ledge where Kharza had stood an instant before.

But the Xorlarrin wizard was safely beyond the lethal shower. Floating high above the battle, he threw back his head and let out a laugh of pure exultation. What wonderful power, what delightful destruction, his creations unleashed! He had possessed these marvelous toys all these many years and never enjoyed them!

Nisstyre observed his enemy's pleasure and took note of his growing confidence. He allowed Kharza his moment, knowing it would soon end. All was going as he, Nisstyre, had planned. The copper-haired wizard had studied Kharza-kzad well, and he had anticipated the older wizard's every attack and parry. He knew the Xorlarrin wizard was a master of battle magic and tactics, and he'd gotten to know Kharza well enough to suspect that the isolation of study, the focused effort needed to craft wondrous weapons of destruction, had left dangerous blind spots in Kharza's education. Xorlarrin might be a master of magic and convoluted drow logic, but he did not have a fighter's instinct for the terrain. The simpler the attack against such an opponent, the better its chances for success.

So thinking, Nisstyre unleashed his next spell. At his command the air of the cavern began to stir, to gain force and momentum. Before the levitating Kharza could react, a mighty wind caught him in midair and flung him still higher, into the waiting arms of the web of shadows.

The fire had thinned and blackened the web, but no physical force could destroy its magic. The Xorlarrin wizard struck the sticky strands and was held there, bouncing slightly and facing the pool of lava. His eyes darted toward Nisstyre; the younger wizard's hands flashed as he formed a spell that would destroy the web. Kharza knew it well, and he understood the danger he was in. His natural ability to levitate had been exhausted. Once freed from the web, he *might* be able to cast a spell of levitation before he fell to his death. He was not sure; he had no idea how long it took one to fall such a distance.

Kharza-kzad had not long to decide, for his pounding heart beat perhaps thrice before the other wizard finished the dispellment, and then he was plummeting toward the deadly pool. The old wizard could see only one chance of survival, and he took it. As he fell, his fingers

closed upon another wand, his greatest creation and his deepest
secret.

It was Nisstyre's turn to laugh now as he watched his rival splash
into the pool of molten rock. He had planned this battle, step by step,
and he had also prepared a spell that would fish the old drow's bones
from the lava. He'd doubted from the beginning that a live Kharza-
kzad would willingly yield up any useful information, but there were
ways of compelling a spirit to speak truth. Soon he would know everything the wizard had learned about Liriel Baenre and her amulet, and
he would be well on his way to possessing both.

Nisstyre's laughter died abruptly. Something was stirring in the
pool of lava. Some dark shape was breaking free of the bubbling surface. As he watched, stunned, the skeletal form of a drow rose slowly
from the molten rock. All flesh had been melted away by the lava, but
the wizard's robes—and presumedly all the magic they contained—
had survived intact. Nisstyre did not know how Kharza-kzad had done
it, but he knew what the old drow had become.

Kharza-kzad was now a lichdrow, a dark-elven wizard who existed
beyond death, beyond the limitations of mind and body. Invulnerable,
nearly invincible, the undead creature could cast at will all the spells
gathered throughout its centuries of life.

The lichdrow soared upward, pausing only upon becoming eye-
level with its dumbfounded enemy. It raised a skeletal hand. Clasped
in the bony fingers was a slender metal rod, still glowing with the
lava's borrowed heat.

"My finest creation," announced the undead wizard in a whisper
as dry as desiccated bone. "A wand of lichdom. Would you care to see
it demonstrated again—on you, perhaps?"

Nisstyre was terribly outmatched, but even now he was determined to have the final word. He clasped a ring of teleportation that
would take him from this place, and he painted a mocking smile on his
face.

"Perhaps several centuries from now, when I have witnessed
Vhaeraun's triumph and have grown tired of life, I might be tempted
to accept your offer. When that time comes, I will no doubt find you
still here."

And with those words, the merchant summoned the magic that
would take him out of the volcano and beyond reach of the lichdrow
Xorlarrin.

In time, the former Kharza-kzad might find his way back to

Menzoberranzan, but Nisstyre knew the wizard had few gate spells at his command. He'd made sure—or at least, as reasonably certain as one drow could be about the secrets of another—that Kharza knew no way back into his own Spelltower. At the present, therefore, Nisstyre felt safe enough in returning to the city.

He might not have gotten the information he needed from Kharza, but there was another drow in Menzoberranzan who knew more about Liriel's plans than she would admit. It was time to get seek out his new partner.

*   *   *   *   *

Shakti Hunzrin had just returned to Tier Breche when the summons came. Along with a dozen other high-level students, she was attending a tutorial session on accessing the lower planes and conversing with its denizens. The subject held little interest for Shakti; indeed, after the events of the last few days, all of her studies at Arach-Tinilith seemed no more than a dreary anticlimax. She would have welcomed almost any interruption.

Almost.

Eight armed female guards—part of the elite forces of House Baenre—came to the very door of the classroom and respectfully commanded Shakti to accompany them. With them was a driftdisc, the floating magical conveyance used by the most powerful of matrons and priestesses. Shakti had never expected to ride on one, and she took little pleasure in it now as she glided in state toward the Baenre fortress, surrounded by her prestigious escort. For in sending a driftdisc, Matron Triel was not honoring her guest but blatantly displaying her own might and position. To Shakti, it seemed the logical first step toward a very public execution. Lloth might have decreed no priestess kill another, but the Baenre clan always seemed to be beyond law.

Her prospects did not brighten when they reached the Baenre fortress. She was ushered into the very heart of the first house—the vast chapel. Gromph pushed past her at the door, looking grim and sullen. Shakti understood why at once: eight Baenre priestesses gathered about the altar. A dark rite would be performed in this chamber that no mere male could witness.

Matron Triel beckoned Shakti to come toward the altar. As the younger priestess drew near, the matron slowly raised her arm. In it was a whip armed with the heads of two angry, writhing snakes.

"Lloth knows what is in your heart," Triel said in her cold, even voice. She began to advance, slowly, a glint of mocking pleasure in her usually unreadable eyes.

At that moment Shakti understood the Spider Queen had witnessed her deal with Nisstyre and had informed the First Matron of her treachery. Because there was nothing else to do, Shakti stood awaiting the first lash of the whip. To her utter astonishment, the Baenre matron turned the whip and offered it, handle first, to the younger drow.

"By the command of Lloth, you are to be elevated to high priestess. This whip will be yours. Ascend the altar for the rite of atunement."

Not without fear, Shakti did as she was commanded. She had witnessed the rite, which was usually administered after the graduation ceremonies. It was not a sight for the fainthearted. But she would have undergone the rite gladly, had she trusted Triel to actually go through with it.

For once, the Baenre matron kept her word, and the circle of priestess enacted the ritual that attuned the weapon to the emotions of its sole wielder.

Much later, the eight priestesses helped Shakti down from the altar. The living snakes that had bound her there slithered off into the shadows, but for the three which had been magically added to the whip. Shakti admired her new weapon with a mixture of pride and awe. Five heads! Few priestesses commanded as many, and such a whip was a sign of Lloth's highest favor.

Triel dismissed the other priestesses with a wave of her hand and then motioned Shakti into a seat.

"We must now talk about your future," she said bluntly. "You need not return to the Academy, except to attend the graduation ceremonies when the time comes. You are free to attend your family business, bearing the full rank and honor of a high priestess. If that business takes you from Menzoberranzan from time to time, so be it. House Baenre and House Hunzrin have worked together in the past. We will do so again, as never before, to the glory of the Queen of Spiders."

The hidden meaning in Matron Triel's words begin to dawn on Shakti. She was supposed to serve House Baenre as a traitor-priestess! From time to time the matriarchy uncovered a spy among

213

the clergy—usually a male priest—who served Lloth on the surface, Vhaeraun underneath. The reversal was almost unknown, and the prospect of gaining such a double spy clearly had Triel salivating with dark glee.

Shakti absorbed this, and again glanced at the snake-headed whip tucked in her belt. Lloth was courting her. *Her!*

Triel continued to speak, outlining Shakti's mission with precise detail and an occasional threat, but the Hunzrin priestess did not hear the matron's words. Another voice, even more powerful, commanded her attention.

It was a whisper at first, a dark insinuating voice in her mind. Soft and seductive, the voice grew in power as it gave to Shakti spells of thought concealment. *Gave* them. Shakti knew beyond doubt she could cast the new spells at will, without rest or study.

These spells are but the first of my gifts. With them you can swear to Lloth, insisted the voice, *yet maintain first loyalty to me.*

The voice continued, giving promises of power, claiming immortality was his to give, even hinting he had not yet found a worthy drow consort.

Shakti had never prayed to Vhaeraun, but with awe she recognized the voice of the Masked Lord. The drow god was not only real, but he was also powerful enough to speak hidden words in Lloth's inner sanctum! And she listened, tempted, without incurring the Spider Queen's wrath. The mind shields of Vhaeraun were clearly more powerful than any that Shakti knew, for the snake heads, which would have turned at once upon a faithless priestess, continued to writhe companionably at her side. Spells such as these could mean the difference between life and death in Menzoberranzan, where every high priestess could read the thoughts of another.

Two deities, marveled Shakti, vying for her allegiance! This put her in an impossibly dangerous position, but it also offered her power beyond her darkest dreams. She might not survive, but she would not refuse.

* * * * *

Nisstyre's interview with Shakti Hunzrin did not go at all as he'd expected. She'd come at his summons readily enough, but she swaggered into his place of power with the whip of a high priestess on her hip.

The wizard carefully masked his fear. For centuries, Lloth's clergy had made a holy task of seeking out and destroying the followers of Vhaeraun. Shakti had no proof against him, but now that she was a high priestess a single word of accusation would be enough to have him flayed alive and hung in pieces from the various corners of Arach-Tinilith.

Well, accusations could be spoken both ways; she *had* offered to turn traitor-priestess.

"If you are sincere about your commitment to Vhaeraun, that thing will hardly endear you to the Masked Lord," the male said dryly, pointed at the writhing snake-headed weapon.

Shakti gave him a smile of supreme confidence. "Vhaeraun is with me," she said stoutly, and then she spoke a word of power that Nisstyre—himself a mighty wizard—had never heard. A dark shadow appeared, flitting around the room and then settling upon Shakti's face, taking the form of a half-mask of blackest velvet. The wizard recognized the manifestation of Vhaeraun, the Masked Lord.

As Nisstyre watched in stunned silence, the double priestess held out her hand, palm up. Cradled within it was a gem, a sparkling ruby about the size and shape of a drow's eye.

"This is but one of the Masked Lord's gifts to me," Shakti said with dark pleasure. "In turn, I give it to you."

Her velvet mask dissolved, reforming into the black shadow. The darkness flowed like smoke to engulf the wizard. Nisstyre's astonishment turned to terror when he realized he could neither speak nor move.

Shakti advanced upon him, the ruby in her outstretched hand. She pressed it to Nisstyre's forehead. With a searing hiss, the gem burned into his flesh and sank deep into his skull. The pain surpassed anything he had ever known or imagined. Only the steadying arms of his unseen, treacherous god kept him from falling to the floor.

At last the ordeal ended, and the white-hot pain in Nisstyre's brain dulled to a burning throb. Shakti smiled and ran her fingers over the part of the gem still exposed. "A third eye," she explained. "The ruby is attuned to a scrying bowl that will enable me to see whatever you see, even in the *Night Above*."

It was that term, more than anything, that convinced Nisstyre the drow god was truly with Shakti. Only the followers of Vhaeraun referred to the surface lands as the Night Above. The god had spoken with this priestess and had made her his own despite the weapons of Lloth she wielded. Which deity claimed Shakti's deepest allegiance,

Nisstyre could not know. That uncertainty made the priestess dangerous beyond reckoning.

"Wherever you go, my eyes will be upon you," Shakti continued.
"Through the power of the gem I can speak into your mind at will,
and I can inflict terrible pain. If you try to betray me, you will die,"
she announced with the newfound calm and confidence of the truly
powerful.

She settled into Nisstyre's own chair, pointed to a lesser chair, and
bade him take a seat. He did so, without any act of will on his own
part. "You have received the gift of Vhaeraun. Now it is Lloth's turn."

The wizard received this announcement with silent dread. If his
own god had made him a virtual slave to this female, what might the
Spider Queen do? Then came the second surprise: Lloth's gift was
information.

Shakti told him all she knew about Liriel Baenre's amulet, even
gave him copies of the notes the girl had written. The particulars of
the young wizard's experiments were not spelled out, but this much
was clear: Liriel's amulet was indeed the one Nisstyre had stolen from
the human warrior, and it gave her the power to take both her innate
drow magic and dark-elven wizardry into the Night Above.

Nisstyre received this news with an excitement that transcended
his pain and humiliation. This was the key he sought, the thing that
might lure the proud drow from their subterranean homeland! And if
this device could be duplicated, what wonders might he accomplish!
He envisioned an army of drow, a silent and invisible force sweeping
the surface lands. With such a thing, Vhaeraun's kingdom—and his
own reign—was virtually ensured.

The wizard looked into Shakti's glowing crimson eyes and saw
there a lust for power to equal his own. "The interests of Vhaeraun
and Lloth need not conflict," he ventured. When Shakti did not interrupt, he continued with more confidence. "You know what this amulet
could mean. If it falls into the hands of the matriarchy, it will only
increase their power, fuel the endless chaos. The city will continue
much as it has for centuries. But with such magic in *my* hands, I could
entice an army of drow to the Night Above. You are young; before you
end your second century of life this army could return and march to
your command. You could come to rule Menzoberranzan."

"And from Menzoberranzan, the Underdark," Shakti added confi-
dently. "The First Directive of Lloth has been ignored for too long.
Most drow will welcome the chance to conquer the Lands Below."

"I have many alliances on the surface world," the male continued. "Supplies, slaves, information—you will need all these things to accomplish your goals. The more power I have, the more assistance I can offer you."

The priestess nodded. "Your kingdom above, mine below."

Despite everything, it was a most satisfactory arrangement. Nisstyre smiled, and the sharp pain in the center of his forehead fled as they spoke the words that bound their pact.

* * * * *

Shakti hurried to her private chamber in the Hunzrin compound. She rapped sharply on the wall, and in response to her summons, the dark naga slithered up through its tunnels and into her room.

"What have you found for me?" she demanded.

The naga promptly coughed up a map of the surface world. When Shakti smoothed the scroll flat, the creature flicked out its long blue tongue, marking a spot near a large forest.

"Here be many caverns," hissed the snakelike mage. "Ssasser been there, *born* there. Close to surface, no radiation magic. Many time Ssasser see drow come through gates there. If drow female be wizard, then this way she might have gone. Ssasser take quaggoth fighters, travel through magic gate." The dark naga paused for a thunderous belch. He spat out a set of combs, beautiful, costly things made of the shells of giant Underdark turtles and studded with gems. "These Ssasser take from drow female's house. The quaggoth fighters get from them the female's scent, track her down."

It was a logical plan, but Shakti's nearsighted eyes narrowed in suspicion. The naga had received most of its magical training in House Hunzrin, and priestesses seldom used spells of teleportation. Through the power of Lloth they plane-walked, moving to the lower planes and back with ease, but they seldom had the wizardly skill needed to command the gates that took them from one place to another on the material plane.

"And where would *you* have gotten such a spell?" She did not wait for an answer. A simple mind-reading enchantment took the image of a spellbook from the naga's thoughts, and she ordered the creature to turn it over. Sheepishly, the naga hacked again and yielded up the stolen book. Shakti did not open it, for she knew better than to read unlearned spells.

217

"Let's see what you can do with it," she told the naga.

The creature nosed open the book and began to read the arcane symbols. But the needed gate spell was beyond its power; the dark naga whimpered with pain and curled into a writhing mass of looping coils.

Shakti sighed and yielded to the inevitable: she would once again have to hire the expensive wizard. She hated parting with more gold, and she simply could not afford to involve an outsider in her current plans. But what else could she do?

The naga, once he recovered from his spell-inflicted agony, was only too glad to go off to summon the drow mage. In the meantime, Shakti sent a servant to bring around a pair of mated quaggoths.

House Hunzrin kept and bred the bearlike creatures for use as guards and shock troops. Quaggoths were ideal for both. Seven feet tall, heavily muscled and protected by tough hide covered with thick white fur, the quaggoths were fearsome in appearance and were strong, fierce fighters. They also had an unpleasant surprise in store for anyone who managed to wound or anger them.

Shakti gave the creatures the combs Ssasser had pilfered from Liriel's home. The quaggoths had keen noses and were excellent trackers, provided she was able to set them in the right direction. It was time to test the power of Nisstyre's ruby.

The priestess took a small scrying bowl, as red and as black as dried blood, and placed it upon the map the naga had stolen. She cast the spell that would enable her to locate Nisstyre. Ssasser's map glowed, marking the spot where the drow wizard now stood. The naga had done his research well, for the glowing spot was in the caverns the snake-creature had named. Apparently Nisstyre held similar opinions concerning Liriel's destination.

When Ssasser returned with the wizard, Shakti handed the drow the spellbook and told him to open a gate near the spot marked on the map. Intrigued, the male leafed through the book until he found the proper spell. After a period of study, the wizard cast the enchantment. A shimmering oval appeared in Shakti's chamber.

"Will the gate close of its own accord, or does that require another spell?" she demanded.

"It will last only a few moments, then dissipate," the wizard assured her.

Shakti nodded approvingly, and the snake heads at her belt began to writhe in anticipation. The new high priestess seized her weapon, enjoying the feel of the cool adamantine handle in her hand, and she lashed out at the hired wizard.

The five snake heads dove in to fasten their fangs in his flesh. Numbing, burning pain coursed through the drow male. Unable to move, unable to cast a spell in his defense, he slumped to the ground. The sight drove Shakti into a frenzy of vicious delight, and she lashed at the defenseless wizard again and again.

When it was clear he was dead, Shakti tucked the weapon away. Her chest was rising and falling rapidly—more from excitement than from the effort of killing the male—but a rare expression of calm suffused her face. She felt sated by the wizard's death, utterly content for now but also eager to kill again.

"Take the male through the gate with you," she instructed Ssasser. When the naga hesitated, puzzled, she added, "You and the quaggoths might enjoy a snack before starting your hunt. Leave no trace of him for anyone to find."

The naga grinned fiercely and sank his blue fangs deep into the dead drow. Lifting his burden, Ssasser struggled to the gate and slithered through eagerly. But the quaggoths hung back, obviously leery of the unfamiliar magic.

Shakti seized her pitchfork and stabbed one of the reluctant creatures—the male, of course—in the backside. The quaggoth let out a roar of pain and plunged into the shining oval. His mate glanced at the glowering drow, then stepped through the gate without further hesitation.

Finally alone, the traitor-priestess placed her new weapons in a row, along with the magic pitchfork that had hitherto been her only claim to power. She admired them—the pitchfork, the snake-headed whip, the ruby scrying bowl of Vhaeraun—and debated which among them was her favorite.

It was pleasant exercise, for in truth she really did not have to pick, although the day might come when she would have to make such a choice. Until that day, Shakti intended to enjoy all her weapons, all her power, to the fullest extent.

Chapter 18

THE NIGHT ABOVE

fter his interview with Shakti, Nisstyre wasted little time in leaving Menzoberranzan. First he sent his merchants out of the city, not wanting any of them sacrificed to the double ambitions of the traitor-priestess, then took a relay of gates that led to his surface stronghold.

When Nisstyre emerged into the Night Above, the blinding intensity of a spring twilight was muffled by the leafy layers of a deep woodland canopy. Here the drow followers of Vhaeraun had built a settlement, above ground, that in small scale began to approach the glory the drow had known before they were forced Below. Among the trees were twisted, spiraled fortresses crafted of stone and magic, as wondrous as the homes in any elven city. The drow had little fear of discovery, for the High Forest held a thousand other secrets.

As darkness approached, the drow began to emerge from their homes to go about the night's business. Most of the settlement's inhabitants were males: restless young nobles unhappy with their subservient role in traditional drow society, renegades from destroyed noble houses, ambitious warriors both noble and common who wondered why the drow did not yet rule all of the Underdark. They were all dark-clad in common garments, and as followers of Vhaeraun they practiced and celebrated the arts of stealth and thievery. Yet not one drow among them wore a *piwafwi*, and the changing of guards at the watchtowers was accomplished by ladders rather than levitation, for they had lost their heritage of natural magic. The drow were not what they once had been, but they were still to be feared.

There were few females in the village, and of them only two were drow. One of the Masked God's main directives was to increase the drow race, particularly on the surface. And so, unlike most drow, Vhaeraun's people sought contact with other elves. Children of such unions tended to breed toward drow. Taking a long view, it was one way to eradicate the pale races of elves!

Nisstyre took his god's instructions one step further: he kept a small harem of surface elves in the settlement. It was not ideal—Vhaeraun indicated there should be equality between males and females—but it was proving effective. With the coming of night, the village's children were awakening. They ran about in play, staging mock battles and elaborate games of stealth and ambush. There was not a full drow among them, but most of the ebony-skinned elflings were as drow in appearance and temperament as any child of Menzoberranzan. There were among them a couple of black-haired, pale-skinned elf children, even a dusky half-drow lad. The boy was tolerated in the community, for Vhaeraun was not averse to a little human blood in his followers. It was a matter of necessity, for few drow females were willing to follow the Masked God into the Night Above.

Not that any of the village females were all that devout. Most of them were silver elves, and without exception the elfwomen were wretched outcasts who for one reason or another had no other place to call home. It was, Nisstyre acknowledged, hardly an auspicious way to begin a kingdom.

Yes, the lack of drow females was a problem, one Nisstyre planned to end. With the inducement of Liriel's magic, he could entice more of the proud and powerful females into the Night Above. Drow tended to be far more prolific than other elves, and only their constant, incestuous warfare kept their numbers low. Once the drow became a united people, their strength would quickly reach nightmare proportions.

With this pleasant thought in mind, Nisstyre gathered together a band of hunters and summoned the settlement's ranking priest, a drow of middle years known only as Henge. The cleric made cautious comment on the ruby glowing in the center of Nisstyre's forehead.

"A third eye," Nisstyre said casually. "A wizardly device. You need not concern yourself with it." The priest looked doubtful but did not press the point.

"You must travel swiftly through the night toward the village of Trollbridge. Not to pillage," Nisstyre added swiftly, noting the fierce smiles on every face. "Travel to the hills surrounding the human village and search there for a lone drow female."

"Find a single drow, in that network of caves?" balked the priest.

"It should not be a difficult task. From what I know of Liriel Baenre, I cannot imagine her content with a hermit's life in some remote cave. She is armed with considerable magic and will be extremely difficult for the humans to capture and kill. I would prefer, of course, that you find her before she finds the humans. You will know her by an amulet she wears: a small golden dagger in a rune-carved sheath that hangs from a gold chain."

As he spoke, Nisstyre reflected upon how little prepared Liriel—or any female drow, for that matter—was for the world Above. The proud females could not begin to fathom the surface dwellers' hatred and loathing for the dark elves. Drow expected to be feared; they were not prepared to be despised and hunted. Downtrodden males, who had survived decades of miserable existence Below, fared somewhat better than their more privileged counterparts. Despite his confident words to his hunting band, Nisstyre knew the importance of finding the princess soon, before her pride and arrogance brought about her destruction.

So with a few quick words of instruction, he set the four fighters on Liriel's trail. He thought he knew where she might have gone. There were many gates the female might have used, for dark-elven wizardry had opened portals to distant places such as Calimshan. But the price for such incredible power was correspondingly high. The caverns near Drygully Tunnel were the easiest areas to reach through magical travel. They were open, near the surface, and had little interference from the Underdark's radiation magic. At short notice, it might have been the best anyone could do. He felt fairly certain Liriel would have fled using that route.

When the hunters were on their way, Nisstyre and Henge went to the privacy of the wizard's own home. Henge looked none too pleased with the task ahead but he kept his opinions to himself. Nisstyre took note of this and saw no need to comment. There was little liking between the two drow males, but as long as the priest did not openly defy him, Nisstyre was content.

The wizard took out a medallion embossed with a curving, stylized dragon. It matched the tattoo on the face of his lieutenant, Gorlist, and enabled him to find the drow fighter at any time. The wizard fingered the metal and chanted the words that would take him and the cleric to the fighter's side.

The pair of drow materialized in a small cave. There they found Gorlist, along with his two companions, strapping on weapons in preparation for the night's journey. The drow lieutenant did not look particularly surprised to see his leader.

"How long must we maintain this ridiculous facade?" he snapped. "It is effort wasted."

"Our plans have changed," Nisstyre said coolly. "You will retrace your steps toward the caverns with all possible haste. I have reason to believe you will find Liriel Baenre there or nearby. Find her, and bring her to the forest settlement."

Nisstyre noted the fierce gleam in the fighter's eyes and vowed to instruct Gorlist in the art of balancing revenge with necessity. He led the way out of the cave, stooping low to duck through the small entrance.

A rustle of leaves was his only warning. Nisstyre spun to see a black-haired human bearing down on him, his pale club lifted high and cold fire in his blue eyes. Although it seemed impossible to the drow wizard, he recognized his attacker as the crazed warrior whom he himself had buried alive in an icy tomb in a distant forest glade.

The drow raised one hand, and dark fire spat from his fingers to engulf the persistent human. The man's club swung right through the flame, arcing downward to meet the wizard's head.

Nisstyre heard the thud of impact, registered the way the rocky ground sped up to meet him. He suffered no pain and supposed he should be grateful, but all he felt was cold wrath. The wizard clung to this emotion as he went down into the darkness; he knew desire for revenge was a powerful force, perhaps the only one that would help him fight his way back.

* * * * *

Fyodor kicked aside the crumpled form of the copper-haired wizard and took in the scene before him in a glance. The heat of the berserker rage fueled his body and sped his mind, so it seemed as if the world slowed down around him, giving him time to react, to attack. In his altered state, Fyodor never felt pain, although he knew from the smell of singed leather that the drow wizard's bolt of dark fire had struck his shoulder. Nor did he feel fear, even though his mind coolly registered that he was outnumbered indeed by the three well-armed drow before him.

The first of the dark elves came on, twin blades in his hands and a cocky smile on his ebony face. As the drow advanced he put his weapons through an elaborate routine: crossing, spinning, slashing the air. The show was clearly meant to taunt and unnerve his victim, much as a barn cat might play with a captured squirrel. Despite the red haze of the battle fury that filled and possessed him, Fyodor could not help but note the drow's brilliance. Even perceived in slow motion, it was a dazzling display of swordcraft. The dark elf warrior possessed a finesse Fyodor could not begin to understand, a skill he could not hope to match.

But no fear came with this realization. The young berserker registered the drow's flailing arms, the trailing light of the enchanted weapons, and he reasoned there was a chest somewhere in the midst of all that activity. So Fyodor hefted his sword high, sighted down a spot in the very center of that incredible swordplay, and heaved with all his might. The mighty weapon flew toward the drow, its path as true and straight as that of a thrown spear.

Instantly the whirling elven blades crossed in a defensive parry, and the three swords met with a clash of metal and a spray of sparks. But the drow's skill and speed could not deflect the sheer power of the blow. The blunt sword tore through the dark elf with such force that the hilt's crosspiece struck his chest with an audible cracking of ribs.

Fyodor had his cudgel in hand before the first drow fell, before the other two could register the death of their companion. He advanced, compelled to fight until none remained to stand against him.

Perhaps the second drow fighter perceived this, for he was not so quick to draw his blades. He snapped up a tiny crossbow and fired several darts, one after another, so fast that the flights of the individual arrows were hard for the eye to follow. Perhaps the sleep-poison faded outside the Underdark, but the drow still possessed his deadly aim and he was confident his tiny arrows would dive deep into the human's eyes, tunnel between his ribs, slice open the vital arteries in his throat and groin. No poison, perhaps, but the human would be dead before he could notice that something about the attack might be lacking.

The drow could not know Fyodor perceived the flight of the darts as a leisurely, graceful glide. He batted them aside, moving his club back and forth with seemingly impossible speed, and he did not for one moment slow his advance on the two remaining fighters. A mighty upward sweep of his club caught the drow archer in his mid-section, first doubling him over and then sending him flying up and back. The dark elf fell heavily, several yards away, his body twisted into a position no living elf could have achieved.

Fyodor whirled upon the last drow—a short-haired warrior with a dragon tattoo emblazoned on one cheek—and raised his cudgel high for a smashing downward blow. With a quick, steady stride, the human advanced.

For the first time in his century-long career, Gorlist considered retreat. The moment passed quickly, and the drow fighter gripped his spear with both hands. He'd taken the weapon from a slain forest elf, and had it magically reinforced for strength and speed. This crazed opponent would test the weapon as it had never been tested before.

Gorlist snapped the spear up before him, holding it like a quarter-staff. He whirled it, once, in a defiant exhibition of his skill.

Once was all the time he had. The human's driftwood club descended in a pale blur. Gorlist spread his hands wide and blocked the blow with the center of the spear's staff. The magic held, but the force of impact sent bright pain coursing through the drow's arms and down his spine. His knees buckled, and he went down.

The dark-elven fighter saw the club descending again. He rolled clear, and as he did he grasped the hilt of a dagger in his benumbed fingers. With the incredible speed and agility for which the drow were famed and feared, Gorlist rolled several times and came up in a crouch behind the human.

He eyed his enemy, measured the distance between himself and the man's ankles. His enspelled dagger could easily cut through boot leather and sever the tendons beneath. Hamstrung, this human would not fight so well. Gorlist launched himself forward and delivered a vicious backhanded slash.

To his astonishment, the man's reactions were even faster than his own. The human fighter leaped and whirled in a single movement. With incredible timing, he jumped over the drow's lunging

225

attack and stomped down with both feet. Gorlist hit the ground hard, full length, and the human landed with him, a booted foot on each of the drow's kidneys.

And the proud drow, who scoffed at pain, let out a howl of pure agony. The human danced aside, and Gorlist saw the club arc down toward him again. Even if he'd been able to move, the weapon came too fast for him to avoid or deflect it.

Gorlist felt the shatter of bone as the club struck his rib cage. This time he did not cry out, but he took little pride in that accomplishment. There was no time for that, no time for thoughts of any kind. His head was jerked sharply to one side as the human hauled him upright by his hair.

Holding the slight drow easily at arm's length, the strange warrior took several strides forward. Gorlist's booted toes barely touched the ground, but he noticed the human looked much smaller at such close range. It was an odd thought, coming to him dimly through the pain of his many injuries, but Gorlist tucked it away. He had survived many fights and he had done so by knowing his enemies. It might help someday to know that this one was not the seven-foot warrior of first perception. And no matter how bad his hurts, Gorlist remained aware of the battlefield, and he suddenly realized what the human intended to do with him.

A few paces away was a steep ravine, with a fall of nearly ten feet to a shallow, rock-strewn creek. Gorlist knew the danger of such a fall. One of his broken ribs would almost certainly pierce a lung and bring upon him a slow but certain death.

Desperation gave strength to the battered drow. He seized the first weapon that came to hand: a tiny, thin knife tucked into the seam of his jacket sleeve. The drow brought it up and slashed across the man's chest. The coarse leather jerkin, the garment of a human peasant, deflected the cut as effectively as drow chain mail.

Frantically the dark-elven fighter slashed out with his meager weapon. He managed to connect a few times, scoring bloody lines across his captor's arms. Yet the human did not slow, did not register the pain by so much as a flicker of an eyelid. He merely took one hand from the drow's hair and seized the flailing wrist, easily crushing the bones and forcing the tiny knife deep into the fingers that gripped it. But Gorlist was beyond pain now, and he registered neither the ruin of his hand nor the sound of his knife falling to the rocky ground.

The man stopped and pulled Gorlist close, face-to-face, and then heaved him up and away. There was a moment's flight, and then came the punishing tumble down the rocky slope.

The drow came to sudden, jarring stop against a boulder in the center of the shallow creek. He tried dragging himself to shore, but the effort sent him into a spasm of coughing. Gorlist tasted his own blood, and knew any further effort was futile.

Almost gratefully, the drow sank into the stream. The icy water numbed his pain and swept him toward oblivion, toward whatever reward awaited the faithful of Vhaeraun.

* * * * *

When all was silent, Henge, priest of the Masked God of Night, crept cautiously from the cave where he had hidden during the battle. He was by nature a wary sort of drow, and the sight before him convinced him of the wisdom of discretion.

His brother Brizznarth, who was famed for his stunning sword-play, lay in a pool of his own blood. Since the young drow was clearly beyond help, Henge did not linger over him or waste any energy on grief. There was only one other drow fighter in sight, and he did not seem to be feeling any better than Brizznarth. So Henge moved on to the still form of his leader. He crouched beside the red-haired drow and realized—with decidedly mixed emotions—that Nisstyre was yet alive.

"What *can* be cured must be endured," he muttered, in a dark parody of a human proverb.

There was a smear of blood on the wizard's temple, and Henge's seeking fingers found an impressive knot on the side of Nisstyre's head. The wizard would have a headache the size of Tarterus when he awoke, but he'd only been stunned. The club had hit a glancing blow. If that battle-mad human had connected directly, it would have split Nisstyre's skull and scattered his brains so far that the remaining pittance might transform the wizard into a credible priest of Lloth, mused Henge with a touch of dark humor.

A quick examination assured the priest that Nisstyre had sustained only the one injury. The priest framed the wounded drow's head with his hands and began to chant a prayer to Vhaeraun, a plea for healing and restoration. The Masked God was with him; Nisstyre's eyes opened, focused on the priest, and then narrowed in suspicion.

"You are unharmed," he muttered thickly. "Did you join the battle at all?"

Suddenly the cleric wished he'd had the foresight to daub himself with some of the blood his younger brother had shed so freely. "Only the two of us survived," Henge said, calmly sidestepping the wizard's accusation, "and neither one of us got off much of an attack."

"The human escaped?"

Nisstyre's voice rang with incredulity. Brizznarth was the finest blade under his command, and Gorlist was fully the match of any five human warriors. The tattooed fighter had proven this, time and again. Nisstyre simply could not credit that his elite drow force might have met defeat at the hands of a single human.

He hauled himself to his feet, ignoring the throbbing ache in his head. That Brizznarth and Codfael were dead was plain to see, but he would not accept Gorlist's fate until he beheld the body with his own eyes.

"Where is Gorlist?"

Henge pointed toward the ravine. The wizard staggered over to the edge and peered down into the stream.

"He breathes," Nisstyre snapped. "See to him at once!"

The priest spread his hands in a gesture of helplessness. "I have used all my healing spells for the day."

"Then use this, and be quick."

Nisstyre produced a vial of glowing green liquid from his spell bag and thrust it into the cleric's hand. He watched intently as Henge slid down the rocky incline and carefully poured the liquid into the fighter's mouth. The outcome was important, for Gorlist was valuable to the Masked Lord's cause. He was also Nisstyre's son, a fact that would have mattered far less if Gorlist had not been so skilled a fighter.

The injured drow groaned and began to stir. Nisstyre cast a spell that brought Gorlist's battered body floating up and out of the ravine. The wizard noted the pink froth at the fighter's lips. He stooped and ran his fingers over the younger drow's torso.

Three, maybe four ribs broken, Nisstyre thought grimly. He hesitated for just an instant before reaching into his spell bag for a second potion. This one was in a vial shaped like a candle's flame, and it gleamed like captured fire. It was a potion of last resort, for although it healed grievous wounds in remarkably short order, there was a price to pay for such healing. The rapid knitting of bone and tissue was agonizing, and the magic was fueled by the life-force of its recipient. The cure stole more energy, and caused more pain, than many wounded drow could bear. It killed at least as often as it cured.

But Nisstyre had an idea. He handed the vial to the cleric, who had just scrambled up over the edge of the ravine. "Pray to Vhaeraun," he commanded. "Ask the God of Thieves to steal the life-force of another being to empower the potion. And if we are fortunate," Nisstyre muttered to himself, "the Masked Lord will take the life-force of the orc-sired human who did this!"

Henge took the vial and began to chant in prayer. The wizard busied himself with another sort of preparation. He cut a length of stout green stick from a scrubby tree nearby and peeled off the rough bark. Gorlist would need something to bite on during the agonizing cure.

The wounded fighter drifted back to consciousness, and his gaze settled on the fiery vial in the cleric's hands. A gleam of fierce approval lit his eyes, and he gestured for the priest to administer the potion at once. Henge hesitated in midchant.

"Do it," commanded Gorlist in a faint, blood-choked whisper. He spat and then tipped back his head so Henge could pour the potion into his mouth. The priest complied, and the fighter downed the fiery liquid in a single swallow.

Convulsions gripped him at once. The other two drow lunged for the fighter and tried in vain to hold him down. Gorlist tossed them aside without thought or effort, utterly unmindful of their presence in the midst of the agony that seared through his every vein and sinew.

Since he could do nothing but wait, Nisstyre found himself a comfortable rock and sat down for the duration. He had seen many fearful deaths—most of them of his own plan and execution—but never had he witnessed such suffering. Yet he watched impassively as the magic fire seared through his son's body.

Finally Gorlist lay limp and still. "Did he survive?" ventured Henge.

"He did."

The answer came from Gorlist himself. The fighter spat out splinters of green wood and climbed slowly to his feet. Nisstyre noted the bloodlust in his eyes. It would be difficult, he realized, to keep the headstrong young drow from pursuing the human who had so grievously wounded him. Nisstyre hungered for the taste of revenge, as well, but he needed Gorlist to focus on an even greater prize.

"By all reckoning, I should have died," Gorlist said. He walked over to the wizard, all the while unbuckling the leather bracers that protected his arms. "I say you owe my bloodprice. Since I have no heirs, I'll collect it myself."

Nisstyre did not doubt what the fighter would demand. "The human was badly wounded," he lied. "Although he escaped, he will not long survive."

The fighter shrugged away this news and thrust his fist high, turning it so Nisstyre could see the thin line of scar that ran down his forearm.

"I want *her*," Gorlist said through clenched teeth.

The wizard rocked back, momentarily at a loss for a response. Nisstyre tended to indulge his followers, encouraging them to enact revenge as the spirit moved them. Drow needed a focus for their inbred hatred, an occasional vent for their simmering rage. It was unfortunate Gorlist had chosen such a valuable target.

"Then you will lead the search to find her," the wizard told him smoothly. "However, you are *not* to kill her. She is too important for that, both for the magic she wields and the children she may bear to follow Vhaeraun. You know the importance of bringing drow females into the Night Above. I will not have her destroyed."

Gorlist scowled.

"There are more ways than one to humble the little princess," Nisstyre said softly. "I want this female for Vhaeraun, and for my own pleasure, but I am not averse to sharing. In time, you shall have your revenge."

The fighter's eyes widened as the meaning of the wizard's words became clear. Drow routinely inflicted horrors upon their own people and slaughtered the surface races merely for the pleasure of the kill, but what Nisstyre suggested was beyond the unspoken code of dark-elven behavior. No female, not even one conquered in battle, was taken against her will. Centuries of indoctrination had forged a taboo that was seldom questioned and rarely violated. Females wielded power in their society, and all female drow, even commoners, were viewed as the mortal incarnations of Lloth.

And yet . . . "We follow a god, not a goddess," Gorlist mused aloud.

"You begin to understand," Nisstyre said approvingly. But as he spoke, his hand lifted to rub the ruby that gleamed in the center of his forehead. He wondered if his "partner" had heard his words, and if so, how Shakti Hunzrin would regard such heresy.

It would take him time, remembering to tailor his words and actions to please a priestess of the drow goddess. It was not a task Nisstyre relished.

Chapter 19

FULL CIRCLE

yodor awoke sometime later that night, shaking with chill and the familiar, dull sickness that followed a berserker rage. He struggled to his feet, dimly understanding what had happened. Often it was that berserker warriors wandered, still in the grip of the battle rage, until brought down by exhaustion or by the wounds suffered in battle. This time he had wandered long and far, for the shallow creek that bordered the battlefield had widened to a cold, deep stream, and its restless waters reflected the light of a waxing moon risen high in the sky.

Quickly the young warrior took stock of his injuries. His head throbbed, and the skin on one side of his neck burned with fierce pain. He touched it, gingerly, felt the raised blisters and remembered the gout of flame the drow wizard had thrown. Fyodor noted that the fabric of his shirt and jacket had been slashed repeatedly, and the garments were caked to his arms with dried blood. He unlaced his leather jerkin and peeled off the damaged garments. As he did, several cuts opened and began to bleed anew. None of them were terribly deep, but all needed tending.

Fyodor took from his pack a travel samovar—a small, narrow tin kettle prized by the Rashemi—and dipped up water from the stream. He soon had a fire going, and he heated the water along with herbs that were both healing and good to drink. When the tea was strong and hot, he poured some over a cloth and carefully cleaned the cuts. One arm was not so bad, and he bandaged it as best he could. The other required a bit more work.

Thankful he always carried a spare flask of Rashemi firewine, Fyodor took a large swig of the potent spirits. Then he threaded a curving needle and began to stitch up the deepest cut. It was not an easy task, with his hands shaking from exhaustion and chill. Fyodor recognized that his body was in shock; if he did not warm himself at once, he would die as surely as if a drow sword had pierced his heart.

When the cuts were closed and bandaged, the young fighter gathered up all the deadfall wood in the area and built the fire into a roaring blaze. Then he stripped to the skin and plunged into the icy waters of the stream.

The shock stole his breath and sent the blood racing through his limbs. Fyodor waded to shore, comforted by the familiar, invigorating sensation of outer cold and inner heat. The Rashemi were a hearty race, and both men and women avidly pursued the sport of snow-racing—grueling relays undertaken in winter, slightly clad and on foot. Fyodor excelled in such sport, but knew that in his current state he could not abide the night chill for long.

The young fighter hurried to the fireside and picked up his sword, intending to warm himself with a practice routine. But the weapon was too heavy for him to wield effectively except in the midst of a berserker fury; the stitches on his arm itched and burned with the strain of merely lifting the sword. So he discarded it for his cudgel and began a simple but vigorous routine of swings and parries.

Before long the exercise and the heat of the fire sent rivulets of sweat trickling down Fyodor's chest. Again he plunged into the stream, and again he sparred against an invisible enemy. Finally he slumped by the fireside, warmed but utterly weary. He wrapped himself in his cape and poured a mug of strong tea from the samovar. Sipping it, he allowed himself for the first time to think back over the battle.

Fyodor remembered it dimly. There had been several drow, one of them the copper-haired wizard whom he had battled in faraway Rashemen. As this thought registered, the young berserker's brow furrowed in puzzlement.

That couldn't be right. He had followed five drow into the Underdark. By his own eyes, he had accounted for all five: two killed by giant bats in the cavern, and three dark warriors fallen in battle this very night. Five drow. The wizard made six.

As Fyodor pondered the matter, other details, equally as disturbing, came back to him. He remembered the elaborate tattoo curving up along the side of one drow face. Fyodor was fairly certain none of the dark elven thieves had been so marked. And the drow fighter's hair had been cut short, so short that Fyodor had barely been able to get a solid grip on it. All the drow he'd seen in Rashemen had worn their hair long and tied back. Was it possible he had followed the wrong band of drow, or were his memories of the night's battle distorted?

The young warrior glanced at his sword and remembered slaying the sword-wielding drow. He had no memory of taking it from the dark elf's body. This was disturbing, but Fyodor knew it was often so. Weapons were precious and expensive, and berserkers retrieved them apparently by instinct. Still, it bothered him that he could not remember.

Then another fact hit him with the force of a blow. He had retrieved his weapons, but he had neglected to attend his most important task. He had not searched the bodies of the drow for the Windwalker amulet!

Fyodor's head sagged forward, and a groan of pure despair escaped him. His berserker rages were becoming worse, more uncontrollable. He remembered less each time and wandered farther; now he had become so engulfed in the fighting frenzy that he'd lost sight of his quest. He *had* to recover the amulet soon, or before the battle fever raged too hot and fierce. He did not want to think about what he himself might do in the moments before death claimed him.

In some corner of his mind, Fyodor resolved to trace his own steps back to the battlefield and remedy his omission at once. If the Windwalker amulet were there, he would find it. But his battered, exhausted body simply would not heed this command. Nor was the pale moonlight sufficient for tracking.

At first light, he vowed as he sank quickly toward slumber; at first light he would once again follow the trail. If the gods were with him, he might yet find a way out of the peculiar slavery that was his heritage, and his curse.

* * * * *

Shortly after dawn, Fyodor traced his way back to the battlefield. To his amazement, he found only two drow bodies, and the footprints of three sets of elven boots retreating toward the east. He set off in pursuit at once, not bothering to puzzle over the addition of yet another drow.

When he realized the dark elves were circling back, he abandoned any effort at tracking and took the straightest route toward the caves that led back down to the Underdark. He made good time, for unlike the drow, he did not have to seek a place to hide with the coming of each dawn. Even so, he took little time for rest. He was determined to catch the drow band before they slipped back into the deadly labyrinth that was their homeland.

Two days, Fyodor figured, or perhaps a little more, and he would again stand at the entrance to that horrific world. As he strode steadily over the rough terrain, he wondered what type of battle would await him there, and how many more dark elves might join the elusive band he had hunted for so many days.

* * * * *

Liriel staggered up into the bright moonlight some two days after she had been thrust from Menzoberranzan. Kharza's teleportation spell had sent her to a place near the caverns where she had staged a battle for the benefit of Fyodor of Rashemen. She had followed the path the human might have taken, up a steep winding incline and into a vast network of caves that lay among the hillsides of the Lands Above.

Not once daring to stop, she'd fled the Underdark and the ravenous, murderous drow greed she had inadvertently awakened. Kharza's warnings had echoed through her mind like mocking laughter as she'd run wildly through the tunnel and up into the labyrinth of caves. Her instinctual sense of direction took her unerringly upward toward the light.

Slowly Liriel edged out of the cave, alert and vigilant despite her exhaustion. She recoiled at the sight beyond, and her lips moved in a silent cry of dismay.

The landscape stretched before her was like nothing she had ever seen or imagined. Rolling, rock-strewn hills seemed to go on endlessly, and looming far overhead was the infinite depth and breadth of the night sky. This was nothing like the forest, with its comforting walls of trees and vines, and its glades that were like caverns carved out of the thick foliage. This was vast, open, and barren.

Liriel's eyes ached in an effort to take in the enormous distances. From the maps she had studied, she knew she'd emerged somewhere west of the great woodland where the Chosen of Eilistraee danced. There were fewer trees here, and none of them had the mystic grandeur of that wondrous forest. The plants reminded her of verdant dwarves: small, tough things that had won their place through grim struggle with rock and soil.

Then voices came to her on the night wind—harsh yet musical sounds that could only be drow. For a moment Liriel thought her pursuers had found her. Then she remembered the strange, linear path sound took up here in the open air, and she knew the voice came from beyond the cave.

She pulled her *piwafwi* close about her and spoke the words that would grant her invisibility. Even so, she shrank back behind the sheltering rock and crouched low to wait and watch. It might be that these drow were like the ones she had encountered in the forest: helpful and welcoming. Liriel hoped it would be so, for she felt very alone and vulnerable in this dismal land.

Soon the dark elves came into sight. Lithe and dark-clad, their white hair covered by the cowls of their capes, the drow walked with admirable stealth. Even so, Liriel knew at once these were not drow of the Underdark. There was no aura of magic about them, and although the night was bright, their eyes shone with the red light that indicated the use of the heat-spectrum. Even Liriel, whose eyes were trained to candlelight, could see perfectly without infravision in the bright light of the moon. Were these hunters' senses so dulled that they could not?

Wrapped in her *piwafwi* and shod with enchanted elven boots, she had the advantage of invisibility and silence. She crept closer to see what these strange drow might be about. They grew uneasy as she closed in, looking furtively about and fingering their weapons, as if their hunting instincts perceived what their senses could not.

How long must we wait? signaled one of them in the drow's silent language of gesture and facial expression.

The wench will come this way, insisted another. *We will search as long as we must.*

Four males, daring to waylay a female? It was outrageous,

unthinkable! Wrath burned bright in Liriel's proud heart, focusing her thoughts for the first time since she'd left Spelltower Xorlarrin.

She unwrapped a package of darts that had been coated with sleep poison and fitted the first of several into her tiny crossbow. This would be the second test of the amulet's power, for the drow poison was magically distilled in places of high-powered radiation. Its essence did not survive in the open air.

With quick, sure motions, Liriel fired the dart. The tiny arrow found its mark, and one of the dark hunters leaped in surprise. He reached behind him and tore the dart from his backside, looking at it in almost comical disbelief for a moment and then pitching senseless to the ground.

The female grinned and gave her golden amulet a grateful pat. She fired three more darts and watched as the last three hunters reeled and tumbled. When all had succumbed to the sleep poison, she threw back the folds of her sheltering cloak and strode forward, determined to get some answers. She straddled the drow who'd been last to fall and slapped him back toward consciousness.

The dark elf's eyes flickered open. Groggy, fighting the poison, he struggled to focus on his tormentor.

"Who are you looking for?" she demanded in the drow tongue.

His eyes settled on the small golden dagger hanging about her neck. "I . . . think . . . you."

Liriel rocked back in dismay. How could it be that even surface drow sought her? She grabbed handfuls of her captive's cloak and shook him, hard.

"Who sent you?" she demanded. "Who?"

But the male was beyond speech; the poison had taken him. Liriel swore and rose to her feet. With deft, certain movements she searched the four sleeping drow. Each one wore a symbol hung about his neck on a thin leather thong, much as she wore her symbol of Lloth. But these were not Eilistraee's people, of that she was fairly certain. The priestesses of the Dark Maiden claimed to help those in need, and they were nothing like these deadly, furtive drow. What, then, were these hunters, and what was their interest in her?

Liriel contemplated the sleeping drow. Practicality demanded she kill them. They were hunting her and would no doubt continue to do so. But somehow this action went against her natural impulse. When they awoke, if they came after her again, she would kill them without a qualm.

She glanced up into the eastern sky. The brilliant sapphire blue of night was fading away; soon the dawn would come. Liriel was eager to see this wonder, but she was wise enough to do so with a ready shelter at hand.

So she slipped back into the cave and made her way quickly through the winding passages that wove under the rocky hillsides. At last she came to a likely spot: a cave with a single opening placed high on a slope. It faced east, granting her a clear view of the coming sunrise, and it was also readily defensible.

Liriel wrapped herself in her cloak and settled down to await the dawn. Yet sleep claimed her, as surely as her darts had taken down the drow hunters. Exhausted by her two days of nonstop flight, weary with grief and loss, she fell into the dreamless sleep of the drow.

* * * * *

Fyodor had barely stepped into the cave when the attack came. There were two of them—tall, man-shaped creatures with white fur and the heads of fierce bears, and they rushed at him with deep, rock-shaking roars. Both carried crudely made swords that they swung with enthusiasm but no noticeable finesse. The Rashemi was not reassured by this. His eyes quickly measured the combined length of arm and sword and reckoned the creatures' reach exceeded his own by well over a foot. Most swordsmen asserted that skill, not size, was the key to victory. Fyodor conceded this to a point, but reach *mattered*; he didn't care what anyone said to the contrary.

But there was nothing else to be done, so he drew his own sword and stepped forward to meet the first wild swing.

* * * * *

Liriel was jarred from slumber by familiar sounds: the roar of enraged quaggoths, and the clashing of swords. For a moment she thought she was back in the Underdark. Then she was fully awake, and wondering what in the name of all dark gods a deepbear was doing so far from its native territory.

Ever curious, the drow wrapped her *piwafwi* tightly about her and ran lightly toward the battle. The quaggoths were hunters who lived out their lives Below. If one of them came to the surface, it was almost certainly at the command of a more powerful being. Since only drow bothered to capture and train quaggoths, Liriel had a pretty good idea who the deepbear might be hunting. What puzzled her was who or what had intercepted the beast.

She followed the sounds of battle to the very mouth of a cave. There stood Fyodor of Rashemen, battling not one, but a mated pair of quaggoth fighters.

Elation, sudden and unexpected, swept through Liriel. She tossed back her cape and took out one of her bolos. Twirling it overhead, she stepped out into full view.

Fyodor's eyes widened when he saw her, and the moment of hesitation earned him a bruising swat from the flat of a quaggoth's sword. Liriel winced. Had the creature more skill in handling the weapon, if it had turned the angle of the sword just slightly, the human would have been cut neatly in two. This was one fight best ended quickly.

So she gave her bolo one more twirl and let it fly. The weapon wrapped around the quaggoth's sword, and the momentum of the whirling rocks tore the weapon from the creature's paw. Looking positively relieved to be rid of the cumbersome thing, the monster bared its fangs and advanced upon the human, looking more than competent with the weapons granted it by nature.

The drow grinned fiercely and pulled a handful of throwing knives from her belt. "The deepbats were just practice," she shouted to Fyodor as she hurled the first knife at the attacking quaggoth. "Let's see what you can do in a *real* fight!"

Chapter 20

TEAMWORK

iriel launched her knives, one by one, at the quaggoth's back. Each found its target, but the creature's thick fur and deep layers of muscles kept any of the small blades from hitting vital points. The bearlike fighter roared with pain, but it continued its advance on Fyodor.

The female quaggoth, however, snarled its rage and charged the little drow who'd attacked its mate. Liriel resolutely stood her ground, a knife in each hand. A flick, and the two small blades took flight, sinking into the quaggoth's red eyes. The beast shrieked and pawed at its face.

Liriel pulled her short sword, knowing she must finish the creature before it entered its death frenzy. Blinded or not, a battle-mad quaggoth was deadly in its strength and fury. She darted toward the wounded creature, sword in hand, and slashed it once, twice, across the belly. The quaggoth slumped, furred hands clutching frantically at the gaping wound. With one last stroke, Liriel cut its throat.

Behind her she heard an angry hiss. She spun to face a hideous visage, like that of a dark blue fiend, with scaly skin and ears like long pointed horns. Its red eyes gleamed with malevolence, and its snake-

240

like body swayed as it spoke an arcane phrase in a sibilant whisper. Liriel had never seen a dark naga, but she knew it for what it was—a magical creature of the Underdark that was in its own way as dangerous as a rampaging quaggoth.

The naga's thin lips pursed, and a thin stream of burning black fluid shot toward the young drow. A venom bolt.

Liriel snapped up her sword and swatted at the stream with the flat of her blade. A spray of droplets—a mixture of acid and melted metal—flew back toward the naga. The creature screamed and recoiled, and Liriel hurled aside the rapidly diminishing weapon before the corrosive venom could reach her hand. The insidious liquid could consume flesh as readily as it ate through metal.

The naga recovered fast and began to hiss out the words of another spell. To Liriel's astonishment, she recognized this spell. It was one her father had created. She remembered it well, though she had been little more than a babe when she had first heard those words. That spell, and the terror and confusion that had followed it, was her earliest memory.

In response to the naga's magic, a cluster of rocks melted, elongated, and flowed into the form of a giant snake with a nightmarish elven visage. The stone naga slid toward its drow prey with the screech of rock scraping against rock.

To buy a moment's time, Liriel hurled a throwing spider at the hideous golem. The magic-enhanced weapon bit deep into the creature's throat. It would surely have killed a living creature; the golem had no blood to shed. It bared its fangs and kept coming.

But Liriel countered; she repeated that most-hated spell and summoned a golem of her own. Rock spilled from the wall of the cave like mist, forming itself into an elfmaid of pale gray stone. The stone drow ran to defend its mistress, and the golems collided with an echoing crash.

The stone naga quickly encoiled the elf-shaped warrior and tried to squeeze, but there was no give in the slender stone body. Its head reared back, and then it struck with wide-flung jaws. The next moment it spat out shards of its own rocky fangs. The drow golem wrapped slender hands around the stone naga's throat and tried to strangle it, with no more success than its opponent. Together the magical creatures rolled and thrashed, equal in strength and mindless obedience.

Meanwhile the dark naga mounted its own attack. It darted

forward, holding high the barbed tip of its poisoned tail. Liriel dove to one side, rolled, and came up holding the quaggoth's discarded sword. Lifting it high overhead with both hands, she lunged forward and slashed into the naga's deadly tail. The heavy blade went through scale and bone, then met the stone floor with a muted crack. The naga shrieked and writhed with pain. Nearby, its severed tail twitched in an uncanny echo of the creature's anguish.

With the dark naga out of the fight for a while, Liriel had time to consider Fyodor. He was holding off the quaggoth male, but his sleeves were tattered and his arms bled freely. She snatched another bolo from her belt, twirled it briefly, and let it fly toward the quaggoth. The long strap wrapped again and again around the creature's neck, gaining momentum with each turn, and the weights on either end hit the quaggoth's head with a pair of satisfying thunks. Still, the deep-bear did not go down. It merely gurgled and tore at the straps. The leather thongs snapped easily, and Liriel knew the death frenzy had come upon the creature.

She threw a second bolo, this one at the quaggoth's ankles. The beast faltered momentarily, then continued, in a mixture of hops and shuffles, to close in on Fyodor. Liriel ran forward and leaped at the creature's back, kicking out with all her might. At last, the quaggoth stumbled and went down.

The drow scrambled up and seized Fyodor's arm. "Come *on!*" she shouted, tugging him along as she kicked into a run. He tucked his sword away and followed her in a headlong flight from the cave.

But Liriel stopped outside, some hundred paces from the opening. "Wait. I'm going to drop the whole thing," she said grimly.

Fyodor watched as the girl sped through the gestures of a spell. She thrust out both hands, and arcane lighting coursed from her fingers, flashing into the cave's dark mouth again and again. Dust flew; solid rock crackled and split. Finally the cave collapsed in an avalanche of dirt and stone.

The drow lowered her hands, and her whole body seemed to wilt. Fyodor put an arm around her and eased her to the ground. He had seen Rashemen's Witches perform such feats in battle, and he realized powerful magic took its toll on the caster. That so young a girl could command such magic was astounding.

"*Wychlaran,*" he murmured with great respect, crouching down beside her.

She focused on him with effort, her golden eyes distant and

glazed. "What?"

"It is a term of honor, given to the Witches who rule our land. Is it so with your people? Do such as you rule in your land?"

The drow flinched. "Not at the moment," she muttered, looking away. "Forget the 'terms of honor.' My name is Liriel."

Fyodor repeated the name, taking obvious pleasure in the lyric sound of it. "It suits you well."

"Oh, good," she said dryly. "I was hoping it might."

She glanced at him and caught the glint of humor in his eyes. He did not seem at all offended by her sarcasm or ill at ease in her presence. She noted how young he was—little more than a boy, actually. A boy with the muscles of a dwarf and the scars of a warrior. So many contradictions, these humans. This one's blue eyes were clear and ingenuous, his manner of speaking forthright. In Menzoberranzan, such behavior would be regarded as simpleminded. But Liriel could not be fooled twice. She noted the taut readiness of the young man's muscles, the way his hand lingered near the hilt of the wicked hunting knife tucked into his sash.

Just then a rumble of stone came from the ruined cavern. Horror and disbelief froze Liriel in place for just a moment. A second rumble galvanized her, and she leaped to her feet. "The quaggoth," she said urgently.

Fyodor stood with her, but he regarded her with puzzlement.

"The bear-creature!" she shrieked. "It's coming!"

"But that cannot be," he said. His eyes were wary, as if he were waiting for her to try some dark ploy.

Liriel hissed with frustration and launched herself at the stubborn human. They fell together, rolling away from the cave in a tumble of arms and legs. She thrust him away from her and curled into a ball, covering her head with her arms just as the stone-filled mouth of the cave exploded outward. A spray of dirt and rock arched toward them as the quaggoth burst from the ruined cave.

The deepbear was filthy and battered. Patches of dark red stained its fur, and a jagged spur of bone gleamed through the torn hide of one arm. Yet the creature seemed unaware of its condition; it merely kicked aside a boulder and staggered away from the cave, nose twitching as it scented the air for its prey. The quaggoth's eyes gleamed red even in the bright moonlight, and its coarse, filthy fur stood up straight, making the seven-foot creature appear even larger and more fierce than it was. In its one good hand it held the battered naga by its mangled tail, lashing the ten-foot creature back and forth as if it were a whip.

"You wouldn't listen," Liriel hissed at Fyodor.

Nor was he listening now. With quick, fluid movements Fyodor rose to his feet, sword drawn. The young fighter's eyes became cold and hard, and to Liriel's astonishment he seemed to grow to a stature than matched that of the enraged quaggoth. No fool, the drow scrambled out of the path of the coming conflict. She threw herself behind some boulders and watched as the human charged forward.

The bear-creature jerked back the dead naga, then snapped it toward Fyodor with incredible force. The man was ready. He pivoted hard to the left and swung his sword low and back. As the naga's dead head shot forward, he sliced up to meet it. The broad dull blade cut cleanly through the scaly armor, and the severed head flew upward in an impressive arc.

"Mother Lloth," Liriel breathed, watching with wide eyes and growing excitement.

Fyodor ran in close, sword leading. The quaggoth batted the weapon aside with its paw, ignoring the deep gash that opened across its palm. Again it flailed the dead naga. Ichor splashed freely from the severed neck, but the human was in too close for the macabre whip to do him much harm. The quaggoth tossed aside the snake body and backhanded the man with its bleeding paw; the blow connected hard and sent Fyodor reeling.

Sensing an advantage, the quaggoth sprang. But the human had already regained his balance. He nimbly sidestepped the lunge, and the quaggoth measured its length on the rocky ground. Fyodor closed in, sword raised high for the finishing stroke.

But the deepbear rolled onto its back and pulled its knees up high and tight against its body. It kicked out hard and caught the man full in the chest. Fyodor flew backward, his back hitting a tree with an impact that threw his arms wide and knocked the sword from his hand.

The quaggoth once again pulled in its knees, this time to spring up onto its feet. The creature waded in, fangs bared in a silent snarl and massive arms flung wide in a grim parody of an embrace.

Fyodor pushed himself off the tree and barreled in, clasping the bear-creature around the middle. They went down like wrestlers, each grappling for a killing hold. Several minutes passed as they thrashed, equally matched in rage and strength.

Finally the man pinned the massive creature, both paws above its head. The quaggoth's furred head tossed from side to side, and although its jaws gnashed and snapped, it could gain no purchase. For the human's head was firmly pressed beneath its chin, forcing the shaggy head upward. Fyodor's head shook, savagely, several times, and blood began to flow down the furred neck of his captive. The quaggoth's struggles slowed to a shudder, and finally ceased.

Liriel pressed her hand to her mouth to keep from crying out in triumph. Fyodor had torn the creature's throat out!

Yet some instinct warned her to keep silent, to stay out of sight. She watched from hiding as Fyodor rose slowly to his feet. He seemed to shrink in size right before her eyes, and he stared at the dead creature for a long moment, as if he could not fathom where it had come from. Then his shoulders slumped, and a low, despairing groan burst from him.

"What?" Liriel marveled, baffled by this response.

Then the human covered his mouth with both hands and darted into the bushes. That, Liriel could understand. The quaggoth smelled bad, even from where she stood. The *taste* of it would probably turn an ogre's stomach.

She waited until the human was finished and had staggered back into the clearing. He looked better, if extremely pale. Liriel stepped into view, applauding softly. Fyodor spun to face her. He looked so startled, she realized he'd forgotten entirely about her. Though she was hardly accustomed to such inattention, she was in a mood to be generous.

"Very impressive," she complimented him.

The young man's eyes looked haunted. "You saw?"

"Yes, of course. It was wonderful to watch. From a safe distance, of course."

"How can you say such a thing?" he cried. "By all the gods, I tore the thing's *throat* out!"

The drow shrugged, not seeing the problem. There were more important matters to attend to. Night was fading, and so was the sleep-poison holding the drow hunters. "We need to take shelter. I know a place."

When he hesitated, Liriel snatched his wrist and pushed up the tattered sleeve. There were marks where the quaggoth's filthy claws had scored him, along with an older, deeper cut that badly needed restitching. "Look—you're hurt, I'm tired. Try to be sensible."

Indeed, Fyodor was weaving on his feet, for the familiar sickness that followed a berserker rage was upon him. "A truce," he agreed wearily.

Too exhausted, too sick at heart to care whether the treacherous drow kept faith or not, Fyodor let her lead him to a cave nearby. With a snap of her fingers, the dark wizard lit a small fire. While Fyodor warmed himself, she deftly tended his hurts. From her travel bag she produced some trail rations—strips of dried meat he recognized as rothe—and they ate in silence. Feeling somewhat revived by the food and fire, he took a few swallows from his flask. He turned to offer some to the drow, but found she had left his side. He watched, puzzled, as Liriel settled down at the mouth of the cave.

"It's silver," she murmured in an awed tone. "The sky is truly silver!"

Suddenly he understood. This was her first sunrise, and her tense, expectant pose suggested it was an experience she had long awaited. Not wishing to disturb the elf's pleasure, but desiring to witness it, Fyodor came quietly to sit beside her. Her eyes watered as if she were in pain, but she did not turn away from the dawning light. Without looking at him, she seized his arm and pointed to some rosy wisps of cloud.

"Look at the smoke there! What *is* that color?"

"Those are clouds, and they are pink. You've never seen the color before?"

"I've never seen anything like this before," Liriel said, not once taking her eyes from the brightening sky. "Look there! The sm—the *clouds* there are purple, and gold. It is always like this?"

"Dawn? No. It is different each day. The colors come again when the sun sets."

Liriel barely had time to absorb this marvel when the sun itself crested the hills. A sliver of red, brighter than molten metal, edged into the sky. She cried out in a mixture of pain and wonder. Her eyes burned fiercely, but she would not look away.

Fyodor was touched by the drow's innocent joy, and loath to end the moment. But he took the girl by the shoulders and turned her firmly to him. "You must not stare at the sun, even now, when its light is faint. Even those born under its light cannot bear to do so."

She cast one last, lingering glance at the wondrous sun as she followed Fyodor into the cave. "Its light is *faint?*" she echoed incredulously.

Back in the soothing darkness, she turned her full curiosity upon the human. In answer to her eager questions, he told her what had befallen him since their last meeting. Her reaction was slight when he spoke of a red-haired drow wizard, but Fyodor did not miss it.

"You know him."

"I'm afraid so. That could only be Nisstyre. Only he would know where to find you," she said bitterly. She told him about the wizard's part in arranging a false trail that would lead Fyodor out of the Underdark. "I thought you'd be safer on the surface," she concluded with a wry grin. "I may reconsider that opinion."

This news baffled Fyodor. "Why would you do such a thing?"

Liriel shrugged and tucked a bit of gold chain deeper into the neck of her tunic. "You tricked me. I admired that. But all that is done and over. I have work to do."

The drow took a small bag from her belt and selected a large, beautifully cut blue diamond. She placed the gem in her palm and chanted softly. After a moment, the jewel crumbled into sparkling dust. Liriel arose and carefully sprinkled the powdered diamond in a nine-foot circle around the fire. Then, humming an eerie melody, she began to dance. Dipping and swaying, she wove an intricate pattern of beauty and magic. Fyodor watched, as fully enchanted as if the spell had been cast upon him.

Finally she sank to the cave's floor, tired and satisfied. "No wizard's eyes can penetrate that circle, not even Nisstyre's. We should be safe enough here."

"Is he so powerful, this Nisstyre?"

"He is drow."

Liriel said this with a mixture of pride and grim foreboding that Fyodor found unsettling. What did it mean, truly, to be drow? He had no real understanding of this fey lass; at their second meeting she was more of a mystery to him than before. So intently did he study the girl that several moments passed before he realized she was observing him with equal interest.

"Do all humans fight as you do?" she asked, her eyes alight with curiosity.

Fyodor stared down at the fire. "No, praise the gods," he said shortly.

"Then how? What magic do you possess?"

He could not bear to speak of it now, after what he had done. The berserker rages took from him his will and his wits: now it seemed they would steal his very soul. What he had done this night was simply not human. "It is a long tale, and I am very tired," he said simply.

Liriel accepted this with a nod. "Later, then. You really must get some rest. But first, tell me: do you sleep, or do you enter reverie?"

"Reverie?"

She paused, searching for words. "You dream."

"Ah! Well, that I do, waking or sleeping," he said with a faint smile. "It is said in my land that there are two kinds of people: those who think, and those who dream."

The drow thought this over, her white brows meeting in a frown of puzzlement. Dark elves either slept or rested in reverie. Whatever was the human talking about? This, and a thousand other questions, danced ready on her tongue. It was clear, however, that Fyodor could not answer them now. But a sudden, outrageous plan popped into her mind, and she voiced it at once.

"We can travel together for a while," she said happily. "There are so many things you can tell me!"

The man smiled, clearly charmed by her beauty and enthusiasm. "Are you always so eager to learn?"

"Always," she promised. They shared a companionable grin, and Fyodor was honestly tempted to accept.

"I cannot," he said with regret. "I must find this Nisstyre and the other drow I fought before."

Liriel's smile vanished. She had forgotten for the moment what the human sought: the amulet she wore beneath her tunic. Nor was he the only one who wanted it!

"Then here, with me, is definitely the place to be," she said grimly. "Why do you think Nisstyre showed up, why he sent the drow hunters back to these caverns?"

So, she was hunted. Why, Fyodor did not understand, but the cold anger the drow wizard had ignited in his heart burned a little brighter. "I will travel with you, then," he said. "When this Nisstyre dies, we may both be free."

Her eyes flashed. "Then it's a conspiracy!"

"In my land," he said, his lip curved in a faint smile, "we call it an alliance."

Liriel nodded agreement. "That works for me."

The fire was fading, so Fyodor picked up a handful of dry twigs to add to it. A tiny brown spider crawled out of the bundle onto his hand.

Absently he flicked it off. The blow crumpled the delicate arachnid and sent its body tumbling into the gathering flames.

Liriel froze, her golden eyes wide with horror. Then, shrieking in wordless rage, she leaped at Fyodor. Her hands curved into talons and slashed toward his face.

Fyodor grabbed her wrists and held off her flailing hands, but the force of her attack sent them tumbling. The Rashemi was larger and stronger; even so, he had to battle the furious, thrashing elf for several minutes before pinning her securely under his body. Tiny though she was, it took all his weight to hold her down.

Contained but not subdued, Liriel fixed a blazing, defiant stare upon her captor. Fyodor returned her gaze with equal intensity. Always he was alert for an attack from this unpredictable drow, but as he studied her face he read not treachery, but wrath.

"What?" he demanded.

"You killed a spider! The punishment for your crime is death," she spat at him.

Fyodor's face fell slack with astonishment. "You cannot be serious," he sputtered.

"Spiders are sacred to the drow goddess, you ignorant peasant!"

The man considered this with sober interest. He'd been through much of late, and his nerves had tightened nearly to breaking. In his current state of mind, the drow's claim struck him as utterly, delightfully absurd. "Am I to understand," he said slowly, "that you worship *bugs?*"

Maintaining her dignity under the circumstances was no easy matter, but Liriel was equal to the task. Her small chin lifted imperiously. "Yes, of course. In a manner of speaking."

Fyodor stared at the drow for a moment, then dropped his head to rest in the tangled waves of her hair. His body began to shake. Laughter started in his belly and erupted into a full-throated roar, and he rolled helplessly onto his side, holding his ribs and rocking back and forth.

The moment she was free of his weight, the drow leaped to her feet, a throwing spider ready in her hand. The sight of this weapon sent the man into fresh gales of mirth.

Liriel glared at Fyodor, too baffled by his strange behavior to respond properly to his blasphemy. So she merely stood and waited for the human's incomprehensible laughter to subside.

At length he came to himself, wiping tears from his eyes. "I can return to Rashemen without delay," he said, and his blue eyes twinkled despite the sober set of his face. "For now I have surely heard everything."

Chapter 21

THE WINDWALKER

isstyre strode along in the strong morning light, his face protected and hidden by the folds of his hood. Despite the efforts of his drow priest, Nisstyre was not yet strong enough to cast the powerful spells needed for magical travel. He and his fighters were reduced to hiking back to the caverns. It was risky for drow to be about during the day, and all of Nisstyre's dark-elven comrades—particularly Gorlist—grew increasingly restive as the day passed.

When finally they reached the first of the cave-filled hills, the late-afternoon sun cast long shadows across the rocky landscape. The wizard, whose eyes were most accustomed to cruel daylight, was the first to see the four still figures lying in the distance. Nisstyre cursed softly and fervently when he recognized the drow he'd sent in search of Liriel Baenre.

He hurried over. To his relief, all were still breathing. Even better, the small shaft of a dart protruded from one hunter's shoulder. Nisstyre stooped, tugged it free, and sniffed at the arrowhead. The distinctive scent of drow sleeping poison—a potion based upon

Underdark magic—still clung to the tiny weapon.

"She actually did it!" muttered the wizard.

So pleased was Nisstyre by this discovery that he kicked the hunters awake with less force than he might otherwise have employed. The poison that felled them lasted only a few hours, so it was likely Liriel had not gone far. That is, she could not have gone far *on foot.* Nisstyre prayed Liriel had not traveled from this place by magical means. There were ways to track wizards who trod magic's silver paths, but such were beyond even his skills.

A shout of triumph interrupted his troubled thoughts. Gorlist called him over and pointed to the small, faint mark of an elven boot.

Nisstyre came, but his hands flashed in furious, silent communication as he reminded the young fighter of the importance of stealth. Gorlist nodded in agreement, but he waited through the chastisement with all the patience of a drawn arrow.

Quick to recognize effort wasted, Nisstyre waved the eager drow on to the hunt. He made very certain, however, that he stayed close to Gorlist. Now that he knew the full measure of Liriel's worth, Nisstyre could not risk losing her to the young fighter's thirst for vengeance.

It was odd, Nisstyre mused, that Gorlist had fixated his wrath upon Liriel, rather than on the human fighter who had so grievously wounded him. As he walked, Nisstyre's thoughts lingered long upon that strange human, and on the amulet the human had once wielded and that Liriel now possessed.

He also speculated on the possible connection between two such disparate beings. Obviously they had met, for who else would merit the elaborate ruse Liriel had staged to discourage pursuit into the Underdark? She knew of the human and feared him; that much was clear. But how had they met, and what might transpire if they met again? It was impossible a proud Baenre female might join forces with a human male, and that was well. The wizard did not like the prospect of Liriel's dark-elven magic acting in concert with the human's incredible battle rage. Vhaeraun's followers were too few to risk in battle against such odds!

* * * * *

Throughout the day Liriel and Fyodor took turns keeping watch, taking what little rest they could. The drow trusted her magic circle to keep out prying eyes, but such offered little protection against physical attack. Both of the travelers stayed wary, not only of the dangers that surrounded them, but of each other.

Since they could not sleep, they talked. Fyodor related one tale after another. Some were heroic in nature, others frankly comic, but all had layers of meaning that intrigued the drow. Equally fascinating to her was a recurring theme: the comparison Fyodor constantly made between "those who think, and those who dream." Drow— except for those declining few who took their rest in the form of elven reverie—did not dream in either their sleeping or waking hours. They thought and plotted and schemed, and then they slept. Liriel herself did not enter reverie, but she wondered if her determination to follow a rune quest qualified as a dream of sorts. If this were so, then perhaps she was also a dreamer at heart. It was a concept utterly foreign to a Menzoberranzan drow, yet it seemed to fit her, and it filled a void she had never before defined.

So did the laughter they shared many times throughout that day. In turn serious and playful, Fyodor viewed the world with wry, dark humor not so very different from her own. His deep bass chuckle joined hers frequently. This was not the drow way, for dark-elven humor was usually a contest, a pleasure taken at the expense of another. She even enjoyed Fyodor's teasing, which was utterly devoid of the malicious intent common to her kin.

Fyodor told her about his land, and the lands he had passed through, and the battles he had seen. Although she recognized in his words a love of travel and adventure to equal her own, Liriel was surprised to note he had little apparent interest in the art of fighting for its own sake.

"If you do not care for swordcraft, how is it you fight so well?" she demanded.

The young man shrugged. "Rashemen is a small land, surrounded by powerful enemies. Every Rashemi learns to fight at an early age."

"So do drow. There is more to you than that," Liriel stated calmly. "I have seen a few humans in Menzoberranzan. Some fight better than others, but all die easily enough. You cling to life with more fortitude than seems natural."

Fyodor sat silently for a long moment, regarding her with a calm, measuring gaze. For a moment Liriel recalled the mind-reading spells of Lloth's clergy, and she wondered whether this human was weighing her in some invisible measure of his own. It seemed unlikely a mere human male, a rough-clad commoner at that, could command such magic, but Liriel was no longer so quick to draw conclusions. When the young fighter nodded and began to speak of matters closely held, she had the strangest feeling she'd passed some sort of test.

The drow listened closely as Fyodor told her of Rashemen's berserker warriors, and the strange malady that severed him from the brotherhood that defended his land. He had been sent away; no longer able to control his battle rages, he had become a danger to those around him.

"That's utter nonsense!" Liriel interrupted heatedly. "After seeing you in battle, I can't think of another fighter I'd rather have at my back!"

The young man sent her a faint, fleeting smile. "You do me honor, little raven. But consider the dangers. I must fight until all who stand against me are gone. This is not always the best course, for me or those who fight with me. But what I fear most," he said softly, "is what I may become before the fighting stops. You saw what I did to the bear-creature. I swear by my soul, I would never have done such a thing had I been able to choose my own course. And if I cannot order my own actions now, how soon before I cannot tell friend from foe?"

Liriel nodded. "I see your problem."

"Then you will also understand the purpose of my *dajemma*. The Witches who rule my land sent me to find an ancient amulet that can store this dangerous power, so I can once again call it forth at will."

Oh, she understood, all right. Liriel's heart suddenly felt leaden beneath the weight of the stolen Windwalker. "You don't say. An amulet that stores magic," she echoed dully.

"That is so. How its magic works, I do not know."

Perhaps not, but *she* did. It gave Liriel little pleasure to know she understood more about the Windwalker's magic than did Fyodor, perhaps more even than Rashemen's Witches. The amulet was hers now, purchased at staggering cost, and so it must remain. And yet . . .

"What happens if you never regain the amulet?" she demanded.

He shrugged and poked at their campfire. "It means my life, and whatever aid my sword might have given my troubled land."

Liriel rose abruptly. She walked toward the mouth of the cave, motioning Fyodor back when he would have followed her. After all that had passed between them, she needed a few moments' solitude to put things in order.

The day was nearly spent, but just beyond the cave all was brilliant, golden light. The drow gazed out as long as she could bear it, trying to wean her eyes to the light of surface world. It would be many days before she could walk out beneath the sun in comfort. The question that troubled her now was whether or not she would walk alone.

She could not abandon her own quest, for doing so could well mean her life. Knowing what she did of her people's power-mad greed, Liriel doubted she could ever return to the Underdark, with or without the coveted amulet. Nor could she long survive on the surface without her drow magic. She was a wizard, not a warrior, and although her skills at arms were considerable they were not sufficient to sustain her in this hostile world. No, she could not give up the Wind walker.

Indeed, why should she? Fyodor of Rashemen was a human, a male, and a commoner, and thus by any measure Liriel had ever known, he was unworthy of her notice. Why, then, this unwonted concern for his success? It was a question that puzzled and angered the young drow.

But most of all, what frustrated Liriel was this: that one person could not increase unless another were diminished. It had ever been so, and until now she had never questioned this simple fact of life. Now she railed against harsh reality and searched the winding pathways of her dark-elven mind for another way.

And yet, when at last Liriel returned to the soothing darkness of her shared camp, she did so with the Windwalker amulet hidden at the very bottom of her travel bag.

*   *   *   *   *

At twilight Liriel and Fyodor stole from the cave and retraced their path toward the ruined cavern. As they neared the battlefield, a cloud of interrupted ravens rose from their feasting with loud squawks of displeasure.

Fyodor's face settled in grim lines as he surveyed the day-old carnage. Liriel suspected the Rashemi did not relish this reminder of his latest battle frenzy, but she strode quickly over the rock-strewn ground toward the bodies of their fallen foe. There were answers there that she must have.

She ignored the battered quaggoth remains and knelt beside what was left of the dark naga. The creature's blue scales were dull and dusty, but formidable armor still. Using her stoutest knife, Liriel chipped and pried and tugged until she managed to peel off a section of the scales. She sliced into the naga's body and pulled from it a large sack that looked more like a traveler's pack than anything normally found in a once-living creature.

Fyodor drew near, intrigued, as Liriel stretched wide the sack's one opening and began to shake out its contents. He'd dreaded returning to this place, but he understood the drow's need to find out who was pursuing her. Indeed, he himself wished to know more about the drow wizard called Nisstyre, and what it was he wanted with Liriel. So Fyodor watched intently as she shook out a number of odd items: a long, broad dagger; a small arsenal of knives; several vials of potions and poisons; a tightly scrolled map; a bag full of platinum coins; another stuffed with gems; several spell scrolls; and a small book. Ignoring the other treasures, Liriel reached for the book and paged through it. Her shoulders sagged.

"What is it?" Fyodor asked softly.

"This is a spellbook, a duplicate of one I carry. It is the work of archmage Gromph Baenre. My father."

The drow's voice was cool and even, but Fyodor did not miss the faint note of despair in it. "Perhaps it was stolen from him," he offered.

Liriel shook her head. "Gromph is probably the most powerful wizard in a mighty drow city. A naga's magic is a pale thing in comparison. No, this creature could only have gotten the spellbook with Gromph's knowledge and contrivance."

"He is your father; he wants you back," Fyodor reasoned.

"He wants me *dead!* What did you think the dark naga and the two quaggoths were—a diplomatic envoy?"

Fyodor could think of no words of comfort for such a betrayal, so he stood silent while the practical drow gathered up the naga's treasures. Liriel slid the dagger into her weapon belt to replace the sword she'd lost in the cavern. The knives she tucked into numerous pockets and straps cleverly hidden about her person. She did not seem to care that Fyodor saw how and where she was armed.

The young man read in this act not only mental agitation, but a measure of trust. It astounded him that this girl, who had just taken a devastating betrayal with stoic calm, would put her confidence in him. Fyodor had come to value the dark elf's intense, zestful approach to life, but only now did he glimpse the true measure of her resilient spirit. What her life among the drow had been, he could not imagine. What she might *become,* he suspected, could shape the tales his children's children might one day tell.

Liriel packed away everything, leaving the spellbook until last. She picked it up, hesitated, then handed it to Fyodor. "This is too valuable to leave, but I cannot bear to carry it."

There was no note of weakness in her voice; it was calm, matter-of-fact. The Rashemi approved and admired her for it. He took the book and placed it at the bottom of his travel bag. That done, he extended his hand to the drow.

Liriel hesitated, then her slender fingers closed on his and she let him raise her to her feet. Nor did she immediately pull her hand away. Side by side, the companions walked into the gathering darkness.

* * * * *

An hour passed, and then another before Fyodor broke the silence that lay heavy between them. "Where were you bound before Nisstyre set upon your trail?"

Ruathym, thought Liriel, but she was not yet ready to divulge her ultimate destination. She named Waterdeep, and he nodded thoughtfully.

"It is a long trip. We must travel by day if we are to keep ahead of those who hunt you. We'll need supplies and horses. There is a village nearby, Trollbridge, where I can purchase both."

The drow girl stared at him in confusion. "But what of your own quest? I thought you wanted to confront Nisstyre's thieves!"

"And so I will. First I would see you safely to your destination, while it is still in me to do so. Are there people in Waterdeep you can trust?"

"I think so, but what about your—"

Fyodor touched a silencing finger to her lips. "Don't concern yourself for me; my interests will be served. Where you go, Nisstyre will follow. Is that not so?"

"Yes, but—"

"Enough!" He threw up his hands in mock exasperation. "Did we not agree to work together?"

Liriel merely nodded. It sounded so easy, when Fyodor spoke of it. Her mind whirled with the possibilities such an arrangement suggested. If two persons could truly combine their skills and strengths, how much more could they accomplish than one alone! Perhaps there *was* a way . . .

Elaine Cunningham

Yet as they hurried toward the village, memories of her life in Menzoberranzan kept coming back to her. Despite her flippant disregard for clerical life, the Way of Lloth had been imprinted deeply in her mind and heart. She had seen the sacrifices Lloth required, the brutally imposed isolation demanded of those who served the Lady of Chaos. The power of the drow matriarchy came at a price, and only Lloth's priestesses understood the full extent of the goddess's cruelty.

Liriel could not help but wonder what price might be demanded of her for thinking to join her path with that of a human male. Worse, for thinking her dream could grow to make room for another. And, most heretical, for daring to dream at all.

No, what Fyodor suggested was not so easy, after all.

Chapter 22

THE SPIDER'S KISS

he drow and the Rashemi walked throughout the night, and by first light they could see the outlying fields that heralded the existence of a farming village. They paused on a hillside overlooking a green, sweet-smelling place Fyodor called a meadow. Beyond the meadow, over the swell and fall of several smaller hillocks, Liriel saw a sparkle of white and blue that could only be the Dessarin River. The drow's sharp eyes scanned the landscape and marked a place that would suit her purpose: a small, sheltered clearing on a tree-covered hill overlooking the river.

"You must stay here," Fyodor cautioned her. "The people of Troll-bridge have suffered much at the hands of drow raiders and would not take kindly to your presence."

Liriel accepted his words without quarrel. "Just as well. I'm too tired to walk another step." She punctuated her claim with a wide yawn, and at Fyodor's urging she wriggled through the vines that all but choked a low-hanging yew tree. The sheltering shade would protect her from the sun, and her *piwafwi* would lend her invisibility. There she could rest in relative safety.

When Fyodor was satisfied that all was well, he hurried down the hillside toward Trollbridge. The time of moondark had passed, and he hoped the villagers' fear of dark-elven raiders had passed with it. Yet he could not help but feel uneasy going there with drow hunters so close upon his heels. The beleaguered townsfolk had troubles enough; Fyodor did not wish to bring his own upon them.

He heard the sounds of the village before the walls of the palisade came into sight: the squeak of wagon wheels, the blended hum of a crowd of voices, an occasional note from the pipes and strings of itinerant musicians. Fyodor quickened his step. The merchants had come at long last, and with them the spring fair.

* * * * *

At first, Liriel had only the best of intentions. True, she had chosen a place of escape on a distant hillside, and she prepared a gate that could carry one or two persons there, but that was a reasonable precaution, no more. She fully intended to remain in her hiding place, to catch up on her sleep. When her natural curiosity asserted itself, she repeated Fyodor's warning about the humans' fear of drow, and she thrust aside her desire to see a human marketplace with her own eyes. And she stuck to her resolve for a good half hour.

Liriel took off her *piwafwi* and flipped it over. The marvelous, glittering cloak had a nondescript dark lining and was perfect garb for blending into a crowd. She put on the inside-out garment and pulled up the deep-cowled hood to shield her face from the sun. Next she rummaged in her travel bag for a pair of gloves to cover her dark skin and to soften the distinctive elven shape of her hands. Finally, the young wizard cast a minor cantrip that lent her face the look of a human. She took a tiny mirror of polished bronze from her bag and regarded her new appearance. She grimaced, then burst out laughing.

At the sound, a flock of small brown birds nesting among the vines took startled flight. Liriel watched them go, then left her hiding place and made her way down the hill toward the place Fyodor had called Trollbridge.

* * * * *

Trollbridge was hardly the grim, besieged fortress of Fyodor's last visit. The merchant caravan brought not only goods and an opportunity for trade, but also news of the lands beyond and a lighter spirit that—although it might not approach the gusto of a Rashemi festival—was nonetheless gratifying to the weary young warrior.

Fyodor noted that this caravan brought the usual hangers-on: armed travel guards looking for a place to drink and a bit of company; artisans plying such diverse crafts as tinsmithing and fortune-telling; traveling bards of all sorts, from gossip-mongers to jugglers to musicians. The villagers were out in force, too, garbed in their finest and displaying their winter crops and crafts to best advantage.

Fyodor went about his business as quickly as possible. He did not use the platinum coins Liriel had taken from the naga—such would attract too much notice in a village market. His own silver was more appropriate to the purchases he needed to make. First he bought two horses: a piebald mare and a chestnut gelding, fast and sturdy beasts both. He gave the stableboy a handful of coppers and bade him to take the horses beyond the village walls and stake them at the far-eastern edge of the meadows. The boy was too delighted with his unexpected riches to question such a request; indeed, Fyodor himself was not certain why he made it. He felt ill at ease, despite the spirit of light-hearted gaiety that ruled the day. Quickly he bought a few other things: some ready-made clothes to replace his much-mended garments, a lady's cloak with a draping hood to protect Liriel from the sun, dried travel rations, twine for setting snares, a piece of tanned deerskin for patching boots and clothing, and a few sundries such as would be needed on a long trip. Fyodor's needs were few and his habits frugal, yet he could not resist a final purchase. It was a pendant, the last remaining piece in the collection of a dwarven jewelsmith. Fyodor saw at once why the gem had not sold, but its very flaw made it perfect for Liriel. He parted with the asking price cheerfully.

Although eager to return to the drow's hiding place, Fyodor had walked since dawn without stopping for food or rest; an equally long road lay before him. So he made his way to the village tavern for a mug and a quick bite. Saida, the innkeeper, recognized him and shouted to one of the serving girls to find him a seat on the level above. He squeezed his way through the crowded taproom and up the stairs. One of the bedchambers had been crammed with tables, and Fyodor found an empty seat near the window. Below him was the kitchen wing, and beyond that the market. He watched the cheerful scene idly as he ate his bread and cheese.

Suddenly he froze, his hand halfway to his mouth. He pushed

aside his meal and leaned closer to the window.

There, near the center of the village common, was a small, slender figure swathed in a dark cape. Definitely female in outline, the figure could have been old or young, dark or fair. Her sheltering garb did not single her out, for many of the revelers were similarly clad—the winds blew straight off the river that day, and the air was crisp and chill. But she drew puzzled stares, all the same. Her step was too light, her movements too fluid and graceful.

At that moment the female paused at a stall and reached out a gloved hand to examine the wares offered. A passing sell-sword came up beside her and seized her extended wrist. He leaned in close and spoke words that Fyodor could not hear, then beckoned with an insinuating toss of his head toward the tavern.

Up came the female's cowled head in an imperious gesture Fyodor knew all too well. He leaped to his feet, jostling a mug-laden serving girl. She responded with a squeal of protest that rose into a full-throated scream when Fyodor pushed past her and kicked out the many-paned window.

Below him was the roof of the single-story kitchen; it was steeply pitched and ended not so very far off the ground. He barreled through the broken window and slid, feetfirst, down the rough-tiled roof.

On his way down, Fyodor saw the amorous sellsword scowl and jerk the female toward him. Her dark cowl fell back. Waves of lustrous white hair sprang into full view, framing a face that was blacker than moondark.

At that moment Fyodor hit the ground, taking two stout merchants down with him. He rolled free of the tangle and leaped to his feet, drawing his dark sword as he rose. Ignoring the shouting, fist-shaking merchants, he began frantically shouldering his way through the crowd to the place where Liriel stood revealed.

His progress was slow, for word was spreading through the crowd and with it a panic all out of proportion to the small, dark figure in their midst. Many people turned and ran, trampling the slower and weaker as they fled from the much-feared drow. For several minutes, the crush and press of the panicked villagers held Fyodor immobile.

Then came another, uglier turn of mood. The area around the dark-elven girl soon emptied, and the villagers saw she was one alone. A lifetime of hatred, generations of remembered wrongs, flowed toward the drow female. Like hounds baying at a treed snowcat, they began to close in. Knives flashed in the late-day sun.

Fyodor heaved a pair of gaping minstrels out of his path and surged forward just as Liriel stripped off her gloves and began the gestures of a spell. Some of her attackers also recognized the beginnings of magic and fell back, and for a moment a path lay clear between Fyodor and the drow. Her eyes met his, took note of his drawn sword, and flickered with indecision. Then she slashed the air with one slender black hand, dispelling the magic she had gathered. She closed her eyes and pressed both hands to her temples, as if to shut out the ravening crowd.

A sphere of impenetrable darkness surrounded her at once, a twenty-foot globe that enshrouded much of the courtyard. The crowd recoiled from the uncanny sight, some screaming, many making signs of warding against the drow evil.

"One man's nightmare is another man's opportunity! I say let's get her!" shouted a familiar voice. A dark-bearded man pushed his way to the inner edge of the crowd, leveled an arrow at the globe, and let fly at the place where Liriel had stood. Fyodor recognized the bounty hunter and started for him at a run.

From the far side of the globe came a man's grunt of pain, and a woman's scream. "She's killed him! The drow has shot my Tyron!"

Fyodor grabbed the bounty hunter's arm before he could nock a second arrow. "You bloody fool!" he thundered. "Your arrow passed right through the darkness into the crowd beyond."

The man lowered his bow. Eyeing Fyodor's drawn sword, he stroked thoughtfully at his beard. "You again, eh? Give me a better suggestion, boy, and I'll see you get one of the wench's ears."

Rage, pure and utterly his own, flowed through the young fighter. He hauled back his sword and smacked the bounty hunter just above the belt with the flat of his blade. The hunter folded as the air rushed out of him in a wheezing gasp. Fyodor placed himself between the midnight sphere and the crowd, his sword held menacingly before him.

"Liriel!" he shouted, not once taking his eyes from the grim-faced villagers. "Are you hurt? Are you *there?*"

"Well, where else?" she snapped. Her voice seemed to come from several feet above the ground, near the upper edge of the globe of darkness. "Get *in* here, would you?"

With a final, warning glare at the villagers, Fyodor stepped backward into the sphere of dark-elven magic.

Elaine Cunningham

The sunset colors were spilling into the churning waters of the Dessarin by the time Fyodor returned to the camp with their horses. Liriel was fascinated by the strange beasts, so different from the mounts of the Underdark, but tonight other matters consumed her thoughts. Fyodor had been strangely quiet since they'd stepped from her escape portal into the clearing. The drow assumed he was angry with her for sneaking into the village. She knew she would be furious, were the tables turned. Never before had she admitted to being wrong, and she found it wasn't an easy thing to do. She waited until they had eaten, and had taken turns snatching a bit of sleep, and then she gave it a try.

"I endangered us both today."

"You saved us both," Fyodor corrected her. "With your magic, you could have escaped the village the moment you were discovered. You stopped when you saw me."

Liriel opened her mouth to reply, realized she had nothing to say, and shut it. Her actions, now that she regarded them, seemed rather strange. "Well, what else could I have done? For all I knew, you'd go into a suicidal snit in the midst of all those people!"

"I would have welcomed the rage," he said bitterly, "but it would not come at my command."

"But you *tried?*" the drow asked, incredulous that he would do such a thing. Self-preservation was the first law of drow society; what he tried to do would almost certainly have meant his death.

Fyodor just shrugged. They sat in silence for a long moment, listening to the gathering chorus of frogs along the riverbank and watching the waxing moon rise above the hills.

After a time he took a tiny velvet bag from his sash and handed it to the drow. "This is a small thing I found in the market."

Curious, Liriel loosened the string and upended the bag. A length of thin, gold chain spilled into her hand, and with it a large jewel that echoed the rich golden color of her eyes. It was an exquisite piece, for although the chain was old, it was of fine elven make, and the stone looked as if it had been cut and polished by a dwarven craftsman. And in the very heart of the jewel was a small, perfect black spider. Liriel caught her breath. Yellow stones were rare in Menzoberranzan; this was an ornament any priestess or matron might envy!

"How is this illusion done?" she demanded, turning the stone this way and that.

"It is no illusion," Fyodor said. "The stone is amber. It is common in my land—pretty, but of no great price."

"But the spider?"

"It is real, caught in the stone by an accident of nature. Amber was once sap—the lifeblood of trees. At least," he added softly, "that is the answer given by those who think."

She recognized the familiar, rising note in his voice, and added the words to come: "And those who dream?"

Fyodor was silent for a long moment. "A tale is told in my land of a certain warrior. After the rage of battle left him, he wandered, wounded and confused, deeper into the forest than any man should walk. In time he came to an enchanted place and came to rest beneath a mighty tree. He saw in the distance a maiden of shadows and moonlight, more beautiful than any he had glimpsed either waking or in dreams. Now, it is said in my land that a man dies when his life surpasses his dreams. Thus the warrior passed from life with the image of the maiden before him, and the sightless tree wept golden tears. Whether in sorrow or envy, who can say?"

For the first time in her short life, Liriel was at a loss for words. The day's events, the carefully considered gift, and the graceful tribute in Fyodor's story had touched her and left her deeply confused. For a moment she wished with all her heart she were back in Menzoberranzan. Her home city, with all its chaos and conflict, was easier to understand. She knew the rules there and played them well. She had no idea what to do with the conflicting emotions inspired by this strange world.

But Liriel was not one for introspection. She pushed aside the uncomfortable new feelings and took refuge in something she understood.

The dark-elven girl rose lithely to her feet. Her armor, weapons, and clothing tumbled about her, and soon she stood, clad only in moonlight, before her companion.

Fyodor's eyes darkened. At last, thought Liriel with relief, an expression she knew! Desire burned with the same dark flame, be the male in question human or drow. Yet the young man made no move toward her. He did not look away, but he was clearly uncertain whether or not to accept what she offered.

A moment's panic threatened to claim Liriel. Passion was familiar, reassuring territory, one of the few emotional outlets permitted among the drow. If not this, she wondered, then *what?* She simply did not know another way.

Then Fyodor held out his hand, and with a cry of mingled triumph and relief she went to him.

The moon rose high, bathing their campsite in gentle light, but they did not notice the passing of time. The human knew none of the elaborate games the drow played, and Liriel found she did not miss them. This was something entirely different, both exhilarating and deeply disturbing. There was an honesty between them, an intimacy as merciless as sunlight. It scorched her soul as painfully as dawn stung her eyes. It was almost more than she could bear, yet she could not turn away.

Liriel struggled to gather herself, to regain some vestige of control. They tumbled together, and she rose above him and claimed command of the intimate dance. But even then his intense blue eyes held her in an embrace that was uncomfortably close. The drow closed her own eyes to take refuge in darkness.

Fyodor saw this, and he did not need the Sight to recognize the sheer self-preservation in the gesture. He had accepted Liriel's offer of herself as the gift it was, though he did not understand what the giving meant to the drow girl. Nor was he sure what place this night would have in his own life. Yet, in the uncanny way of his people, he knew without understanding that his destiny was somehow linked with this dark-elven girl. The sheer insanity of that thought did not trouble him; Fyodor was well accustomed to taking life as he found it.

Inexplicably, he thought of the snowcat kitten he had befriended years ago, knowing full well it could never be tamed. He'd accepted this with the calm resignation that was the heritage of the Rashemi people. He did not fault the cat for following its nature, or wish the animal could be other than it was. But he did not hold back his heart then, and he did not now. *Those who thought* knew embracing a drow was utter madness. *Those who dreamed* understood life's joy was measured in moments.

Fyodor raised a hand to stroke the dark elf's cheek. A faint smile touched Liriel's lips, and he traced it with a gentle finger. Her golden eyes opened, focused, and then turned hard. She put his hands away from her and looked him full in the face. For a moment, Fyodor thought he saw a hint of moisture behind the cold amber. Then Liriel clenched her hand into a fist and drove it toward her lover's temple.

A burst of bright pain exploded in Fyodor's head, searing his senses and eclipsing the moonlight. When the light and pain faded, he knew only darkness.

* * * * *

Liriel rose to her feet and dashed the back of her hand across her eyes. Bitterly she cursed herself for letting down her guard, for betraying her drow upbringing. The cost—as she'd expected—had been high.

The drow glanced toward her discarded clothing, but there was no time to dress, no time even to seize a weapon. So she merely stood, as coldly proud as any high priestess of Lloth, as the first of the dark-elven hunters slipped into the moonlit clearing. She did not fear them. After all, she had her magic, and it would take more than a few drow fighters to overcome a wizard of her ability.

The drow hunters—six, all told—formed a cautious ring around the campsite. Liriel recognized the four she had felled with sleeping poison, as well as the male with short-cropped hair and the dragon tattoo on his cheek. She glanced at his arm and gave him a faint, mocking smile, which broadened when his comrades flanked him and forcibly kept him from drawing his sword against her. But her smile vanished when a copper-haired, black-eyed drow pushed past the hunters and into the circle. Another wizard tipped the balance decidedly in the fighters' favor.

"Nisstyre," she hissed. "Come to offer me more *assistance?*"

"Whatever you require, dear lady," he said, and bowed. "But first, to remove unnecessary distractions."

He turned to the barely controlled Gorlist and pointed to the human. "You've found him at last. See if you can manage to kill him while he sleeps." His tone was deliberately harsh, clearly intended to direct the fighter's anger away from the female.

"You needn't bother," Liriel said coldly, marveling at how steady her voice sounded. "He's already dead."

Nisstyre's gaze swept the pale, still form of his human nemesis, then he turned a speculative gaze upon Liriel. "The Spider's Kiss, eh? A strange ending to a moonlight tryst! I heard you have adventurous tastes, my dear, but this exceeds the tales. Still, I almost envy the poor sod," he concluded gallantly. "Some things may well be worth dying for."

Elaine Cunningham

Liriel did not care for the gleam in the merchant's eyes. She lifted her chin and reminded herself she was a daughter of House Baenre.

"In that case, I wish you a long and healthy life," she said in the haughty tone Baenre females had honed through centuries of undisputed rule. "If you came seeking revenge against the human, you are too late. He is dead. Thank me for saving you the trouble, and be on your way."

"Actually, I seek a certain magical trinket," Nisstyre said softly. "An amulet, shaped like a dagger?"

She answered with a derisive sniff and spread her arms wide, as if inviting inspection. "As you can see, I don't have it on me," she said mockingly.

"A pity. I always find that searching for information is most entertaining," the wizard replied. He held out one hand and made a show of adjusting his many rings. One of them, a thick gold band set with a sparkling black gem, was chillingly familiar. Liriel's eyes widened as she recognized her former tutor's ring. The wizard noted this and smiled. "I assure you, he has no need of it."

So Kharza was dead, Liriel acknowledged with mingled sorrow and fear. How brutal had Nisstyre's "search for information" been, and how much had Kharza told him about the amulet before escaping into death?

Enough, it would seem. Nisstyre flicked at the ring's large black stone, and the jewel swung back on a tiny hinge. He took a pinch of powder from the hidden compartment and cast it into the air. The eerie, faint blue light of a find-magic spell filled the clearing. Most of Liriel's things glowed: her chain mail, her elven boots, her *piwafwi*, many of her knives and throwing weapons. But the amulet—even hidden as it was in her travel bag—positively blazed with azure fire.

Nisstyre stooped and picked up Liriel's bag. He spilled the contents onto the ground. Gold coins and sparkling gems cascaded out, and the eyes of the drow thieves lit up with open greed. Nisstyre waved them back and snatched up the brightly lit amulet.

"You're wasting your time. You can do nothing with it!" Liriel said coldly.

"Perhaps not. But far to the south is a city ruled by drow wizards skilled beyond your reckoning or mine. When the amulet's magic is mine, I will be able to wean the People from their false dependency on Lloth. And at last," Nisstyre concluded triumphantly, "the drow will reclaim a place of power in the Night Above!"

This was too much for Liriel to absorb. "*You* worship Eilistraee?"

"Hardly," the wizard said dryly. "We follow Vhaeraun, the Masked Lord, drow god of stealth and thievery. Eilistraee's insipid wenches think only to dance in the moonlight and give aid to hapless passersby; we have a kingdom to build!"

Nisstyre turned to Gorlist. "Gather up everything that glows. I want to study every magical item she possesses."

A bubble of panic rose in Liriel's throat. "You're going to leave me without any magic?"

"Not at all," Nisstyre assured her. "There is a place among Vhaeraun's followers for any drow who forsakes the Night Below. In your case, a high place! I myself would be pleased to take you as a consort."

Liriel laughed in his face.

For a moment she thought the wizard would strike her. Then he bowed again, this time mockingly. "As you wish, princess. But in time, you will learn drow can survive only by banding together in force, and you will come to me." He took a small scroll from his belt and held it out to her. "This is a map. With it you can find your way to a nearby settlement of Vhaeraun's followers. You may keep your nonmagical weapons and your wealth—you will have need of both if you are to reach the forest stronghold."

She struck the parchment roll from his hand. He shrugged and turned away. "Have it your way. But sooner or later, princess, we will meet again."

"Count on it," Liriel muttered under her breath as the last of the drow hunters slipped from the clearing.

She waited until all were beyond sight and hearing, then dropped to her knees beside Fyodor and began to shake and slap him toward consciousness. All the while, she whispered fervent prayers of gratitude—to any and all drow gods who might be listening—for the fact that Fyodor had stayed obligingly "dead" until the danger was past.

After a few moments of this treatment, the Rashemi groaned and stirred. He sat up, clutching his temples. His clouded eyes settled on Liriel. Memory crept into them, and then puzzlement. "In my land, such things are done differently," he murmured.

Liriel rose abruptly. He reached up and caught her hand. "Why?" he said softly. "I ask of you only this, that you tell me why."

She brushed him aside and began to collect her clothes. "For what it's worth, I just saved your life," she snarled. "Nisstyre and his drow thieves came upon us. They would have killed you, had I not

269

convinced him I'd saved him the trouble."

Fyodor still looked bewildered. "But how could he believe you'd slain me, if he came upon us at such a time?"

"Because it happens." She stopped lacing her tunic and met his gaze squarely. "Such sport is not unknown among my people. One of these games has been named the Spider's Kiss, after the spider who mates and kills."

The man stared at her, clearly aghast. Liriel steeled herself for his response. From what she'd learned of her human companion, she expected revulsion, horror, wrath, perhaps utter rejection.

But he merely shook his head. "Ah, my poor little raven," he said softly. "What a life you must have known!"

What Liriel could not understand, she decided to ignore. "Get up," she said bruskly. "If we hurry, we might still catch them."

Fyodor regarded her strangely. "I know why I must face the drow. But why should you take such a risk?"

"They took all my magic! My weapons, spellbooks, even my boots and cloak!"

"But these are mere things," he pointed out.

"Nisstyre has the Windwalker," she said flatly. It was dangerous to tell him this—she had not yet figured out a way to share the amulet's magic—but she saw no other choice. "I saw a dagger-shaped amulet in his hands. Or is this also a 'mere thing,' not worth retrieving?"

Chagrin flickered in Fyodor's eyes, and he reached for his sword-belt. "My apologies, lady wizard! Your need is as great as mine."

They scrambled down the hill after the thieves—Liriel gritting her teeth against the pain of rocks and brambles tearing at her bare feet— and came to an abrupt stop at the water's edge. The drow were already in the river, many yards from shore, poling light wooden crafts toward the swifter water in the river's center. Nisstyre caught sight of them and called a halt.

"Brava, princess!" he called, smiling ruefully. "You tricked me well! Yet by my reckoning, you have lost." He held up a small, dangling object. Moonlight glinted off the dull gold of the ancient dagger. "Until you get this back, I would say the victory is mine!" Nisstyre blew her a kiss, then signaled his drow to pole the boats into the swift-flowing current.

"*Get it back*," Fyodor echoed softly. He turned incredulous eyes upon his companion. "You had the amulet, all this time! You kept silent, after all I told you. But why?"

Liriel held her ground, but she was finding it inexplicably difficult not to squirm before his accusing gaze. "I had my reasons."

The young man took a long, steadying breath. He reached for her hands and clasped them between his. "Liriel, I do not deny this may be so," he said carefully. "By your lights, these reasons might have been good and sufficient. But I tell you truly, this is too much for me to bear. Here we part ways."

Liriel pulled her hands free and clenched her fists at her sides. Her first response was anger. Intrigue was the meat and drink of Menzoberranzan, and even her most casual friends took this in stride. Why couldn't Fyodor just be reasonable?

"We both need that amulet," she pointed out, hoping to appeal to his practical side. "If we compete, only one can win."

The young man nodded, somberly conceding her point. "You will do as you must, little raven, and so will I."

She stood staring for a moment, unable to believe he was thrusting them into competition. His eyes held both sadness and resolve, and Liriel knew instinctively that none of her threats or wiles could change his mind. She was not prepared for the wave of desolation that swept over her.

Not knowing what else to do, Liriel turned and darted off downstream in pursuit of Nisstyre and the stolen Windwalker.

Chapter 23

DIFFERENT WAYS

s the hours of night slipped past, Liriel made her way southward along the river. She moved quietly, lightly, yet she cringed at the sound of each faint footfall; she was accustomed to walking in complete silence. Her feet were bruised and bleeding, but she kept walking until she could go no farther. Huddled at the base of a tree, she wrapped her arms around herself for warmth and took stock of her position.

Her drow magic was gone. She could not summon darkness, or conjure faerie fire, or levitate. Stripped of her magical items, she could not walk silently or cloak herself in invisibility. Not to mention the more mundane value of boots and cloak! Her spellbooks were gone, along with the spell components that would enable her to cast wizardly spells. But perhaps her clerical magic had not forsaken her.

Liriel remembered the words of Qilué Veladorn, claiming that Eilistraee heard and answered her faithful wheresoever they went. Could Lloth also hear, so far from the chapels of Menzoberranzan? The girl tried a simple incantation that summoned spiders—a blessing Lloth granted to any drow. She whispered the words of the spell, then strained her ears for the skittering sound of delicate legs. There was only the chirp of crickets and the lonely hoot of a hunting owl. She was truly alone.

The drow drew her knees up to her chest and dropped her head to them. She felt very small and utterly lost beneath the vastness of the night sky.

After a moment a fragment of melody slipped unbidden into her mind. Liriel recognized the wild, haunting music played at the moonlit revels of Eilistraee's priestesses. On impulse, she rose and began to dance to the rhythm of the remembered song. Closing her eyes, she whirled and dipped and leaped. As she did, the pain in her battered feet subsided, then slipped away. Liriel was not surprised; caught up in the private ecstacy of the dance, all things seemed possible.

From a nearby hillside, Fyodor watched her. The moon had sunk low in the sky, and the fey dancer was silhouetted against the pale light. Another female danced with Liriel, clearly elven in form but taller by half than a mortal drow. Fyodor did not know what this meant, but he took comfort in the fact Liriel was not alone.

*   *   *   *   *

Carried swiftly on the waters of the spring-swollen Dessarin, the merchants of the Dragon's Hoard made their way southward. Henge, drow priest of Vhaeraun, watched with interest as Nisstyre argued with the tattooed lieutenant. The priest's hatred of Nisstyre was almost as strong as his devotion to his god, and he eavesdropped on the small mutiny with shameless enjoyment. Gorlist, it seemed, wanted the princess and her human lap-lizard destroyed. That struck Henge as reasonable enough. True, the female would be useful for breeding purposes, but they had her magic, and that, in Henge's opinion, was sufficient. He'd seen more than enough of drow females during his years as a slave in Ched Nasad. If Gorlist wanted to kill one of the two-legged spiders, may Vhaeraun be with him.

Yet the cleric could not move openly against his captain. He'd tried, once, only to find he'd exchanged one sort of slavery for another. Many years ago, Nisstyre had lured Henge into Vhaeraun's service, extracting an oath of blood-bond in payment for escape from Ched Nasad. Any failure of loyalty carved deep, magically inflicted cuts onto Henge's body. The priest still bore the scars of his early rebellions and small failures to serve; after many years, however, he had learned exactly where the parameters of the bond lay. There were still some small things he could do, and he watched and waited for an opportunity.

Suddenly Nisstyre's voice faltered, and his hands went to the eye-shaped gem embedded in his forehead. Gorlist, obviously thinking himself dismissed, left the wizard's side with an abruptness that set the boat rocking dangerously. The cleric beckoned the young drow over. He handed Gorlist a silver ear-cuff.

"This is a small thing that you might find useful. No matter how skilled the warrior, certain tasks are dangerous. Wear this, and any wound you receive will heal."

Pride and practicality warred in the fighter's eyes. Then Gorlist cast a surreptitious glance at Nisstyre and slid the ear-cuff into place.

*　*　*　*　*

Back in Menzoberranzan, Shakti had had little time to spare for her merchant partner. Her mother, Matron Kinuere, was delighted with the addition of a high priestess to her arsenal and encouraged by the favors shown them by House Baenre. She promptly began plotting a war against House Tuin'Tarl. The unnatural peace would end sooner or later, and those who were prepared to act with little notice would gain advancement.

Shakti, therefore, had been inundated by the demands of her new responsibilities. She did not mind, but rather listened well, learning skills she intended to wield herself someday, and on a much grander scale. But she did not forget her hunters; when no word come from Ssasser, she gave up the naga and the quaggoths as lost. Nisstyre, however, she could and would keep within her hand.

When at last the priestess had an hour to call her own, she took out the black-ruby scrying bowl and cast the spell that linked her to the drow merchant. A strange scene came into view: small boats traveling a river bright with sparkling lights and swift-running water. With Nisstyre were several drow fighters, and he was arguing with one of them. To get his attention, Shakti sent a quick burst of pain to the ruby eye. The wizard winced, and his hands rose to touch his forehead. The movement brought the golden amulet dangling from one hand into Shakti's line of vision.

"You have done well," she complimented him, and her words were carried to his mind by the telepathic link. "And now?"

I take the amulet to the south, to have its magic studied by drow wizards there. When its secrets are known to me, I will return to Menzoberranzan.

Shakti nodded. She was confident the wizard would do as he said; how could he not, when she could follow him wheresoever he went and slay him with a thought? Yet there was a formal, cautious feel to his mental response that she distrusted.

"And what of Liriel Baenre?"

She will not *be returning to Menzoberranzan.*

The traitor-priestess threw back her head and cackled with delight. Desiring to see for herself the details of her enemy's death, she cast a clerical mind-reading spell and sent it along the crimson path. Vhaeraun had been generous; of all the gifts granted her by the God of Thievery, Shakti relished most these small plunderings of the mind and the spirit. From Nisstyre's memory she plucked his last image of Liriel. The princess, although decidedly more bedraggled than Shakti had ever seen her, was very much alive and pacing like an angry panther along a rock-strewn shore. Shakti's mood plummeted and her red eyes narrowed.

"You lied to me! She lives!"

Have I said she didn't? As I recall, you required only that Liriel not return to the city. That has been assured.

"It is not enough!" shrieked the priestess, clutching at the rim of the scrying bowl with both hands.

A surge of rage flowed through the magic portal and struck the wizard like a thunderbolt. The ruby gem in his forehead flared and seemed to burst into crimson flame. Nisstyre screamed in torment, then slumped, apparently lifeless, into the arms of his puzzled drow followers.

Shakti snatched her hands from the bowl and regarded the fading scene with horror. She had not intended to strike, and she had clearly gone too far. Gingerly she reached out one fingertip to touch the scrying bowl. She felt the hum of magic power still sing through the dark red crystal. That was a relief; it meant the tie had not been severed, that Nisstyre still lived. Yet only through his eyes could she see into the Night Above. Until Nisstyre regained his senses, he was of no use to her.

Sobered by this near disaster, Shakti settled back in her chair and regarded the scrying bowl. She had much to learn about her new power and how to wield it to best advantage. But this one thing she *had* learned: *it was not sufficient.* Nisstyre was an important ally, but, like all mortals, he was vulnerable.

As she stared thoughtfully at the scrying bowl, the priestess began to ponder other ways to gain access to the power and resources found in the Night Above.

* * * * *

The coming of dawn roused Liriel from a brief, exhausted slumber. She picked her way down to the river to drink and wash. There, placed neatly on the rocky bank, she found a new cloak and a pair of low boots rudely fashioned from soft leather. There was no doubting who'd left them for her.

The drow shook her head in confusion. Humans apparently had a lot to learn about the art of competition! But she donned the gifts and continued downstream. As she walked, the roar of the water grew louder. The river flowed rapid and shallow here. On the far shore, not too far away, were Nisstyre's hunters, shouldering their small boats to portage around the dangerous stretch of water.

Liriel crouched behind some bushes and thoughtfully studied her foe. It would be an ideal time to attack. Though she had little magic left to her, she cudgeled her mind for an innovative way to use a minor spell. The roar of the water made thought difficult, however, and hearing impossible. Bereft of her magic, the drow felt keenly the loss of these other senses.

Fortunately her elven eyes were as keen as ever. At the very edge of her peripheral vision, she saw a familiar, dark figure creeping toward her. Liriel spun as the tattooed male came at her with drawn steel. She pulled her dagger and parried. With a quick, circular sweep of his sword he knocked the blade from her hand, then stepped in closer and seized Liriel's wrist.

Gorlist pressed the keen edge of his blade against her skin. "Shall I mark you, wizard, as you did me?" he demanded. "How can you stop me? Where is your magic now?"

He was taunting her, but Liriel saw the humiliation in his eyes, and she understood what this was about. Drow fighters took pride in their lack of scars—she had probably been the first to lay a blade on him, and in doing so had dealt his pride a dangerous blow.

"What will your master say?" she demanded. "Nisstyre will be furious if you harm me!"

"Perhaps he will be, but not for a while," the male said cryptically. "Nisstyre would not thank me if I marred your skin. He might, however, be pleased to find you humbled." With a cruel smile, he sheathed his blade and dragged Liriel to him.

Her eyes widened with shock and outrage when his intent became clear. There was no time to draw a weapon, no time to cast a spell, but Liriel was not without defenses. She crossed her middle finger over her index finger, braced them into a rigid weapon, and drove her lacquered nails deep into Gorlist's eye.

He roared with pain and lashed out blindly; his fist connected solidly with Liriel's ear and sent her sprawling. Gorlist dashed the gore from his face and leaped at her. Ignoring the ringing in her head, Liriel kicked up and out with all her strength. Her aim was true, and she was rewarded by another scream of pain—this one at least two octaves higher than the last. Gorlist hit the ground nearby, groaning, and curled up as tightly as an overcooked shrimp.

Liriel scrambled to her feet and turned to flee. The male grabbed at her, and his hand managed to close around her ankle. With her free foot, she stomped on Gorlist's wrist, but her soft deerskin boots lent little conviction to the attack, and she did not break his hold. Quickly abandoning that attempt, she kicked him in the face. She got in several more blows before Gorlist managed to capture her free foot, as well. With a quick, sharp jerk he pulled both feet out from under her. Liriel's arms flew out wide and she fell straight back. Her head met the rocky ground with a sharp crack. The force of the blow—although cushioned a bit by her thick white mane—left her stunned.

The male crawled over to her and drew a long knife from his belt. Pure malevolence glowed in his one good eye. Liriel knew a moment's relief—he meant only to kill her, after all.

"Get away from her!" demanded a deep bass voice.

Gorlist looked up, startled, as a familiar-looking human hurtled toward him. The drow was faster, though, and he brought the wicked knife up.

Yet Liriel was also drow, and just as fast. Summoning all her strength, she managed to strike Gorlist's arm aside an instant before Fyodor would have impaled himself on the knife. The two fighters rolled clear of her, thrashing and struggling for position. She watched intently; the outcome was by no means clear. The human was a head taller and probably outweighed Gorlist by half, but the elf was more agile and nearly mad with rage, pain, and wounded pride.

Liriel waited expectantly for Fyodor's berserker frenzy to come and settle matters. It did not. This worried her; Gorlist still held the knife, and it was only a matter of time before he found an opening.

So she crawled over to the fighters, ignoring the throbbing in her head and the weird sparks of light exploding behind her eyes. She pulled a knife from her sleeve, watched for an opening between the grappling fighters, then thrust the blade between them. She drew it back hard against Gorlist's throat. The drow managed a gurgled protest, then fell limp.

Fyodor pushed away from the dying drow. For a long moment, the rivals for the Windwalker regarded each other in awkward silence.

"Next time, don't announce your arrival," Liriel suggested icily. "Kill first, and if unanswered questions remain you can always hire a priestess to chat with the spirit."

He responded with a faint, bleak smile. "It is not my custom to strike from behind. We do things differently, you and I."

"So I noticed! It's not drow custom to give any advantage to an enemy, much less leave them gifts."

"Yet you wear these gifts."

"Of course. I'm practical," she stated. "As you're always pointing out, there are those who think, and those who dream. Well, together we've got one of each. I suggest we stop this foolishness and tend to business. Together."

"But how can that be, if there is no trust between us?" he demanded, his blue eyes searching her face.

The drow crossed her arms and stared him down. "So, what's the score now?"

Fyodor blinked and drew back. "The score?"

"The score. You know: I've pulled your *tzarreth* out of the fire four times, you've saved mine three—that sort of thing." She lifted one white eyebrow. "It says something, doesn't it?"

The light began to return to Fyodor's eyes. "Are you saying I should trust you?"

The drow shrugged.

"I suppose if we continue as we have been going, neither of us will possess the Windwalker," he said cautiously.

"Now you're talking!" Liriel could not suppress a smile of pure elation. "Then it's settled!"

"Is it? If only one can possess the Windwalker, who will be that one?"

"Let's worry about one thing at a time," Liriel advised him. She squinted downriver. The drow hunters were almost beyond sight. "Nine Hells! We'll never catch them! Where are those long-legged lizards of yours?"

"The horses fled—probably the drow ran them off." He hesitated. "There is another way. We could build a raft. It is risky, with the water running white and fast."

Her eyes sparkled with reckless glee. "Let's do it!"

Working furiously, they dragged deadfall wood to the bank and lashed it together into a rude platform. Fyodor tied long loops of rope onto the makeshift craft for handholds, and the two of them waded out with it into the river. They had not gone far before the rushing water threatened to tear the raft from their hands.

The Rashemi shouted for Liriel to get aboard. She scrambled on the back of the raft and wrapped a rope around her hand. She grabbed Fyodor's vest and helped haul him up.

Then they were off, tossed like a leaf on the foam. Fyodor tried vainly to steer, using his cudgel to push away from jagged rocks. Mostly, they just held on as the little raft bounced and spun. The river quickly turned rougher, and the raft lifted and dropped in the turbulent water, like an unbroken horse trying to throw a rider. Above the roar of water Fyodor heard Liriel's wild, exultant laughter. The raft reared up high for a breathless moment, then splashed down hard. Water swept over them in an icy rush.

Fyodor fought with his rope, hauling upward with all his strength to bring the front edge of the raft above the water. If it dipped too low, the raft would flip and they would be tossed into the river's frigid depths. He struggled for several desperate moments before he had the little craft bouncing along again. With a sigh of relief, he glanced back over his shoulder at Liriel.

She was gone.

His heart seemed to leap into his throat. He lunged for her rope and gave it a mighty tug upward, hoping against hope she might have kept her grip. Liriel's head broke the surface of the water, and she gasped in huge gulps of air and foam. Sputtering and coughing, she hauled herself back toward him, hand over hand. As she rolled onto the raft, she batted away Fyodor's hand and pointed. Her eyes were wild, and she shrieked a single word that was lost in the noise of the rapids and the pounding of his heart.

Fyodor turned, and his eyes widened. The river turned shallow ahead, and rocks jutted out of the water like so many grave markers. Beyond was a curtain of spray, and the deep, thunderous roar of falling water.

The wooden raft screeched as it scraped against rock, and then the lashing gave way. Liriel and Fyodor were thrown into a whirlpool of splintering wood and rending water. They tumbled over the shallow riverbed, scraping over gravel and hitting one bruising rock after another. Then, suddenly, they were free, plunging down through the spray-filled air.

They hit the water hard and sank deep. Fyodor fought his way upward, gasped in air, and saw that he was alone. He grabbed his floating cudgel, hooked an arm over it, and plunged his head under to look for Liriel.

The drow floated just beneath the surface of the water, her arms hanging limp and her white hair floating around her in a nimbus. Fyodor snatched a handful of hair and dragged her to the surface. Slowly, painfully, he began to swim to shore.

Because Fyodor's home village lay on the shore of a small, icy lake, he had learned from childhood the realities of life upon water. He turned the drow onto her back and began to press rhythmically. Finally water poured from her mouth, and she gasped in air. She rose up on her hands and knees and crawled weakly away. Fyodor turned aside, granting the proud elf privacy to rid herself of the water she'd swallowed.

Utterly exhausted and aching in every bone and sinew, the young man sank down on a fallen log. His rest was brief; a revived Liriel ran toward him, her eyes blazing.

The drow leaped at him, sending them both tumbling to the sandy shore. She seized Fyodor's tattered shirt with both hands and dragged him close. His first thought was that the treacherous drow had turned on him again, and this time he could not fault her. He had persuaded her to go onto the impossibly dangerous river, and she had nearly paid with her life. His death, should it come at her hands, would not be undeserved.

Then, to his utter astonishment, Fyodor noted that his companion's eyes burned not with rage, but with excitement.

"Again!" she gasped out, and gave him a little shake. "Let's do that again!"

With a groan, Fyodor fell back on the bank. He eyed the irrepressible drow, not sure whether to embrace her or give over to helpless laughter. So he did both.

This time, Liriel's laughter joined his.

Chapter 24

PROMENADE

hey did not see Nisstyre or his hunters again for the duration of the trip. That was just as well, for the rigors of the road were quite sufficient for Liriel's taste.

Fyodor spent most of the first day tracking down their horses, and although Liriel was glad for the speed this granted them, she almost wished the wretched beasts had made good their escape. In the Underdark, she was considered an expert rider, but a horse's gait was vastly different from the smooth, darting movements of a lizard mount. At the end of the first day's ride, Liriel ached in muscles she had never before acknowledged. But as the days passed, her body became hardened to the jarring trot, just as her eyes adjusted to the bright light.

The long westward ride brought other changes to the drow, as well. Liriel had never been one to sit and think; now she had little choice. Yet try as she might, she could find no words for the night she and Fyodor had shared in the moonlit clearing. Finally she asked him, bluntly, what the human customs were in such matters.

The question did not seem to surprise him, but he was long in answering. "These things are not easily explained. Ask ten men what it means to spend a night with a maid, and you will likely get ten different answers."

"Thanks, I'll take your word on that," she said with a shudder. *Once,* in her opinion, offered more confusion than she could handle.

Fyodor responded with a deep, wry chuckle. "Please, little raven! A man has his pride."

The drow frowned. "I didn't mean—"

He waved her into silence. "You need not explain. I think we both were surprised by what we found together. There is a bond between us, for good or ill, and so it will remain. Understand that I've never taken such things lightly, but I think it best to agree that we came together as friends, and let the matter end."

Liriel thought that over. It seemed reasonable, and it felt right. Still . . . "I've never shared passion with a friend before," she mused.

He lifted one brow. "With whom, then? Your enemies?"

A short, startled burst of laughter escaped the drow. "Yes, that pretty much sums it up."

"Ah." Fyodor nodded solemnly, but his eyes twinkled. "This explains much."

Liriel acknowledged his teasing with a wry smile and was more than content to let the matter rest. Talking about it cleared the air between them and that, for now, was enough. The challenges ahead were daunting, and she could not afford to be distracted by things she could not hope to understand. The insights she *had* gained were disturbing enough.

For Liriel had come to accept the possibility she might never regain her drow powers. Every night, when they stopped to rest the horses, she coaxed Fyodor to practice swordcraft with her. Nisstyre had left her those weapons that bore no magic—a few knives, the long dagger she'd taken from the naga—and she was determined to wield them as best she could. Day by day, her strength and skill improved, and the desultory swordplay of a spoiled princess began to harden into a drow's fierce art. Liriel planned to make her way as a wizard; the naga's treasure would purchase spell components and spellbooks in the markets of Skullport. In time, she might regain a level of power similar to the magic she'd once wielded. Until then, she had to survive.

But not until they neared Waterdeep did Liriel realize she had not lost *every* drow gift she possessed. The art of intrigue, once learned, was not soon forgotten.

She and Fyodor approached the city from the north, riding cautiously through verdant farmlands, skirting the well-traveled roads. At last they caught sight of high towers rising up over the broad fields of green. They urged their weary horses closer and reined them to a halt on a small, wooded hillside.

Laid out before them, looming over a broad plain and several busy trade roads, was Waterdeep, City of Splendors. An exuberant smile lit the drow's face. She flung her arms wide, as if she could gather the whole into her embrace.

How wonderful it was, this city perched between sea and sky! The air here had a delightful salty tang, and it carried a low, restless murmur that could only be the voice of the sea. The city itself was bigger than Menzoberranzan, and bustling with activity. Wagons and horses carried a steady stream of people through the gates. Liriel's arms dropped to her sides.

"The gates," she murmured, seeing the problem at once.

"All who wish to enter must pass armed guardsmen," Fyodor added in a troubled tone. He glanced at his companion. Even with hood and gloves, she could not pass as human without the aid of a spell. And her spells had all been used in the hazardous journey westward.

The drow nibbled at her lower lip as she studied the city walls. Surely there was some weak point, some way she could slip in unnoticed. But no, the walls were high and thick, and the surrounding plain offered little cover. She watched the merchant caravans and pondered smuggling herself in. No help there—the guards searched each wagon carefully.

Muttering an oath, Liriel turned her attention to the plain. It was grassy and smooth, dotted with small clusters of bushes and a few shade trees. In that pleasant spot were raised a number of pavilions: tents fashioned from bright cloth and decorated with elaborate coats of arms. Milling about the idle tents was a throng of humans, dressed in vivid silks, lush furs, and jewels. The spring breezes bore the scent of savory foods and the sound of music and revelry. Wealthy, idle people enjoying an outdoor feast, Liriel concluded.

Then the music changed, taking on the stately, measured tread of a promenade. Liriel's eyes narrowed. She noted the dizzying variety of the humans' costumes—some of which were enhanced by magic—and the way the dancers paraded past a flower-draped dais. A slow smile curved her lips. The dark elves had a similar custom: formal dances known as *illiyitrii*. Most of these were political affairs fraught with dangerous, nuanced posturing, but occasionally a promenade was an excuse to compete in less lethal ways; wealth, beauty, and ingenuity were flaunted through clever disguises and extravagant costumes.

Suddenly Liriel knew how to get into the city.

The drow watched and waited until a man and woman, giggling over some wine-induced bit of wit and clinging to each other for support, made their unsteady way toward the privacy of the bushes clustered at the base of the hill. The woman was small and slim, dressed in a gown of clinging white silk. On her head was an elaborate headpiece, now slightly askew, that mimicked the ears, mane, and horn of a unicorn.

"Wait here," Liriel hissed at Fyodor.

Before the Rashemi could respond, she slid from her horse and made her silent way down the hillside. Fyodor heard a couple of faint, dull thuds. After a few moments' silence, the drow emerged triumphant, her arms full of shining silk.

Fyodor eyed her warily. "You didn't—"

"Kill them?" she finished cheerfully. "Effort wasted! Those two were barely standing; all they required was a little push. They'll waken with not much more of a headache than they've already earned through overindulgence. And I left a handful of coins to cover their losses," she added dryly. "Something tells me you wouldn't take kindly to a little harmless thievery."

The drow promptly stripped off her travel-worn clothes and pulled the gown over her head. She combed out her hair and let it fall in a wild cascade around her bared shoulders, then fastened her amber-encased spider pendant about her neck. Hushing Fyodor's protests, she handed him the "borrowed" robe—somewhat grass-stained but still exquisite—to put on over his travel clothes. Then she took a length of red silk and wound it around his head, turban fashion, and fastened it with a jeweled pin.

"There," she said in a satisfied tone. "That's just how it looked on the other man. I've no idea what you're supposed to be, but I suppose the humans will."

"You wish to join the festival, and slip into the city among the others," he realized. "But what about your disguise?"

Liriel smiled slyly. "I'm a drow, of course. It's quite an exotic costume. And authentic, too!" she added with a touch of irony.

Understanding lit his eyes, then wry admiration. They exchanged a conspiratorial grin and crept down the hill to join the merrymakers.

* * * * *

For the next hour, Liriel danced, sipped wine, accepted inane compliments on her "costume," and watched Fyodor with amazement. He fit into the gay company as easily as a sword in its sheath: laughing and drinking and telling tales. Before long, he'd gathered about him a group of young noblemen, each striving to outdo the others with boastful accounts of his own adventures. Fyodor passed around his flask of firewine and listened with rapt attention to their lies. The drow heard the word "Skullport" whispered, and her eyes glinted with amused understanding. Her plan would get them into Waterdeep, but Fyodor was looking to the task beyond.

Someone brushed aside her hair and dropped a kiss on the nape of her neck. Instinctively, she spun around with a snarl.

A tall man with gray eyes and wheat-colored hair fell back a step, as if startled by her vehement reaction. Liriel recognized him as one of the nobles who had shared tales with Fyodor. Though his wavering stance and the nearly empty goblet in his hand suggested he'd had more than his share to drink, there was a shrewd expression in his eyes that Liriel noted and mistrusted. Then the sharp look vanished, and the young man smiled engagingly at her.

"Oh, I see. You're in character." He raised his hands in mock defense and pretended to cringe. "I must say, Galinda, you've outdone yourself this time. That's a marvelous costume! But shouldn't you carry some sort of fearful weapon to add realism—a whip or some such?"

For the first time in her life, Liriel actually envied high priestesses their snake-headed whips. She bared her teeth in an approximation of a smile. "The trouble with whips is that you never seem to have one handy when you really need it," she cooed.

The man threw back his head and laughed. "How true! I've often thought that very thing, myself."

His leer was comic and good-natured, his laughter infectious. Liriel suddenly misplaced her anger. A genuine smile curved her lips, and she regarded the handsome male with a touch of speculation.

Fyodor chose that moment to appear at her side. Once again, the drow glimpsed a flicker of penetrating intelligence in the stranger's gray eyes as he took the Rashemi's measure. Before anyone could speak, an exceedingly tipsy woman with bright red hair and an abundant display of cleavage lurched over to claim the young man's arm.

"There you are, Dan," she cooed. "I've been looking everywhere for you!"

"Was this our dance?" he murmured absently.

The redheaded woman smiled like a hungry troll. "Unless you had something a bit more . . . *interesting* in mind?"

The invitation was crude and unmistakable, and it got his full attention. He claimed the woman's hand and bowed low over it. "Myrna, my dear, *phlar Lloth ssinssrickla,*" he said fervently, and then raised her fingers to his lips for a gallant kiss.

A bubble of startled, delighted laughter burst from Liriel. *When Lloth giggles,* he'd said in response to the woman's amorous advances—hardly the tribute the simpering, overheated wench apparently believed it to be. Oh, he was clever, this one!

Liriel's laughter died abruptly. This one was *too* clever.

With three words, spoken in oddly accented drow, the fair-haired man had said much and revealed even more. He knew what she was, and was putting her on notice of this. He had also tested her, beyond the obvious trial that recognition of the drow phrase offered. The blasphemous little jest would have surprised a scowl from a truly devout follower of Lloth. Although Liriel supposed her mirth had spoken well for her, she was annoyed with herself for falling into the human's multilayered trap. She simply hadn't expected such subtlety among these vapid folk. And how the Nine Hells had a human learned a few words of the drow language?

Fyodor, sensing her agitation, slipped a steadying arm around her waist. "My lady?" he inquired, leveling a challenging stare at the taller man. "Is all well?"

The stranger turned an engaging smile on the wary drow and her apparent champion. "It is indeed, my friend. Wonderful story Regnet told earlier, wasn't it? Oddest thing is, most of it was actually true! And at the risk of repeating myself, Galinda, that costume is simply the best you've ever come up with. A bit disconcerting at first, to be sure, but the Dark Maiden look suits you. Well, enjoy the party, both of you."

With those cryptic words, the man slipped away into the crowd, firmly steering the red-haired woman toward the circle of dancers and

287

away from the private, silken pavilions she so obviously preferred. But Liriel had heard the message in his parting words, in all its layers of meaning. The tension drained from her, and she leaned back into the reassuring circle of Fyodor's strong arm.

A servant dressed in flowing robes and a medusa headdress wandered by with a tray of seafood tidbits. Suddenly Liriel felt ravenous. She helped herself to several bits of spiced squid, and as she munched she eyed the blond man's retreating form.

"You know," she mused, "I think I could live in this city."

* * * * *

Rats, a swarm of them, scrabbled at Liriel with tiny, grasping hands. The drow hurled several of the little creatures off her and leaped from her narrow stone perch into waist-deep water. She caught her breath at the incredible stench and resisted an urge to hurl a handful of throwing knives at the squeaking vermin that had forced her into the sludge. But there was no sense losing her weapons in the water and muck of Waterdeep's sewers.

"This was not one of your better ideas," she grumbled at Fyodor.

The Rashemi did not turn around. He slogged along steadily, surrounded by a circle of torchlight. "It is the route Regnet's story suggested. It may not be the best way into Skullport, but at least a drow can take it without attracting notice."

Liriel cast a venomous look at Fyodor's back. "Oh, sure! I look right at home in any of your basic cesspools. No one we meet would give me a second glance!"

"Come now, little raven," he said teasingly. "Where is your sense of adventure?"

She responded with a drow idiom that defied translation. The Rashemi, however, got the gist of it and wisely put several more paces between him and his disgruntled companion.

Without warning, something grabbed Liriel's leg and yanked her beneath the water. An unseen creature dragged her, kicking and thrashing, to a hole in the tunnel floor, then sank into deeper water with its prey.

Liriel pulled a knife from her boot and sawed frantically at the clinging appendage. Other, similar arms encircled her. The drow understood the nature of her captor and went limp. Her lungs burned with a need for air, but she forced herself to remain still, to let the thing pull her close. Through the murky water she saw the bulbous eyes and beaky mouth of a giant squid. When she was within arm's reach, she slashed it viciously across the eyes. At once the squid released its deadly "meal." Thick black ink jetted through the water as the wounded creature scuttled away.

Liriel fought her way to the surface and gasped in long, grateful breaths of the foul air. She crawled out of the water and found a ledge on the uneven blocks that formed the sewer wall. A length of slender tentacle, severed but still twitching, was wrapped around her calf.

"I think I ate some of your relatives at the costume promenade," the drow muttered viciously. She grabbed the tip of the tentacle and peeled it back. The underside was covered with suction cups, and blood welled up from several tiny, circular cuts on her leg. Liriel gritted her teeth and ripped the thing off in one quick motion. The pain was much greater than she expected, and she let out a howl.

At last Fyodor looked back over his shoulder. "You shouldn't make so much noise," he cautioned her. "No telling what we might run into down here."

Liriel set her jaw and leaped back into the water. As she sloshed along in Fyodor's wake, she entertained herself with thoughts of wrapping the severed tentacle around his neck.

* * * * *

Moonlight, as beautiful as it was improbable, appeared suddenly before them, spilling in a sheet of silver over the murky waters of the sewer. Fyodor pulled up short at the unexpected sight, but the drow, who was more learned in magical matters, shoved him unceremoniously through the shimmering portal.

They emerged from the gate to find themselves on the banks of a vast subterranean river. The faint light of luminescent fungi lit the cavern beyond, in which was a city carved from stone. The city was unmistakably drow, smaller than Menzoberranzan and lacking the wondrous light of faerie fire, but to Liriel's eyes it was no less beautiful.

"What is this place?" Fyodor murmured.

"This is Eilistraee's Promenade," said a low, musical voice behind them, "and we have been expecting you."

The companions spun. There stood a beautiful drow female, taller even than the Rashemi, with silver eyes and hair of spun moonlight.

She was flanked by dark-elven guards wearing fine chain mail and armed with swords and longbows.

Fyodor's hand went instinctively to the hilt of his sword. To his surprise, Liriel gave a cry of delight and threw herself into the female's arms. Heedless of her own finery, the elfwoman enfolded the bedraggled girl in a sisterly embrace.

"Qilué! How did you hear of us so soon?"

"Word of your arrival was passed to us by the Harpers."

Liriel drew back, her brow furrowed in puzzlement. She'd suspected the fair-haired man with the laughing gray eyes and the devious mind would somehow send word of her arrival to Eilistraee's followers. He'd more or less hinted at this, with his oblique reference to the Dark Maiden, but Qilué's reference to musicians made little sense.

"Harpers?" Liriel echoed. "Why should harp players bother themselves with such matters?"

"There are many who share that sentiment," the older female said dryly. "But it was a tale strange enough to pass along. It is not every day a drow female enters Waterdeep looking for a path to Skullport, accompanied by a human male who carries a flask of *jhuild* firewine and speaks with the accents of Rashemen. You, then, must be Fyodor. Liriel has spoken of you. I am Qilué Veladorn, priestess of Eilistraee. We serve the Dark Maiden, goddess of song and moonlight, and in her name give aid to all who need it."

The young man dropped to one knee before the regal drow. "The Dark Maiden is not unknown in Rashemen. And I think I have seen you before, Lady," he said slowly; then, remembering the unnatural height of the shadowy elf, he added, "or someone who bears your close likeness. Several days past, I watched unseen as Liriel danced in the moonlight. Another danced with her. I was far away, but I would not soon forget that face."

The elfwoman lifted one snowy brow. "Is it so? What you saw could only have been the Dark Maiden's shadow. The task ahead of you must be of great importance to earn so plain a sign of Eilistraee's favor."

"Will someone please tell me what all this is about?" demanded Liriel.

"Later, child," Qilué admonished. "Tell me how can we aid you."

Liriel hesitated. The Chosen of Eilistraee could travel as they wished and take with them the magical blessings of their goddess—

the Windwalker was of little use to them. Perhaps she could trust Qilué and her people. She glanced at Fyodor. He gave her a barely perceptible nod of encouragement.

"Fyodor and I both need the Windwalker amulet: he, to tame battle rages gone out of control; I to carry dark-elven magic with me wherever I go. I believe I've discovered a way to make these powers permanent. For us both," she added, meeting Fyodor's puzzled stare directly.

"To what end?" the priestess asked.

Liriel returned her gaze to Qilue. "What do you mean, to what end? Fyodor is a berserker warrior, a protector of Rashemen. I am a wizard whose magic comes from the Underdark, and from the heritage of the drow. We merely wish to be what we are."

"Your friend desires to serve his land," Qilué pointed out. "How will *you* use the power granted by the Windwalker?"

Liriel blinked. Power was the goal of every drow she knew, and it was pursued for its own sake. No one pondered what they'd do with it, beyond wielding it to gain still more. Though Qilué's question was strange, Liriel found she had an answer.

"The amulet has been stolen by a drow wizard called Nisstyre, captain of a merchant band known as the Dragon's Hoard. I know what *he* wants to do with it: he hopes to coax the drow from the Underdark to follow the ways of his god, Vhaeraun. From what I've seen of Nisstyre and his drow thieves, this would not be a good thing," Liriel concluded grimly. "If I *must* justify my claim to the Windwalker, then taking it from Nisstyre would be a good start!"

"A *start!*" exclaimed one of the guards. A tall drow male, clad in a hauberk and helm of black mail, stepped to Qilué's side. "My lady, that name is known in Skullport. Nisstyre is a wizard of Ched Nasad, and his guards number at least four score. Worse, it is rumored the name of his company is taken from his hidden hold: a cavern somewhere beneath the city that was once a dragon's lair. Many have followed these rumors in search of treasure. None have returned. Who knows what magical defenses might guard a dragon's hold?"

"Well then," Qilué said calmly, "we had better lay our plans well."

Chapter 25

THE DRAGON'S HOARD

n a cavern buried far below the streets of Skullport, the drow priest Henge paced the small chamber where Nisstyre lay in a deathlike stupor. The wizard had improved but little since the night he'd been mysteriously struck down. Every day since, Henge had kept reluctant watch over him.

Nor was he the only one watching. At times the priest sensed an unnerving, malevolent presence, an evil hunger, behind the ruby embedded in Nisstyre's brow. Someone, somewhere, had reached through that gem and struck down his captain. Had the blow been clean and sure, Henge would have been delighted; this lingering vigil, however, was becoming unbearable. The ships of the Dragon's Hoard were loaded and ready to sail for the far south, but only the secretive Nisstyre knew the identity of their contacts there. There was nothing to do but wait, and dark elves were not known for patience.

The door to Nisstyre's chamber swung open, and a tall drow stalked into the room. Henge took in the elf's tattooed face, the patch over one eye, and the livid scar slashed across his throat.

"Ah, Gorlist. Here at last. The cuff of regeneration did its job, I

292

see. Your wounds seem to be healing nicely."

The younger drow scowled. "But not without scars!"

"Yes, you're amassing quite a collection of those," Henge observed, "but considering the location of that throat wound, I should think you'd count yourself fortunate to have come off so lightly. I take it the wench is still alive?"

Gorlist ignored the cleric's taunts. He snatched up Nisstyre's travel bag from the bedside table, rummaged about in it, and took out a small, crimson vial shaped like a candle's flame. "Give him this. Those meddling drow from the Promenade are making inquiries in Skullport. If there's trouble, we'll need the wizard."

The priest balked. "This potion is more likely to kill than cure! You should know that as well as anyone."

"I survived it. He may, also. You needn't worry about breaking your blood-bond, or fear punishment if the wizard dies of the potion," Gorlist said bluntly, getting to the real issue behind the priest's hesitation. "Nisstyre is my sire; I have the right to order his treatment. You are absolved from responsibility."

Henge shrugged and uncapped the vial. It *was* past time for Nisstyre to rejoin the Dragon's Hoard, and his painful journey back should be most entertaining to observe. If some of the healing agony traveled through the ruby eye to the unseen watcher, so much the better.

* * * * *

In the garrisons and armory of the Promenade Temple, in the streets and hidden places of Skullport, Eilistraee's followers prepared for battle. At first Liriel was unimpressed by Qilué Veladorn's forces. The temple guard—a motley collection of dark elves, humans, dwarves, and halflings who called themselves Protectors of the Song—numbered fewer than sixty. In Menzoberranzan most of the lesser noble houses had several times that many soldiers, supported by the magic of wizards and high priestesses. Granted, every priestess of the Dark Maiden was trained to the sword, but the so-called Chosen of Eilistraee had no slaves to spend as battle fodder, no wizardly weapons of destruction, and virtually no offensive clerical spells. The Chosen trusted in their goddess, in their skill at arms, and in each other. It was, in Liriel's opinion, a formula for disaster.

Yet as she watched the preparations, the young drow began to understand the true power at work. Every person in the temple was

293

utterly devoted to Qilué and completely focused on the task ahead. No energy was siphoned off in small intrigues. No one seemed concerned about improving her status and influence. Each had a role and played it well, with an eye to the greater goal.

To Liriel, this was a revelation. She herself was beginning to come to terms with her alliance with Fyodor. From their first meeting, despite their vast and innumerable differences, she'd been drawn by the kindred spirit between them. The thing that Fyodor called friendship was an astonishing paradox: each gave, and neither was diminished. To the contrary, together friends stood to become more than the sum of their individual strengths. This flew in the face of everything Liriel had ever learned or experienced, but she was beginning to accept it as truth. And dawning on the far horizon of her mind, as she watched the Chosen come together in preparation, was the possibility that something similar to friendship could exist on a larger scale. The young drow had no words for such a thing, but she suspected this discovery might also be part of her journey, might become part of the rune she was fashioning with each passing day.

In the meanwhile, Liriel prepared for battle in her own way. The temple had a small library of scrolls and spellbooks, and the young wizard committed to memory several spells that might be useful. She also spent time poring over her book of rune lore, seeking a way to adapt the spell she'd devised to store her Underdark magic in the Windwalker amulet.

After two days of frantic activity, Elkantar, Qilué's drow consort and the commander of the Protectors, called all together in the temple's council chamber. The spies who'd been dispatched throughout Skullport to gather information on Dragon's Hoard activities spoke first.

"Nisstyre has not been seen since the day his band entered the port. Word has it he is ill and remains in the merchant stronghold," supplied a drow soldier.

"That might explain my news," added a stout, well-armed halfling. "The Dragon's Hoard merchants have two ships at dock. They've been ready to sail for days now. Seems they're waiting for something."

"Or some*one*," put in a grim-faced human. "Nisstyre's lieutenant, a tattooed drow warrior called Gorlist, was seen entering Skullport just this day. He has stood in for Nisstyre on other trade journeys, so they might well set sail now."

Liriel and Fyodor exchanged a dismayed look. "But you killed him!" the Rashemi protested.

"Well, apparently it didn't take," Liriel said, throwing up her hands in exasperation.

"We have more important problems," proclaimed a little-girl voice. This came from Iljrene, a tiny, kitten-soft doll of a priestess. With her elegant gowns and silvery ringlets, the delicate drow seemed the most unlikely of battlemasters. Yet with her first word she commanded the attention of every person in the room. "It is confirmed that a deep dragon—in drow form—walks among the Dragon's Hoard merchants."

A murmur of dismay rippled through the room. "We haven't the numbers to bring against such a foe. How should we fight a dragon?" said Elkantar in dismay.

Suddenly Liriel remembered a promise she'd made not long ago, without much thought or sincerity. With a crafty smile, she turned to the commander. "Give me two hours, and I'll *show* you how! Fyodor, I need the spellbook you've been carrying for me, and Qiluć, may I have access to the temple's store of spell components? I need to adapt a known spell to create a new dimensional door. If someone has a spell scroll for a *sending*, so much the better. It'll save me a trip back into the Underdark."

"The Underdark!" The high priestess leaned forward and fixed a penetrating gaze upon Liriel. "I think you ought to explain."

The girl smiled into Qilué's concerned face. "What better way to fight a dragon," she said slyly, "than with another dragon?"

* * * * *

The city of Skullport was a trading center unlike any that flourished in the light of the sun. There, in a cavern far below the ports and streets of Waterdeep—deeper even than the bottom of the sea—merchants from dozens of races gathered to ply their trade. No race, no matter how powerful or rapacious, was denied access to the city's ports, and no cargo was considered too illegal, immoral, or risky. Rules of "safe ground" made trade between enemies possible; however, intrigue, even small-scale, outright warfare, was part of daily life. Few denizens of Skullport cared to intervene in the quarrels of others. In the case of the more deadly races—such as beholders, illithids, and drow—the city's residents were more than happy to look the other way. And if two drow females—one of whom was a purple-skinned, button-nosed elf with round, faintly reptilian eyes—wanted to indulge in a round of wild tavern-hopping, no one felt compelled to comment.

"Slow down, Zip," Liriel cautioned her companion, catching the purple wrist while the goblet was still south of the female's lips. The purple "drow" had downed enough wine to put away an entire battalion of dwarves, and Liriel had little desire to set a drunken dragon loose upon Skullport.

Zz'Pzora pouted, but the sparkle in her round eyes didn't diminish in the slightest. The dragon-in-drow-form was having a wonderful time in this marvelous cesspool of a city. Gorgeously clad in a gown and jewels borrowed from Iljrene, supplied with coins that bought her an astonishing variety of high-potency libations, the dragon was free to wander at will among races who, in the Underdark, would have either fled from her or tried to destroy her. The deep dragon—mutated by the Underdark's strange magic, cursed with two heads and conflicting personalities—had lived most of her life in enforced isolation. When Liriel's magical message came to Zz'Pzora's grotto, the dragon's flighty, left-headed persona seized the chance to mingle with other races, to indulge in adventure and revelry; the practical, more traditionally minded right head kept a firm eye on the promised share of another dragon's hoard. In the hours since she'd emerged from Liriel's portal into the Promenade, the dragon's dual voices had spoken as one. Even Zz'Pzora's drow form, which boasted a single head, seemed to symbolize the creature's rare unity of mind and purpose.

At the present moment, the dragon and the drow reclined on ale-stained couches in a ramshackle tavern known as the Grinning Gargoyle. True to its name, the taproom boasted scores of the ugly, winged stone statues, perched on every lintel and rafter. Liriel suspected any one of them could take flight at will. Considering the caliber of patron, she'd almost consider this an improvement. The tavern was teeming with rough-mannered dark elves: commoners, former soldiers, riffraff of all kinds.

Zz'Pzora gestured with her goblet to one of several drow standing near the hearth. "That's him. The one they're calling Pharx. Look at his eyes."

Liriel squinted. The male's eyes were red, like those of most drow, but when the firelight hit them just so, she could see that the crimson orbs were slashed by vertical, reptilian pupils. "All right, that's him. Now what?"

The drow-shaped dragon responded with a carnivorous smile.

"Now I make the gentleman's acquaintance." She tossed back the rest of her drink and rose from the table.

Liriel caught her arm. "Take this gem with you. If you manage to get into the dragon's stronghold, leave it there."

"Oh, I'll manage," Zz'Pzora said in an arch tone. "Where else could we have the space—and the security—to resume our true forms? Purple or not, I'm the best thing in town! Don't bother waiting up for me." The drow-dragon smoothed the folds of her borrowed gown and slinked across the room.

True enough, the "drow" called Pharx seemed delighted by Zz'Pzora's unsubtle advances. In moments, the pair slipped away through one of the doors that lined the back wall of the Grinning Gargoyle. Liriel lingered in the tavern for a while to watch the dark elves who had been with Pharx, taking note of their number and weapons. When she was satisfied she could learn no more, she returned to the Promenade to study battle spells.

Much later that evening, a smug and sated Zz'Pzora gave her report to a gathering of the Chosen. "There is a hidden tunnel leading from the Grinning Gargoyle to Pharx's lair. It's small—barely big enough for an elf to crawl through—but comfortable enough for a deep dragon in serpent form. Pharx has a lovely home. He gave me a tour of the caverns." Zz'Pzora smiled and admired her manicure. "It's been a long time since he's enjoyed the company of another dragon."

"The details of your encounter, however entertaining, must wait for another time," said Iljrene in her little-girl voice. The battlemaster spread a sheet of parchment on the table and thrust a quill at the drow-dragon. "Draw."

Not even a dragon was immune to the power behind Iljrene's lilting commands; Zz'Pzora complied without argument. The complex she sketched out was impressive. To the east of Pharx's lair was a series of tunnels leading to three main chambers. The deepest and best protected was the hoard room, a vast cavern filled with the treasures Pharx had collected over the centuries, as well as the bones of those who'd hoped to claim some of the treasure as their own. Above the hoard were two smaller caverns that served the merchants as living quarters and warehouses. Two tunnels led out of the merchants' quarters, one up toward the docks and another, an escape route, winding down to some still deeper dungeon.

Iljrene studied the drawing for a moment. "We'll send two patrols to attack the merchant ships. That will draw their fighters up through

297

this tunnel. When the way is clear, Liriel will open a portal into the hoard room, then find and engage the wizard."

"She should not go alone," protested Fyodor. "What if guards remain?"

"That is unlikely. Nisstyre's people have no reason to suspect we know the location of his stronghold," reasoned Iljrene. "They will see no further than the attack on the ship. They carry slaves, among other cargo, and they know that this alone is enough to arouse the ire of the Dark Maiden."

"And why should he post guards, with a dragon in residence?" added Elkantar, leaning close over his battlemaster's shoulder to study the drawing.

"Exactly," Iljrene agreed. "Which brings us to the dragon. Zz'Pzora, you will ensure that Pharx remains in his lair. Keep him engaged, in battle or otherwise, until the way is cleared and our forces arrive."

The drow-shaped dragon eyed the battlemaster's exquisite, silvery gown with open greed. "Lend me that dress, girlie, and it's a deal."

"Done. Liriel, are you ready to face Nisstyre?"

The young wizard smiled grimly. "I'd be happier if I had the amulet, but I'm as ready as I can be. Did you leave my gem in Pharx's hoard room, Zip?"

"Yes, and it nearly killed me to do it," grumbled the dragon's right-headed persona, emerging for a moment to mourn the treasure that had slipped through her purple fingers. "A black sapphire!"

"What would you have me do?" asked Fyodor. The young warrior had spent the past few days on the fringes of the group, watching the preparations intently. What he saw reassured him greatly, for the dedicated drow commanders reminded him of the Fangs of Rashemen—the canny chieftains who defended their tiny land against much stronger foes. Still, he was not sure of his place in all this.

Elkantar shook his head. "We could certainly use your sword, friend, but it's best you remain in the temple, far from battle. If the battle frenzy should come upon you, could you tell one drow from another?"

The Rashemi had no answer for this argument, but his blue eyes burned with frustration as he listened to the drow plan each stage of their attack. Never, not in all the months since his berserker magic went awry, had Fyodor felt so utterly helpless. He searched his storehouse of old tales, hoping to find an answer there. Inspiration, when at last it came, did little to set his mind at ease.

When the meeting ended and those present scattered to prepare for battle, Fyodor beckoned one of their number into a private corridor. As he laid out the terms of his offer, his mind rang with the warning of an old Rashemi proverb:

He who would bargain with a dragon is either a fool or a corpse.

* * * * *

The ships of the Dragon's Hoard were well guarded. Fully loaded and tied at the dock, they presented a tempting target. Drow mercenaries walked the docks, and dark-elven archers kept watch from the aft castles and crow's nests of the waiting ships. The merchants of the Dragon's Hoard were not unaware that Eilistraee's drow had expressed earnest interest in their business, and they did not have to think long to understand why. Packed in the hold of one ship was a score of drow children: unwanted males who would bring a fine price as slaves in the far-off cities of the south. The priestesses of the Dark Maiden took a dim view of such things and were foolish enough to attempt a rescue. So far they'd shown admirable restraint, but there was no predicting what the drow of the Promenade Temple might do.

Not far from the ships, far beneath the surface of the fetid water, Iljrene and ten of her fellow priestesses clung to the rocky seabed and waited. According to Liriel's deep dragon, the tunnel from the merchants' stronghold ended here, in the solid rock of the harbor's floor. Each merchant of the Dragon's Hoard wore a magical pendant that allowed him to pass through the rocky wall at will. It was Iljrene's task to harvest of few of those pendants.

Armed with short swords and a spell that enabled them to breathe underwater for a short period of time, the priestesses waited anxiously, straining their ears for the sounds of battle above. Iljrene trusted Elkantar—he was her commander and she had fought under him for nearly a century—but this task required precise timing. If Elkantar's patrol did not strike soon, the lurking priestesses would run out of air. Yet they could not come to the surface, for doing so would alert the Dragon's Hoard mercenaries and put Elkantar's people in peril. So Iljrene schooled her thoughts to icy calm, and bided her time.

Elaine Cunningham

*   *   *   *   *

Under the command of Elkantar, a double patrol of Protectors swam toward the docked ships. They'd come in from the Sea Caves, down the watery gates that transported ships into Skullport's hidden harbor, and in from the dark water beyond the docks. His forces paddled stealthily toward the ships: a score of drow, their silvery heads covered by tight, dark hoods; six men; and a halfling—all adventurers rescued by Eilistraee's priestesses and pledged to the Dark Maiden's service.

As he swam, Elkantar took the measure of the forces arrayed against his band. At least a dozen well-armed drow mercenaries patrolled the docks, and as many walked the decks of each of the two ships. Their ranks were supported by minotaur guards and deadly, dark-elven archers. The battle would be costly, yet Elkantar did not for a moment reconsider his course. Qilué Veladorn was not only his consort, but his liege lady. He had sworn to her; he would gladly do anything—even die—for her. But *this* task he would have done regardless. The long years fell away as the drow remembered another, similar vessel. That time, Elkantar had been chained in the cargo hold: a warrior-trained youth, nobly born but too rebellious for his matron mother's liking. What he had endured during his slavery, and how he'd finally made his escape, pressed heavily on him now.

But this was a time for action, not for memories.

The bow of the ship nearest him was pointed away from the docks and was the area least heavily guarded. A lone minotaur paced the deck of the forecastle. Elkantar raised a small, crossbow-shaped harpoon and took aim. The bolt flew silently toward its target, trailing a length of nearly invisible spider-silk rope. The barbed weapon tore into the bull-man's massive chest. Instantly dead, the creature slumped against the railing, head lolling out over the water. He looked for all the world as if he were a seasick sailor reconsidering his last meal.

Elkantar swam right up to the ship. He tugged at the rope; it held, and he scrambled up the curving hull to the forecastle. Using the minotaur's body as a shield, he hauled himself over the railing. At once an alarm sounded, and an arrow streaked down from the crow's nest, missing him but sinking with a meaty thud into the lifeless minotaur. Elkantar returned fire with a handbow, rapidly sending dart after dart toward the archer.

Meanwhile, his band had found the web of ropes alongside the ships and had swarmed up onto the decks. The ship guards rushed to do battle, and the drow guarding the docks surged up the gangplanks onto the ship, drawing their weapons as they ran. Swords clashed as the drow battled hand to hand.

The Chosen might have held off the fighters, but the archers in the crow's nests picked off the valiant invaders one by one. Elkantar watched, helpless, as an arrow took one of his fighters through the throat. He turned to his second—a tall, grim halfling who had followed him up the rope—and pointed toward the crow's nest. The halfling nodded and dropped to one knee behind the sheltering bulk of the minotaur. The small archer sent arrow after arrow toward the mast, effectively pinning the deadly archer down.

Meanwhile, a small band of priestesses followed Qilué through the dark waters. One of them, supported out of the water by two of her sisters, managed to toss a rope around the bowsprit. Qilué went first, climbing lithely up the rope and leaping onto the ship's forecastle.

The sight before her stole her breath. Elkantar, her beloved, ran with acrobatic grace up a rope that sloped steeply from the aft castle to the top of the mast. His knife was drawn; he clearly intended to take out the troublesome archer. It was the sort of risky and valiant plan she'd come to expect from her consort, and, considering the storm of arrows raging around the mast, it might well be his last.

The priestess knew a moment of despair. She had loved and lost far too often in her many centuries of life; she could not bear to lose Elkantar, as well. But such choices were not hers to make. So Qilué drew her singing sword and held it high, taking strength as its song—the eerie, haunting tones of an elven soprano commingled with the call of Eilistraee's hunting horn—leaped forth.

The magical sound galvanized the priestesses who followed her. Five more swords flashed in the faint light, joining in a chorus that rang out pure and strong above the clash of battle and the screams of the dying.

* * * * *

Far below the shipboard battle, Iljrene and her priestesses hugged the harbor floor and watched the hidden portal. Suddenly drow mercenaries, no doubt responding to a summons from the beleaguered ships, burst from the solid stone. The drow fighters rose quickly through the water, intent upon the shadowy forms of the ships.

Iljrene counted carefully as thirty drow swept past her hiding place on their way to battle. From all the information her spies had gathered, it seemed unlikely that more than forty drow remained in the stronghold. The final ten, therefore, were the targets. When these had passed, the battlemaster nodded, and each priestess swam quickly toward her chosen mark. The females struck from behind, each of them slicing a drow throat and releasing a magical pendant in one blow. Iljrene had no quarrel with such tactics; this was an ambush, not a duel of honor.

Triumphantly the priestesses swam down to the portal. Clutching the pendants, all ten of them hurtled through the invisible magic door. They rolled, drenched and gasping for air, onto a rocky-floored tunnel.

Right into the path of two-score onrushing guards.

The drow males pulled up short, startled by the unexpected arrival of the Promenade forces. Iljrene leaped to her feet and brandished a sword, taking advantage of the merchants' surprise to buy a moment's time for her equally nonplused priestesses.

Four-to-one, she acknowledged grimly as she faced off against the closest male. Granted, the narrow tunnel gave the females some advantage—no more than four could fight at once—but the mercenaries could replace their slain as quickly as they fell. As she slashed and darted and danced, the tiny battlemaster determined to lower the odds as much as she could before another priestess was forced to step into her place.

* * * * *

Gold coins, a mountain of them, shifted beneath Liriel's feet. Magic weapons, priceless statues and vases, and exquisite musical instruments were heaped around the base of the golden, gem-studded hill. The drow released a long, silent sigh of relief; she'd gotten into the dragon's hoard room.

Liriel stooped and picked up the glittering black sapphire at her feet, the gem Zz'Pzora had planted there. Properly enspelled, the sapphire had been the final ingredient to opening the portal into Nisstyre's stronghold. But Liriel did not pause to savor this triumph. Cautiously she made her way down the treasure heap, sliding on the shifting coins with each step. Usually the slightest disturbance of a dragon's hoard brought the fey creature roaring toward battle. The sounds coming from Pharx's lair suggested Zz'Pzora was tending to her assigned task with unusual vigor and relish. The male dragon was well and truly distracted.

Not wanting to chance too much on the capricious Zz'Pzora, Liriel made her way quickly through the tunnels that led into the merchants' quarters. Far above, muted by the stone, she heard the faint sounds of battle, but the corridors were deserted. Then, at the base of one of the closed stone doors, she saw a sliver of light. She crept close, and eased the door open.

In a small chamber sat the copper-haired wizard, wrapped in a shawl and studying the Windwalker by the light of a single candle.

"Having any luck?" Liriel said mockingly.

Nisstyre started at the sound of her voice and spun to face her. He was thinner than when she'd last seen him, and his black eyes burned in his haggard face. The ruby embedded in his forehead flared with angry red light. "How does it work?" he demanded, brandishing the amulet. "Its secrets yield to no drow magic!"

"I'll gladly give you a demonstration," the girl challenged. "Give me the amulet, then test me in battle!"

"I have no wish to harm you."

"Afraid to try?" Liriel taunted.

The wizard scoffed and held up his left hand. The gold and onyx ring that had once belonged to Kharza-kzad Xorlarrin glinted in the candlelight. "I bested your tutor. Can the student do better?"

Liriel shrugged. "Look at it this way: you want information, and the only way you'll get it from me is to kill me and converse with my spirit."

The gem in Nisstyre's forehead flared again, brighter this time. He winced, and his face contorted with pain and frustration. He hurled the amulet at Liriel, accidentally knocking over the candle and plunging the room into utter darkness.

"Very well, I'll fight her!" he shouted. "Watch if you must, but by all the gods, hold your wretched tongue!"

Liriel peered at the wizard. He was not talking to her, but to some unseen person. Someone who could hear what she said, perhaps see what she did. Someone who wanted her dead. Her gaze flickered over to Nisstyre's ruby eye, and a plan began to formulate in her mind.

Quickly she stooped and picked up the Windwalker amulet. The drow magic captured within—her own magical essence—coursed through her in a blissful tide of power. Dark-elven spells danced ready in her mind; faerie fire and darkness vied for a place at her fingertips.

For the first time in many days Liriel felt complete. She dropped a quick kiss on the tiny golden sheath and hung the amulet around her neck. Then, with a quick sweep of her hand, she sent the first of her magic weapons hurtling toward Nisstyre.

A pulse of crackling black energy sped toward the wizard. Nisstyre was faster still. He disappeared, and the magic missile passed through his lingering heat shadow to explode against the far wall.

At that moment the walls of the room began to shudder. Cracks appeared in the ceiling, spreading out like tree branches. The floor beneath Liriel's feet buckled and shook violently, and her ears throbbed with a dull booming roar that sounded as if the very stone cried out in torment.

Liriel's first impulse was terror and an overwhelming desire to flee. Only once before had she experienced such a tremor, but all her life she'd heard stories of the disasters that occurred when the earth shifted. Patrols lost, tunnels collapsed, whole cities buried. The drow, who spent most of their lives trapped beneath tons of rock, feared nothing so much as this.

Then she remembered the amulet and her restored powers. Summoning her ability to levitate, she rose just above the quaking floor and glided swiftly and calmly toward the doorway. She emerged just as the ceiling gave way. Stone fell with a thunderous roar, sending a cloud of dust into the empty corridor.

But beyond Nisstyre's chamber, all was calm and still. Liriel took a deep, steadying breath. The "earthquake" had been a magical attack, limited to that one room. She silently applauded Nisstyre for his strategy—the attack was calculated to utterly unnerve a drow opponent—as she made her way back to the hoard room. For what other site would Nisstyre choose for spell battle? And what better warrior to have at his back than a dragon? The wizard anticipated the advantage of overwhelming odds. He could not know a second dragon had entered the fray.

Yet as Liriel sped down the silent corridors, she had little hope Zz'Pzora would even the score. So far the mutant dragon had been unfailingly helpful, but Liriel knew the creature could turn treacherous at odd moments. Their alliance had been built on the assumption that neither could be trusted. To her sorrow, Liriel knew the dragon as well as she knew herself.

* * * * *

Even in his weakened condition, Nisstyre was a formidable opponent. The moment the young drow stepped into the hoard room, she was buffeted by the sweep of giant wings. Liriel dropped and rolled, coming up with a handful of throwing knives ready. She launched three of the weapons at the giant bat—a nighthunter, the largest and deadliest of the Underdark bats—before she realized the creature was merely an illusion. The real danger came from fifty paces beyond. Perched on the pile of golden coins, Nisstyre slowly lifted a wand and pointed it in her direction.

Liriel struck a seductive pose. "I've reconsidered your offer," she purred. "If you still desire a consort, I'd be honored to accept."

As she'd expected, the ruby eye on Nisstyre's forehead flared with sudden light. The wizard's hand faltered, and he wove unsteadily, as if buffeted by the force of the unseen watcher's anger.

"I still have the map you gave me," Liriel lied sweetly. "In just a few days, we can be together in your forest stronghold. We can share the amulet, as you promised. Think of the power we can wield together! And as I promised, I'll help rid you of the *other.*" She pointed to the ruby, which by now was almost vibrating with rage.

"She lies," whispered Nisstyre, his face contorted with agony. "Yes, yes—I'll prove my loyalty." Again he lifted the wand and sighted down his target.

But Liriel had reached for a weapon of her own—a deadly, uniquely drow spell she had never dared try before. She snatched up a tooth from a pile of dwarven bones and hurled it at the wizard. Instantly his outstretched hand jerked into a flexed, tortured claw. His wand fell among the coins, but Nisstyre's attention was wholly absorbed by his own hideous metamorphosis. His thumb shrank, becoming a rounded head with a greedy, pincer-shaped mouth. His fingers elongated, then divided in half to become eight thin, hairy appendages. What was once a wizard's dexterous hand was now a hairy black spider. Mindless in its hunger and need, the creature twisted toward its host's arm and began to feed. For a moment Nisstyre, horror-struck and dumb with pain, merely stared at the *death spider* eating its way up his arm. He began to stammer out a chant that would dispel the deadly enchantment and restore his hand—if not the flesh already devoured.

Liriel, meanwhile, searched for her next weapon. She *knew* that wand—it was one Kharza had made—and she knew what Nisstyre's next attack would be. Frantically she dug through the piled treasure.

Zz'Pzora had said there was a mirror—had the treacherous dragon lied?

Now healed, Nisstyre stooped, sliding several feet down the golden pile as he scrambled for his wand. With his undamaged hand he snatched it up and pointed it at Liriel. A gout of flame, hotter than the breath of a red dragon, sped toward the dark-elven girl.

At that moment Liriel found what she sought. Her fingers closed over the gilded frame, and she snapped the mirror up before her at arm's length. She closed her eyes and turned her head away from the searing light. The dragon-breath spell struck the silvered glass and reflected back toward its sender.

The wizard's black eyes widened with pure panic as the magical fire struck the golden coins at his feet. Instantly the metal melted, and Nisstyre sank deep into the bubbling, molten mass. His shrieks, as he suffered the agony intended for Liriel, were horrible to hear.

The results of a dragon-breath weapon were spectacular but brief. In mere moments the golden pile had cooled enough to bear Liriel's weight. She climbed the treasure heap and stooped over the dying drow trapped there. The ruby eye seemed to be rising out of his forehead, and its glow was dimming in concert with the wizard's ebbing life-force. Liriel plucked out the ruby and smiled into its fading light, as if into the face of the unseen watcher.

"You lose," she said succinctly. With that, she tossed the lifeless gem into the pile.

* * * * *

Crawling on his belly, Fyodor crept through the tunnel that wound through solid stone toward the dragon's lair. Zz'Pzora had preceded him in the form of a huge, purple snake. It had been odd, watching the purple drow shapeshift into a serpent. Her *current* form would no doubt be even more unnerving. Fyodor, for all his travel and his years of fighting, had never seen a dragon. They were not so plentiful in these times as they were in the old tales. Soon he would see not one, but two of the creatures. One of them, he was pledged to kill; the other had pledged to kill him.

It was not the death most Rashemi berserkers would choose for themselves, but Fyodor was content with his fate. Although he was far from his beloved land, he would die in battle, and with honor. It was enough.

Finally he came to the end of the tortuous journey. Beyond the tunnel was the dragon's lair, a huge cavern riven with jagged, fanglike stalactites and cluttered with the bones of Pharx's recent meals. Within the cavern were two dragons, encoiled in reptilian embrace. One of them was undoubtedly Zz'Pzora—a beautiful creature with two heads, iridescent purple scales, and enormous wings the color of amethyst. She was huge—at least fifty feet from the tip of her tail to her dual snouts, but it was Pharx who stole Fyodor's breath. The male dragon was fully twice Zz'Pzora's size, armored with dark maroon scales and armed with teeth the size of daggers and claws like curving scimitars. This, Fyodor realized with awe, was the creature he had vowed to help slay.

A faint hiss came from the distant tunnel, and then screams of mortal anguish. Immediately Pharx lifted his head, like a giant hound scenting the breeze. "My gold," muttered the creature in a rumbling voice. He disentangled himself from the purple dragon and sprinted toward the tunnel in a lurching run, head down to avoid the low-hanging ceiling. "My gold is melting! We must protect it!"

As the dragon neared his hiding place, Fyodor leaped into the cavern and pulled his sword. With all his strength he swung, bashing the creature between the eyes. Pharx pulled up short, shaking his head and huffing in astonishment. The blunt-edged sword had not broken through the dragon's armor, but for a moment the dragon was dazed and cross-eyed.

Zz'Pzora seized the moment. She spread her wings and leaped at Pharx like a pouncing hawk. Her claws found a foothold on the male's vertical plates of belly-armor, and her wings enfolded his spiked back. Her two heads dove in for his throat. Nothing but a dragon's teeth could pierce a dragon's armor, and Pharx, despite his enormous size, could not shake the smaller female. One head he might have dislodged, but not two. Locked in a deadly embrace, the enormous creatures thrashed and rolled. Zz'Pzora's wings were pierced, then shredded, by the male's spiky armor, but still she clung—teeth grinding and two heads tossing violently as she sought to rip through the male dragon's scales.

Fyodor circled the titanic battle, watching for a chance to strike, but so entangled were the two creatures that he could not hit one without harming the other. Finally Pharx's tail thrashed out, away from the clinging Zz'Pzora. The Rashemi leaped, hacking at the scaly appendage. It was not much, but perhaps it would distract the beast

307

and give Zz'Pzora some small aid.

Pharx's enormous maw opened in a roar of rage and pain that shook the cavern. Then the creature lowered his jaw toward Zz'Pzora's back and exhaled deeply. A noxious, crimson mist flowed from the dragon's mouth. It clung to the female's back, and wherever it touched scales melted away like snow in a spring rain. Both of the female's heads screamed, and Zz'Pzora lost her hold on Pharx's throat.

The Rashemi stepped in, sword leading. His black blade dug deep into one of the holes Zz'Pzora's teeth had worried open, and he leaned in hard until the sword struck bone. Fyodor gripped the hilt with both hands and threw his weight to one side, wrenching the sword in a deadly arc through Pharx's throat. Blood poured from the creature's fanged mouth, quenching the strange fire that ate through Zz'Pzora's scales.

The female disentangled herself from her dying mate, and the fierce joy of battle shone in her four eyes. "Let's go," she rumbled, leading the way unsteadily from the cavern. "Liriel is in there. No sense letting her have all the fun!"

* * * * *

Slowly and at great cost, Iljrene and her forces made their way down the tunnel toward the hoard room. The tiny priestess had been cut more than once, and her garments were wet with mingled seawater and blood. Yet she did not falter, did not seem to register pain when she was wounded, or when one of her sister priestesses fell. She had a mission and she would fulfill it. Once the ship was breached and the drow children rescued, Qilué would lead a band of drow into the merchants' stronghold. Iljrene planned to ensure they did not walk into overwhelming odds.

* * * * *

Liriel looked up as Zz'Pzora ducked her way into the hoard room. "Got the wizard, I see," the dragon's left head observed in a slurred voice "Pharx is dead, too."

The drow smiled. "We make a good team, Zip."

"That we do," the dragon's heads agreed in unison. The creature seemed about to say more, but her left head swayed, then drooped, sagging lifeless onto her bloodstained purple scales.

The right head looked down and grimaced. "I was afraid of that," she said, and plunged down faces-first into the pile of gold.

Liriel's eyes widened at the horrible wound on Zz'Pzora's back. The scales had melted away, and the flesh looked as if it had been eaten away by some corrosive acid. The drow darted forward and gathered up the lifeless head of her friend.

"Damn it, Zip," she mourned.

A flicker of light returned to the left head's eyes. "My life has numbered more than twenty thousand days," the dragon said, and her voice was content. "This was the best of them all." With those words, half of Zz'Pzora died.

The right head stirred and lifted out of the golden pile. "A word of advice," the dragon added in a rapidly fading voice. "Don't trust that human of yours. An utter fool! He offered to follow me into Pharx's lair and help in battle if needed. In return, he offered to let me kill him if he should raise a sword against any of Qilué's drow. Talk about a win-win situation!" The right head grinned, and not in Liriel's direction. "You're on your own now." With that, the reptilian eyes glazed as the right head followed her counterpart into the darkness.

For a long moment Liriel sat and rocked the enormous head in her lap. So often she'd considered the high price to be paid for trust and friendship, but it had never occurred to her the price might be demanded from another. Then the sound of battle grew louder, breaking through the drow girl's pain and grief. Liriel realized Iljrene's forces had met resistance, after all.

The drow gently laid Zz'Pzora's head down and rose to her feet. She recoiled, for she found herself face-to-face with Fyodor. Suddenly the dragon's last, comradely words made sense.

"Get out of here!" she shrieked, pushing him toward the tunnel. "Stubborn, stupid . . . *human!*"

"It is too late," Fyodor said in a despairing voice. His gaze turned to the approaching conflict, and his hand closed on the hilt of his sword. Before Liriel's eyes, he seemed to take on height and power. The battle rage was coming upon him, and it would no doubt be his last.

Liriel's fingers closed around the Windwalker. For one last moment, she savored her dark-elven heritage.

"The ritual to bring on a battle rage! Do it!" she commanded.

Fyodor gave her a startled look, but he was too far beyond his own control to question the order. Witches commanded the Rashemi berserkers, and he had long ago accepted Liriel as *wychlaran*. So he lifted his deep, bass voice in song, singing in the language of his homeland the hymn of battle to come.

The drow, meanwhile, opened the amulet. She snatched the flask of magically distilled *jhuild* from Fyodor's sash. She quickly twisted off the top of the amulet, then unstoppered the flask with her teeth and tipped it slowly, carefully over the tiny sheath. Liriel had no idea if this ritual would suffice to store and control the berserker magic. If it worked at all, it would be temporary. At least it would buy Fyodor's life and those of the drow he would slay in his frenzy. No one else, Liriel vowed fiercely, would pay for the choices she had made.

Suddenly Fyodor's song stopped, and the Rashemi's eyes turned dull and hollow. Liriel caught him as he fell, not caring that the precious flask of *jhuild* clattered down among the treasure. The dark hair at the back of Fyodor's head was parted by a deep gash, and through the swift flow of blood Liriel caught a glimpse of bone.

She looked up. Over them stood Gorlist, a bloodied sword in his hand. "Your turn," he said with dark satisfaction.

Cold wrath coursed through the drow girl, pushing aside her grief. "Hand to hand," she challenged, and the fighter accepted with a nod and a smirk. With careful, deliberate movements Liriel stoppered the amulet, locking her Underdark magic firmly into place. She rose and pulled her dagger. The two drow crossed weapons with a ringing clash, and the deadly duel began.

Liriel knew at once that Gorlist's skills far outclassed her own. At first it was all she could do to hold off his furious, pounding slashes. The male was taller, heavier, and more experienced. But Liriel's hours of practice told, and she fought with more skill than she'd thought she possessed. Yet she knew she couldn't outfight Gorlist. Her only chance was to out-think him.

From the corner of her eye, she saw Qilué step through the portal, followed by her priestesses. They did not see her, or hear the sounds of the fierce duel over the clamor of the larger battle just now spilling into the treasure hall. The drow females drew their singing swords and rushed toward the tunnel entrance to intercept the mercenaries that Iljrene herded relentlessly downward.

Suddenly Liriel knew what she must do. Slowly, deliberately, she let Gorlist work her backward toward the invisible portal that led out to the Dragon's Hoard ships. Qilué's presence here meant the vessels had been secured, offering safety and escape.

When she reached the portal, Liriel feigned a stumble. Gorlist, triumphant, lunged in for the killing blow. With the speed of thought the girl levitated into the air, whirled, and kicked the fighter through the portal. Gorlist disappeared as if he had never been.

Liriel, still magically aloft, cast the spell that would close the portal and lock out her adversary. When that was done, she floated down and cast a quick glance around the cavern. A few merchants still fought, but most had fallen to the singing blades of the Dark Maiden's priestesses. At last she was free to go to Fyodor's side.

She ran to him, stooped down, and found he still breathed. Her arms encircled her friend, and her bright head bowed in the sincerest prayers of her life. Her entreaties did not name the goddess, but Liriel had no doubt who listened and heard.

It was thus that Qilué found her. The priestess placed a hand on the girl's shoulder. Liriel looked up, clearly uncertain what the priestess might do now that the battle was over. She clutched the Windwalker, and her golden eyes blazed defiantly. "Nisstyre is dead, the followers of Vhaeraun routed. The Windwalker is Fyodor's and mine now. We've earned it!" she snarled.

The priestess smiled down at the fierce young drow. "Not yet," Qilué said, "but I strongly suspect that, in time, you will."

Chapter 26

PATHWAYS

he black ruby crystal gleamed bright as blood in the light of a circle of candles. Shakti Hunzrin bent low over the bowl, her nearsighted eyes drinking in the scene magically laid out before her. Nisstyre was dead, and Liriel's final taunt still echoed in the priestess's ears. But the sight before her was ample proof that she had not lost, after all.

In the dark circle of the scrying bowl was a hideous face, the face of Shakti's new ally—a creature from another plane. Not the Abyss, but another, lesser traveled place. Few drow knew of such beings, and fewer still dared to consort with them. Those who did trod a razor-thin ɔath. On the one side was the promise of immense power; on the other, madness and servitude. The risks were great, but so was the potential reward.

Shakti Hunzrin had developed a taste for both, in nearly equal measure.

*　*　*　*　*

Back in the Promenade Temple, the followers of Eilistraee mourned their dead and tended the wounded according to their usual custom: they sang and they danced. Music, eerie and haunting, filled the cavern for days. Some of the songs were prayers for healing, others praise to the Dark Maiden for victory.

The Chosen found strength and solace in their dancing, but they also took time to tend to practicalities. The dragon's wealth was added to the temple treasury to be used in aiding the many who fell prey to the dangers of Skullport. Some of the coins would help pay the expenses of rearing and training the more than dozen drow children who had been added to the Promenade's ranks. Elkantar took charge of this task himself, tending the children with a fierce devotion reminiscent of a brooding she-dragon watching over her eggs.

Nor was Liriel idle. She worked and danced alongside the silver-haired drow, doing whatever was needed. She ventured out into Skullport from time to time, seeking adventure and planning her next steps. She could not forget that most of her journey lay before her, that the rune she needed was as yet unformed.

She also haunted the hallway outside Fyodor's room. His wounds were mending, but slowly, and only on the third day after the battle was she allowed to see him. There was much she needed to tell him, so he could understand what lay ahead.

The Rashemi listened as Liriel told him what she knew of rune magic. First the shaping, in which a rune was formed through a journey of discovery. Then the carving of the rune on the sacred tree Yggsdrasil's Child, using as a tool the chisel hidden inside the Windwalker amulet. Finally, the casting of a spell that forged insight into power.

"So you see, I have to go to Ruathym. I've booked passage. The ship leaves in a few days."

Fyodor nodded and took her hand. "It is right for you to go, little raven. In my land, no *wychlaran* would consider giving up her power for another, as you would have done in the dragon's cavern. I will never forget that, or you."

The drow stared at him. Understanding came to her, then rage. Snatching free her hand, Liriel leaped to her feet, head held high and eyes blazing. "After all this, do you still think so little of me? Or do you doubt I'm wizard enough to wield the Windwalker for us both?"

"It is not that," he said somberly. "I doubt neither your friendship nor your powers. But the journey you describe is not one I wish to make."

313

Liriel fell back a pace. It had never occurred to her that Fyodor might not wish to come with her. "To see the land of your ancestors!" she wheedled.

"It is a worthy *dajemma*," Fyodor agreed slowly, warming to the entreaty in her eyes, "but I do not want to endanger you so. You take a great risk, to travel with me as I am."

So *that* was it, Liriel thought with relief. Humans worried about the strangest things! *Risk!*

"It hasn't been dull," she agreed happily, sitting down on the edge of his bed. "You've got to get better fast, for the ship leaves as soon as the captain is released from a certain dungeon. I'd have thought it nearly impossible to get arrested in Skullport, but Hrolf the Unruly has a certain flair for such things. Let me tell you . . ."

With a smile, Fyodor leaned back against his pillows, well content to yield the role of storyteller to another. His excitement grew as he listened, for the plans Liriel unfolded far exceeded any dreams for *dajemma* that he, the dreamer, had ever dared to fashion. Whether or not he ever regained control of his berserker magic, the journey she described would be well worth taking.

But what pleased him most of all was the knowledge that their journey together was just beginning.

ScFic
C   Cunningham, Elaine
          Daughter of the drow.

                    95-2298